A GAME PLAYED FOR KEEPS . . .

Her black negligée blended into the black satin sheets. Pinpoint spots flattered her stretched-out legs, emphasized her cleavage, threw hollows under her cheekbones, and picked up her eyes.

"Welcome home, *husband*," she said throatily.

"I want a divorce."

"That's not the deal," she said quietly. "And if you don't go through with your part, someone's going to get hurt."

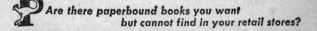

ROUGH CUT

by

Andrew McCullough

A KANGAROO BOOK
PUBLISHED BY POCKET BOOKS NEW YORK

ROUGH CUT

William Morrow edition published 1976

POCKET BOOK edition published September, 1977

This POCKET BOOK edition includes every word contained in
the original, higher-priced edition. It is printed from brand-
new plates made from completely reset, clear, easy-to-read type.
POCKET BOOK editions are published by
POCKET BOOKS,
a Simon & Schuster Division of
GULF & WESTERN CORPORATION
1230 Avenue of the Americas,
New York, N.Y. 10020.
Trademarks registered in the United States
and other countries.

ISBN: 0-671-81197-5.
Library of Congress Catalog Card Number: 76-10725.

Printed in the U.S.A.

Any actor who survived in Hollywood during the period of this novel would have acted on TV shows starring James Arness, Chuck Connors, and David Janssen. They and other theatrical personalities mentioned are, of course, real. The remaining characters have been created by the author and any resemblance they have to anyone living or dead is unintentional and purely coincidental.

This book is dedicated to
Hazeltine and Frank McCullough,
my mother and father,
with thanks for their support, belief, and love
over many a long year

ROUGH CUT

1

Just out of range, two pink Ping-Pong-paddle-shaped fish goggled warily at me. Gently kicking the flippers, I slid toward them through the soft warm yellow-green water. They darted off through a coral arch twisted like a Monterey cypress, stopped dead and started grazing on kelp, peaceful as cow ponies.

I eased toward them. Sliding into range, I raised the spear gun, and—

Suddenly was shadowed. Sick with fear I raced for the protection of the coral. The black shadow stayed with me.

Oh, my God, I am heartily sorry for having offended—

I was struck. Great teeth sheared through my ribs, my guts, my soul. Screaming, I

woke up in my own bed. A snub-nosed blonde I'd never seen before stared at me.

"You were screaming your lungs out," she said resentfully.

"Sorry."

Hangover hurting every step, I walked out across the living room behind the bar and opened a Heineken. It was ice cold.

Where had I started drinking last night? . . . Dominick's? . . . Matteo's? . . . Rusty's?

I turned my mind into a blank screen and waited. . . . Nothing. Complete blackout.

You're letting it get to you. The not working. And having no money when you thought all that was behind you.

1

Outside, the early-morning fog blotted out the surf. A patch was pulled up as suddenly as a Venetian blind, and running flat-out on the wet sand was Iz Liebowitz's Irish wolfhound. I wondered what a successful composer-conductor's dog was doing so far north of the Colony. This hadn't been a fashionable stretch of beach when I bought ten years ago and now cheap, pink stucco condominiums were shouldering aside the too small, too old frame houses that surrounded mine.

"This place looks like a Goddam pigpen!"

The girl pointed angrily at the dozens of old TV dinners scattered over the floor, mixed in with gnawed chicken bones from the overturned drums of Colonel Sanders, the spilled ashtrays and empty bottles of Heineken and Jack Daniel's.

"Right."

"Isn't this you and Jim Arness?" Awed, she stared at an 8 x 10 glossy on the wall.

"Unh-hunh."

"From *Gunsmoke?*"

"Yeah."

"And here's you and David Janssen. From *The Fugitive?*"

I nodded.

"Here where you're wrestling with Chuck Connors—is that from *Rifleman?*"

"No. *Range Rider.*"

"*Range Rider?*" she said blankly. "I never saw that."

"You and two hundred and twenty million other Americans."

"*What?*"

"That was my series."

"Oh." She came toward me with that you-really-need-a-woman-to-take-care-of-you look.

"Lis-sen," she murmured. "Why don't I clean things up and cook us up some breakfast. I'm a fan-tas-tic cook."

I looked at my watch.

"Christ! We've got to get out of here."

"Why?"

"I've got an appointment."

She ran after me. "At six-thirty Sunday morning? Where?"

I thought quickly. "Mass."

"Oh, *Wow!*" Disappointed, she still displayed your true Californian's deep reverence for any religion.

Dressed, she asked sadly, "Lis-sen, would you give me an autographed picture?"

"Sure." I pulled one off a stack of *Range Rider* glossies. "How would you like me to make it out?"

" 'To Audra Lee—the greatest fuck in the world.' "

"Gee, I don't know, Audra Lee. Since Congress passed that new truth-in-labeling act—"

"Oh, you got to!" she broke in desperately. "Or my friends won't ever believe I balled a movie star."

Outside, I spotted a beat-up Mustang next to my car. Grateful I didn't have to drive her home, I said huskily, "Thank you for last night." Slid by her up-turned mouth, nestled against her neck, kissed it with three small, quick kisses and left. It was a bit I'd stolen from Cagney.

Driving south on the Pacific Coast Highway, I saw her, in the mirror, sit slowly on her fender still staring at the 8 x 10.

She was good for half an hour and where the hell can you go in Malibu six-thirty Sunday morning?

I pulled up in front of the just-built church—all curved concrete and stained glass—south of the Pier. Inside a pale fat young priest said, "In the name of the Father, and the Son, and the Holy Ghost." Then sat down. Three teen-age girls with guitars stood up and sang:

* * *

> *"Where have all the flowers gone?*
> *Long time paaaaasing . . ."*

Christ, I thought, it's Episcopalian. But on the way out I spotted the Stations of the Cross. Mother must be spinning in her grave.

I surfed for a long time, hoping that the hot sun on my back and the easy feel of the three-footers might start putting me back together. But four kids moved in on my spot. They were noisy. Full of that phoney, hip-surfer talk. Then, too, they didn't know how to handle themselves so there was a lot of loose wood flying around.

It was ruined so I left. Picking my way through their pretty, stupid, long-haired girls stretched out on the sand, listening to the Supremes on their eight-tracks.

There was a chill in the air. To keep warm I jogged along, the board banging against my shoulder. Ahead twelve men playing touch were turned red by the setting sun. They ran complicated patterns, casting long purple shadows on the sand. They were awfully big and fast. Must be from USC. The quarterback, trapped, turned and tossed a forty-yard bomb. It was settling down right in the receiver's hands when a big black cornerback blew in from nowhere and batted the ball away.

He had to be a pro but I couldn't place him. Must play Canadian. I tossed the ball to him underhand. He smiled at me, showing perfect white teeth. Jesus, but he was pretty. An Omar Sharif profile, lean powerful body with tremendously developed delts and lats, a tiny waist set off by white bikini shorts.

"Hey, Movie Star," he said. "Care to play a little touch?"

"Sure."

"Beautiful. What position?"

"End."

"Fantastic. Red, drop out."

In the huddle I said, "Throw it to me. I'm going to cut inside that black cat."

"Cavalry?" They exchanged an unhappy look. "That's ... uh not such a good idea," said the quarterback.

"What's the holdup?" Cavalry called sharply.

"Nothing." Ducking his head down in the huddle, he muttered, "Seventy-three."

Walking to the line, I thought, Damned if they aren't all scared of him.

On the hike I ran flat-out at Cavalry. Christ, he could backpedal faster than I could run, but I fooled him with a head feint, beat him on the cut and had a good step on him. But the throw was high and behind me. I jumped for it, grazing it with my fingertips—when that motherfucker blind-sided me as hard as I've ever been hit.

When I opened my eyes he was looking down at me, smiling.

"Touch?" I asked.

"Right, Movie Star. We play tackle—someone liable to get hurt." And he laughed.

I limped back to the huddle.

"Can you hit me with the ball two steps past the line?"

"Why don't we call it a day?" the quarterback said.

"No," I said. "I'm not blaming anyone but I get one more play."

As I came up to the line Cavalry, smiling, danced lightly on his toes in the backfield.

The ball was hiked. The quarterback threw it right where I wanted it. I had three steps to get up speed before he was on me. I gave him a knee. He dove for it. My straight-arm snapped his head back. I saw the surprise in his eyes before my left knee went into his face as I ran right through him. At the goal line I touched the ball down, then jogged back. His long black body stretched out on the sand. They were all looking down at him. Then they looked up at me.

"He had it coming," I said.

I didn't know how they'd react but at least I had the sun in their eyes.

"Yeah, he did," said the quarterback, and I saw none of them felt anything for him but fear.

So I picked up my board and headed home.

The fast-dropping light turned the line of houses into the black cardboard cutout for a high school play.

"Buck!"

A kid on the porch of the most expensive house was waving at me. "It's Chris," he yelled. "Come on in. I'm having a party."

I cut across the sand. "How the hell can you afford to rent this? Did you get a series?"

I'd embarrassed him.

"No. My . . . uh . . . father's out from New York. He wants to find out what I'm into with film and where my head's at. So he rented it for a month . . . and I moved in."

It was a young filmmakers' party. Fat, guttering candles threw weak cones of light. Moving in and out of the shadows were long-haired, bearded kids talking seriously to thin pretty girls in tank shirts.

A hand waved from the corner. It was Tuesday Weld. I waved back. There was the sweet heavy smell of incense and grass. Dylan sang:

> "Lay, lady, lay,
> Lay across your big brass bed . . ."

Behind the hacked-up ham, untouched turkey and dozen wine bottles I found a pint of cheap bourbon.

A commercial director said carefully to a serious black girl, "I've completely re-evaluated Leo McCarey. I now place his early work almost on the Preston Sturges level."

I took a belt of the bourbon in front of the fireplace. The heat felt good on my back.

Someone poked me in the ribs.

"You Tarzan?" It was one of the great voices of all time. Early Jean Arthur with a touch of Margaret Sullavan.

I said: "Lord Greystoke to you." And turned around.

Laughing at me was a girl with all the kick and style of the young Kate Hepburn. Great grey eyes, strong high cheekbones; white skin, no makeup; Irish-setter red hair that hung to the small of her back. She wore a hand-knit white sweater and grey flannel slacks.

Chris wailed, "You've met! Dammit, Tabitha, I wanted to introduce you. This is Buck McLeod. Remember? I told you he's going to star in my movie. Isn't he the perfect beat-up Bogart existential hero?"

She looked me over. "He's pretty beat-up."

"I didn't get the last name," I said.

"Weston."

"Buck!" Chris was struck by a new thought. "I've got to talk to you about *The Last Picture Show*. Didn't you *love* it?"

"No."

"Why not?"

"It's a closet-fag picture."

"How can you say that?" she cried.

"There's that sensitive boy who can't get laid until a woman old enough to be his mother takes him by the hand—"

"But that's the whole point Bogdanovich was making!" she said angrily. "That the sterility of small-town American life is castrating."

There was a chorus of agreement from the crowd.

"Any of you ever live in a small Texas town? ... Well, that sterility makes 'em fuck like jackrabbits."

"It's a *masterpiece*," she said.

I said, "If that's a masterpiece then what in God's name is *Rules of the Game? Ikiru? The Seven Samurai? Eight and a Half? Jules and Jim? Grand Illusion?*"

The commercial director said, "But the way Bogdan-ovich recreated those Walker Evans Depression shots!"

"Absolutely!" "Fabulous!"

I leaned toward her. "Let's get out of here."

Startled, she stared at me, then nodded and slipped away.

I went over and introduced myself to Chris's father, who was nice enough as rich fathers go who want to get their sons out of Hollywood and home into the family business. "Of course, I could cut off his allowance. But . . ." He shrugged hopelessly. "That might alienate him."

From a distance I heard Tabitha say: "Let go."

Down the dark hall, in the lit bedroom, Sonny Krause, a hot-shot agent with CMA, held her wrist.

"He's nothing, Tabitha. An over-the-hill Malibu stud."

"Now," she said.

"I won't let you leave with him. You're not only my date. You're my client."

Stepping in, she hit him with her right fist in the solar plexus.

Gasping, he sank slowly down on the bed heaped high with coats.

On our way out the door Chris caught us.

"Tabitha, you *can't* go! I haven't seen you in months, and I've so much to tell you. . . ." He broke off, staring at us. "God! There's a really *fantastic* chemistry between you two! Like Bogart and Bacall in *To Have and Have Not.* I'm going to rewrite my movie and co-star *you.*"

She laughed, ruffled his hair as if he were her kid brother and kissed his cheek. I slung the board over my shoulder and we walked away from the light out across the dark chill sand.

She smiled at me. "Chris thinks you know absolutely everything there is to know about making movies."

"He's right," I said. "I do."

When she saw I wasn't kidding she stopped smiling

and didn't say another word until we were inside the house.

She looked around the room and laughed.

"You really *are* shanty Irish."

She studied the 8 x 10's, sipping her wine, while I built a fire and put Ellington on the hi-fi.

She turned, frowning, from the bookcase.

"Generally, I can tell a lot about a man by the books he reads. But what in God's name do *Great Expectations, The Magnificent Ambersons, The Maltese Falcon, An American Tragedy* and *Moby Dick* have in common?"

"They made movies out of them."

She stared at me, shook her head, then pointed to the picture of Hank and me. "What do you think of Fonda?"

"Best actor in America."

She smiled and in a patronizing Chapin drawl said, "You don't, *actually,* think he's as good as Brando."

"Something I learned when I played tight end with the Forty-Niners."

"What?"

"Never talk football with a stranger until you find out if he knows a fucking thing about it."

She turned quite pale, the freckles standing out across the bridge of her nose.

"I have played six roles off Broadway," she said very distinctly. "All to good reviews. For the last one—Lucinda in *Winter Leaves*—I received an Obie for Best Female Performance of the Season. Does that qualify me as one who knows—in your inimitable phrase—a fucking thing about it?"

"What about film?"

"I am now playing Lucinda in the film of *Winter Leaves*. But I thought you were asking me about acting. Acting is what you do on a stage."

"Don't look down your fucking New York Actor's nose at me."

"I beg your pardon."

"You all come out here with your bullshit about Lee and the Studio and how can one find the spine of the scene in this cheap Hollywood writing?

"But once you're on your feet and the camera rolls, you die. When they don't print your first take, you get mad at the crew who are breaking their ass to try to make you look good. Then you go empty and start pushing; then you get scared and start blowing your lines. Until ten takes later, I have to throw out *my* performance and carry you—line by line—through the scene. *I've had every fucking one of you.*"

As she walked toward the door I threw my glass away. It smashed against the fireplace.

"Don't go. I'm in a black-ass Irish mood and taking it out on you. That's not right. Why the fuck should I jump down your throat? Or those kids? Why should I give a Goddam if you can't tell good film from bad?"

She said quietly, "Because you're an artist."

Startled, I said, "No, I'm not."

Studying me thoughtfully, she walked slowly toward me.

"I think that's it, McLeod. Under that dumb, jock, macho mask . . . you're really an artist."

She stopped a foot away, and suddenly we were deep into it with each other.

We made love on the bearskin in front of the fire, those lovely, long legs wrapped around me, her hard nipples brushing against my chest, her sharply kicking heels driving me deeper and deeper into her, until she arched her back and cried exultantly, "Oh, yes . . . yes, McLeod . . . *yes.*"

Rusty's was jammed. She didn't care much for the fishnets, phoney Polynesian masks, flaming torches and the smiling girls at the bar waving and calling out, "Hello, Buck."

Rusty, lined face worried, leaned over the bar and whispered, "Buck, you gotta let me have something on the tab. I don't want to bug you—"

"Then don't. The back booth's open. We'll take it."

Over drinks, eyes dancing with curiosity, she began firing questions.

"Where were you born?"

"Brooklyn."

"Any brothers or sisters?"

"No."

"What did your father do?"

"Structural iron worker. He was pushed off the George Washington Bridge when I was nine."

She stared at me. *"Murdered?"*

"Couldn't prove it. But the mob was moving into the union. He didn't like it. And he was a very outspoken man. So he took the tumble."

"Were you close?"

I nodded. "Yeah. He was always taking me to museums. Plays. Shakespeare. Trying to educate me."

"What happened after he died?"

"Mother took a job in Great Neck—as a maid—so I could go to a good school."

"Wasn't that rough?"

"She never complained. Five-thirty Mass every morning and a tightly buttoned lip."

"I mean rough on *you*. That's a snobbish town. Didn't the kids look down on you?"

"I could take care of myself."

"Oh, I know *that*. But did you have any friends?"

"Not until high school. When I became All-State end, everyone was my friend."

"Especially the girls, I bet. Did you love it—football?"

"I liked it. But it was a job. I had to get a good football scholarship."

"Did you?"

"Not bad. University of Oregon. Now, I want to hear about you."

Over blood-rare steaks, she told me about the father she loved, a brilliant Wall Street lawyer; the mother she didn't—beautiful but lazy; her education—Brearley

and Bennington, junior year at the Sorbonne; the du-
plex at the UN Plaza, the summer place at Quogue.

"Why, you're nothing but a spoiled-rotten-rich-kid."

"Don't you believe it. Seton's a great believer in the
Pursuit of Excellence. Remember, he taught me to
box."

"Not very well. You lead with your right."

She wanted to know all about the jobs in the lumber
camps, the oil fields. What it was like—shilling in car-
nivals, bouncing in strip joints.

"McLeod, I've never known anyone like you before," she said. "A *bum*. How did you ever become an
actor?"

"I was hustling tennis out at the old Standard Club,
near MGM. I won a bundle for my partner, Nate
Keeler. He was directing a Rory Calhoun football picture. So he put me in it. I ended up with a nice little
bit and Universal put me under contract."

"Is that where you got that tacky name—Buck?"

"They were making a lot of Westerns at the time."

Something made me look quickly over my shoulder.
A big bulky man with too many rings on his fingers
stood too close to the table. Two other men in the
same white coveralls stood three paces behind him.

"Remember me, McLeod?" He had a thin scratchy
voice for a man that size.

Setting both feet flat on the floor, I gave him my
early Jimmy Stewart smile. "Can't say I do."

"From last night?" He was very angry.

I shook my head. Not wanting to take my eyes off
them, I kissed Tabitha on the ear, whispering, "Grab
the bench with both hands and don't let go."

When I turned back the two men had moved in a
step.

"Freddy," the second man said. He was slight,
cleaning his fingernails with a screwdriver. A knifer.
The third was a big, blond, untogether weight lifter.
"Ask him if he remembers your girl."

"Afraid not."

"You were talking to her at the bar," Freddy said. "When I came back from the can you were both gone."

"She must have split with some other dude. I left alone."

Freddy gave me a bad smile, and reached in the neck of his white coverall. When his hand came out it held an 8 x 10 glossy of me in a black cowboy hat. I locked in on his breathing. He read slowly: " 'To Audra Lee, the greatest fuck—' "

I turned over the table. He screamed as the edge chopped into his ankle. I blew by him, throwing an elbow in his gut. The knifer was coming in fast. I down-blocked hard but he cut a slice off my ribs. By then I had his hand and leg-swept him, driving his face into the floor. Blondie grabbed me from behind—too high across the chest. I threw my head back, smashing his nose, then took him over backward. A table splintered under us. As I whirled around I had a fast cut of a man still sitting at the smashed table with a napkin under his chin with a red lobster on it.

Then Freddy hit me above the ear with a left hook; his right dug into my ribs, cutting into me with his profile rings. Mad, I heel-kicked him in the balls.

His jaw dropped open as he fell. I jumped high and landed on his back with my knees. You could hear things break. And it was all over.

As Rusty was telling the customers, "Please sit down, everything's all right," and the Chicano busboys were carrying them out, I turned toward Tabitha.

She was staring at me, her face white and strained.

"What's the matter?"

"I was afraid you'd be hurt."

"By *them?*"

She started to laugh, then suddenly began to cry—hard.

I sat down and took her in my arms. She was shaking. "What's wrong?"

She looked up at me, tears trembling in her eyes.

"I never wanted to fall in love with a man like you."

Later, head on my chest, firelight playing on those lovely grey almond-shaped eyes, she murmured, "Oh . . . me . . . oh . . . *my!* So that's what love is."

I got up and lit a cigarette.

"Tabitha." I walked up and down. "I haven't worked for over a year. It was a lousy three-week job. I hadn't worked for eight months before that . . . and I'm broke . . . and I'm forty-seven years old."

She smiled gently up at me. "That's downright noble of you, McLeod. Your big renunciation scene."

"It's no big renunciation scene. It's the truth. So if you want to call it off now, it's OK. No harm—"

"Jesus, you're dumb, McLeod. We're way past that. Light-years past that. The Goddam problem is tomorrow morning at nine-thirty I leave for five weeks' location in South Africa."

"Oh, Christ."

"I know." She looked at me. "I won't go if you don't want me to."

"Walk off a shooting picture? You'd never work again."

"I don't care. We're more important."

I knelt down and put my arms around her. "We'll be all right."

"Will we? I have a terrible feeling that something's going to happen to you. I couldn't bear that. And I nearly didn't go to that party. Life's scary. Isn't it?"

"No," I said. "Life's great."

She shook her head slowly. "It must be sheer hell for you—not working when you love it so much. That's why you brood and get drunk and into fights, and pick up those tacky girls, isn't it?"

"My father used to say, 'Michael, never talk with a poor mouth.' "

"Michael! So that's your name."

Delighted, she threw her arms around me. "Michael, I'm going to bring you luck."

"Don't say that," I said sharply. "Nobody brings anybody luck. You have to make your own."

She sat back and studied me.

"What do you want to do more than anything else in the world?"

"Oh, for Christ—"

"Answer me."

I tossed my cigarette in the fireplace.

"My own series."

"A *television series?*"

"Yeah. A private eye show. Like *The Maltese Falcon.* Tough and hard and real and gritty."

"What are you doing about it?"

"What?"

She stared at me fiercely. "Not one Goddam thing. Seton thinks that's what's wrong with actors. They get dependent and passive. Sitting—waiting for the phone to ring. You've got to get out and make things happen."

"It's not that easy."

"Easy!" she cried. "Who said life was easy? Get cracking on it. Do you have a script? An outline? A story?"

"Wait a minute," I said. "I optioned a property a couple of years ago for a feature I couldn't get off the ground. But it might work for a series—if I still have it."

"Find out. First thing in the morning."

"Yes, *sir!*"

She smiled. "Now do you see why the WASPs own the world?"

I kissed her. She bit my lip hard. "Fuck me, Michael," she whispered. "Fuck me."

I woke suddenly. The fire had burned down to grey coals and the blue pre-dawn light was separating the beams from the ceiling. She slept snuggled up against me, breathing deeply, mouth open, slightly smiling. She looked about fourteen.

Maybe she's right, I thought. Maybe she will bring you luck.

With the top down I threaded my old Jag through the Strip traffic thick with Porsches and Ferraris driven by bearded CPAs hoping to be taken for the managers of rock groups.

Tabitha, pounding out on my thigh the tempo to *The Night They Drove Old Dixie Down,* sang along with Baez in a lovely, deep, completely tone-deaf voice.

The eight o'clock news led off with the renewed bombing of North Vietnam. Tabitha punched it off.

"It's dumb, McLeod," she said sadly.

"What?"

"The war, and the world, and leaving you to go to Africa with this dumb movie."

"Are you good?"

She shrugged. "Chip Hanneman comes up every day, saying, 'Dah-ling, I just saw the dailies and you are fan . . . tas . . . TIC!' "

"What do you say?"

"I can't watch those little snippets of film."

"That's your job."

"Up-a yours. My job is to re-create my fabulous New York stage performance."

But she listened carefully as I told her why she had to know exactly where the lens was cutting her, and how to find something different to play when you shoot a scene over and over, and how to force the cutter to use pieces you want of a long reaction close-up by dropping your eyes or scratching your nose.

As I pulled up in front of the Château Marmont she threw her arms around my neck.

"You'll make a wonderful father, McLeod. You're a good teacher."

Holding hands, we walked slowly across the vaulted Spanish porch. I opened the high, carved-wood door and a tiny old couple, elegantly dressed in black, strolled out. Enchanted, Tabitha dropped them a curtsy. They smiled at her, bowed and walked away, whispering compliments in Italian.

Tabitha punched me gently in the stomach.

"McLeod, this is the time to say something Irish and charming."

"I love you."

"Why, you *do* have a way with words."

I kissed her for a long time.

The old couple stopped at the sidewalk and smiled at us.

She suddenly shoved me away, screaming: "Bastard! I'm carrying your unborn child. And what do you do? Beat me, steal my money and spend it on another woman." Sobbing, she darted inside.

The old couple glared at me. I smiled to show them it was all a joke but they stared back stonily.

"Pssst!" Tabitha stuck her head out. "Get cracking on that show. And no fooling around. Got it?"

"Got it."

Her eyes filled with tears. "I miss you already," she said miserably. "God bless, Michael."

And she was gone.

2

Angus MacNab, frowning, pince-nez perched on his thin arched nose, studied the papers in my manila folder. Behind his bald brown-spotted head hung smiling, silver-framed, signed photographs of Eisenhower, Kennedy, Johnson and Nixon.

"Buck," he said in a tight, strained voice, "I have very bad news for you."

"The option's lapsed?"

"No. It has three more months. But you have no money. Or to be exact you have ... eighty-seven dollars and eighty-three cents."

"Jesus, Scotty. How the hell could you let it get this bad?"

"Buck, seven months ago—in this very office—I informed you that you were in disastrous financial straits. Remember?"

I nodded. When he was upset he burred his *r*'s heavily, reminding me of early Donald Crisp.

"You said to me—and I have it noted here—'Scotty, buy me some time. Buy me a couple of months. That's all I need.' That was seven months ago."

"You've done a damn good job, Scotty."

"It hasn't been easy. You owe nearly forty-seven thousand dollars. To some nasty creditors. I couldn't let the account girl handle this. I've been on the phone with them myself; and because I flatter myself I have a reputation for a certain probity in this town. And because I told them something good was in the offing and was able to pay them ten—twenty dollars a month ... they held off."

He closed the folder and clasped his hands across it. "Now, what am I going to do when I can't pay them a cent?"

"Tell them I have this great property under option that's all set for a *Movie of the Week* and there's a surefire series in it."

He shook his head. "No one will buy that. Not the way the industry is. Not with your history."

"Tell them a few years ago Clint Eastwood couldn't get arrested. Today he's a millionaire. And I will be, too, as soon as—"

"Buck, you've got to face reality. You haven't any money. And I don't mean script development money. I mean survival money. Money for hamburgers and gas and taxes and cigarettes. How the hell are you going to live?"

"That's easy." I gave him my cocky Cagney grin. "I'm going to borrow five thousand dollars from you."

"I'm sorry," he said solemnly. "But that is completely against company policy."

"Come on, Scotty. It's your company. You make the policy."

"That is true, Buck. Now I'm going to be completely honest with you—"

"You always have been."

He flushed with pleasure. "Thank you. When I say it's company policy I mean that I never have loaned one cent to a client. And I never will."

"It's only five G's."

"Julie Weir *only* needs thirty-five G's for the completion bond on a million eight feature, Slippy Netter *only* needs seventeen G's to put together his new act and the Sands guarantees him four weeks at fifty thousand per; Eva Low only needs nine to cut her new album. If I did it for you, I'd have to do it for them, and I'd be out of business."

"It's OK, Scotty, I understand."

"Buck," he said gently, "you've had a good crack at it. Good parts in features. Your own series. Stop butting your head against a stone wall. You're not going to make it. How about Real Estate?"

I stood. "Sorry to miss the rest of the pep talk, Scotty. But I've got to go get my series on."

It was still early as I walked down the center aisle of Talent Unlimited, Limited. Doors were open as the agents went over the day's work with their secretaries. All the cubicles had the same black modern desk, the same imitation Eames chair, the same Buffet print of the Eiffel Tower. The only things different were the wives and children in the 8½ x 11½ Mark Cross picture holders.

Annette saw me coming. "I'm sorry, Mr. McLeod,"

she called out nicely. "We weren't expecting you. Mr. Kootz is busy."

I threw open the door. Guccis on the desk, Stan was drinking coffee, reading the trades.

"Busy? Stan? *Busy?*"

He said indignantly, "Reading the trades is part of my job."

I slammed the door. "Wrong, Stanley. Your job is to get me a job. Now!"

He was on his feet, selling. "I'm talking you up all the time. All over town. Just yesterday I was talking you up to Dick Zanuck."

"For what?"

"The heavy opposite Chuck Heston."

"I thought Palance was set."

"Ninety percent. But Dick weakened after I gave him the rundown on you. He's showing interest. Definite interest. So much so—as a matter of fact—I'm on my way to Warner's now to show him some film on you."

I smiled at him sadly. "You're lying, Stanley. Dick Zanuck's in New York."

"So it was the day before yesterday."

"He's been there all week."

He crossed his arms and sat on his desk, sullen in his black silk suit. I went to work on his Jewish guilt.

"Stanley, you were a young lawyer, fresh out of the mail room, when we met."

"I remember."

"I liked you. Took you to parties. Introduced you to people. It was through me that you met Artie and Kay. Or am I wrong?"

"No, Buck. And I've never forgotten."

"Then, when I got *Range Rider,* Nate wanted to assign someone with more rank to handle me. But I said, 'No, I'm sticking with Stan.' "

He began to look like Freddie Bartholomew in *Captains Courageous* after Tracy fished him out of the ocean.

"I know I owe you a lot."

"I've never asked for a lot, Stanley," I said quietly. "Just the truth."

"All right, Buck," he snapped. "I'll give you the truth. I can't sell you, anywhere."

"Why not?"

"Because you're *trouble!* Big trouble! You yell at the director. You rewrite the script. You direct the other actors—"

"So what? So does Marvin. So does Newman. So does McQueen."

"But they're *stars.*"

"SO AM I!"

Stan carefully polished his wraparound sunglasses with a yellow sheet of Kleenex.

"No, Buck," he said. "You're an out-of-work actor."

"I'm an out-of-work *star.*"

He shrugged. "Have it your way. Any idea how many ex-series stars are cleaning pools in Encino?"

"The difference between them and me, Stanley, is that I am good!"

"On film you're fantastic. On the set you're impossible."

"Used to be, Stanley. I've reformed."

He looked at me bleakly. "The last time you told me that I went out on a limb; got Quinn Martin to give you the lead on *The FBI* and three days later you beat up Marini."

"He hit me with his cane."

"I don't care *what* he did. For Christ's sake, you can't hit a director in this town."

"I just tapped him."

"You broke his jaw in three places."

"He must have a calcium deficiency."

"That's right. Joke about it! For two months he's walking around town with a wired jaw that might as well be a neon sign. Blinking: Don't hire Buck McLeod! Don't hire Buck McLeod! Then you bust in here and want to know why I can't sell you." He threw his hands up helplessly and fell backward in his chair.

"Buck . . ." he was very quiet, very sincere. "If you think another agent can do better . . . then, buddy, go with my blessing."

The son of a bitch knew I couldn't get anyone else to handle me.

"Stanley, I have complete confidence in you. And I know you need some fresh ammunition." I flashed my Cagney grin again. "So I've got it. A brand-new package. All ours. A *Movie of the Week* spin-off for a private eye series. Rough. Tough."

He sagged lower in his chair. "If it's that property we tried as a feature—it's not good enough."

"It's good enough for Cassidy."

He sat up.

"Cassidy?"

I nodded.

"He's never directed a TV."

"Right, Stanley."

He studied me warily. "Cassidy said he'd do it?"

"Subject to script approval. That's why I'm here. I need a good writer."

"Spec?"

"Yeah."

"Then you can't beat Ted Hornblower."

"Only trouble is he doesn't write too well."

"What do I know? I'm not an artist. I only know that since *Range Rider* he's written well enough to sell three series. Besides, he'd be great for your image. Your old producer who isn't afraid to work with you."

"What about Mordecai Gaunt?"

"Mordecai?"

"Never heard of him? Figures. He's your client."

"Fun-*ny!* It so happens Mordecai only writes comedy."

"He wrote a prize-winning off-Broadway play about junkies."

Puzzled, he riffled through his bottom drawer.

"You're right." He tossed me a playscript. "Take it. You'll like it. It lost money. Ha ha."

He put his hand on my shoulder and launched into his closing pitch.

"I'm getting good vibes out of this. You: the star. Cassidy: the director. Hornblower: the producer. We'll stud it with great cameos. Bette Davis, Milton Berle, some *schwartze* sports star and I guarantee I'll get it on. Once it's on, I smell series. And this time we'll go all the way. And, Buck, I want you to know that all this time I've never lost faith in you. Not for an instant."

"I know you haven't, Stanley," I said gratefully. "And that's why I'm going to let you lend me fifteen hundred dollars."

I'd caught him completely off balance.

"Jesus, I can't do that, Buck. You know Nate has a rule against that."

I looked at him warmly, admiringly. "I'm sure if you wanted to, Stanley, you could figure out a way."

He sighed. "Would two hundred help?"

I stuck it to him.

"For Christ's sake, Stanley! How can you be so Goddam insensitive? I haven't worked for a year. You know that! You know I don't have any residuals! You know I'm out of unemployment insurance. Do you think I'd ask for money unless I was desperate? And what do you offer me? A lousy two hundred bucks."

He kicked his bottom desk drawer shut and turned on me, white and shaking. "Don't try to make me ashamed. Goddamn you. You're the one who's asking. And I'm offering two hundred dollars. Take it or leave it."

I was surprised and proud he showed so much spirit, and sorry that I'd have to break it. But he was no good to me like this.

I dropped my eyes to the floor. When I looked up I was the Mafia executioner from *The FBI*.

"Seven hundred," I said, very quietly. I placed a .38 slug into the nose corner of his left eye.

He swallowed. "Sure." He sat down. "Seven hundred." And he wrote out the check.

Bruce Connor's gym was crowded and noisy. Pulleys whined, weights crashed to the floor, jocks strained at the barbells. Over the muscle boys doing bench presses, I spotted Eddie on the high bar. He had a forty-four-pound weight around his waist and a brand-new, shiny white cast on his right ankle. His back was to me. I walked over and whispered, "Gout?"

He looked down across his shoulder, grinned, then, veins standing out on his throat, muscles straining, twisted up for another one.

Eddie Riordan had been on the Forty-Niners with me. I got him in movies as a stunt man and today he's the best there is.

Gasping, he eased himself to the floor and unbuckled the weight. I rapped the cast. "Fell over your own feet, huh? Drunk again?"

"Hairbreadth Harry."

That was our name for the klutzy lead of a series Eddie gaffed most of the stunts for.

"How'd he get you this time?"

"I'd laid out the whole car hit when he came back from lunch with some girl from *TV Guide* who said, 'You mean you don't do your own stunts?' So he did."

"Buy you a drink."

"You've got a deal."

Eddie had picked out the bar. It was nearby, west of Sepulveda, south of Wilshire, and smelled like an embalmer's. Alkies from the VA sat staring hopelessly into their drinks. In a shallow room behind us drunken hard hats were noisily shooting pool. The bartender weighed about 250, had a Marine Corps tattoo and a terrible toupee parted straight down the middle.

"Jesus, Eddie, you sure can pick 'em."

"The atmosphere will grow on you."

"I'm worried about the barstool."

He laughed.

"Eddie," I said. "Can you loan me fifteen hundred bucks?"

"Sure," he said, pulling out his checkbook.

"Wait a minute," I said. "I don't know when I can pay you back."

"No problem."

Eddie handed me the check. I looked down as he filled out the stub. It read:

old balance	1828
this check	1500
new balance	328

I tore up the check.

"What did you do that for?"

"You can't afford it."

Eddie has fair, freckled skin that turns red when he gets mad; it was getting pink.

"Who the hell are you to tell me what I can afford?"

"Listen to *him!* A gimpy stunt man. With a wife and two kids. Make it three hundred."

"Fifteen hundred."

"Three hundred or I'll tear it up."

Lobster red, he slammed his fist on the bar. *"Who the fuck are you to be tearing up my checks?"*

"Why, you dumb son of a bitch—I'm your best friend."

"Jesus," he said. "I really lucked in." But as he made out the check for three hundred, he started to smile.

3

I drove up Pacific Coast Highway slowly in the clotted late-afternoon traffic, listening to the Beatles sing *Eleanor Rigby* on KRLA, and squinting into the low hot orange sun.

Ted Hornblower moved farther north after each successful season. He'd gone from Carbon Beach to the Colony to Old Malibu Road, then last year made the big jump to Trancas.

As I swung left onto Broadbeach Road, I hit the brakes and stared at the long line of shiny Mercedes and Rolls backed up from his house. A red-coated parking boy opened the door. Wondering what the hell was going on, I walked up the path.

The house was a severely functional glass and steel cube that had won the previous owner an award from *Architectural Digest* that Ted kept framed on the wall.

I pushed open the blinding stainless steel door.

Inside, a pretty sunburned brunette sitting behind a card table said: "Hi, Buck. It's thirty-five dollars."

"What's thirty-five dollars?"

"Admission to the Malibu Free Angela party. Drinks are three dollars apiece but you get ten for only twenty-five. So why don't you make out the check for sixty dollars? It's deductible."

"From what?"

She laughed politely as I made out the check.

Down the hall, three big, scowling Black Panthers—all leather and chains—lounging against the red-iron staircase took my ticket.

In the big room the hot orange sunlight slanting through the tall glass doors threw the hundred and fifty or so people into silhouette.

There was a strange sound in the room. The tan tennis-thin wives in their Puccis stood against the wall, as always, but instead of chatting about children and clothes as they watched their writer-director-producer husbands make deals, they stared silently at the black men in the center of the room; who, blazing in wild clothes, exploded in wild laughter, slapped palms and street-jived, while the pale overlooked husbands surrounding them murmured on about money.

A sexy black girl in skintight white hip-huggers said, "Hi there, Buck McLeod. I'm Nanette. Get ya a drink?"

"If you'll have one with me."

"Beautiful."

"Double Jack Daniel's on the rocks."

She tore five tickets off my roll.

"Too young to count?"

She snapped, "There's a service charge," and, scowling, stalked off.

I spotted Ted in a yellow silk jumpsuit across the room under the Calder stabile and worked my way over to him.

"How are you, Ted?"

He shook his soft, white face unhappily.

"You can't believe the aggravation I've had to endure." He looked nervously around the room. "These damn blacks are all Moslems. Last night they were telling me how the Arabs are going to kill all the Goddam Jews and take back their holy city, Jerusalem. *Their* holy city!"

A flashbulb went off. Blinking, he put his hand across his eyes. Laura rushed up and clutched his wrist. She wore a long red dress with too many big white flowers on it. "Is Jane Fonda here?"

"I haven't seen her," Ted said.

"But she promised," Laura said desperately.

Nervously, they peered about through their contact lenses.

A big black man in a white burnoose stopped before us.

"Time for that speech." He had a deep voice that sounded familiar. His strong, harsh features looked hacked out of coal; his eyes were hidden by shades.

"Ummmmmmm ..." Ted pushed the white toe of his Gucci around the brown tile—studying it.

"*We* ... ah ..." Laura said, with a kindly smile, "don't generally ... ah ... speechify at these affairs."

"We niggers don't have no manners. So let's just tell 'em where it's at and—"

"What has happened to *my* manners!" Laura cried, clutching me. "Buck McLeod, I'd like to introduce you to—"

"Hell," I said. "Now I recognize you. I saw you go on for Brock Peters in *Great White Hope*. You're Har—"

"No!" he cut in haughtily. "I am Kryellah."

Ted put in helpfully, "He changed his name."

"Sure sounds that way." I moved on.

"Hold on!" he called out. "You here because you want to see Angela freed?"

"No," I said. "I'm here to borrow money." And split.

"I was within six paces of the packed bar when Kate Cassidy's lovely voice said tentatively, "Michael?"

She squinted uncertainly into the sun. Tall, lovely—grey hair falling straight to the shoulder of her blue suit—she was the only woman in the room wearing white gloves.

"Kate." I kissed her. "You look wonderful."

"You certainly don't! You haven't shaved in days. Your jeans are filthy. And you've been fighting!"

"Me?"

"Don't try to con me, Michael. Your knuckles are all skinned."

"Stop picking on him, Kate." And Tim stood beside

her, grinning. He never looked quite right out of the
work clothes he wore on the set. The well-cut white
linen jacket from Trimingham's was rumpled in a way
that reminded you of a boy buttoned, struggling into
his Sunday suit. Then, too, his thick thatch of white
hair wouldn't comb down flat either.

As we shook hands, Kate asked, "Why haven't we
seen you for months?"

"Things haven't been going well for him, Kate."
His rough, clipped voice had a slight lilt to it.

"Agh, he knows better than that. Or should. Can
you have dinner with us Friday night, Michael?"

"I'd love to."

"Good. Come early and watch the sunset."

Tim had been sizing me up. "Anything that can't
wait till then?"

I was surprised to hear myself say, "I'm putting together a *Movie of the Week*. If the script's good
enough will you direct it?"

"Why, Michael!" Kate said, shocked. "Tim doesn't
direct television."

"I know."

"Then why—"

"At ease, Kate," Tim said gently. "We'll talk about
it over dinner." He flipped open his solid gold watch.
"We'd better go."

"Tim's guest of honor at the USC Film Society,"
Kate said proudly. "He's going to make a speech."

"Answer questions. After we run *The Last Scout*."

"That's a beautiful picture," I said.

"Oh, you wouldn't say that if you had to sit through
it again."

"Oh, yes, I would."

"Wait till you see something you did damn near
forty years ago. You'll want to change everything." He
added grimly, "You'd better."

"Not the acting."

That surprisingly quick warm smile passed over his
face. "Hank *was* good. The others weren't bad. But

I didn't tell the story right." Suddenly he was deep into it. "The daybreak scene at the corral should have started *before* the patrol; then cut to shoeing the horse—"

"Master!" Mordecai, stinking drunk, bowed deeply, spilling his drink over his bib overalls.

Tim said easily, "Kate, I'd like you to meet Mordecai Gaunt. A good writer."

"Mrs. Cassidy," Mordecai said reverently, "I believe your husband is the only great artist alive in this here city."

Kate, veteran of a thousand such encounters, smiled. "I not only agree with you, Mr. Gaunt, but would love to discuss the matter at length—unfortunately we must leave."

Tim extended his arm, Kate slipped her hand through it, and with a bow they disappeared in the crowd.

Mordecai stared after them admiringly. "He's something, that son of a bitch. He's better than Hawks and Ford put together."

"Don't tell me," I said. "I only made three pictures with him."

"And he hasn't directed one in four years." Mordecai said savagely, "This fucking town."

The black girl came up with my drink. "Here you are, Buck McLeod."

"Why, it's Nanette King," Mordecai said. "The Happy Hooker."

"Fuck off, Jewboy," Nanette said evenly, and walked off.

Clapping his hands, Mordecai sang after her loudly, niggerly: *"It must be jam! 'Cause jelly don't shake that way!"*

Black heads turned slowly in our direction.

"Shut up, Mordecai," I said.

"The cunt hustles in the Polo Lounge."

"So?"

"Last week she rolled me for six hundred bucks."

"Mordecai!" A worried, beautiful girl in a white silk sailor suit clutched his arm. "Come home, darling. Please. You've had too much to drink. You're going to get in trouble." She had an accent I couldn't place.

"Cheese it!" Mordecai said in a stage whisper. "It's my date. Patina—Mike McLeod."

She was a Yugoslav model who'd made a few spaghetti Westerns. Couldn't act.

"How do you do? I thought you were marvelous in *Death and Destiny,*" she said politely. "I saw it in Rome. Was that your voice?"

"No. I only dubbed the English version."

"Which has never been seen." Mordecai laughed and grabbed a glass out of the hand of a thin, blue-black girl in a muumuu.

"Just one minute!" the girl said.

"Rack it up to experience and the NAACP," Mordecai said.

Those black heads swung in our direction again.

"Here," I said, smiling, handing her five tickets. "Have some drinks on me."

Frowning, she walked over to two black men. They started whispering.

"Jesus, Mordecai. Cut it out."

"He was fired today," Patina said, starting to cry. "He's miserable and he won't listen to me, and he won't stop drinking."

"I've got a grant from B'Nai B'rith," he said. "To become the first Jewish alcoholic."

Suddenly spotting Nanette across the room, he shouted, "Nanette, honey, getting a good price on your poontang?"

In the sudden shocked silence that fell over the room, Nanette stalked toward us, black men falling in behind her.

"Keep your mouth shut, Mordecai," I whispered. "Or you'll get us killed."

"Don't worry kid. I'm the White Hope. I'm the Nonpareil."

Nanette slapped him hard across the face.

"What's happening?" asked the Panther who'd taken my ticket.

"Little joke," I said.

"Better make *me* laugh," he said, moving in.

"Or what?" yelled Mordecai. "Going to kick my ass, Boy?"

"Boy!" came from a dozen voices as they rushed us.

Kryellah—his huge hands moving the front men off balance and around as easily as Deacon Jones—said soothingly, "Cool it, brothers. Only reason we're here is to get that lovely lady out of the slammer. Bustin' honky heads ain't gonna do it." He whispered to me, "Get him out."

Mordecai said: "Retreat? Never! The Gaunt motto is—"

I twisted his wrist up between his shoulder blades and rushed him across the room, out through the glistening stainless steel kitchen and didn't turn him loose until we were in the middle of the garage. Mordecai, gasping, leaned back against the green Bentley.

"Oh, thank you," the girl said, "thank you so much. *Mordecai!*"

Eyes closed, he was buckling at the knees. I caught him, slung him over my shoulder, carried him outside and got him tucked into his Porsche.

He was still out as Patina, waving gratefully, drove off.

I'd taken two steps into the garage when the overhead doors dropped down and slammed shut behind me. There was a moment of solid blackness. Then the overhead light bulb snapped on. Standing by the switch was Cavalry.

He wore a black velvet Edwardian suit with a beautifully ruffled white shirt. But his jaw twisted strangely, his lips were swollen and split, and his bulging nose was hidden behind white tape.

"You fuckin' marked me for life." Wire glinted between his teeth.

"You had it coming."

"You got something coming, too." His right hand slid out from behind his back; he had an eight-inch blade in it.

He walked slowly toward me, holding it low, point up.

I was trapped in the narrow slot between the Bentley and the white Volvo station wagon.

"Shee-*it!*" Kryellah said wearily, slamming the kitchen door behind him. "I got one fucking untogether nigger after another on my hands all fucking day long."

"This is private," Cavalry said.

"No, Stevie," Kryellah said easily, moving toward us. "Nothing is private. Not here. Not today. So slice him up tomorrow, someplace else."

"No way."

Kryellah held out his pink palm. "Give it to me, Stevie."

Cavalry slashed at his hand. Kryellah caught his wrist. Twisting, pivoting, he pulled down hard. Cavalry, screaming, flashed over his head. There was a sickening thud, and Cavalry was spread over the front fender of the green Bentley like a wet chamois.

Kryellah sighed and shook his head. His eyes were tired as he looked at Cavalry.

"Can't blame the bastard. You cost him money."

"He a player?"

"No. White women keep him."

"Thanks," I said.

"I didn't do it for you."

"I know."

"But if you *really* would like to express your appreciation—split."

"Can't," I said. "I've got work to do."

"Borrowing money?"

I saw a flicker of a smile as he turned to Cavalry.

Outside on the white clamshell-shaped patio, Ted sipped a glass of buttermilk, eyeing me warily.

"It's a good story," he finally said. "But for a private eye show this late in the season . . . it doesn't have enough clout."

"It does for Cassidy."

He blinked at me. "Cassidy?"

"*If* he likes the script. That's why I want you to write it." I gave him my best smile.

"Spec?"

"Spec."

He stared off in the distance. I could hear his mind clicking like a computer.

"Buck, my business manager will kill me. But since you're my friend, I'll do a treatment."

"Ted, I've got to have a script."

"*Buby,* I just don't have the time. We'll try on a treatment and play it from there."

People began pushing by, pointing out to the ocean.

"It's her."

"You're crazy."

"Who?"

"Honey Holly."

"She's too old to jog. She must be sixty."

"Forty! I see her show every week."

"They put Vaseline on the lens."

"I hear she's a dyke."

"I hear she likes dark meat."

"*Will you shut up!*"

"Oh. Sorry."

"She doesn't like anything. She's a fanatic. Mormon or Christian Science."

"Just since her husband died."

"Naw. She never smoked or drank. Just made money."

"Is she loaded?"

"Loaded."

"How loaded?"

"She's twenty, thirty mill loaded."

"Holy shit."

A hundred yards away, a woman in a blue sweat suit

jogged briskly on the wet flat sand, behind her the bottle-green curve of an incoming roller.

Ted jumped over the low brick wall and, Guccis sinking into the soft sand, ran awkwardly toward her, shouting, "Honey! Wait! It's Ted Hornblower. Remember?"

They disappeared behind a sand dune.

Suddenly, excited as a kid, I leaped the brick wall and ran north, parallel to the beach, behind the sand dunes.

Honey Holly!

Christ, I'd wanted to fuck her since the first time I saw Mickey Rooney chase her around his Model A. She drove me crazy in all those musicals with Tyrone Power and Don Ameche. The combination of that full sexy body in the black net stockings contrasted with that sweet innocent face straight out of the convent made me feel guilty jerking off over her.

Even now at the beginning of her show, when she'd twirl down to the footlights in that strange half-stripper, half-fashion model tight-assed walk, I'd get a hard-on.

I cut left through a gully, came out on the beach and there she was, on my left, running toward me not thirty feet away. Heavy blond hair bouncing over her shoulders, fine full knockers bouncing against her chest.

Sweet Christ, I vowed, *I'm going to fuck that before I die.*

She stopped dead in her tracks and stared at me.

I wondered if I'd said it out loud.

Ted came up huffing and puffing. "Honey! What luck running into you! I'm Ted Hornblower. I was head writer for Clem Bunting when you honored us with a guest appearance."

"Yes?"

"Well, since we're practically neighbors, I hope you'll honor us by coming up and having a drink."

"No, thanks."

She hadn't taken her eyes off me.

"This is my old friend, Buck McLeod."

"I know," she said. "I've seen your show. You're good."

"Not good enough to be on opposite you."

"Oh, *Ted.*" She suddenly turned on all that pigtail, saddle-shoe, squeaky-clean cuteness that was her trademark. "Golly, there is something I'd *love,* but I'm afraid it'd be an awful lot of work for you."

"Name it," he said gallantly.

"Couldja bring me a glass of fresh orange juice?"

"Coming up." He sprinted up the gully.

"Organic—if you have it," she called after him. "Who are all those people?"

"It's a fund-raiser for Angela Davis."

She wrinkled her nose. "If I'd known that I wouldn't have stopped."

"That's not why you stopped."

The skin tightened across her cheekbones as she tried to stare me down.

I thought I knew that face by heart. The beautifully cut clean long nose. The enormous light violet eyes set very far apart. But I was stunned by her lower lip. On camera it was always thin, flat, long. Here it was deep and full. I wanted to sink my teeth in it.

"You shouldn't powder down your lip."

"*What?*" I'd startled her.

I reached out, took her chin in my hand and slowly ran my thumb across her lip.

She jumped back and, shivering, stared at me. Then bolted, running with all her strength back down the beach away from me.

"Honey! I've got it." Ted sprinted across the dunes, Laura at his heels, orange juice sloshing out of the glass he held toward her disappearing figure. "OR-GANIC!"

The phone woke me at six-thirty. The answering service said, "Mr. McLeod, I have a Stanley Kootz on the line. He says it's urgent."

"Put him on."

A few clicks. Then: "Baby! Who's the greatest agent in the world?"

"Myron Selznick."

"He's dead. It's me."

"You're alive?"

"Am I ever! After our productive talk yesterday, Buck, I've been pushing you all over town. I was on the horn all night. And it's paid off! I've got you a job—starting today! And what a job! The biggest show in television. *The Honey Holly Show!*"

I tossed the phone on the bed and, grinning, walked out to the bar and poured myself a Heineken's.

So that's how she works.

I picked up the extension. Stan was yelling, "Buck? . . . Buck? . . . Hello? . . ."

"Stan—"

"I thought you crumpled over with a coronary. Listen, today's their camera day. They been rehearsing all week with Rod Light. You replace him as guest star."

"What happened to him?"

"That backwoods *fegellah!* Who knows? Maybe the fleet's in. Ha ha."

"What's my deal?"

"I got you his billing. Special Guest Star. One hundred percent. Under the title. So, who do you love?"

"What's the money?"

"Seven hundred."

"No."

There was a long silence.

"You better be kidding. I already accepted."

"You can't do that, Stanley, it's not legal."

"Buck, for Christ's sake!" he said desperately. "It's one of our packages so there's no agency commission. You have to look at it like a G."

"I want three G's, Stanley."

I could hear him breathing. "Buck, if I call them back and say, 'We have no deal. He wants three G's,' after they stop laughing, they're going to call Nate. And Nate is going to get mad. And, Buck, if there's anybody in town you can't afford to have mad at you it's Nate—"

"Three G's, Stanley."

"You fucking son of a bitch, don't start getting independent with me. That's my money in your pocket."

"That's why I need the three G's, Stanley. To pay you back." I hung up.

I had showered and was just about through shaving when the phone rang.

"You're set for three thousand."

Stanley was so stunned he forgot to take the credit.

"Buck, *luv!* Could you give me a bit more?"

"No."

There was an awkward silence in the empty theater. The small group onstage huddled around the dim work light as if for warmth. Cora Hardiman, the great old comedienne; Harriet, the hatchet-faced, grey-haired script girl; Pat, the bored assistant director, half hidden in the shadows; all turned and looked at the director.

Carl Ushley, still tap-dancer thin, smiled at me prettily. He wore blue jeans, sneakers and a two-hundred-and-fifty-dollar red knit Italian sweater.

"But of course you can, luv."

"Sorry. We've walked it three times. I can't play it until Honey gets here."

His smile didn't waver. "I agree that would be *ideal.* Unfortunately, we can't always work under ideal circumstances. So let's use these precious minutes before the crew arrives to get out of the way all those dreary questions about character and motivation."

"I don't have any."

"You must have *some!*" he wailed.

"Why? In the first sketch I'm a cowboy at a dude ranch teaching her to ride. I'm too dumb to see she's making a play for me. In the second, I'm cooking a barbecue and even dumber, because I don't stop her from spilling food all over me."

Cora raised her script over her mouth to hide her smile.

Carl studied me, then asked apprehensively, "Do you want to change any of the lines or business?"

"No," I lied, knowing he wouldn't dare change anything until she got there.

"Then do let's run it once more, luv." He turned on his smile. "Pretty please?"

I offered him a face-saver. "Carl, I really need the time to learn lines."

He grabbed at it. "Of course, luv. Take five, gang." He shot off into the dark, a young man on his way.

I sat down at the table and tried to figure out how to fix the second sketch. I was suddenly surrounded by half-a-dozen heavy, grey-haired women.

"Hi, Buck. I'm Phyllis—wardrobe."

"Phyllis what?"

"Just Phyllis." They laughed. "We're all on a first-name basis here. This is Julie, and Mary, and Trudy, and Evelyn."

"Hi, Buck," they said.

"Hi."

"We're all just one big happy family."

"Honey wouldn't have it any other way."

"You're the luckiest man in the world to be working with our darling."

"She's the sweetest!"

"Dearest!"

"Darlingest girl in the whole world."

"She's a lot more than that, girls," Phyllis said severely. "She's a saint."

"I'm a forty-three long," I said. "Thirty-inch waist."

Lights banged on and the crew walked in. I looked over the assistant operators noisily loading the three Mitchells on the ramp at the back of the theater to see if I knew any of them.

"Jesus. We get rid of one *fegellah* cowboy only to get another."

Looking down from the boom was Max, an old-timer with a great, deadpan Ned Sparks delivery. I laughed and we shook hands.

A woman stuck her head in the back of the theater. "She's coming." There was a nervous bustle of anticipation.

"What's she like to work with?"

"A saint," he said dryly. "Ask anybody."

Honey dashed up the aisle. She wore a floppy Mickey Mouse sweatshirt, a baseball cap—brim sticking out over an ear—slacks and high-heeled white shoes.

"Hi, Honey!" everyone yelled.

"Hi, Gang!" she replied, throwing her arms out toward them. She disappeared onstage into a hugging crowd of the crew and the girls. There were squeals of "Harriet!" "Honey!" "Phyllis!" "Harry!" "Ooooh!" "You look wonderful." "Darling!" "Cute." "Oh, how I've missed you!"

"Remember," Max said. "They haven't seen each other since five P.M. yestiday."

Honey burst through the crowd holding out her hand. "Welcome aboard, Buck!"

"Thank you, Miss Holly."

"HONEY!" she cried. "We're all one, big, happy family, here. Right, Gang?"

"*Right, Honey!*" they thundered.

"Didja say hi to Buck?"

"*Hi, Buck!*"

"Oh, Gang . . ." she said softly.

"Quiet! And that means quiet!" yelled the assistant. "Nobody moves."

"Thanks, Pat," she said gratefully, sinking cross-legged to the floor. "Gang, Rod Light came down with the flu and *boy!* Were we lucky to be able to get Buck to pinch-hit! It's going to mean lots more work for all of us. We'll be restaging right through dress. So, Gang ..." She looked up, pleadingly. "Will ya give it all you've got?"

"We sure will, Honey!" they shouted.

She put her hand on my arm. "How do you feel, Buck?"

"Like Ruby Keeler in the last reel of *Forty-second Street.*"

Max turned away, coughing.

"Honey?" asked Carl. "Could we go to work?"

"Oooops! Looks like dat ole slave driver's back."

"That's right! That's me! Dat ole dabble slave driver!" Cracking an imaginary whip, he drove her down the aisle while the Gang laughed.

Pat shoved three middle-aged platinum blondes in blue dresses against me.

"For the two-liner with Buck in the barbecue," he yelled. I thought they were a vocal group. They smiled strongly. Honey and Carl, sitting on the aisle in the front row, looked them over coldly. Honey delicately put her hand over her mouth and whispered something. Carl held up two fingers.

Pat jabbed his thumb at the middle girl. "You stay."

Bravely the rejects trudged off.

"Hi, I'm Buck McLeod."

"Oh, I know," the survivor said. "I think you're great. I loved you in—"

"What the hell is this—a coffee klatch?" barked Pat. "Come on, ya gotta fill forms."

A small woman in a sable coat, with a face like a skull, swept in, followed by a wedge of five men.

"Thelma!"

"Honey!"

They embraced passionately, barely touching cheeks.

"Buck, I want you to meet the most wonderful writer in the world. An old, *old,* dear, *dear* friend: Thelma Zeit."

"First, Buck, let me assure you I am but part of a team of really great writers." She rattled off the names of the four middle-aged worried men: Shooster & O'Hare, Cosgrove & Gerstein. The other man was a scholarly young Jew in a tank shirt. "And here is our hippie! Fresh from *Laugh-In*—Lanny Eccles." He bobbed his head. He was the only one with a pad and pencil.

"Hello," I said, as nicely as Van Johnson in his heyday. "I hope you brought some new words."

"Oh?" said Thelma. "I must be laboring under a misapprehension. I thought the old words were fine."

"For Rod. Not for me, Miss Zeit."

"Thelma!" cried Honey.

"Those lines about my curly hair, dimples and good looks won't play."

"Lanny," Thelma said curtly. "Change them to rugged, strong, masculine, et cetera."

"Thanks," I said. "And the second sketch doesn't work."

They flicked a suspicious glance at each other.

"Why not?"

"Honey spills stew on me, then beans, chili, flapjacks. But I never say a word to her."

"That's right," Thelma said coldly.

"If I yelled at her, told her to stop helping, it would be funnier."

They went into action.

Shooster, pulling his earlobe, said mildly, "I thought it *was* funny. But what do I know?"

"Nothing," snapped Thelma. "You've only been the top comedy writer in town for thirty years."

"Let me tell you something, Buck." Cosgrove put a friendly hand on my shoulder. "Thelma manages to take home a dollar or two a week herself, writing jokes." They all laughed at this but Lanny.

O'Hare said, "Thelma, tell me honestly, do you think it's funny?"

"Hilarious," she said coldly.

Honey gave Carl a look.

"Buck, luv, we're *hours* behind. And I'm sure we can straighten out your little problems in the staging."

We started blocking the first scene while the crew watched us through the cameras. When I picked her up to swing her onto the sawhorse, I held her for a moment—surprised at how flat and muscular her stomach was. When I put her down on the saddle, she stared at me and blew her line.

"Anything wrong, Honey?" Carl called out on the talk-back.

She quickly threw a hand up over her eyes. "The lights are dazzling."

Gray-haired women swooped down on her, holding out sunglasses, cooing like pigeons.

During the next break Phyllis shoved a wardrobe rack against me.

"Could you check Buck's costumes, Carl?"

"Sure thing, Phyl."

She held up a fringed white buckskin.

"*Divine.* Would you mind slipping it on, luv?"

Stripping to the waist, I caught Honey staring at me. She turned quickly away. From behind came a long, low, fuck-you whistle. It was from the blonde with the two lines. I bowed and she laughed.

When we got to the damned barbecue scene, I said, "Look. After she spills the stew, can't we restage this so I pass out the hamburgers? That way I can have my back to her, instead of looking her right in the eye, as she comes at me with the beans."

I lost that one and four others. They left me nailed to the floor. When we got to the end, I picked up the custard pie and indicated mushing it in her face.

"NO!" Thelma ran onstage. "You can't throw it. Just hold it, and she'll turn into it."

"I can't throw it?"

"Absolutely not! No one would laugh."

"Why not?"

"Because everyone loves Honey."

"Everyone," said O'Hare.

"The whole country," said Shooster.

"The world," said Gerstein.

"And they're right!" cried Thelma. "I love her, too. I pray to God every night, thanking Him for letting me write *The Honey Holly Show.*"

"Now, Thelma—" Honey protested mildly.

"I know I'm embarrassing you, my darling. Forgive me, but it's God's truth! Other writers have to create an image. Benny being stingy. Dino a drunk. But I don't have to create a cockamamie thing. Just show what a beautiful human being you are, and watch the American people clasp you to their hearts." Eyes glistening, she turned to me. "Can you understand what I'm saying, Buck?"

"I don't throw the pie in her face."

During the walk-through I tried playing him very dumb. It was a disaster. Everyone but Lanny and Cora told me I was wonderful. Just wonderful.

"Take an hour for dinner," Pat yelled. "And that doesn't mean sixty-one minutes."

I looked at the blonde with the two lines.

"Are you the girl who whistled at me?"

"No," she said. "They fired her."

I walked the horse around the parking lot to get the feel of him, trying to figure some fucking way to play it. There must be some angle. Some attack.

Then something zapped home.

Tabitha had said Olivier played Macbeth as if he knew everything that was going to happen. On *Is this a dagger, which I see before me* he wasn't surprised. It just confirmed what he already knew.

Suppose at the barbecue the moment I saw Honey I *knew* she was going to spill all those things on me.

It just might work.

For the run-through the theater was a quarter full with the usual collection of receptionists, low-ranking agents, hairdressers and the sad-faced women in cheap cloth coats who are either maids or poor relatives.

Carl barked on the talk-back, "Remember, Gang, we can't stop for anything. I've got to get a timing."

Then we were into the first sketch. It was tricky, trying to time the scattered laughs. When I brought the horse on, the lights made him skittish.

"Cut! Cut!" Carl screamed. "Buck, check your marks!"

I looked down. I was miles off.

"Shit, Carl, I'm sorry—"

A siren wailed. A follow-spot hit me. In the glare I could barely make out the cast and crew running at me, yelling: "Shame! Shame! Shame on Buck!"

"Buck . . ." Honey began seriously.

"Quiet!" Pat shouted angrily. "Not one sound!"

"Like every family we have our rules. One of them is no profanity. Dirty words show a lack of control in language. That leads to lack of control in drinking, drugs, sex—all the things that are destroying our country." She smiled slightly. "But, Buck, you know you've done wrong and must be punished."

"So bring on the Penalty Box!" Carl called.

Four of the girls shoved out from the wings a pink cardboard safe with two angels painted on it.

"Your punishment is to apologize to the Girls and the Gang; and contribute five dollars to the Sisters of St. Cyprian, some really dedicated nuns helping colored children in Africa."

"Pay up! Pay up! Pay up!" they chanted.

I pushed five dollars through the slot. They clapped their hands and cheered.

"Now, you must apologize."

" 'Pologize! 'Pologize! 'Pologize!" the gang shouted.

I stepped forward. "I'm sure one sad-ass son of a bitch for saying shit in front of all you nice people."

In the shocked silence all eyes swung to Honey.

She said crisply, "That will be thirty-five dollars more."

As I counted it out, Carl scampered for the control room. "Time's a-wasting, Gang. Let's pick it up with Buck's entrance."

In the dressing room I stared at myself in the mirror. It was no good—too Goddam passive. I smashed my fist into the wall. You wait twelve fucking months to get a fucking scene and they write and stage it so you can't act it. If that fucking fag dance director had staged it right, I'd be running away from her as desperately as Grant ran from Hepburn in *Bringing Up Baby*.

WAIT!

The way Grant played Curtis in *Operation Petticoat*. Like a shrink studying a psychopath—watching everything he did with tremendous intensity because it might give him the missing clue.

YES!

Put it on top of Olivier and it'll work.

A fist pounded on my door.

"Onstage. Show time."

As I came down the spiral iron staircase Honey stood onstage behind the closed curtain with the cast and crew circled around her.

"Buck," she said, "we're waiting for you to join us in silent prayer."

She sank to her knees and put her hand on the floor.

Everybody knelt and there was a big piling on of hands and moving of lips.

"Amen," she said finally. "And, Gang, wouldja give it all you've got?"

She moved away to watch the announcer do his warm-up. She had a big sloppy bathrobe wrapped around her, with her hair piled up under that baseball cap. She caught his eye and he broke off his Anaheim and Azusa jokes.

"Folks ..." he said. "Lots of times I have to say things I don't really believe in. That's my job. But tonight I'm going to really level with you. You're about to meet one of the greatest gals in the whole history of the world.

"I could talk all night about her good deeds. The charities she supports. The hospitals that are standing, today, all over this great land—*only* because Honey got them built.

"*But!* I can't say one single word about her good deeds. And do you know why? Because she won't let me. She's too modest. Now does that give you an idea of the kind of woman she is? *Huh?*"

They applauded.

"So all I can say is here she is, not only a great star but—more important—a great Human Being: HONEY HOLLY!"

She skipped out, blowing kisses. They pounded their hands together and screamed and hollered.

They were men in cheap work shirts with grey crew cuts and steel-rimmed eyeglasses; women with seamed faces, worn hands, and hats with cherries on them. There wasn't one black or Chicano face, one head of long hair. Damned if it wasn't a small-town Kansas revival meeting.

She held up one hand. They stopped instantly. She grinned at them.

"That's the goshdarnedest greeting I ever got. And I just can't tell you how good it makes me feel . . . in *here.*" She grabbed both shoulders and hugged herself. "I was *praying* you'd be just the way you are. I know it's not fashionable these days to admit you pray. The Supreme Court said it's against the law for school kids . . . well, I'm no school kid so I just go ahead and do it anyway."

A skinny woman leaped up, waving her pocketbook. "We know you do, Honey, and we love you for it."

She looked at her in amazement. "You do?"

"Yes!" And they were all on their feet, cheering.

You're good, I thought. *I hate to say it but you're as good as I've seen.*

Ring!

The announcer ran on, holding out an enormous alarm clock.

"Oh, dear! That means the show is about to go on, and we won't have any more time to visit. But before I go could we all sing—together—*God Bless America?*"

The band hit it; they all sang at the top of their lungs, Honey punching out key words with closed fists.

Max, positioning his boom, said, "You're not singing."

"Too choked up," I said.

On the last note she scooted into the wings, where the girls were waiting.

As she ran upstage, hands helped her out of the bathrobe. Took off her cap. Fluffed up her hair. Straightened her dress. Held out long white leather gloves. She shoved her hands into them like a boxer.

"AND NOW COMING TO YOU FROM HER OWN THEATER IN HOLLYWOOD, CALIFORNIA . . ."

Hands placed a hat on her head. A pin skewered it in place.

"YOUR GAL AND MINE . . ."

A mirror was held up. She took a brush. Calmly added a freckle.

". . . AMERICA'S SWEETHEART . . ."

The girls sprinted for safety.

"HONEY HOLLY."

The curtains flew. The band hit her theme. The house, startled by her lightning change, applauded wildly as she walked down to the footlights in her quick-moving, tight-assed way.

"Hi, folks! Tonight's a really super, dooper show 'cause it's our last of the season."

"Boooooo!"

She pouted prettily. "Now that's not fair. You get to take a vacation. Can't I?"

"NO!"

"Oh! You're *terrible*. I wish I *didn't* have such a good show for you. . . ." She relented. "But I do. A few months ago there was a wonderful Western series, *Range Rider*. The star was so rough and tough he scared me. But after rehearsing with him all week . . ."

Leaning forward, she whispered, ". . . he still scares me." (LAUGHTER) "But, seriously, give a warm welcome to . . . Buck McLeod."

I walked out in my tails to the theme from *Range Rider*. The applause swept over me. And I loved it. Even though I could see the applause signs blinking, the ushers waving it in; and knew anyone else would have gotten as much—I still loved it.

I stopped on my mark and bowed to her.

"Then I've got my old buddy back: Cora Hardiman!"

Cora made her entrance, bowing graciously.

"And all the wonderful guys in the band under the baton of dear old Gus Hemsley."

Gus and the musicians all laughed uproariously.

"We're gonna go out west on a dude ranch. Gus has picked a Golden Oldie for me, so don't go 'way. We're gonna have lots of fun. After this word from our sponsor."

Blackout. I ran to my dressing room. Changed.

Waiting in the wings, I felt the old butterflies; heard my cue; crossed myself; stepped out in the lights and said: "Which one of you ladies wants to learn how to ride?"

And we were into it. She was hell to play with—taking a lot of her lines out front. But the horse behaved; and it went by like lightning the way it always does. They laughed at the tag and it was over.

I came back in the white buckskins for the barbecue scene and checked the props.

The curtain flew. The moment Honey turned to me I fixed on her like a bird dog—and I had them. When she dumped the food on me they screamed. But when I didn't react—except to nod—they fell apart. It built from the stew to the flapjacks. When I picked up the pie there was sudden silence.

Fuck all of you, I thought.

And plowed it right in her face. There was a gasp; two beats; then an explosion of laughter. Honey milked it, hinging off me, and it kept building until they cued in the applause and blacked out on it.

As Honey in her sequined evening dress finished *September in the Rain,* the band segued into her theme. I stepped out, back in my tails, and took her hand; Cora took the other; the chorus kids filed on behind us, singing; as we hit the last note Honey slipped forward, said her "Good-bye and God bless us . . . every one."

And that was the show.

The Gang surrounded her. "You were great!" "Marvelous!" "Sensational!" "Cute!"

"Hey," Cora said. "You're no cowboy star. You're good."

I kissed her. "Do you fool around?"

"Better be careful. It might come back to me."

"Luvs!" Carl screamed. "Everyone back onstage in forty-five minutes for notes, changes and the second filming."

In the dressing room I ran the show through my head. Tightening. Shifting a reading. Changing a bit of business.

Satisfied, I lit a cigarette and, stretching out on the floor, wondered when I'd get to fuck her. Then I stubbed out the butt and took a nap.

I woke up an hour later. Wondering why the hell they hadn't called me, I ran down the staircase. But the theater was deserted. The work light shone on an empty stage.

Carl stepped out of Honey's dressing room, clicking shut his attaché case.

"Where the hell is everyone?"

"Why, Buck! Someone should have told you. The show was so tip-top, I said that's it. No second show. No retakes. Tribute to you in a way, luv. Ta-ta."

With a wave he was gone. The door to Honey's dressing room was ajar.

So that's the game plan.

But inside there was only Phyllis, shoving Honey's costumes into plastic bags.

"Honey left five, ten minutes ago."

Surprised, I stood there trying to figure it out. It didn't track.

"Oh, Buck," Phyllis asked suddenly. "Isn't she everything I said she'd be?"

"Phyllis, you didn't do her justice."

Outside, it was cold and fog was drifting in. I leaned back against the stage door. That great high of being at the center of the universe, pushing as hard as you can, using every bit of yourself—all drained away. And I was just another actor who'd done another lousy television show and knew I'd never work again as long as I lived.

I turned the corner of the blocky white building; in the black asphalt acre of the parking lot there were two cars. Mine and a big custom-built white Rolls. Honey stuck her head out of the window. "Hi! My car doesn't start."

"I'll take a look at it. I'm pretty good with motors."

"Never mind." She got out quickly. "I've already phoned the garage. I was wondering, if you're going anywhere near Holmby Hills, if you could drop me?"

She didn't say a word until, on Carolwood, she suddenly pointed to a dark driveway. "Turn there."

I swung hard, barely making it on screeching tires.

A searchlight flared through the windshield. Blinded, I hit the brakes.

A metallic voice said, "Come out with your hands on top of your head."

"It's all right, Harry," she called, waving.

"Oh, I'm terribly sorry, Mrs. Rosenstock. I didn't know the car."

"You did fine, Harry. That's what I pay you for."

The light went off; gates slid open; I drove past a concrete guardhouse where barking Dobermans danced on metal leashes.

The gravel drive curved through clusters of dark trees broken by an occasional spotlit sycamore.

I slid past a bluely gleaming sixty-foot pool flanked by ghostly cabanas with fluttering pennants.

Darkness. Then the glow ahead turned into a red-brown tennis court. A stooped old Mexican carefully scrubbed it with a long-handled brush. The lights spilled off on a formal rose garden, then dark trees slid by the windows again.

Christ, she must have six acres in the heart of Holmby. I didn't know anyone had that much land anymore.

Far ahead floodlit white columns floated toward us. An old maid, white apron fluttering against a black dress, painfully picked her way down the wide, white marble steps.

"Good evening, madame."

"Nora." Stepping out, Honey stopped as if struck by a sudden thought. "Oh! Buck, would you like a drink?"

In the dark entry hall Nora disappeared under a carved wood staircase that curved up thirty feet over our heads and disappeared. Honey, taking my elbow, led me into an enormous room, through solid black shadows broken only by small pools of light revealing pieces of glistening tables, Chinese vases, embroidered footstools standing on Persian carpets. She reached out. Something clicked. Panels swung open. We stepped into a crypt.

A man's golden profile, lit by a flickering gas flame, was centered in the marble wall between a Cross and a Star of David.

Under it:

IRVING ROSENSTOCK

(1916–1969)

Write–Producer–Husband

In Eternally Loving Memory

from

His Little Girl

HONEY

"Did you ever know Irving?" she whispered.

"No."

"He was a saint."

She bowed her head over clasped hands and prayed. Her head bobbed up. She said briskly, "You must be dying of thirst." And tugged me down an echoing unlit hall. Pushed me through a door. Lights blazed on. We stood in a Gay Nineties soda fountain. Honey skipped gaily behind the marble counter, flipping up gleaming brass covers. "What'll you have? Vanilla, chocolate, or strawberry?"

"Bourbon."

"GOSH. When *I* said *drink . . . you thought . . .* And I won't allow a drop of alcohol in the house. *Where are you going?*"

When I came back with the bottle of Jack Daniel's I keep in the trunk for emergencies, she was sipping a soda in one of the high-legged wire-backed chairs.

"Oh! You *startled* me. I thought you'd left."

I smiled at her. "No, you didn't."

I went behind the counter and started building a drink.

"I did, too. Cross my heart. I thought you walked out because you were mad."

"Just surprised," I said. "You're full of surprises." I raised my glass. "Here's to the next one."

"Oh . . ." She blushed and lowered her eyes. "I don't think I should drink to anything I don't completely understand."

"*Lion Country.*"

"What?"

"That was your line in *Lion Country.* The night before you went on safari. Stewart Granger (the guide) raised his glass, and looking right at you, said, 'Here's hoping we all get what we're after.' Bob Preston (your husband) said, 'Why, Sally, you're not drinking.' And you said (blushing and dropping your eyes), 'Oh . . . I don't think I should drink to anything I don't completely understand.' "

"That's *amazing!* That was years ago! I'd completely forgotten it."

"I remember every movie you ever made."

"Bet you don't," she said, smiling. "What was my first?"

"*Andy Hardy's Dilemma.* You were Donna Reed's cousin from Chicago."

"Close. That was my first feature."

"But not your first movie?"

"No. I'd made some shorts as a band singer. That's why MGM tested me. But once I was under contract Ginny Simms and Marvell got the songs and I got the jokes."

"*All at Sea, High Kickers, Snug Harbor.*"

"Say, you do have a memory."

"Then you went to Universal and made *Hip, Hip; Hayride; The Farmer's Son;* and *All-American Girl.*"

"Are you this good on everybody?"

"No," I said. "Just you."

She stared at me for a beat, then leaned quickly over

the counter and squirted seltzer in a glass. "You look like a man who could use a chaser.... Got you that time!"

"Swing Shift Sally."

"Wow!" She set the glass in front of me admiringly. Her breasts rested on my arm. She blushed and moved quickly back.

"Where was I?"

"Swing Shift Sally."

"Oh, yes. That was the first time I worked with Irving. From then on, of course, he produced all my pictures."

"At first nothing but hits: *Tea for Three; Who, What and Where; The Champagne Campaign.*"

She waggled her hand modestly. "We were just lucky."

"For two years you were the top-grossing star in the business."

"That was when *they* began," she said bitterly.

"Who?"

"The *critics.*" She moved quickly about. "Irving and I were making clean, happy movies that all America loved. And they couldn't stand that! So they decided to crucify me ... 'The Oldest Girl Scout in the World'! Can you believe *The Saturday Evening Post* would stoop so low?

"Don't think I cared for *myself.* No. It was Irving who was being destroyed by those vile lies. He'd go white with fury! I begged him not to read them. Oh!" she cried. "Those filthy murderers!"

"Murderers?"

"Yes," she said flatly. "Irving was hounded to his first coronary by a pack of newspapermen who never made twenty thousand a year."

I helped myself to another drink. She turned back, composed.

"But God smiled on us. He helped me nurse Irving back to health. I retired. I loved being just a housewife. Money never meant anything to me. I was content."

She shook her head admiringly.

"But not Irving. Night after night he'd sit in his bathrobe watching TV. One night he turned off the set and said, 'Honey, the Guy Upstairs has been good to us'—he meant God."

"Ah," I said.

" 'I'd hate to think we're repaying Him by abandoning all your fans. Leaving them with nothing to see but pornographic movies.'

" 'But, Irving,' I said. 'What can we do?'

"We sank to our knees and prayed for guidance ... and y'know that very night he wrote the pilot of *The Honey Holly Show*. We put our own money in it, shot it a week later. And three days after we wrapped, Heinz bought it from the rough cut."

"Certainly shows the power of prayer."

"Doesn't it just!"

"That's from *Apple for the Teacher*."

She frowned and stepped toward me. "Buck," she said, "just because I may—now and then—subconsciously say a line from an old movie, I don't want you to get the wrong idea. Basically, I'm a completely honest person."

"Good," I said. I kissed her, slowly sinking my teeth into that soft full lower lip. She sighed and leaned those heavy breasts against me. I slid my tongue in her mouth, she moaned and slipped her arms around my neck. I sucked her tongue into my mouth and chewed on it. Uttering wild little cries, she ground her cooze into me until my cock became hard as a rock.

Then she stepped back and, grinning, held out her hand. "Gosh, Buck. I had no idea it was so late. Thanks for the show and the ride home and the real nice talk. But it's hours past my bedtime so now I have to say nighty night!"

I laughed. "That's from all your pictures."

"*What?*" she said, stunned.

"You'd rub it up against MacMurray and Milland and Douglas all night and when they'd make their move you'd jump back with that same how-can-men-have-such-dirty-minds look! That's why you never grossed a dime in Europe, turned box-office poison and had to go into television. You're the Great American Cock Teaser."

Skin tightened over her cheekbones.

"I suppose those dirty words turn on the extras and stand-ins you're used to." She was haughty, cutting, high-toned Bette Davis. "You happen to be out of your class now. Way out. So good night, Mr. McLeod."

"I'm not going anywhere."

She picked up the phone. "Get out before I have the guards throw you out."

"You're good," I said. "As good as I've seen. But you can't con me. Since you saw me on the beach you've wanted one thing. That's why you fired Rod Light. Put me on the show. Pretended your car couldn't start. That's why we're here."

"And what," she asked icily, "is *that* supposed to be?"

I unzipped my fly and pulled out my cock. Stunned, she stared at it. Then drove her nails straight for my eyes. I ducked but she ripped my cheek. And scratching and kicking, went for me. I grabbed her hands, twisting them behind her back, and kissed her full on that mouth. She bit through my lower lip. I jumped back, spitting out blood. Her knee flashed as she kicked for my balls. I caught her foot and took her to the floor. Jamming my hand in her waistband, I yanked. Cloth ripped. Buttons went flying.

"No!" she screamed, grabbing her slacks as I pulled them to her knees, tore off her panties and went down on her.

She thrashed around wildly, screaming, but my crotch pinned her chest to the floor as my tongue searched through her musky wet cunt hair.

One hand raked my neck; the other gouged for my

eyes, but by then I had my tongue on her clit. I put pressure on until she went limp, then went to work on it.

"Oh, yes . . ." she whispered, caressing my neck. "That's lovely . . . you were right. I want you to do everything to me. . . . And it's been so long. Not since Irving . . . but not like this. I want to feel your beautiful body against mine. Please, take off your clothes?"

"Sure."

She threw the light switch and, in the dark, modestly turning her back, stepped out of her clothes.

"Turn around."

Smiling, she moved toward me. And sweet Christ, but she was something to see. Moonlight shining through the Venetian blinds cast black and white bars across those heavy long-nippled goosefleshed breasts; tiny tumbler's muscles rippled over her sharply outlined ribs; her black bush peeped out between those long showgirl legs glistening with sweat.

"Now, *you*."

I kicked off my boots, yanked down my jeans. As I was pulling my turtleneck over my eyes, I heard a strange scratching sound. I looked up and she was swinging down with all her strength a twenty-five-pound cut-glass candy jar.

I twisted away, getting my arm up as it exploded against my head. I fell backward, blood pouring into my eyes. Her legs—way out of focus—were coming toward me. I cut them out from under her. She fell back, another jar smashing against the brass footrail.

Then I was on her. She was screaming, struggling, scratching as I pinned her down, forced her knees apart and slammed my cock into her.

"No," she gasped. "No. No."

But I stabbed her again and again, until she relaxed and whispered, "Yes . . . do it to me. . . ."

I smiled, because what she didn't know was that I was going to teach her a lesson she'd remember the rest of her life. I was going to pimp-fuck her.

I was going to build her up till she was right on the edge of the greatest O of her miserable life. Then I'd whip it out, button it up and walk away.

It's the worst thing you can do to a woman. They become animals. Worse than junkies. I remember leaving a Ford model writhing on the floor biting the legs of the bed.

My blood was making ink-black dots on that freckled face I knew by heart. Eyes closed, she was smiling; little beads of sweat shone on her.

I went to work on her.

I'd set a pattern, but as soon as she'd hook into it I'd shift it. I'd lay out a fast beat, and when I felt her peaking too soon I'd change it. Take it away from her.

"Oh, God," she cried. "I never knew it could be like this . . . you're beautiful."

I hooked her left and right, until she gasped in excitement, then I moved it around, gently caressing the edges, exploring the outer limits.

"Oh, that's lovely." She relaxed.

I machine-gunned her.

Then stopped dead.

"Oh, no. Darling!" she screamed. "Don't stop! Please! Please!" She began shaking all over, her teeth chattering.

But I waited, then slammed it home like a battering ram.

And kept at it with deep penetrating strokes with all my weight behind them.

"Faster! Oh, that's so beautiful. But faster. Please. Darling! Please!"

Then I gave her the fireworks.

Until I felt it building and rising in her.

"Now," she moaned, writhing against me. "Now!"

So long, Cock Teaser.

As I started the pullout, she grabbed me—*inside*. I mean, I've felt snapping pussies before but never anything like this. It was as if a hand inside her was squeezing my cock. Hard. She tightened the pressure as if she had me in a vise.

I screamed and fell back. She stayed with me, straddling me.

"You're mine now," she crooned. "You belong to me. And I'll never let you go."

And grunting with delight, she came.

Then she used me like a dildo. I was just a big piece of stiff meat that provided her with multiple orgasm on top of multiple orgasm. Until, finally, she slid off me and rolled to the rug—sound asleep.

I stood in the surf, letting the breakers batter against me. Hoping they'd wash the smell of her off me.

Back in the house shivering from cold and exhaustion, I huddled next to the blazing fire, drinking Jack Daniel's. But I couldn't get warm.

The phone rang.

"Yes?"

Static. Woman's voice: "Mr. McLeod?"

"Yes."

More static. "Go ahead, Johannesburg."

Through the static that marvelous smoky voice: "Michael?"

"Tabitha."

"I've just seen the future of the world and it doesn't work. They're headed for a bloodbath. If the blacks aren't in their compounds by sundown they put them in concentration camps. There are former SS men everywhere, and you should see our brave liberal producers kiss ass with them to save a buck on locations.

"God, it's awful. The hatred in everyone's eyes cuts against you like sleet. The only thing that's right and real is love. And where the hell is mine? Halfway across the world. And where have you been? I've been trying to get you for hours?"

"I did a show."

"Darling, how wonderful. You see! I did bring you luck. What was it?"

"The Honey Holly Show."

"Ugh! But it's a start. It's a good omen. But the hell with your career. Tell me how you love me. Tell me how the agenbite of your inwit makes you babble to the stars: 'I love Tabitha! I love Tabitha. I love Tabitha.'"

"I do."

"Is someone there?" she asked quickly.

"No."

"Oh . . . you've been with another woman."

"It was an old hang-up. Something I had to get out of my system."

"It was her! That Honey Holly."

"Yes. But she didn't mean anything. I love you."

"Then, McLeod," she said sadly, "that was a lousy Goddam thing to do."

I finally traced the call back to her hotel but she wouldn't talk to me. I sat there cursing myself and finishing the bottle when the phone rang.

"Hello?"

"Buck, darling, where did you disappear to? I just woke up and you aren't here. Come back for breakfast."

I ripped the cord out of the wall and threw the phone across the room.

By the time I'd finished the letter to Tabitha the room was flooded with hot lemon sun; I walked out and lay down on the empty beach and fell asleep.

5

Heels click-clicking in my purposeful Kennedy stride, I shot down the corridor at TUL, Stanley two steps behind.

"Buck, for Christ's sake, all I ask is for you to give her a phone call. She's been on my back ever since the show. 'Why doesn't he call? Is he in town?' "

"Forget her, Stanley."

"I can't afford to. Neither can you. Honey has six series on the air. That's a lot of parts."

"Stop thinking like an agent. Now, what's this meeting with Nate about?"

He clammed up. I wondered if they had a nibble on the series. It must be important. I hadn't had a meeting with Nate since *Range Rider*.

The smiling male secretary pushed a release switch under the desk and we walked into Nate's office. The modern one. Two doors north was the Early American. He shuttled between.

Getting up from the low red leather chairs, shaking hands, smiling, were Ike Feldstein, head of television; Maury Davis, the plump, horn-rimmed closet queen, head of literary; and a dry hawk of a man I'd never seen before—Schiff, head of legal.

I sat down and the three short Bright Young Men brought me coffee and lit my cigarette.

Nate—plump, pink-faced, white-haired—danced into the room, crying, "Buck, God! But it's good to see you." He shook my hand and elbow, admiringly. "You look thirty. Doesn't he?"

They agreed I looked thirty. He sat down behind the chrome and glass clean-topped desk. There was a slight pause.

I said, "I suppose you're wondering why I called you all together."

"What?" asked Nate, startled.

"It's a joke," Stanley said.

"*I* called the meeting," Nate said indignantly.

"He's just kidding," Maury said soothingly.

Ike said to me, laughing, "I should get you a comedy series."

"I'll settle for a series."

That struck a nerve. They all turned and looked thoughtfully at Nate.

"This treatment Hornblower came up with on this private eye show got me enthused," said Nate.

"Me, too," said Maury.

"We all were enthused," Ike said. "Tremendously."

"Good," I said.

"And that enthusiasm was not misplaced." He tapped the fingers of his right hand on the top of the desk. I waited.

"Buck, you want it straight from the shoulder. OK. I can sell it to CBS—but not with you."

"What about NBC and ABC?"

"They turned it down flat."

"I even tried UBC," Ike said. "Greengauge won't look at a private eye. But CBS loves it."

"Perry Lafferty's crazy about it."

"But not about me."

"Nothing personal," Nate said. "This season the networks are committed to stars."

"I'm a star."

"I'm talking thirty-, forty-, fifty-G-a-week stars."

"Jimmy Stewart! Tony Curtis! Glenn Ford! Shirley MacLaine! Tony Quinn!"

Maury said, "You're no kid anymore."

"I'm a helluva lot younger than Stewart."

"You're at that awkward age," Nate said. "Too

young to be Robert Young. Too old to be James Brolin."

Stan said soothingly, "We all know it's a jolt to the ego, but let's consider the positive aspects—"

"No," I said.

"Now, Buck," Nate said.

"Now nothing! CBS is making a hundred lousy fucking *Movie of the Weeks* starring no one you ever heard of. I come up with a property that they love. Want for a *series*. And you mean to tell me—you can't sell it?"

Nate didn't blink. "Not with you."

Ike slapped me on the knee. "But don't think we won't get you one sweet deal."

"Right on!" said Stan.

"The way Perry feels I bet I could get you a G an episode."

"No," I said.

Nate said slowly, "In a situation such as this I'd insist Buck have a piece."

"Ya hear that? Ya won't have to lift a pinky. Surf all day, hump that young pussy all night, and open up a check once a week for maybe two G's. Plus participation."

"I don't want the fucking money. I want my show on."

Ike said, "Perry Lafferty will be heartbroken if he doesn't get this property."

"My ass bleeds for Perry Lafferty."

The atmosphere got very chilly.

Schiff looked at Maury. Maury said, "This puts me in a difficult situation because I represent the *author,* and since CBS wants *his* property—"

"Where is Ted?" I asked.

They looked around as if they expected to find him crouched behind one of the red leather chairs. A Bright Young Man murmured something about some root canal work he believed he had to have done.

Schiff, staring at me through his bifocals, said, "Legally, in a case like this, there are precedents that we should sell the series and let an arbitrator decide the amount Buck is entitled to."

"Fuck you, lawyer. That presentation is based on a property I own. That story is filed under my name at the Writers Guild. Try and sell it without me, I'll hit you with so many injunctions CBS won't dare touch it."

"Buck!" cried Nate with a smile. "Any schmuck can keep shows off the air. The trick is to get them on."

"Then get it on!"

"I can't with you."

"You sure as hell can't without me."

"Considering your financial situation," Stan said deliberately, "you can't afford to say no."

"No," I said.

Little sidelong glances click-clicked around the room.

Nate shrugged and smiled. "All right, Buck, have it your way," he said mildly. "But it's going to be a long, cold summer."

I was about twenty minutes late when I pulled up in front of Eddie's little white stucco house off Woodland in the Valley. My goddaughters banged out the screen door and ran down the cement walk, squealing, "Uncle Mike! Uncle Mike!"

I reached over the gate and hauled them up. There was much passionate hugging and kissing. They smelled superbly of freshly ironed dresses, talcum powder and that little-girl smell as distinctive as that of puppies.

Maria came out, hands on her hips, smiling but shaking her head. "Luciana! Antonella! Shame on you. Let him alone."

I set them down and gave Maria a big kiss.

Eddie was sitting out in the backyard under the huge orange-and-green heavily fringed beach umbrella I'd given them for Christmas years ago. He was drumming his fingers on the round white metal table the pole went through.

"Sorry I'm late."

"That's OK," he said grouchily.

Maria came out carrying a green bottle of Verdicchio and a corkscrew. She was a big-boned woman with a lot of flesh on her, not fat but the kind of thighs and breasts sculptors go crazy over. It was a pleasure to watch her move.

The girls followed her slowly in single file, seriously and carefully carrying the wineglasses and the big wooden salad bowl.

The wine was lovely. Clean, dry, probably a touch too cold—but the way I like it. The salad was fresh cracked crab with a sharp, dry mustard-mayonnaise.

While we ate, the girls filled me in on their lives: teachers they loved, teachers they hated; changes in Disneyland; the dog they were going to get—argument over the virtues of cocker spaniel versus Scottie.

Bored, Luciana, the world's best five-year-old courtesan, leaped in my lap, kissed me passionately on the mouth and murmured, "I love you, Uncle Mike, and I'm going to marry you."

Maria pulled her off and said sternly, "We do not joke about marriage in this family. Especially about your Uncle Michael's marriage."

"Why's that, Maria?" I asked innocently.

"Because," she exploded, "it's high time you grew up, found a nice girl, got married and started raising children, instead of chasing those bimbos around."

"Bimbos?" asked Antonella.

"Bimbos!" said Luciana. They fell into each other's arms, howling with laughter.

"I think you're absolutely right, Maria," I said. "That's why I've decided to get married."

She screamed, "Who is she? What's her name? How long have you known her? Where is she? Why didn't you bring her over? Eddie, why don't you say something?"

"How the hell can I?"

I told them about Tabitha as best I could without getting too flowery about it. When I finished Maria asked quickly, "Can she cook? Will she convert?"

"Maria," Eddie said quietly, "Mike and I have things to talk about."

"Of course." She stood, smoothing her skirt. "Come, girls."

The girls stood, smoothing down their skirts, then curtsied. "Good-bye, Daddy. Good-bye, Uncle Mike." They kissed us, somewhat aloofly. Minds already set on different goals. I wondered what?

We waved as the Volkswagen bus disappeared around the corner with them waving furiously.

"I just hope I do half as well as you on the wife situation."

"You must be out of your fucking mind."

I stared at him. I'd never seen him so mad.

"Marriage! What the fuck do you know about marriage?"

"Not much, but—"

"Not one fucking thing. Marriage is responsibility. Being faithful to one woman. Paying bills. Bringing up children. And money. Money. And more money."

"Jesus, Eddie, what the hell's bugging you?"

"You are. You've had one fucking job in a year. You're up to your eyeballs in debt. And you're going to get married? Forget it. Just fucking forget it."

He threw his arms out like an umpire signaling safe.

"OK, Eddie," I said. "Let's have it. Whatever you've got up your ass."

He stood there for a second looking at me, then nodded and walked into the house. It was serious, whatever it was.

He came out with a bottle of Jameson and a quart of ale and four glasses. We knocked back a good shot of Irish; and while I was drinking the chaser, Eddie said in a tight, high voice, "When the doc was working on this"—he slapped his cast—"he spotted some warts on my belly he didn't like the look of. So he had me take some tests. I got the results today. It's Big C."

"How bad?"

"They don't know. I'm going into St. John's Friday. They're going to take out what they can. Maybe they've caught it in time."

"Does Maria know?"

"I don't think so. I told her it's a hernia and I've been faking the symptoms. But I can't tell if she believes me or not." He smiled suddenly. "I never lied to her, so I haven't any pattern to go by."

He poured us some more Irish. A yellow jacket came nosing around. He shooed it away.

"Mike," he said. "There's a favor I have to ask."

"You've got it. Anything happens to you, don't worry. I'll take care of Maria and the girls."

"How? Hustling broads?"

"I'll find a way."

"Forget it. Maria can go back to nursing. Her mother will help with the girls. I've got some money to carry her over the worst part. . . . That's not the favor."

"What is?"

"If it's really bad . . . terminal . . . I want you to kill me."

I stared at him.

"Jesus, Eddie, how the hell can I agree to a thing like that?"

He exhaled slowly, then turned and looked at his rosebush.

"My old man died from cancer of the intestine. The doctors all lied. To him. To us. They kept him alive for eight months. He had tubes in his arms, up his nose, his ass. . . ."

He turned to me, his blue eyes very calm, very clear. "Maria and the girls are not going through that."

I nodded. "OK."

I held out my hand, but he made me swear it on the Bible. Then he poured another round. We clinked glasses and tossed it down.

"Anything else?" I said when I had my voice under control. He shook his head. So I stood.

"Got to be on my way," I lied. "I have an interview."

"So-long."

I started toward the gate.

"Wait. There is something." He called out, grinning. "Give me a real Irish wake. Maria won't want to. But talk her into it. It's good for the widow."

Suddenly we were hugging each other hard, and slugging each other on the back and shoulders. Maria always teased us about how Italian men were always kissing their friends, but American men didn't dare show emotion. Well, no Italian loved anyone more than I loved this ugly, sawed-off son of a bitch.

Then we were standing apart again, embarrassed.

"Got to split," I said. "Thanks for lunch."

"Glad you could make it," Eddie said. "See you."

I drove like a madman through the parched brown mountains until the black yellow-lined road curved through the last of the high rocks and the land fell away in flat shelves to the Pacific, steely blue in the late-afternoon light, stretching on either side as far as I could see and ahead to infinity.

As I shot through the huge old gates I hit the brakes hard and skidded sideways, just missing a shiny new Cyclone fence. Through it I could see the gardens, and the old adobe mission and the long arched porch that led to the chapel. I yanked at the bellpull. I could hear a faint jangle far away, then became conscious of another sound, and I saw above the steeply pitched red tile roof a swarm of yellow bulldozers ripping through the old vineyards, slashing the softly rounded hills into flat foundation sites.

"Yes?" A gaunt sharp-nosed man in brown friar's robe, sandals, with a rope tied around his waist, stood impatiently behind the fence, a black Doberman at his heels.

"I'd like to use the chapel, Father."

"It's closed."

"I thought it was never closed."

"It's now open to visitors nine A.M. to eleven A.M., three P.M. to five P.M.," he said crisply.

"It's only a few minutes after five, Father, and it's terribly impor—"

"No exceptions are ever granted to the rules."

"But I've got to pray for a man's soul."

"In that case . . ." He smiled sourly. "I'm sure it can wait until tomorrow." And he walked away.

"Are you an ordained priest?"

He stopped, surprised. "Yes, of course."

"Then in the name of Christ, Father," I yelled, "go fuck yourself."

The black dog threw himself at the fence, trying to bite me through the wire. And he was right. If I'd gotten my hands on that son of a bitch I would have torn his head off his shoulders.

He put a whistle to his lips and blew on it. It didn't make a sound, but called the dog off. The man hurried around the white corner of the main building, brown skirt flapping around his thin, white, bare ankles.

It was so dark that coming out of the hot sunlight I could barely make out Rusty behind the bar.

"Double Jack Daniel's on the rocks. And a Heineken's chaser."

"No."

"No jokes, Rusty. I need that drink. Fast."

"It's no joke, Buck. You're shut off."

"Because of last night?"

"Because of a lot of things. You haven't paid anything on your tab. You cause trouble. You scare off some of the customers."

"I'll give you a couple of hundred when I get the check from *The Honey Holly Show*. Now get those fucking bottles on the bar. Fast!"

"Trouble?" asked a deep voice from the shadows.

"Nothing we can't handle," I said.

"I didn't ask you. I asked him." Coming toward me through a shaft of sunlight was a cop about six-four. A couple of paces behind him in lockstep was his partner. They both had their shades on.

"Oh, look," said the partner, smiling. He had an interesting purple scar running off from the corner of his mouth. "It's that big tough movie star who's always beating up fags."

"Damned if it isn't. What's his name?"

"Damned if I can remember."

"Buck," I said, smiling. "Buck McLeod."

"Right," said the big one. "The one who thinks he's tough."

"Wrong," I said, still smiling. "The one who knows he's tough."

"Buck," Rusty said nervously, "I'll give you a drink if you'll go without causing trouble."

"Trouble?"

"I'd like to see him try to start some trouble." The big bastard hooked his thumbs in his cartridge belt.

That just cost you, I thought. I'll blow past you, nail your partner, and be putting my fist through your ugly teeth while you're getting your thumbs out.

Suddenly I thought of Eddie. What the fuck good are you going to be to him in jail? So I turned and walked out.

"Thanks, Buck," Rusty called.

"Thanks for what?" said the second cop.

"Buck, you just pay off a little something on that tab, and you're welcome back. Because we're friends. Right?"

I spat on the threshold.

When I pulled into the parking area, big yellow signs were stapled all over my fence and garage door. "THIS PROPERTY HAS BEEN SEIZED AS SECURITY AGAINST

Unpaid Taxes and Will Be Disposed of at Public Auction on July . . ."

The phone was ringing.

"Mr. McLeod, this is Hodgkins. The manager of the answering service? Well, I just finished talking to Miss Honey Holly. Our switchboard is just jammed with messages she's left for you. She's giving a party at her house this evening at seven. She left several messages saying if she didn't hear from you, she assumed you'd be there. But she's beginning to wonder. . . . I'd be more than happy to relay any message, and—"

I hung up.

I knelt by the fireplace, facing the setting sun, and prayed for Eddie for a long time.

Then I sat at the bar and had a drink. Evening fog had clouded the sun and the waves had a steely, cold look.

I wondered where Eddie'd go, if he died. Purgatory? . . . Paradise? . . . I couldn't picture that. I saw him, somehow, out there—part of the movement of the waves moving in, the breakers curling, the gulls swooping . . .

The phone rang. I waited for a long time before I picked it up.

"Yes?"

"McLeod, you *can* write. That was a lovely letter. I accept your apology and *yes.*"

"Yes?"

"We are now betrothed. So hie your ass to the nearest confessional and post the banns. And stay as pure as the driven snow until I get back. That will be in about four weeks."

"Four weeks."

"You talk like a boob, it's a good thing you write like an angel. Listen, darling, this picture is a disaster. I'll never work again. And I don't give a damn. I'm just going to lie around your shanty Irish beach house and have children. I've got the names picked out. Joshua, Zachary and Matthew; and Abigail and

Amanda. That's just for starters. How are you with diapers and bottles, Michael?"

I threw the phone into the center of the plate-glass window behind the bar. Glass splinters exploded around me. I wiped them off the bar, laid my head down on it and, for the first time since my mother's death, cried.

As I pulled up in front of the spotlit white pillars, Honey was running down the steps, a gauzy white shawl standing out straight behind her.

"Buck, I'm so glad you came. But where have you been? Why haven't you called? I've been frantic—" She broke off and stared at me. "But you're not dressed for dinner."

"No," I said. "I just came to say good-bye."

"Good-bye!" she cried. "Didn't that night mean anything to you? It was the most beautiful of my life."

"Mine, too. But I loused it up by falling in love with you."

"Silly! How could your falling in love louse anything up?"

"Because deep down inside I'm square. Old-fashioned. Just like in the movies. When I fall in love I want to marry the girl."

Startled, she said slowly, "Marry me?"

"Don't worry. I know you're way out of my class. You told me. So, so long."

"Wait a minute. *Please!*"

"No. Seeing you again hurts too much. Good-bye."

And I gunned down the drive.

It was a little overboard, but a print.

6

The next afternoon when I walked into the drawing room, Honey was sitting on a rosewood sofa behind a silver tea service and a tray of cucumber sandwiches.

"Don't you look nice, darling. I'm glad you wore your blue suit. It's just right for a business meeting."

"Business meeting?"

"That's what Greengauge will turn it into."

Nora scurried in with a bottle of champagne in an ice bucket.

"Put it there," Honey said, pointing.

"Hello, Nora."

"Sir!" She was startled at being called by name.

The tall, black-lacquered grandfather clock boomed four times.

"My God," I said. "It sounds like Big Ben."

"It is." Honey arranged the folds of her bottle-green dress. "I had it taped in London."

A carillon chimed. There was the sound of the front door opening, voices murmuring. Then a big man stood leaning against the arch. I was surprised at how fat he was. Network presidents this season were young and athletic.

"Honey!" he cried. "How lovely you look! Poised behind the tea service like a heroine from Henry James."

"His favorite author," said the very good-looking blond man in a pink linen suit entering behind him.

"It's been *far* too long!" Greengauge crossed the long room quickly. There was muscle under his jowls

74

and belly. He wore a beautifully cut double-breasted grey sharkskin suit.

"Josiah!" Honey held out her hand, wrist arched.

He bent down and kissed it, his bald head shining pinkly for an instant in her spotlight.

"Josiah," Honey said, "I'd like you to meet—"

"Buck McLeod needs no introduction," said the other man quickly.

"Indeed not!" Greengauge took my hand in a powerful grip. "How grand to meet you, sir. I've been a fan of yours for years."

"Josiah was very high on *Range Rider*—as was I." The other man, smiling, held out his hand. "I'm Hal Hundsley."

"What has happened to my manners? Hal here is my good right hand."

"And vice-president in charge of West Coast operations," Honey added.

Hundsley shrugged modestly. Up close he looked older, probably thirty-five. His thin blond hair was fluffed out to cover his high narrow skull.

"Hal, we must commission someone to paint her portrait. Sitting there in *that* exact pose. Pity Sargent's dead."

"Yes," said Hundsley.

Honey laughed. "You should hear what he says to Lucy."

"Nothing like that."

"Only because you can't persuade her to leave CBS," Honey said naughtily.

Greengauge chuckled deep in his chest. "What care I for Lucy as long as I have you?" Suddenly serious, he sighed. "But do I? That's the question."

"Exactly," said Hundsley gravely.

"Buck—I hope you'll forgive me for calling you Buck but I know we shall be friends—Honey will only sign a *yearly* contract with us. And every season, at about this time, I'm summoned here—"

"*Summoned!*" cried Honey.

"Ha ha," said Hundsley.

"Where she tells me that she has made up her mind to retire, and will never perform again—"

"And I mean it!"

"I wonder, Buck. Because after harrowing negotiations she agrees to return for just one more season, *if* we put on the air some ghastly new program she's produced."

"You're *terrible,* Josiah. Buck, don't believe a word he's saying."

"Ha ha," said Hundsley.

"Forgive me. I was only explaining to Buck why I emitted that enormous sigh of relief when I saw him and realized this was a social occasion." He beamed at me. "Or," he asked lightly, sitting on the sofa, "is it?"

Honey dropped her eyes. There was a long wait before she said in a small voice, "Buck has asked me to become his wife . . . and I have accepted."

Greengauge slowly stood. "Ah, Honey," he murmured. "It's what I've always wanted for you."

"It's just marvelous," Hundsley said.

While they kissed her, I popped the cork and poured the champagne.

Greengauge slowly raised his glass to Honey. "Hail to thee, blithe spirit, and may God bless this troth!"

"Hear, hear," said Hundsley.

Tears sparkled in Honey's eyes. "Oh, Josiah, I never thought you'd take it like that. You are indeed a kind and generous friend."

"Generous." His eyes flicked to Hundsley. "Why generous?"

She slipped her hand under my elbow. "Surely, you see this is the end of *The Honey Holly Show*. From now on, I'll be Mrs. Buck McLeod . . . homemaker."

"I see nothing of the kind. Marriage doesn't mean retirement."

"Josiah, stop pretending. It's time to ring the curtain down. There's nothing worse than watching an actress of what the French call *un certain âge* hanging on too long."

"As God is my witness, if that were the case I'd be the first to tell you. But, Honey! Look at you! Slim as a girl! A cheek like a peach blossom."

She shook a finger at him. "Nevertheless, every year I get older."

"You're like a great wine, Honey, age only improves you. Today you have more of that glow, that shimmering radiance that only the greatest stars possess."

"And that's just how I'm going out. Number One in the national Nielsen's."

"Honey," Greengauge said solemnly, extending his hand toward the window, "what about . . . *them?*"

She looked sadly out into the garden.

"The millions of shut-ins, widows, hardworking people who live harsh, bleak, hopeless lives, who look forward all week to one thing! Spending that hour with you! They love you, Honey. Can you abandon your fans?"

"Oh, you are cruel," she said. "You do know how to hurt." Suddenly she darted about the room. "How did we get on all this upsetting talk of *fans* and *contracts*. Yes, Hal, I know that's your job, bullying people and worrying about money. But, Josiah, I thought *you* would understand."

She stopped behind the love seat, catching the pink pinpoint perfectly. She looked imploringly at him.

"I'm a woman in love! I'm going on my honeymoon!"

"Lord knows," Greengauge protested. "I want you to taste life to its fullest. But"—he slowly spread out his hands—"society, in its infinite wisdom, has decreed that honeymoons cannot last forever. And once you are back here in Holmby Hills. A woman of your drive and discipline and talent! *A housewife!* You'll be bored, restless, miserably unhappy! That's what concerns me."

"Don't worry, Josiah," she said lightly. "I'll keep busy producing the other shows."

He blinked. She'd caught him off guard.

Hal snapped, "No way. You go. They go."

"And just what do you mean by that?"

"You blackmailed us into taking those dogs to begin with. If you cancel out, you can kiss them good-bye."

Honey took a step toward Hundsley.

"*Joe and Josephine* is a solid hit."

"Because it inherits your ratings. *Surfside Six* reruns would be a hit in that time slot."

"*Billy's Beanery* is building beautifully."

"You mean it has a terrible rating. And not even you can find a word to say for those three dog-eared Westerns. If I cancel all six shows, the FCC will pin a medal on me."

"Klipsruder won't," she said softly. It was the second time she'd startled them. "And neither will Kidder or Stone."

"Honey," Greengauge said reproachfully, "you and Hal have had your differences, but I can't believe you'd go behind my back and talk to clients about a family matter."

"How do you think it makes *me* feel," she said tearfully. "I thought this would be such a lovely, happy, *fun* time because I do think of you as my family." Her voice broke. "But Hal had to go and turn it into a nasty ole business meeting. My engagement!" Sobbing, she threw herself into my arms.

I picked up my cue. "I think you'd better go."

"Hal," Greengauge said severely, "this reproof is richly deserved. Please accept my apologies, sir, and my felicitations."

After the door closed behind them, Honey moved away, drying her tears.

"It must be pretty upsetting. Losing six shows."

"Oh," she said, "I'll keep two." She thought for a moment. "No. Three."

* * *

I found Maria in the corridor at St. John's, leaning against the white wall outside his room, saying her Rosary.

"He's left the recovery room," she said. "Should be down any minute."

She was very pale. I squeezed her arm.

"Stop worrying. A hernia's nothing."

"*Hernia!*" She shook her head scornfully.

I lit a cigarette. "Did you know all the time?"

"Sure. He lies like a ten-year-old." She smiled a tight-lipped smile, and shook her head again. "Hernia."

A skinny black kid in hospital whites came around the corner wheeling Eddie up on a stretcher.

Maria, cupping her hands around the knobs of his shoulders, bent down over him—and very slowly, very gently put her cheek against his.

I squeezed his hand, hard.

His skin was a greenish yellow and his eyes were out of focus.

"It was a spinal," he said in a voice I never would have recognized. He kissed Maria's cheek. "Hey. Don't cry. I'm fine."

His eyes cleared, and over the back of her head probed into mine. I knew what he was asking.

The doctor was young, balding, smoked a pipe, was impressed by Movie People and had seen *The Honey Holly Show* I did.

When I got back, I took a deep breath, put on a smile and walked in.

Eddie was propped up in the far bed; Maria, in her yellow silk dress in the chair beside him. Three bony old men, in bad shape, looked up at me vaguely as I walked past their beds, then turned back to their television sets.

Eddie asked, "Did you see the doctor?"

"Yeah. He'll be around to tell you everything in fifteen or twenty minutes."

"I want to hear it from you. Now."

I looked at Maria.

"No more secrets," she said. "I was a nurse. Remember?"

Eddie nodded. So I said, "They couldn't get it all out."

Eddie closed his eyes.

"But there's a good chance it will respond to chemotherapy and cobalt treatments."

"Sure," Eddie said tonelessly. "How long do I have to stay?"

"Not long. A week. Maybe less. Ten days at the most. They want to see how you react to treatment. They're getting very good results with chemotherapy these—"

"Skip the commercial."

"I'm giving it to you straight. The treatments are hell. You'll be sick as a dog. They'll make you irritable, depressed."

"But only for a day," Maria said.

He patted her hand. "Let Mike do the talking."

"She's right. That's just what he said."

Eddie thought it over. "What about work?"

"Hard to say. He doesn't understand much about stunt men. Hard, physical labor is out at present. But driving a motorcycle off a bridge might be OK."

He stared me straight in the eye. "That it?"

"That's it."

He nodded slowly. "Thanks." Then he smiled brightly. "OK. You two can split for a while. I'm fine. Just tired. Going to take a little nap." He closed his eyes.

In the corridor she said, "I want to be with him for the next hour and then go tell the girls. Can you come back at one-forty-five and spell me till four-thirty?"

"Sure. You OK?"

"Yes," she said defiantly. "And so is he."

Honey's pine-paneled Colonial pub room was full of white-haired sunburned men in plaid dinner jackets and their wives.

Honey led me around by the elbow, introducing me. First, I met her oldest and dearest friends: Ken and Judy Klipsruder (Klipsruder Flashlights sponsored *Billy's Beanery*). Then there was old Mr. Hydesdale, of Hydesdale Savings and Loan, with his hawknosed daughter, Emily, who had married the son of Judson Hotels; from Phoenix and Palm Springs came the Truscotts, he'd been Goldwater's biggest backer; while up from La Jolla was Admiral Kinlock (retired); then there was Catspool, who'd built the Marina; Clint Merrimac, who'd managed somehow to slip out of the conglomerate that bore his name before it collapsed; the Kidders, of Kidder Petroleum, who lived in Houston but summered in Bel Air; and Larry Huddlestone, who'd won last year's Newport–Honolulu race, and his much older wife.

They all kidded Honey about finally repealing Prohibition and serving real drinks.

"I have another surprise. We're going to watch Walter Cronkite."

There were scattered boos.

"Damned Democrat," growled Klipsruder.

On the big set sunk in the wall above the mantel, Cronkite said: "In Hollywood. TV Superstar Honey Holly announces she is going to marry Buck McLeod, an actor."

The rest was drowned out by cheers. Everyone kissed Honey and shook my hand.

We ate in an enormous dark dining hall. Suits of armor stood against the oak-paneled walls. So many banners hung from the heavy beams I expected C. Aubrey Smith in Bengal Lancer full dress to bound up, glass in hand, and shout, "Gentlemen, the Queen."

Instead, Admiral Kinlock spoke at length on the blessings of matrimony.

Before he had finished, Honey herded us into a room full of crystal chandeliers with red satin walls where we watched a screening of *Klute*.

When the lights came on and the projection screen

slid back in the ceiling, Judy Klipsruder poked me in the chest. "What do you think of Jane Fonda?"

"Great."

"She may be—as an actress," she said bitterly. "As an American, I just wish she'd go back where she came from."

"Where's that?"

"Hanoi."

As we stood on the front steps saying good-bye, Klipsruder slapped me on the back again. "From now on, Buck, old boy, we're going to be seeing one whole lot of each other."

"Yes, indeedy," Judy said. "We play bridge with Honey three or four times a week. For hours."

"I don't play bridge," I said.

"Oh, dear!"

"Don't worry, Judy," Honey said. "He'll learn."

The cops standing on the curb—between us and the kids running along the sidewalk trying to peer into the Rolls—bowed and smiled at Honey like doormen.

Twenty feet from Grauman's, a white glove flourished and I stopped.

The wooden stands set up on both sides of the marquee were packed, but hundreds more spectators crushed together, pushed against the ropes, jostling for a better view. Searchlights slashed into the sky. An announcer surrounded by a TV remote crew was interviewing Bob and Natalie.

The white glove waved me on.

The announcer shouted on the PA: "Behind the wheel of that Rolls-Royce sits the luckiest man in the world! Why? Because he's going to marry America's Sweetheart . . . *Honey Holly!*"

As she stepped out the spotlight hit her, and they screamed. I've been to a lot of premieres in my time, but I never heard a scream like that. It struck against me like a wind.

They reached out over the ropes, frantically trying

to touch her, shoving autograph books at her hands. Dried-up women screaming her name. Openmouthed men, veins standing out on their throats.

The announcer shook my hand. "Talk about your great receptions, Honey. They love ya. And so do I and so does Buck. Right, Buck?"

"Right."

"Beautiful! *Beautiful.* Honey, can ya tell us when the great day's going to be?"

"Soon. Very soon." She looked up at me adoringly. Flashbulbs exploded. "Now that I've found him, I'll never let him go."

You had to hand it to her, she had a bad line for every occasion.

The fans screamed. She waved to them. "How do you like my guy?"

They fell silent and stared at me. A searchlight swept their sullen faces; empty eyes sparkled like marbles.

A stringy woman called warningly, "You better be good to her, mister!"

After the picture we walked into the green-and-white tent pitched on the parking lot and sat at Honey's table. The Klipsruders, Truscotts and Huddlestones were already eating. Greengauge, at the far end, called out, "How is it CBS beat us on the wedding story?"

"Gee, Josiah, I don't know. Ask Benjy."

Benjy, a very thin, white-haired fag, very elegant in his velvet dinner jacket, knelt between Greengauge and Hundsley, murmuring apologies.

Someone set down a plate of lukewarm chicken curry.

"Darling, I thought you knew. Always eat first. The food is never any good. And you don't want to be photographed chewing."

Squads of photographers surrounded us. Flashbulbs went off in volleys. Important Beautiful People came up in platoons, kissing her, congratulating me. Benjy stayed at Honey's elbow, discreetly whispering a name she might have forgotten, tactfully easing away someone who'd overstayed his allotted time.

Ross Martin walked out on the dance floor and introduced Jack Lemmon, who introduced George Burns, who introduced Dean Martin. Dean sang three songs and called the others back, and they began auctioning off five miniature poodle puppies.

Spotting Greengauge moving off, waving good-byes, I excused myself.

I caught him at the curb as he was stepping into his limousine. Hundsley sat inside, an open attaché case on his lap.

"Why, Buck, how kind of you to come out to say good-bye."

"I have to talk to you. It's important."

Hal looked up at me curiously. Greengauge apologetically clapped me on the shoulder. "Unfortunately, I'm on my way to the airport. Hal here will set up a meeting just as soon as I return from New York."

"It won't wait." I stepped in and sat down; the doorman closed the door, and the car pulled out into the traffic.

Greengauge studied me carefully.

"How are the negotiations with Honey for next season going?"

Greengauge smiled, sliding the cellophane wrapper off a long black cigar. "These days negotiations have become so financially complicated the only fellas who know how things stand are the tax experts."

"Wrong," I said. "I know. Honey's not going to sign."

Hal laughed harshly.

"You must forgive Hal. But at just about this stage of negotiations, every year someone very close to Honey tells us the very same thing."

"She doesn't get married every year."

"No," Hal said. "But there's always something."

"Honey's planning to spend this year in Europe."

Greengauge, unimpressed, clipped the end off the cigar. "Plans can always be changed."

"She has her heart set on spending the fall in London."

Greengauge chuckled.

"Forgive my cynicism, but each season my stars tell me they won't be back because they have their hearts set on touring in Shakespeare; playing Beckett off Broadway; doing a documentary on ecology. Yet next fall there they are—back on UBC. Don't think it's due to my powers of persuasion. Dear me, no—it's because what their hearts are really set on is . . . *money.*"

Hal said coldly, "Especially Honey."

"What would you say if I told you she's spent fourteen thousand dollars to rent a London town house for September, October and November?"

Greengauge smiled.

"No way," Hal said, laughing.

He stopped when I handed over the Xeroxed copy of the cashier's check.

"That cunt!"

"Hold your tongue," Greengauge snapped. "It's bad form to speak so of a man's fiancée. Besides . . ." He shifted his great bulk expectantly toward me. "Buck didn't come along just to tell us that."

"No," I said with a warm Will Rogers grin. "I came to help."

"One needs all the help one can get these days . . . especially with Honey."

"If Honey stays here she'll do the show."

"Agreed. But . . ." Hal clicked a lighter; Greengauge sucked flame into his cigar. "What would induce her to forgo this honeymoon she has her heart so set on?"

I took out of the inside coat pocket of my dinner jacket the presentation of the private eye show and handed it to him.

His eyes flicked down the page, then back to me. He

had very hard, very cold green eyes. He picked up a small black mike.

"Hans, pull over to the curb, please."

"I wouldn't want you to miss your plane."

"I won't," he said. "It will wait."

He read through it carefully, passing the pages over to Hal. When he was finished he said, "I'm no program man, of course, but it seems first-rate to me."

"Absolutely." Hundsley was still reading.

"What was I saying this morning, Hal?"

"Find a series for McLeod."

His forefinger tapped the pages. "This is that series."

"No doubt about it, Josiah. Except, I don't quite see how this solves the Honey problem."

"If I'm shooting that series, we can't go to Europe. Honeymoons take two."

Hal shook his head. "There's no time to shoot a pilot. Edit it. Sell it, and—"

"That's right," I said. "You'll have to put the series on cold."

"Jesus, that's dangerous!" He stared at me. "Do you know how dangerous that is?"

Greengauge said delicately, "How would I explain my role in all this to her satisfaction?"

"You tell her I brought the show to you. You thought it had possibilities for next season. Someone in New York misunderstood, showed it to a sponsor who insisted on putting it on this year."

"Jesus!" Hal said. "Honey could get so sore at Josiah she'd jump over to CBS. And walk right out on the wedding."

"That's why we don't tell her until it's over."

Hal's jaw dropped open. He looked to Greengauge for instructions.

Greengauge blew a perfect smoke ring that rolled a slow three feet before it dissolved against the glass behind Hans' neck.

"Well?" Hal asked nervously. "What do you think, Josiah?"

Looking straight ahead, he said carefully, "It's certainly . . . *audacious.*"

Hal, relieved, said, "Right. Much too risky."

Greengauge looked suddenly at me with glittering eyes. "No. We'll do it. I've learned life generally rewards audacity."

"I'm glad you feel that way, Josiah," I said. "Because part of the deal is I get the time slot following Honey."

Greengauge threw his head back and laughed until tears started to run down his fat cheeks.

When I stepped back into the tent, Honey, standing in the spotlight, was speaking seriously to the hushed crowd.

"Many years ago I met a shy, gentle young nun. You couldn't mistake her. She was one who dares to Dream the Impossible Dream. Today her dream has come true. And tonight I have a wonderful surprise! It's a great honor for me to introduce the founder of the Order of St. Cyprian. Flown to our hearts from the heart of the Dark Continent—courtesy of Pan Am—a real live saint: Mother Superior Rosamunde."

Gus Hemsley gave the downbeat; the boys struck up *Ave Maria;* Benjy shoved out onstage a frail old woman in white robes, who shielded her spectacled eyes from the spotlight.

Honey hugged her while she peered out, puzzled at the standing, shouting, whistling crowd.

Click. Click.

Went the Hasselblad in the hands of the skinny, intense young man in white jeans.

"Once more, please," Benjy called. "And smile. It's your first date."

I picked a rose from her rosebush and, smiling, handed it to her.

Click. Click.

Smiling, Honey and I silently strolled across the carefully clipped lawn.

When a sequence was finished, the girls from Honey's show, laughing and chattering, surrounded her, patting away the beads of sweat, helping her change, powdering her down; while a bored wardrobe man clothespinned the back of my sport coats borrowed from Dorso's.

Click. Click.

Honey and I smiled at the Klipsruders and Truscotts in dinner jackets in the drawing room.

We were acting out Benjy's scenario of our courtship.

In the article he wrote for me, "How I Came to Fall in Love with the Real Honey Holly," I said I'd met her at dinner at my old friends the Klipsruders, and gradually got to know her at the home of mutual friends.

Click. Click.

In the article he wrote for her, she told how friendship and respect suddenly became love when Rod Light was struck down by illness; she turned to me for help and I saved her show.

Click. Click.

"That's it for you, Buck," Benjy said, smiling.

As I got in my car he caught up with me. "Interviews tomorrow." He handed me a typed schedule. "I'm starting you with the small-town stuff: Peoria, St. Joe, Chattanooga. As soon as you've got it down pat, we'll move up to the big boys: *New York News, Chicago Tribune*. Even *Time* and *Newsweek* are dying to talk to you."

"That's me," I said. "America's Sweetheart."

"Oh, no, my pet. You're America's Sweetheart's boyfriend." He smiled thinly. "And don't you forget it."

The receptionist must have sounded the alarm, for by the time I got to Scotty's office I was surrounded by giggling mini-skirted secretaries.

"Congratulations, Mr. McLeod!" "Oh, it's so thrilling!" "She's fantastic!" "She's been my idol since I was a baby!" "She's so cute!" "Could ya get me her autograph?" "Me, too!" "Please!"

Scotty, pouring us a drink from his crystal decanter, said, "I can't tell you how happy I am about this. She's a fine woman. A woman of character—"

"Scotty—"

"She's just what you need. She's going to be a steadying influence on you."

"I wonder."

"I know. Now I want you both to be my guests. Mine and Helen's, that is, of course. For dinner at her favorite restaurant. Scandia. Chasen's. The Bistro. You name it."

"Thanks, Scotty. I'll check out her schedule, but what I came here—"

"I know how busy she must be. So any last-minute cancellation is perfectly all right. My feelings won't be hurt. Just give me a call and we'll be there in ten minutes." He clicked his glass against mine. "Here's to a long and successful marriage."

"Scotty, I came to borrow five thousand dollars. Now, I know—"

"A *very* good idea," he said, smiling. "There are always expenses that crop up before the ceremony." He opened up a big bound checkbook and began writing.

I'll be Goddamned, he's more star-struck than the secretaries.

Eddie was lounging in bed, looking through the *Times*, a tray of untouched food before him.

"How do you feel?"

"Not too bad."

"Well," I said with a grin, "I've got something that's going to make you feel one whole helluva lot better."

I handed him the check.

He looked at it, then up at me.

"Christ, I must be a whole lot sicker than I thought."

"What do you mean?"

"I must have had a raging fever and in a fit of delirium asked you to lend me four thousand dollars. Because I can't remember it. Is that what happened?"

"Now listen, Eddie," I said. "Don't get that way about it."

"I'm just asking you if that's what happened."

"Now, don't start yelling—"

"Because if it didn't, who the hell you think you are to start handing out money—Jesus Christ Superstar?"

"Eddie, you've had an operation, you're in the hospital, there are going to be bills."

"Who the fuck are you, Medicare?"

"I'm your friend."

"No." He was beet red and shouting. "Any friend of mine would know better than to lend me money before I asked for it."

He tore the check in two and threw it in my face.

"You are the most hard-nosed, mean motherfucker—"

A gunmetal-grey plate warmer flew between us and clanged against the wall.

"Will you bastards pipe down?" The old geezers were all glaring at us. "We can't hear a word of *The Price Is Right*."

That broke us up.

7

Smiling my Cagney smile, I threw open the door of Greengauge's office.

"Surprise! Surprise!" Honey called.

And it was. Fifty faces smiled back at me.

"Buck, my boy, so glad you could get here on such short notice." Greengauge stood at the head of the long conference table. Honey, at the foot, patted the empty chair next to her, invitingly.

"Let me introduce the boys from New York."

The gray-haired Chipp-suited men at the conference table smiled.

"Warren, vice-president of Planning; Hendricks, vice-president, Programming; Waters, vice-president, Sales; Fimberg, vice-president of Publicity; and Harris, vice-pres— Arleigh, just what the hell are you in charge of?"

"Why, Warren, Hendricks, Fimberg, Harris and Hundsley."

There was a company laugh for the company joke.

"And their lads." He waved a casual hand at the handsome, razor-cut, serious young men in the background. "The fellas who really run the shop."

Honey said, "I've just got to tell Buck before I bust. Josiah has come up with the greatest idea in the whole world! UBC is going to televise our wedding!"

"Like *Bride and Groom?*"

Everyone frowned at me.

"Certainly not," Greengauge said sternly. "It will be an hour and a half, broadcast live, like the Academy Awards. And it will be an equally important event. It will set standards that Americans will be wed by for years to come in dress, decorum and elegance."

"You want elegance," Fimberg said intensely, "you got to go Episcopal."

"No way," Thelma said.

"No!" Fimberg said fiercely. "When Grant marries Hepburn in *The Philadelphia Story,* what is it? Episcopal. When—"

Carl said sharply, "Excuse me for butting in. But I do think as director of *The Honey Holly Show* I might have a teeny bit better understanding of Honey's fans than some of the newcomers. And I assure you they will not stand still for an Episcopal wedding."

"Why not?" cried Fimberg.

"Too aristocratic."

"Right!" said Thelma. "Honey's down-to-earth. Homespun. Just folks."

"So," said Carl, "it should be non-denominational."

Fimberg stared at him in horror. "You mean with a *judge?*"

"No. Handle it just the way you would on *Marcus Welby.* Have a clean-cut, WASP-y minister in a black suit and a white collar and no one can tell if it's Methodist, Baptist or Presbyterian."

"Fine with me," Honey said.

"Then the game plan is non-denominational Protestant," Greengauge said briskly. "What church?"

"Oh!" Honey said quickly, girlishly. "Can't I have it outdoors in my rose garden?"

"Of course!" said Carl.

"Cute!" said Thelma. "Oh, I could just hug you."

"I'm afraid that's out," a vice-president said.

"Why's that?" Honey asked. "Mr. . . .?"

"Hendricks. This is a live telecast, Miss Holly. What if it rains?"

"Great!" said Thelma. "Gives us suspense. Millions of mommas chewing their fingernails all week. Will it rain on Honey's wedding?"

"But if it *does* rain," Hendricks said coldly, "there's no show."

"We just need a cover set," Hundsley put in.

"Use the house," Thelma said. "She'd look fabulous floating down the staircase.

"Oh, yes!" cried Honey. "Couldn't we? Please, Mr. Hendricks?"

Hendricks beat a hasty retreat. "Yes, of course."

Carl spoke up defiantly. "I hope it does rain! During the ceremony I'll keep cutting outside to the empty, deserted, rose garden—with the raindrops gently falling on the rose petals. It will give the show a real Fellini quality."

"Carl, dear." Honey ran her fingers carefully down the pleat in her skirt. "I wouldn't cut away from the wedding for anything but a commercial."

"Oh, you can't do that!"

Everyone stared at a pale young man in a cheap blue suit sitting far back.

"Why not?" asked Carl.

"One cannot cut away from a religious ceremony for any reason."

"Religious ceremony!" Harris said angrily. "A wedding's classified as a religious ceremony?"

"Absolutely," said the young man. "And one cannot cut away from it. Especially to a commercial. It's all in the Code."

"Then, of course, we shall not do it." Greengauge looked at Hal.

Hal said, "I think we'd better identify ourselves before we speak out."

"I brought him with me," Hendricks said. "Thought he might come in handy. He's head of Religious Affairs. Name's Denison."

"Shoe," the man said. "Deni*shoe*."

"Tell me, Denishoe," Greengauge said affably, "how long will a religious ceremony such as this run?"

"Between nine and eleven minutes."

"Jesus!" said Fimberg. "What do we do for the other hour?"

There was an uncomfortable silence.

"I've got it." Thelma shouted, jumping to her feet. "We get a Bert Parks to emcee. Bert grabs the first guest—Fred Astaire. 'Fred,' he says, 'day like this must start you wending down Memory Lane? Right?' Fred chuckles, nods and tells a very warm, very human story about his first day on the set with Honey. Bam! Cut to film clip of Honey and Fred doing that dance where they play Ping-Pong. Cut to commercial. Dissolve up on Bing. Bing plugs his orange juice. Whatever. Cut to film clip of Honey and Bing singing that Hawaiian number. It's *beautiful,* I tell you! It's got everything. Names. Nostalgia. Singing. Dancing. Great cut-aways to commercials. Know what we've got on our hands? A *This Is Your Life* wedding!"

She sat down, the writers leaning forward to pat her shoulder. The others watched Greengauge.

Hal said, "What do you think, Josiah?"

Greengauge gave a little start. "You must forgive me, I wasn't really listening. Proust's madeleine kept running through my head."

"The old Chevalier song?" asked Fimberg.

Greengauge smiled. "Hardly. No, the narrator of *A La Recherche du Temps Perdu,* my favorite novel, would dip a madeleine in his cup of tea ... suddenly time present would dissolve into time past. And ..." He slowly brought his hands together. "We have time past in our own hands."

Puzzled glances ricocheted around the room.

"I'm afraid, Josiah," Hal said, "you're just a touch too intellectual and esoteric for us peasants."

"Damn it, man. Why should we publicize a score of old movies—which you can be sure Paramount and RKO will charge an arm and a leg for—when we have our own time capsule? Twenty years of *The Honey Holly Show.* Think of *those* highlights, gentlemen! She not only dances with Fred, sings with Bing. But remember Honey's dance with Brando? Her sketch with the Burtons? Her duet with Streisand? Cary Grant's only television appearance? A cavalcade of Honey's greatest moments. What a show!"

"And!" yelled Fimberg. "What a hype for the syndication sales!"

Hal said, "It's brilliant!"

Greengauge cut off the admiring murmurs with a wave.

"I want only one person's opinion. Tell me, Honey, what you honestly think of it?"

All eyes swung to Honey.

"I think it's so super that I'm asking you here and now to give me away."

"It will be the crowning honor of my career."

Outside in the hot sunlit parking lot, Honey raced the motor.

"Buck, stop being stubborn. I can't be married in the Catholic Church. And that's all there is to it."

"Because it would offend your fans from the Bible Belt?"

She drew a circle with her trigger finger on the back of my hand. "No," she said softly. "Because I was married to a Catholic before Irving, and he's still alive. Oh, Buck, don't look like that. I was sweet sixteen and never been kissed and he was a trumpet player."

I stared at her. "Where is he?"

"Don't worry. He won't say a word. He has TB. Lives near Tucson. I send him a little something every month to keep him quiet. Irving had the records lifted. And nobody else knows about it, but Mother Superior Rosamunde."

I said stupidly, "Mother Superior Rosamunde?"

"Sister Rosamunde, then. She was the witness."

She leaned up, kissed me with a soft open mouth. "Let's leave the Truscotts early tonight."

I watched the glistening white Rolls shoot off through the black-faced parking lot, wondering about Honey's contributions to the Sisters of St. Cyprian. Wondering how many other people were getting a little something every month to keep their mouths shut. Wondering what secrets Benjy could tell me. Or Nora. Or, for that matter, Greengauge.

As I drove around the corner the girls jumped up from the curb, shouting, "Mummy! It's Daddy! Daddy's home!"

As Eddie opened the door they piled in hugging and kissing.

Maria called, "Gently, girls, gently!"

The screen door boomed open and the yelping puppy streaked down on us. I grabbed him before he jumped up on Eddie. He licked my face gratefully.

"Who the hell is that?" asked Eddie.

"That's Heathcliff."

"He's an Old English sheepdog. Uncle Mike got him for us."

"But we picked him out," Luciana said. "Do you like the name Heathcliff?"

"I certainly do," Eddie said, arms around them, walking up the sidewalk. "From *Wuthering Heights?*"

"Partly," said Antonella. "But also because being a sheepdog he'd like the heath and cliffs."

The backyard had a big cardboard sign: "WELCOME HOME DADDY." Red-white-and-blue paper ribbons were strung from the top of the umbrella to the fence. A table was groaning with antipasto.

"My God, Maria!" Eddie said. "I can't eat all that."

"Who said you had to? All I ask is that you try the prosciutto with wild fig after this."

"Champagne?"

"It's a celebration, Daddy!"

Heathcliff put his slobbering muzzle on Eddie's knee and stared up at him adoringly.

"Uncle Mike," Luciana asked. "Are we all going to your wedding?"

"You certainly are. And, Eddie, I want you to be best man."

"I'd like that," he said.

"What Church?" asked Maria.

"It's going to be in Honey's rose garden."

"Performed by a priest?"

"No," I said. "Minister."

"Then Eddie can't be in it," she said quickly.

"Maria—"

"You can't! You'll be excommunicated."

"Father Flynn wouldn't—"

"He won't have any choice. It'll be in all the papers. The Cardinal will—"

"Maria," he said gently.

"No!" she shouted. "You can't get excommunicated, *now*."

"Or I won't get last rites?"

She turned away.

"Hey." He went over and put his arm around her. "Maria," he said quietly. "When my best friend gets married, I stand up there beside him. Even if we all have to become Mohammedans."

As I pulled up in front of the Beverly Hills Hotel some luncheon was breaking, and middle-aged women in expensive dresses kissed good-bye while green-uniformed car boys impatiently held shiny Cadillac doors open, or raced off clutching yellow tickets.

Benjy hustled me off, the ladies oohing and pointing after me.

"This is the shower the Overseas Press Club is giving you."

"Giving me?"

"Don't worry, darling, we're paying. They're the biggest collection of freeloaders west of the Potomac. By now, I trust, you know all your lines. If someone throws you a rough question, don't panic. Mother is here."

We went in the side entrance. Down the green-carpeted hall there was quite a crowd slowly squeezing into the Crystal Room.

"I'll stash you in the can. I want you to make your entrance after they're all seated. You surprised me, I didn't expect you to be on time."

"Punctuality is my most endearing trait."

"If that's true, darling, your marriage has no chance."

Inside the john an assistant director stood jumpily before a stall.

"Hi, Mr. McLeod. I'm Harry Carter. Remember, I was the second on *The FBI* you—"

"*McLeod!*"

The black marble door to the can swung open. Tabitha leaped out and threw her arms around me.

"Oh, my God, darling, but it's good to see you. Oh, McLeod, how I've missed you. Oh . . ." Then her voice got muffled as she began kissing me short, little kisses all over my face.

"What are you doing here?"

"Peeing, darling. The can for the courts is fucked, and the one up here is crammed full of fishy-eyed female gossip-writers—Oh, you mean why am I *here?* We flew in at dawn. There was a scene where I beat the pants off Kurt playing tennis, and he threw a tantrum about it. So we're reshooting it."

"Negative scratch," Harry put in tactfully.

"Ha!"

"We've got to get right back on the set before we lose the sun," he said nervously.

"Run down and tell them I've just passed a kidney stone. But, trouper that I am, am hobbling toward the camera."

Harry shot out the door. She threw her arms around me, nearly knocking me into the urinal. Two double-breasted businessmen came in talking, stopped dead in their tracks and gaped at her.

"It's perfectly all right, gentlemen," she purred. "I'm a transvestite."

She scampered down the hall, dragging me after her, giggling like a schoolgirl. "Oh, God is a director at heart. Staging our reunion in the crapper. What is it, McLeod? What are you looking so hangdog about? Why the hell can't I ever get you on the phone?"

We were outside. Below us on the tennis courts a shooting crew was impatiently waiting, reflectors shining on Kurt center court in tennis gear.

"Tabitha, haven't you heard?"

"What, darling? Remember me? The brave little tyke out battling rhino and lions in the Serengeti?"

"I thought you knew."

Down below the crew spotted her. *"Tabitha!"* they shouted.

"I'm getting married."

Her eyes went a bit out of focus, as if I'd hit her.

"Hurry up, Tabitha," called the director. "We're losing the sun."

She let her breath out slowly. "I don't understand, Michael."

"I'm getting married next week," I said stupidly.

Harry raced up the aisles toward us.

"That Honey Holly?" I nodded. "You can't do that, Michael." She said as patiently as if she were talking to an eight-year-old, "You don't love her. You love me."

Harry grabbed her arm. "We gotta shoot this now. Then talk to Buck." He pulled her down several steps. She twisted out of his grip.

"No, Buck," she called, her face desperate. "You can't do this. It's *wrong!*" Harry had her elbow and hustled her down the steps.

The crew, kidding, applauded as she reached them.

Benjy came up to me.

"Are you all right?"

"Sure." I started walking away.

"If you're ill I can cancel it."

"I'm fine," I said. "Don't cancel anything."

As we turned the pink stucco corner, I looked back. They were shooting. She and Kurt were rallying. They hit back and forth from the baseline, forehand, backhand, cross-court.

Christ, I thought, and we could have played great tennis together, too.

8

During the next weeks she'd come back when I'd least expect it. Like a knee that's been operated on. You run on it. Cut on it. Put pressure on it. Punish it. And it's fine. Then during a time-out you kick mud off your cleats and pain shoots through you like an arrow.

So, walking off the court at a celebrity tennis tournament or twirling Honey around a Bel Air dance floor to the chug-chug Lester Lanin beat of *Just in Time,* suddenly I'd have to be careful of how I moved and smiled.

And I was smiling too much, drinking too much, and worrying about my show too much. Hal, constantly on the phone, chattered away about how marvelously things were progressing; but my meetings with Greengauge were—somehow—always postponed at the last minute.

I caught up with him at the luau UBC tossed Honey at the Bistro.

As we worked our way down the line of handshaking, dinner-jacketed vice-presidents, Hal asked, "Haven't the design boys accomplished wonders with their Polynesian motif?"

"Sure have," I said. "It looks just like Trader Vic's."

After Greengauge had kissed Honey and she was engulfed by adoring station managers, he turned, beaming. "Buck, my boy, how have you been?"

Not letting go of his hand, I moved him a few yards away to a secluded spot by the totem poles. "Not well,

Josiah. My nerves are jumpy; my sunny disposition has turned mean and nasty."

Hal appeared, holding out glasses of champagne.

Greengauge frowned. "Must be the strain of the approaching nuptials."

"No," I said. "Like all actors, I'm sensitive. Shot full of anxiety."

"Sounds as if you need a security blanket," Greengauge said disapprovingly.

"By God, you're right, Josiah. What I need is a contract."

They exchanged a quick glance. Josiah smiled. "Then you shall have it." He held out his hand. "You'll have your series on the air this fall."

"Good." I shook his hand. "When do I get the contract?"

Hal laughed. "You already have the best contract in the world—Josiah's word."

"I want it in writing."

"Just who the hell do you—"

"Hal," Greengauge murmured, "Buck doesn't understand the traditions of our industry. I've made multimillion-dollar deals with Henry Ford the Second on a handshake."

"But he OK'd the Edsel. I want it in black and white."

Josiah studied me, then asked slowly, softly, "And if you *don't* get what you want . . . what then, Buck?"

"I take the show straight to Perry Lafferty."

Hal said, "You're bluffing. CBS already turned it down."

"That was before I became America's Sweetheart. And . . ." I brushed some imaginary lint off his bottle-green velvet dinner jacket. "Before I could offer them *The Honey Holly Show*."

Greengauge tried to stare me down. "You can't deliver her. And my advice is: you better not try."

I gave him the smile Cagney gave the bartender in *Public Enemy* who wouldn't buy his beer.

"I'll tell Paley what you said, Josiah."

I hadn't taken three steps before he cried, "Buck! Your nerves *are* taut as a drumhead. If it means all that much to you . . . Hal, put the legal fellas on it."

"First thing tomorrow."

"Tonight," I said. "I want it first thing tomorrow."

When the lunch interview at the Bella Fontana was over I walked quickly out through the lobby, past the bellboys pushing little aluminum carts piled high with suitcases; past the middle-aged women sitting heavily alone on the ornate sofas, waiting.

"Buck! Hey! It's me!"

The cute blonde behind the cigar counter was running toward me. "Don't you remember? You balled me. Audra Lee?"

"Sure, Audra Lee, how's it going?"

"Just fan-*tas*-tic, Buck! I have that autographed picture of you hung on the wall. And guys who wouldn't look at me twice before are going crazy, trying to get into my pants."

"I'm glad to hear that, Audra Lee."

"And it's *all* due to *you*. You're *famous* . . . look!"

She pointed to the rack of fan magazines. All I could see were smiling heads of Honey and me. We'd pushed Liz and Dick, and Ari and Jackie, and Dean and Jeannie and Cathy right off all the covers. There wasn't even a Lennon sister in sight.

As we pulled up in the drive, the rose garden was swarming with men. A dozen TV remote cameras, cables trailing behind them, were warming up on test patterns. On the tennis court white-coveralled men were fitting together the wooden squares of a dance floor. Swearing stagehands, stripped to the waist, were shoving around lights, reflectors and phony rosebushes while earphoned floor managers nipped at their heels like terriers.

One shook my hand. "Welcome, Mr. McLeod. I'm

Hanrahan. This Mr. Riordan? Fine. Your wardrobes and dresser are in the pool house. We're running a little behind schedule. So it'll be twenty or thirty minutes before we get to you."

Carl's voice screamed on the talk-back, "I will not put up for one minute more with this noise. Do you hear me? I want absolute silence. *Now! This instant.*"

No one paid any attention.

Carl went on. "That's better. *Much* better. We're starting interview five. So proceed to Rosebush Four."

Equipment moved out in three different directions.

"No!" shouted Hanrahan, running after a camera.

Hal in a brown houndstooth hacking coat strode around a hedge.

"Buck, I told Honey, Carl couldn't handle this. We've got our best remote crew here and he's lost. We need a sports director. But Honey—"

"Hal, have you got my contract?"

"I've had a million other things to attend to. This—"

"You've been promising me it for ten days—"

"Simmer down, sweetheart. Josiah's bringing it. He has to be here for rehearsal." He smiled. "He's giving the bride away, remember?"

The UBC sports announcer Biff Branigan stood in front of a rosebush that had a big 4 hanging on it.

"Quiet!" Carl screamed on the talk-back. "Start interview five."

A floor manager threw a cue.

"Cary," Biff said to a tired old character actor, "on a day like today I think everyone's thoughts tend to go wandering down Memory Lane. I was wondering where yours are?"

The actor, squinting at a Teleprompter, read woodenly: "Funny you should ask, Biff, because I was thinking of Honey's first day on the set of our first movie together."

"She must have been just a kid."

"And nervous as a kitten. But as soon as she opened her mouth I was spellbound, because I saw stardust sprinkling down on that cute, curly head—"

"Cut! screamed Hal. "You mean to tell me Grant's approved this shit?"

Desperate shouts. A green-and-white tent was bellying in a sudden breeze. Men sprang to seize ropes, pound in tent pegs.

I found Honey standing in her duplicate wedding dress before the non-denominational altar. She was studying her close-up on a monitor; a knot of worried men watched her; she shook her head.

"I'm afraid that's just not going to do—Oh, hi, Darling!" She ran over and kissed me. Click Click Click went three still photographers working with Benjy.

"And, Eddie." She held out her hand. "How nice to see you. Would you be a dear, Eddie, and take Buck off to the pool house and see that he gets into his wardrobe and stays out of trouble until we need him?"

"Yes, ma'am."

"Thanks ever so." She turned back to the waiting men. "Now, I have a feeling, and it's only a hunch. (What do I know about lighting?) That the fill is too flat. Why don't we lower the key three feet, bring it a teeny bit this way, and take the backlight up two points?"

In the pool house, the dresser, plump and nervous, was waiting with our cutaways and striped trousers.

"We'll have different shirts and ties tomorrow, Mr. McLeod. But these are exact duplicates. For the lighting man."

"Fine," I said. "We can get dressed by ourselves."

He slipped out the door like an eel.

"How about a drink?"

Eddie smiled as I went behind the bar.

"Shit. It's been stripped clean. There's nothing here but Fresca. I'll call up to the house."

"Save your breath." He slung his suitcase up on the

bar. "My orders were very explicit. 'Make sure he doesn't get a drop to drink.' "

He opened the suitcase and pulled out a bottle of Jack Daniel's and two six-packs of Coors.

As I poured the drinks he said, "Hey! That's you."

The big monitor set up in front of the fireplace showed stills of me from the Great Neck High yearbook in football uniform.

Eddie turned up the sound.

"Buck's athletic prowess gleamed even more brightly on the playing fields of the University of Oregon."

Old newspaper stills of me catching passes. The music went dramatic; there were newsreel shots of Pearl Harbor.

"Buck, as patriotic as he was tough, enlisted in the Army the day after Pearl Harbor."

"Hooray!" Eddie shouted. "You're *brave*."

Fast cuts of Iwo Jima, North Africa, Sicily, Marines landing on beaches, paratroopers falling out of planes, D Day in Normandy.

"You really got around," Eddie said admiringly. "You were everywhere."

I threw a beer can at him.

Newsreel shots of advancing infantryman.

"A frontline dogface with the Thirty-fourth Division, Buck fought bravely in Africa and Italy, and received the Purple Heart twice for wounds received in action."

Cut to close-up of a Purple Heart.

"How come they left out your good conduct medal?"

"I wouldn't let them. I'm brave but I'm modest, Eddie."

He threw a beer can at me.

"Buck's superb playing was just what the pros were looking for. And he became a slashing star of the famed San Francisco Forty-Niners."

Hanrahan stuck his head in. "Time to go, Mr. McLeod."

They cut to a game clip. Brodie faked a hand-off.

"Goddammit, Eddie. It's the Green Bay game."

Brodie dropped back, threw. Toe-dancing on the sideline, I caught it. The cornerback tried to knock me out of bounds; somehow I twisted around him. The safety shot in, and I straight-armed him. He sat down hard and I took off.

"For Christ's sake, for years you've been telling me how you straight-armed him. He fell down."

"Could we get going?" Hanrahan asked nervously.

I ran into the striped end zone, then turned and looked back downfield to see if there were any penalty flags.

"No slamming the ball down. No war dance. You weren't very dramatic."

"I was a sweet, shy kid, Eddie. And stardom hasn't changed me. I still am."

Hanrahan led us to our positions behind a hedge. The band struck up some churchly music. Hanrahan cued us. Eddie and I marched out toward the non-denominational altar where a cleancut young minister stood smiling.

As soon as we stopped, Carl screamed, "Buck, luv, for God's sake, can't you ever find your marks?"

"Right on 'em."

"No, you're not! Won't someone—*please*—show him where his marks are?"

Three blue-blazered floor managers jumped out. "He's on his marks."

"Then what is going on? A *conspiracy?* Must *all* the cameramen *always* be on the wrong lens?"

Sullen cameramen twisted their lens turrets, muttered into their mouthpieces.

"Permit me to introduce myself," said the minister. "I'm Teddy. Teddy Coffin. No relation to the activist one at Yale. Ha ha."

Carl shrieked on the talk-back, "I don't care who was right or who was wrong. *I don't care, I tell you!* I just want to go on with Honey's entrance. QUIET! PLACES! CUE THEM!"

Gus Hemsley gave the boys the downbeat and they struck up *The Wedding March.*

The big silver side of the Houston blocked Honey from sight as it dollied down the aisle with her; it tongued back, slid away and there she stood, holding Hal's arm.

"Where's Greengauge?" I said.

"Sssh," Honey whispered.

Hal, looking straight ahead, spoke out of the corner of his mouth. "He's tied up."

I grabbed him. "What the fuck are you trying to pull?"

Carl screamed, "Stop it! *Stop it! Stop it!* Have you gone insane?"

Honey leaned forward quickly and sniffed my mouth.

"Eddie! You promised you'd keep him sober!"

"Oh, I did, ma'am," Eddie said politely. "If he were drunk he'd smell so bad you couldn't get within ten feet of him."

The bar at Dom's was crowded. Bright young agents and game-show producers stood shoulder to shoulder with Jack Lemmon and Walter Matthau, hoping something would rub off on them. All of the red-checked tables were full but mine. In the middle booth Rod Serling and John Frankenheimer, sunburned, sat frowning, talking thoughtfully.

Dom leaned over the bar. "I can't hold your table any longer, Buck."

"He'll be here any minute."

"I've held it half an hour."

"Five more minutes, Dom?"

"Two and that's it." He moved off.

A hand slapped me on the back; I whirled around but it was some damn kid in a black flaring blazer, with a white turtleneck and a hard little blonde.

"Hi, Buck. Remember me?"

"I never remember anyone who says, 'Hi, Buck, Remember me?' "

"Ha ha. Henry Rose. Used to work with Stan before I moved down the block to CMA. I came over to congratulate you, buy you a drink, introduce the wife—Hey, aren't you going to shake hands?"

"I never shake hands with agents."

"Why not?"

"Because they're all cunts."

The smile drained away, and he stood there not knowing what to do until she dragged him away.

"Charm," Eddie said. "Some people have it and some people—"

"Leave it alone."

"No way," he said. "Anytime you act like a prick, I tell you. That's the arrangement."

"Mike," Dom yelled from the far end of the bar. "Phone."

I grabbed the extension off the wall.

"Josiah?"

"Yes, Buck, I'm—"

"Where the fuck are you?"

Slight pause, then, patiently: "In a rather important meeting that, alas, is still going on. I'm afraid I can't make dinner."

"Have you got my contract? Just answer yes or no."

"Yes."

"Then I'm coming right over to pick it up."

"It's not quite finished."

"When will it be ready?"

"Excuse me, gentlemen, I'll be right with you." His tone swiftly shifted gears. "Buck, what time do you show up for rehearsal tomorrow?"

"Eleven o'clock."

"I'll meet you at nine-thirty. If you have objections to any details we can iron it out then. Sorry to have to miss your bachelor dinner."

The phone clicked down.

"Dom," I yelled. "The table's all yours. Sorry to

have hung you up. Could you bring us a double round of boilermakers? Jameson and ale?"

"Now," Eddie said patiently, "would you mind telling me just what the hell is going on?"

When I finished, he nodded slowly. "So that's it ... your own series ... I should have known."

"My old man used to drink 'em like this." I dropped the full shot glass into the ale.

Eddie smiled. "Mine, too." He dropped his in with a plop.

"I remember the first time I saw him do it. It was St. Patrick's Day. At Hurley's on Sixth Avenue. My old man loved it because when Rockefeller was buying up all the land for Rockefeller Center, Hurley wouldn't sell. At any price. So today there's this little Irish bar with the skyscrapers around it shooting up sixty stories."

"To your father," Eddie said.

We clicked glasses and drank.

We dropped the second shot glasses in, clicked glasses and drank again.

"What did he want you to be when you grew up?"

"President. Doesn't every father?"

Eddie, serious, shook his head.

"Hell, I don't know. . . . Someone fighting for the poor and oppressed . . . maybe an organizer for Chavez. Some kind of Sir Galahad."

I smiled to show him how foolish it all was but he didn't smile back. So I pushed the shot glass around on the brown wood varnished bar, feeling fucking awful, remembering what he and Mother had hoped I'd become ... and what I was.

"Give it up," Eddie said gently.

"What?" Startled, I looked up.

"Her. The wedding. The whole fucking thing."

"Leave it alone, Eddie."

"No," he said. "It's not just the morality. Leaving the Church. Marrying to get a show on. Though that's bad enough. You just can't do it."

"I'm going to."

"You can't, Mike," he said patiently. "That cunt will kill you."

"OK, Eddie, you've said your piece. Now fuck off."

He nodded, got up and walked through the crowd to the door. As he opened it he turned back.

"You call that other girl," he said. "That Tabitha."

I threw my glass as hard as I could at his face; he moved his head a few inches and it shattered the window in the door behind him. Everyone shut up and stared at us. The only sound was Sinatra singing:

> *"In a spin*
> *Lovin' the spin*
> *I'm in. . . ."*

Eddie said, "If that's your fast ball—you better have a curve." And left.

After Dom threw me out I went to the Raincheck and put in some serious drinking with the out-of-work actors, but couldn't find a good fight. I tried Cyrano's but the Strip was quiet. Looking for trouble, I worked my way out toward the beach by way of the Batrack, Chez Jay's and that place in Santa Monica with the blind black piano player who isn't there anymore.

"Hold on, Buck." The blonde with the big knockers and the nervous husband frowned as she chewed on her swizzle stick. "I don't understand. You said: 'You mean . . . Dot? Dot? Dot?' "

"Picture after picture. End of *Sodbuster,* Julie Adams looks at the little frame house and says: 'Now, there'll be peace fur a spell—you can add that new room we'll be needin.' I look at her and say: 'You mean . . . Dot Dot Dot.' "

"Dot? Dot? Dot?"

"Has to be three. It's in the Writers Guild contract. English playwright at Paramount once used four. They ran him out of town."

Next bar I sat alone. I was Muni as Pasteur. Edward

G. Robinson as ... whoever it was invented the magic
bullet. A scientist. Coolly studying the way alcohol kills
off everything. Coordination. Speech patterns. I closed
my eyes; held my arms out; brought my fingers together. Missed by miles. I opened my eyes and could
see the peripheral vision was going. Going . . . going . . .

Funny how alcohol could kill everything but the Tabitha pain.

I was in complete blackness. Complete quiet. I
swept the heavens with my radar screens. "I know
there's something out there, Barnes. I don't know what
. . . but . . . *something.*"

You name a bad line and I've said it. But the radar
screens were turning into funnels. No . . . megaphones.
Like Rudy Vallee used to use. Way down there by the
mouthpiece I was picking up something. Have to rack
it into focus. I strained, hard, and . . . *alla kazam!*
Sharp as a knife staring down at me was a scared Chicano parking boy.

"Mr. McLeod, you're in no shape to drive. I'll call
you a cab."

"Fuck off, sonny. Just get me up."

He pulled me out of the gravel.

I drove up the Pacific Coast Highway. Hands carefully spaced out on the wheel. Cleverly, I kept it right
at fifty because the cops will pick you up if you go too
slowly. I'd acquired a little double vision so I kept one
eye closed.

But something else was wrong. All I could see out
the windshield was dribs and drabs of lights. Green
and yellow and orange dots. I closed the other eye. But
there were just more of them.

"I don't know what they are, Barnes. But they're
proliferating like cancer."

Always been proud of that reading even though it
took five takes. But I can't see a Goddamned thing except these dots. Alcohol must have penetrated the optic

nerve. I'm looking at my own retina, that's what those dots are. Dot's all, folks.

I hit the brakes hard. Shit, I'm too smart to drive if I'm going blind. I'll run home. Little jog'll do me good.

It takes a while to get the door open but finally I stand out on the pavement, and Goddam—it is pouring! It's beautiful! The rain belting away at me. The road ahead all black and wet, shining, reflecting my headlights.

> *"Singin' in the rain,*
> *I'm singin' in the rain . . ."*

I'm Gene Kelly in my raincoat and Debbie's in her raincoat and arm in arm we're walking toward camera with the rain coming down, singing our little hearts out.

> *"What a wonderful feeeeee-lin,'*
> *I'm haaaaa-py again . . ."*

I break into a fast tap step and . . . SHIT!

I hit that pavement like a sack of cement. Debbie must've tripped me. What the fuck did she do that for? Wait a minute. There's another guy in a raincoat in the number. He's the bastard tripped me. It's . . . it's . . . Phil Silvers! OK, Phil, you prick . . . NO! That's *Cover Girl* looking for the pearl with Rita and dancing around the mailbox for Christ *Make Way for Tomorrow.*

Brrrr . . . cold on the wet concrete. But I'm fucked if I get up until I figure out who that son of a bitch was who tripped me and give him his lumps . . . Dan Dailey? . . . No.

Headlights far away coming out of the dark rain. OK. Let's pan them in. Careful. Little more center frame. Pretty shot. Filling the frame fast. Zooming in to one headlight. Light hits the horn. Brakes squeal. Swerves off, shooting sheets of water in my face. But I hang onto the shot as the lights spin away, turning into a yellow XKE doing a beautiful slow-motion figure eight.

Christ, what a beautiful shot. Surtees will pin a fucking medal on me for that shot. ONE FUCKING MINUTE. Can't shoot a shot like that if there's anything wrong with your eyes.

I crawl over to the car, stick my head in, twist the wiper knob and the dots dissolve into streaky half-circles and I can see the road ahead.

Laughing, I drive down the highway.

RUSTY'S red neon sign floated toward me in triplicate. I swung off hard and stopped as close to his front door as I could get, which was pretty Goddam close.

Inside, it was empty except for four or five guys at the far end of the bar talking to Rusty.

Rusty hollered, "Why, it's Buck! Hi, Buddy. Long time no see. Congratulations."

"The reason it's long time no see, Rusty, is because you're a cunt. Want to make something of it?"

"No, Buck," he said politely.

"What about your friends? They're cunts, too. They want to make anything out of it?" Nobody said anything. "Just in case you're not sure how I feel about you—" I pulled out my cock and pissed on the floor. It made a nice sloshy sound and a nice, hot, bitter smell.

I turned my back and walked slowly toward the door. Waiting for them to rush me. Waiting to punch the Tabitha pain out. But then I was at the door. I looked back but all those faces in the bad yellow light against the shadows weren't moving.

So, screaming like a siren, I jumped in the car and took off, really burning rubber.

The rain hit against my nude body hard as hailstones as I stumbled blindly toward the sound of the breakers. Lightning lit the black seas, the smoking foam-topped breakers, the empty sweep of sand.

Blackness again and thunder exploding against my skin, then my feet were in water, the backwash nearly sucking them out from under me. A wave slammed against my shoulder, spinning me around. I swam into the warm, wet blackness, the pelting rain stinging my face. Christ, it was black. I touched bottom, turned around, but there wasn't a star or a light from a house or a car on the road. Just blackness as thick as pitch.

Suddenly the water boiled down to my knees. My ankles.

Lightning flashed. A coal-black wall thirty feet high was hurtling down on me. I ran toward it. Then dove. Low. A foot from the bottom. Trying to get under it. But the turbulence exploded against me like a depth bomb. I swam for the surface but was held down and—helpless as a dead baby—turned slowly over and over. Lungs bursting, I started to panic. Suddenly I was above the surface. I gulped in mouthfuls of air. But it was so wet with spray and rain there was no air in it. Suddenly I felt absolute, complete terror. There was no *gravity*. I couldn't tell which was up, which was down. What was air. What was water. I was disintegrating into particles of fear.

"Hail Mary, full of grace, the Lord is with Thee, Blessed art Thou—"

The ocean seized me; shot me ahead like a torpedo; smashed me against the bottom.

I came to, throwing up on wet sand; waves trying to suck me out again. I crawled away, pain shooting through my right shoulder. Safe in dry sand I collapsed, and lying face down, thanked Him for a long time.

Finally I sat up. It had stopped raining. Lightning showed me I'd been swept down the beach a mile from the house.

I got to my feet and started walking home. Staggering because I was weak as a baby.

But I felt marvelous. Light, clearheaded, empty in a warm, good way and very close to Tabitha.

Life was really so simple. How dumb I'd been to let it get so complicated. Tabitha was right. I couldn't marry Honey because I didn't love her. I loved Tabitha and she loved me, so we'd get married and have some sons and live happily ever after . . . God willing.

Then I threw my head back and laughed from the sheer, sweet joy of life. And ran, sometimes stumbling, sometimes falling, but always running because I couldn't wait to tell Tabitha the good news.

Deep in the soft, warm, yellow-green lagoon, I eased around the coral shoulder after the pink Ping-Pong-paddle fish. The shadow fell across me. Frozen with fear, I forced myself to look up. But there on the surface was Tabitha!

Her beautiful naked body shone from the sunlight behind her, shining through her lovely red hair floating all around her as she soared down to me. O sweet Christ, my love is—

I was struck. Gutstruck. Deathstruck. Shark's teeth tearing through spleen. Kidney. Liver. Spine. Falling toward the bottom the huge grey shark passes between us, Tabitha's eyes widen in horror, the thin red line across her white belly opens into a great black gap and her guts come tumbling out endlessly, from her throat comes the death rattle

KRREX KRREX KRREX

It was the phone. Lying on the floor next to me in a patch of hot sunlight. I slammed it in the cradle. My right shoulder hurt, so I turned over on my left side to go back to sleep.

The phone rang immediately. I waited for the service to pick it up. But it rang and rang and *rang* and RANG—

"Why the fuck don't you pick it up?"

"Oh, it's you, Mr. McLeod. Thank God!"

Clicking. Buzzing. Mumble of voices. "We've got him."

Greengauge: "Where are you?"

"My place."

"He's at Malibu . . . can you drive?"

"Of course I can—"

"Have you a car?"

"Yes."

"Then get in it and start driving."

"What the fuck's wrong with you?"

"Your wedding goes on the air in twenty-five minutes."

I jumped up. "Don't worry. I've never missed a show in my life."

I ran in the bedroom, pulled on some jeans and ran out the back door.

I was doing ninety up the Pacific Coast Highway when, red lights rotating, a black-and-white pulled alongside; and, siren shrieking, led me straight into Holmby Hills. On the street outside the guardhouse there must have been six or seven hundred fans. Screaming, they jammed around me, shoving autograph books in my face. It took a dozen cops to break me through.

9

In the pool house, Eddie in his cutaway said grimly, "I was hoping you wouldn't make it." He handed me a big glass of Jack Daniel's and ice. I drank it in the shower while the needlepoint blasted the sand out of my hair. When I stepped out, Eddie had another glass and a razor ready.

The monitor blared: *"I'm standing before the Beverly Hills mansion of America's Sweetheart . . . Honey*

*Holly! Pouring into her spacious gardens—to celebrate
the wedding of the century—are movie stars, Broadway luminaries, political—"*

"Turn it off."

The dresser was just finishing tying my ascot when
Greengauge, Hundsley and a man I hadn't seen before
walked in. The new man was white-haired, very thin,
wore a chalk-stripe grey double-breasted suit he must
have paid seven hundred dollars for in London. He
carried a leather briefcase that cost more.

Hal said bitterly, "Where the fuck have—"

"Hal," Greengauge said, "this is not the time for re-
criminations. The past is past." He held out a thin
package wrapped in silver foil. "With felicitations for
the future."

It was a gold Patek Philippe wristwatch. Hal and the
man murmured appreciatively.

I put it in my pocket. "I've been expecting something else."

Greengauge chuckled. "I know. Allow me to present
Mr. Coulter, senior partner of Dickinson and Coulter.
The most prestigious law firm on Wall Street."

"Now, Josiah, none of that." He had a scratchy
voice and a Groton accent. "I'm just another hardworking lawyer." He sat down behind the poker table.
"With some business to transact."

"Quite so. Hal."

As the door closed behind them, he looked coldly at
Eddie. "Alone."

"This is Mr. Riordan. He stays."

Coulter considered this, then unlocked the briefcase
and dealt long legal pages out on the green felt ta-
bletop.

"I must apologize for arriving at the last minute but
the Attorney General kept me in Washington longer
than I'd expected. Then, too"—a chiseled smile darted
across his face—"you were expected earlier. But this
shouldn't take a moment. Purely routine. I just need

your signature on the standard waivers." He uncapped a gold fountain pen.

"What standard waivers?"

"Your right to community property in case there should be a divorce. An agreement to incur no debts that Miss Holly could be held liable for." The smile flashed again. "We shall, of course, liquidate your current debts."

"There's a check here made out to me for one thousand dollars."

"You accept that as your share of Miss Holly's estate, in case of her death, and agree not to contest the will."

I turned over the last page. "That's all?"

"I told you it would just take a moment."

"Eddie," I said. "Get Greengauge in here."

"If you have any questions I'm the one to answer them."

I walked to the bar and freshened my drink.

"You understand these must be signed before the wedding?"

The door opened; Greengauge and Hundsley were silhouetted against the sun for a second as they stepped in.

"Josiah," I said quietly, "does this mean you don't have my contract?"

"Certainly not. It just makes no sense getting into it until you've squared everything away with Coulter here."

"Let's get into it."

Coulter said pointedly, "Evidently I haven't made myself clear, Mr. McLeod. There can be no wedding until you sign these papers."

"You made yourself clear."

Hanrahan threw open the door. "Twenty minutes! Oh—" Stunned at being in the presence of Greengauge, he swallowed, smiled, darted out.

"The contract." I held out my hand.

Greengauge nodded. Hal pulled papers from inside his white silk double-breasted coat.

As I read through them, I could feel their eyes on me. The only sound was the murmur of voices on the monitor.

Eddie said, "Doris Day broke down remembering the first show she did with Honey. She's bawling like a baby. It's very moving."

I let the contract fall on top of the other papers.

"You're cute," I said. "For three weeks you keep me on the hook, then twenty minutes before the wedding you shove it up my ass and break it off."

Hal said quickly, angrily, "That's a damn good contract. We give you five hundred a week, fifty-two weeks a year, an unlimited expense account and—"

"Fuck me out of my show."

Greengauge said soothingly, "Buck, I'm sure your show will be on the air this fall."

"Then put it in the contract."

"It says we'll use our best efforts."

I laughed. "You're cute—but you're fucked, because she's not going to back you."

"I wouldn't be too sure of that."

I scooped the papers off the table.

"Eddie, don't let anyone leave."

I ran through the rose garden, into the kitchen, startling the shirt-sleeved caterer's staff setting things out on silver trays; took the back stairs three at a time; but in the hall blocking Honey's door stood a chunky blue-suited ex-FBI man.

"Sorry, Mr. McLeod, my orders are no one not on the list can go in."

"That doesn't mean the groom."

"No one means no one." To soften it he added with a smile, "Besides, it's bad luck for the groom to see the bride before the wedding."

"Not this time." I pulled out the wristwatch and dangled it before his fat red Fordham Law face. "Present."

Dazzled, he stepped aside.

As I opened the door the dozen women fussing with her wedding dress screamed and jumped in front of her.

"Get out!" "Go 'way!" "You shouldn't be here!"

Honey murmured something. Glaring at me, they slipped away into her dressing room.

"Gee," Honey said, "I feel so . . . *shy*. Seeing you like this just before the wedding."

"Do you know what's in these papers Coulter gave me to sign?"

Confused, she shook her head.

"If we get divorced, I waive community property. If you die, I waive—"

"Stop it!" She clapped her hands over her ears. "How can you talk about such terrible things on our wedding day?"

"Because Coulter says if I don't sign these we can't get married."

She stared wide-eyed at me through her veil. "How can he say that?"

"You tell me."

"Oh, Buck, please stop being so cold and angry. You're getting me all upset. I don't know what he's doing."

"Good. Then I won't sign them."

"Wait! Oh dear, you're getting me so confused. He gives me all sorts of things to sign and I always do and it always works out beautifully. This must be like insurance. Once he wouldn't let me drive the Rolls one step out of the garage for my protection. I guess you'd better sign."

I took her by the shoulders and looked her right in the eye. "Honey, are you afraid I'm marrying you for your money?"

Her head snapped back as if I'd slapped her.

"Oh, Buck," she whispered. "How can you even *ask* such a question?"

"I had to know." I picked up the phone, dialed the number of the pool house.

Greengauge said, "Yes?"

I held out the phone.

"What do you want me to do?" She looked at it blankly.

"Tell him I'm not signing and we're getting married."

"Stop it!" she screamed. Doors flew open. Open-mouthed women ran in. The FBI man appeared, tugging a .32 out of his shoulder holster.

Honey sobbed, "I couldn't sleep a wink last night—seeing your crumpled body lying on some freeway. All morning I've been frantic. Wondering where you were. Why you didn't call. Phoning hospitals and morgues. Now, minutes before our wedding, you burst in and start bullying me about contracts and clauses and papers to sign. Oh, darling, I beg you—stop; because . . . I . . . can't"—she staggered backward—"take . . . any . . ." Her eyelids fluttering, the back of her hand flew to her forehead, and with a little sigh she crumpled neatly to the rug.

Shrieking women swarmed over her, slapping her hands and face, calling for smelling salts.

I ran down the stairs. You had to hand it to her, she knew how to pull a faint.

As I sprinted through the rose garden, the PA blared: *"Here is a man who married Honey . . . but . . only in a Warner Brothers musical. Today he's Governor of the great State of California. The Honorable Ronald Reagan . . ."*

I cut behind a hedge into a little glade, sat down on the sundial held up by marble cherubs, and forced my hurting, hungover brain to try to think my way out of this.

The pool house was dark and clammy cold from the air conditioning. It took my eyes a second to make out the three of them on the barstools drinking martinis.

Eddie, locking the door behind me, said, "Greengauge got a call five minutes ago. From Honey."

Greengauge, hands thrown out, came toward me.

"Well, Buck, now you know how things stand."

"That's right." I dropped the contracts on top of the green felt table. "But you don't."

"Meaning?"

"I've written out a contract for you to sign."

Without waiting, I read with no expression: "I, Josiah Greengauge, president of the United Broadcasting Company, agree to put on this fall over the full network twenty-six episodes of a private detective series, created, owned and starring Michael McLeod. Budget to be comparable to *The FBI* and *Mannix*. McLeod shall have complete artistic control. If any of the above terms are not fulfilled UBC shall pay McLeod three hundred thousand dollars damages. Dated—"

Coulter and Hundsley laughed. But Greengauge, head cocked, lips pursed, asked alertly, "What makes you think I'd sign that?"

"If you don't, there's no wedding."

Eddie said, "Good idea."

Greengauge said abruptly, "If you don't go through with this, just what do you think you'll be worth in this town?"

"A lot," I said. "I'll have had a million dollars' worth of publicity."

"America's Sweetheart," Eddie said.

"But Sunday night is the only thing that keeps UBC alive. If Honey leaves, it collapses. Then what are you worth?"

"A rhetorical question, because she won't—"

"She wants to marry me. If you fuck up her wedding, she'll cut your throat."

Greengauge laughed explosively and slapped me on the shoulder. "You're a fighter to the end! And God knows I admire you for that. But you're an amateur when it comes to negotiations. You've put me in an impregnable position. Buck, much as *I* like you, you're a failed actor; a man in desperate financial straits; a man with a long history of violence. How could I allow Honey to put herself in a situation where her accidental death could enrich you by as much as thirty million dollars? I would submit, sir, as her trusted friend I had no alternative but to cancel the wedding when you refused to sign those waivers."

"But I signed the waivers."

I'd coldcocked him. He stared stupidly as Coulter stepped quickly to the table and looked through the papers. "They're signed."

Josiah sank heavily into the chair opposite me.

"The reason there won't be a wedding is because you double-crossed me."

"Honey will understand," he said without much conviction.

I stuck it to him. "You'll have made her a bad joke. And when they start laughing, you're going to take the fall . . . and you know it."

I slid the papers across the table and held out Coulter's fountain pen. He threw it down so hard it bounced to the floor, then cursed me in a thick, choked voice.

I stood. "Let's go."

"About time." Eddie opened the door; sunlight streamed in.

Hanrahan, standing outside, shouted, "Two minutes!"

Greengauge, moving faster than I thought he possibly could, jammed me in the doorframe. Hard belly pushed against mine, pupils glittering like nailheads, he whispered, "You walk out on me and you'll be through. And I don't mean just in this town. I mean through, washed up, finished for life. Hold a gun to my head, will you? I swear, I'll have you crucified."

I believed him. Scared, I tried to come up with my Cagney grin.

"You're good, Josiah," I said. "But you're bluffing."

His eyes bored into mine for a long beat.

"Yes," he said finally. "I am." Then quickly crossed to the green-topped table and signed the contract.

"Do you, Michael, take this woman, Honey, to be your lawfully wedded wife from this day forward, for richer, for poorer, in sickness and in health—until death do you part?"

"I do."

The reception line was a blur of Ronnie and Duke and Frank and Sammy and Dean and Lucy and Loretta; and Jimmy Stewart, Art Linkletter, Edgar Bergen, Fred Astaire, Robert Montgomery. Everybody who was anybody who wasn't young or a Democrat.

When the line stopped I hustled Mordecai, surprisingly elegant in his usher's cutaway, to the deserted pool, sat him down on the diving board and told him what I wanted.

"Why me?"

"I liked your play about junkies."

"I'll be damned." He sucked on a joint. "How much time would I have?"

"Five days."

"Forget it."

"Cassidy's directing."

Awed, he said softly, "Cassidy . . . directing my script."

"If you can write it in five days."

"Seven."

"Six." We shook on it. "And don't tell anybody."

I got back just in time to help Honey cut a ten-tier wedding cake with a samurai sword MacArthur had given her for a USO tour.

Then, smiling, I danced her around and around the huge green-and-white tent until the tape and 16 and 35 crews were satisfied.

* * *

Changed into my getaway suit, I stood, smiling, beside Honey at the top of the staircase. Far below, flashbulbs exploded like tracers. Women's eyes stared up, focused hungrily on the bouquet in Honey's hands. She tossed it high over her shoulder, grazing the chandelier. A wild scrimmage broke out below. Thelma drove in, using her elbows like Bobby Hull. But a lanky girl leaped above the spearing hands, nailed it and walked off triumphantly; the women stared after her, furious that she was young and of no importance.

Outside we dashed through volleys of rose petals, into the long black Mercedes limousine, and waved, smiling, as it rolled down the gravel drive.

It had been decided we'd spend our honeymoon at Honey's beach house in the Colony.

The round black-lacquered door was opened by an angry old Chinaman in a white coat that buttoned to his neck.

I carried her across the threshold.

The setting sun blazing through the Venetian blinds cast hot white lines of light across the thick black shadows, turning the Chinese Modern room into a Dietrich set lit by Von Sternberg.

We followed the houseboy, in whispered argument with Nora, as he carried our bags up the white circular staircase.

Honey disappeared in a corner of the enormous red-and-gold master. I fell across the huge, round, black satin bed; stared in surprise at the mirrored ceiling; and passed out.

Honey woke me. She'd unbuttoned my shirt and was sliding her nails slowly across my stomach. She was in a slinky negligee with feathers on the shoulders that reminded me of the one Ginger wore in *Top Hat*.

There was an excited light in her eyes as she bent down and gave me a long, hungry kiss.

"Forget it," I said. "I'm too beat."

A little half-smile played across her lips.

"Oh, no, Buck," she whispered sweetly. "That's not

the way it works. I want it. And when I want it—you give it to me. . . . Understand?"

And I understood and I gave it to her.

10

I woke up with the taste of her in my mouth. Brushing my teeth, I unlatched the French doors. A sharp north wind was pushing chunky clouds across a hot blue sky, breaking up the beach into fast-moving, shifting patterns of light and shadow.

The surf was running high; glass-green breakers pounded in with the rumble of heavy artillery.

I pulled on my trunks and went downstairs.

Honey in a white two-piece bathing suit sat in the shadows of the white-columned pavilion at the far end of the pool. She was jotting notes on a clipboard.

I took her hand. "Come on."

"Where?"

"Swimming."

"I don't know how."

I stared at her.

"You can't swim?"

She shook her head.

"My father was going to teach me the summer I was ten. But instead Mother dragged me off all over Kansas and Nebraska, entering me in Shirley Temple contests."

"Were you good?"

"If I didn't win, we didn't eat," she said tartly.

Touched, I jumped in the shallow end of the pool. "Come on." I held out my arms. "I'll teach you."

"It's too late."

"No, it's not."

"They're here," she hissed. "Hi, Guys!"

Marching down the shallow white steps from the house were Nate and Stan, four or five vice-presidents from TUL, and Coulter.

"How very sweet of you to leave your families on Sunday morning and come all the way out here to help Buck. The least I can do is rustle you up some breakfast."

"Couldn't." Nate patted his stomach in explanation. "We ate at Hillcrest."

"Had a little pre-conference conference," Coulter said.

The others nodded, blinking in the sunlight, standing around her, smiling in their suits and ties.

"Oh, you don't have to look at me like *that*. I know this is no place for *wimmin folk*." She kissed me. "They're going to tell you how to put together your interlocking corporations and hold onto your holding companies. I never could understand a word of it." They laughed, very conscious of her in her bathing suit as she walked off.

Then there was the squeal of rubber-tipped chairs shoved back on the marble and the clicks of Guccis being opened. They took turns droning on about how I had to become a corporation; then that corporation had to form a joint corporation with UBC with a high evaluation on goodwill to justify the cash flow; but because of tax problems all the profits had to be siphoned into a holding company.

I watched the blue water across the pool lap into the gutter wondering: *what kind of women he liked; if he'd been married; what he drank; his favorite movies ... No. The hell with that—that'll come in time along with the walk and the look. But what about the core? His mother? ... His father? ... No. Go deeper. Start at the beginning. Does he believe in God?*

Conscious of silence, I turned. The circle of faces were all staring at me, waiting.

Stan broke the quiet with a laugh. "Beautiful! *We're* talking about twenty G's a week take-home pay—and *you're* bored!"

They smiled indulgently.

"Understand," Nate warned, "that's not what you're getting. That's what we're asking. I'm going to have to fight like a tiger to get half that."

"Oh, come now," Coulter drawled, "hasn't Mr. McLeod already done that for you?"

Nate bristled. "Hell, no! This isn't Wall Street. This is a jungle. Where you gotta bite and gouge and go for the jugular—"

I stood up. "I want two things in there. One: Eddie Riordan is gaffing all stunts but write him in as associate producer at seven and a half a week. So in case he gets hurt or we lay off a week he still gets paid."

"No problem," Stan said eagerly. "What's number two?"

"I want it all spelled out and nailed down that I have the OK on every script, actor, set, setup, cut—"

Stan, startled, said, "They'll never give you final cut."

Coulter snubbed him. "He's already got it. Oh, by the way, Mr. McLeod, you'd better give me your copy of the contract—for safekeeping."

"My business manager has it," I lied.

"Listen, Scotty, Nate and his boys and Coulter, he's—"

"I know who Coulter is."

"—Just left."

"What the hell were they doing out there?"

"Setting up all sorts of interlocking corporations."

"You didn't sign anything?"

"No. But they sure as hell wanted me to. Coulter also wanted the contract."

"You didn't give it to him?"

"No. I'll bring it in tomorrow. Get it notarized and Xeroxed; then put the original in the safe."

"Oh, *I* know what to do; but I'm not so sure *you* do."

"What's that supposed to mean?"

"You should have let me know about the meeting."

"I didn't know about it. They just walked in."

"Then you should have delayed it until I could get there ... provided, of course, you still want me to represent you."

"You dumb Scots bastard, you're my friend. I'm counting on you to keep those bastards from stealing us blind."

I showered, shaved and dressed. When I walked down the white staircase I was surprised to see Honey standing in the living room, one elbow on the mirrored fireplace, talking in a low voice to Thelma and the writers who sat on the big white sofa that no one had bothered to take the plastic cover off.

11

The Hornblower stainless-steel door slid open, and Laura stared at me. She wore an old bathrobe and hair curlers, and clutched the theater section of *The New York Times*.

"Ted!" she wailed. "You'll never guess who's here."

Ted sat in his study at a red IBM electric typewriter. On the brick wall behind him photographs from Steichen's *Family of Man* were arranged around his two Emmy nominations.

"Finished the script?"

"Fun-*ny!*" Laura, laughing, lit a Sherman brown. "We found out about this less than twenty hours ago. Remember?"

"Ted's written *Range Riders* in less time."

"But that was when we were young and hungry and so was the world. Can I get you a drink?"

"Bloody Mary, but the visit's not social."

She left, giving him a warning look.

He stuffed tobacco in a pipe with his thumb. "I've been fooling around with the concept," he said, watching me warily. "And I've come up with a great character. The guy who cleans up your office. Cooks for you. An old cop. Shot up. On a pension. Has a limp. He loves you, worries about you; but what's really fresh, he'd rather cut out his tongue than say a kind word to you. He's salty. Crusty. And—"

"Walter Brennan in *Rio Bravo.*"

"I'll admit there are some similarities, but he'll *play.* Hundsley doesn't like him; he wants a black girl like the one on *Mannix.*"

"Ted," I said carefully, "I don't want you talking to the network about anything until you've cleared it with me."

He puffed on his pipe thoughtfully, then forced a fatherly smile. "Now, Buck," he said gently. "As creator-writer-producer and co-owner of our show I do have the right to talk to—"

"Do you want it straight, Ted?"

"Oh, by all means."

"It's not our show. But my show. It's not part yours, part mine. It's all mine."

He blinked at me in surprise. "Buck! I can't believe I heard you correctly. We have a contract. A *deal.*"

"That deal died the moment you tried to cut me out of it."

He jumped up. "That's not true! I had no idea Nate took it to CBS for Glenn Ford. I swear it!"

"Stop lying, Ted," I said. "We haven't the time."

"Cut!" Laura gaily slipped in with a tray of Bloody

Marys, crackers and cheese. "Can the men in my life take a ten-minute break?"

"No," I said.

She set down the tray and went out, sliding the doors shut behind her.

"I believe," Ted said stiffly, "that before we were interrupted . . . you were calling me a liar."

"Right. Now, here's where we stand. Forget the old deal. I have a signed contract with UBC for twenty-six episodes. I have to start shooting two weeks from tomorrow; and I want you to produce."

"Surprise, surprise," he said bitterly. "Why?"

"You know the ropes, you're good at getting scripts, and you're the best pressure rewrite man in town. I'll pay your price. I'm generous. And you'll have a percentage of my profits."

"No piece of the show?"

"No one has a piece of the show but me."

"Are you taking executive producer credit?"

"No. Just star. You can have whatever billing you want. But on cast, scripts, everything, I'm the boss."

"And if I don't like this . . . ah . . . arrangement?"

"I'll set someone who does by six-thirty." I put some Brie on a Triscuit and ate it.

Ted sat heavily on the desk. "Jesus." He stared at me, sadly shaking his head. "I just can't believe you're the same Buck I did *Range Rider* with three years ago. I thought we were *friends*. I thought we had a great relationship. You were the star. I was the producer. And when I asked you to do something you did."

"And we were off the air in thirteen weeks."

"One Goddam minute," he said angrily. "I've had three hits since then."

I smiled at him. "Ted, don't think I don't know if this show bombs, you'll have another next season at thirty-five hundred per. But for me, it's the end of the line. That's why I'm calling all the shots. Now are you in or out?"

He stared at the beach, tapping the stem of the pipe against his teeth. "In, I guess."

"Good. I'm glad." As we shook hands, I called, "Laura, for Christ's sake, stop listening at the door and come in."

She ran in, kissed us, and we all had a drink together before I threw her out and we went to work on the script.

Cassidy rocked gently on the shadowed veranda as I told him the story. Behind him the quarter horses moved restlessly in the corral. Beyond them the ocean reflected the setting sun like a knife blade. Toward the end Kate came up and, worried, sat on the railing.

When I finished Cassidy said, "Not bad."

Kate said, "You're not seriously considering directing a television show that doesn't even have a shooting script?"

He winked at her. "Now, Michael, why do you want me to direct?"

"You're the best." He waited. "I really need you, Tim. I haven't worked in over a year. I'm rusty. My timing's off."

Kate asked murderously, "Aren't there dozens of bright young television directors dying to polish up your timing?"

"Sure."

"Then why don't you bloody well get one and leave Tim alone?" she raged. "How can you be so damned selfish? Do you know the features he's turned down in the past few years? Because of some little flaw in the script? To end up doing *what?* Something he has to shoot in five days."

"Nine."

"You hear that, Tim? That's the end of it. I won't allow it. Nine days. That's too much pressure. Remember what the doctor said—"

"At ease, Kate."

He said it gently but with such authority she bowed

her head, wrapped her arms around her legs and stared down at the red-brown tiles.

"Tim,'" I said, "it's my one chance in life to do something good."

"*Good!*" Kate said. "It's a cheap private detective show."

"So was *The Maltese Falcon,*" I said. "I want it to be that good. Hard and tough and fast and funny. But even if it isn't, at least it won't have any cheap dialogue and dumb chases and bad acting. Now, I know that's not much—"

"Hell," said Cassidy. "That's a lot."

"Well," I said. "It's not *Hamlet.*"

"No," he said. "But what is?"

Kate stood up suddenly. "Please don't do it, Tim."

"Now, Kate." Cassidy slid his arms around her and kissed the side of her forehead. "You know it'll do me good to get out of here and back on a deck. Stop bitching about how TV cuts up my old pictures, and start shooting a new one."

"You're right, dear." She gave him a good smile. "I don't know what's come over me. I must have been remembering those last days on *Stampede.*"

"One thing, Michael." Cassidy turned, struck by a sudden thought. "I won't shoot at Magnitude."

"No problem," I said. "Neither will I."

"Then"—he held his hand out behind Kate's back—"you've got yourself a director."

Hal sprawled behind the conference table, elegant in his pink madras suit with matching tie and shirt. Two dark-suited vice-presidents, Timkins and Porter, flanked him. They stared at us coldly as we sat down.

Hal said, "I don't know if there's any sense even discussing the show."

"Why's that, Hal?" Ted asked.

"Buck's salary demands are so outrageous—"

"Ridiculous," Timkins snapped.

"—that we'd save time if we started negotiating *them.*"

"I don't talk money, Hal. You'll have to discuss that with my agent."

"Well, la-di-fucking-da," he drawled. "Ain't we grand?"

"Boys," Ted pleaded. "I've got a lot of writing to do. The agents always manage to work out the deals. Can't we firm up the concept?"

"Very well." Hal suddenly threw up his hand. "I see Buck's house as a whitewashed old Spanish, high atop the Palisades. Exterior: Dufy-ish white sails against blue ocean. Interior: all off-white, eggshell wrought-iron chairs, and *gigantic,* creamy, French Provincial wardrobes. The chandeliers—"

"Hal," I said, "I don't know what you're smoking, but I'm making a show about a beat-up private eye who lives in a hundred-and-twenty-dollar-a-month apartment south of the Strip, has two suits and trouble paying the phone bill."

"Then you're dead in that time slot. Timkins, show him the demographic breakdown." Timkins slid a thick leather-bound notebook across the table. "What you don't understand, Buck, is that you're inheriting Honey's audience. Now, we've analyzed them by age, sex, race, income, and buying patterns. We know what they want. It's glamour! Luxury! Beautiful clothes! Beautiful People! And that's what we're going to give them."

"What you don't understand, Hal, is that you're not making the show—I am."

"Oh, no, dear boy, this is a UBC show and—"

"Fuck off, Hal. I have creative control."

"Not to be unreasonably withheld," Porter screamed.

"Now, now, let's not get upset," Hal said softly. "Buck's new at all this. Let's start from the beginning. UBC wants a *happy* show . . ."

* * *

"I think they're right." Honey looked up from her cantaloupe and cottage cheese in the vast dining hall. "There's so much gloom and misery in the world, why put it on Sunday night after my show?"

"To depress people."

"It's not a thing to joke about. There must be something terribly wrong with your show to make Hal— Hey! Where are you going?"

"Out."

"Not tonight. The Kinlocks are coming over to play bridge. Remember?"

"You forgot," I said. "I don't play."

12

The big old hawk-nosed man in the worn brown suit sitting behind the scarred desk handed back my SAG card and driver's license and studied the clippings. Outside the small second-floor office on Vine near Sunset a red neon sign blinked in on walls lined with 8 x 10 glossies of long-forgotten starlets.

He gave me the clippings. "Now, just what would you want me to do?"

"Let me watch you at work. Answer my questions."

He stared at me noncommittally. "For that you'll pay my regular fee of one hundred and seventy-five dollars a day?"

"One hundred."

He scratched the corner of his mouth. "One and a quarter?"

"OK."

"Now stop looking at the guy at the door. You'll scare him away."

"He's been back three times."

"I know." He tapped the silver-framed autographed picture of Jean Harlow on his desk. "I have this angled so it works like a mirror. I have my desk set so they can look me over without having to face me."

"I was thinking of working out of my apartment."

"Too personal. It's got a bed in it. Makes women think about sex. Scares them off. At first, anyway. When I took this office it had a solid wood door. I made 'em take it off and put up the glass one. Just so they could look me over."

The small hatched-faced man in brand-new overalls stuck his head in the door. "Which one's Partridge?"

"I am. What can I do for you?"

"I dunno." He looked at me suspiciously. "Who's he?"

"My partner. Harry Waters. You can talk freely in front of him."

The man sat awkwardly on the edge of the battered brown leather armchair and told a long rambling story about how he lived out in Ojai and had a television and hi-fi store and this young clerk that he was sure was stealing components.

"Well," Partridge said finally, "we *can* handle that. But it's expensive. Means putting a man in the store. Then he might not do anything because there *is* a man there."

"Then you won't handle it?"

"I didn't say that. Though it is a bit out of our line. Our speciality is surveillance."

"Surveillance?"

"Suppose this clerk was stealing because a woman was involved. We'd follow him. Find out who the woman is, where they met and for how long. Give you all the details."

"Oh." The man abruptly walked out.

Partridge pulled a pint of Four Roses from a drawer and poured it into paper cups.

"What did you make of your first case?"

"He was lying."

"Better get used to that. They all do."

"Why?"

"They spin some cock-and-bull story while they're sizing you up."

"Why did you pitch surveillance?"

"If you had a hi-fi store and a clerk that you thought was stealing, you'd go to the cops or fire him. Only reason you'd come to me would be to try and regain the stolen property. Cops don't give a damn about that."

"He didn't seem to either."

"That's right. You notice anything else?"

"Why the new overalls?"

He smiled. "Disguise. Make me think he's poorer than he is. That he's from Ojai."

"He's not."

"I'd bet someplace a lot closer in. Like Van Nuys. . . . And he's probably got the store." He thought for a moment. "But instead of a clerk tipping the till, he's got a young wife that he thinks is playing around. He'll come back in about twenty minutes and pay my advance in cash because they have a joint checking account."

He was right on everything.

As we walked in the next morning, Hal snapped, "Now, on top of your outrageous salary demands I understand you refuse to shoot at Magnitude?"

"That's right."

"Why?"

"It's the worst lot in town."

"How in God's name can you say that when we do fourteen series there including your wife's?"

"I've seen the shows."

"Christ!" he screamed, throwing himself back in the

chair. "If you're going to fight me over every little thing, I'm just going to have to alert Josiah that I don't see how we can get the show on." Sulkily he looked out the window.

Ted lit his pipe. "I've come up with a compromise on the concept." Hal looked at him suspiciously. "I stayed up most of the night simplifying the two positions. You want the show glamorized, theatrical, escapist. Buck sees it realistic, semi-documentary. It's James Bond versus Sam Spade."

Hal said coldly, "And how do you compromise that?"

Ted puffed out a cloud of smoke. "Think *Bullitt*," he said calmly.

"*Bullitt?*" Hal said.

"*Bullitt,*" Ted repeated.

Timkins said, "*Bullitt* was big financially."

Porter said, "Very."

Ted said, "It was nominated for five Academy Awards."

Hal said thoughtfully, "That's right, *Bullitt* did have a certain style. Almost hard-edge Pop Art. And *you* have some of McQueen's existential quality." He began to brighten up. "Perhaps I can get Yates to direct it. That flick with Dusty and Mia was a disaster, so—"

"I've already set Cassidy."

Timkins and Porter shouted:

"You can't set a director." "Artistic control only gives you a *veto* over our selections."

"Oh, shut up!" Hal snapped. "Cassidy would be marvelous. He's my idol. Maybe," he added wistfully, "he can give this damn thing some class."

As I walked into the soda fountain Honey handed me a Jack Daniel's on the rocks and kissed me.

"Darling, I'm so proud of you, getting Hal to go along with your concept. How did you ever swing that?"

"It's my Irish charm."

She pouted. "I wish you were more charming about Magnitude. Wouldn't it be fun shooting on the same lot?"

"No."

"Buck!"

"It's the worst lot in town and——"

The phone rang. It was Scotty.

"What the hell is this Baker company set up for?"

"Something to do with the cash flow."

"And the Oran?"

"Scotty, don't ask me. Ask Nate and Coulter."

"Oh, I've been asking. And getting some very fishy answers. I don't trust any of them——or the way they've set up these interlocking corporations."

As I hung up, Honey said, "What's the matter?"

"Scotty thinks Coulter and Nate are doing a job on me."

She laughed and ruffled my hair. "Oh, darling, he's just being a business manager. They all think everything's a big swindle and the lawyers are crooks and the agents are cheating you. It's just a big act they put on to make us think they earn all that money we pay them."

"Not Scotty. He's honest."

"I didn't say he wasn't. That's just the way they are."

As the orange-and-white car barrier at Magnitude went up, Neely stepped out of the guard's glass cage.

"Beautiful to see you, Buck."

Neely had the nervous, guilty face of an Irish drinker; and the long dyed hair, mod handlebar moustache and expensive brass-buttoned blue blazer only made him look more like a Gay Nineties cop on the take.

He signaled me to pull up in the no-parking zone before the tall black-glass building.

A bent old black man in a pink swallowtail coat took us up in the carved rosewood private elevator.

It opened directly into Saul's enormous office. I felt

that I was stepping into a black-and-white movie. The walls were white, the furniture black, the floor-to-ceiling windows that watched the lot were tinted black; even Saul, springing across the room, hand outstretched, looking like a very thin, grey-haired Kissinger, wore black suit, white shirt, black tie.

"Buck, I believe in cutting straight through to the heart. I've been informed you don't wish to shoot here and I don't believe a word of it."

"It's true."

"Trouble I expect from my enemies, not my friends."

"We're not friends, Saul."

"What are you talking? I was at your wedding. Remember? Since I am your friend—"

I jumped. He was stuffing handfuls of ten-dollar bills in my pockets. Neely chuckled.

"What the hell are you doing?"

"I've got the most efficient lot in town. We crank out film at the lowest cost per foot. Ask our competitors. They admit it. Here everything's automated. Computerized. What's that mean to you? Since you got a pice, it means money in your pocket."

I dumped the money on the floor. "I want the best film that can be made. I don't care what it costs. To give you an idea of the quality I'm after, Cassidy's directing my first show. You're not geared to deliver it, so—"

"Who says? Don't listen to my enemies. I know, all over town they put me down because I was once an agent. They say: That Saul! How does he have the temerity to sit at the summit of a lot like Magnitude? I'll tell you why! Because I once *was* an agent, I'm *you*-oriented. In the old days I would have been out battling studio heads to get you what you wanted. Now, I can *give* it to you."

"I bet you can at that."

Neely smiled.

"Oh, a little joke. Go ahead. Enjoy yourself. The Irish are great kidders.

"But seriously! You want a Tiffany operation and because I run a Sears, Roebuck lot you think I can't give it to you. Wrong!

"There comes a time in every man's life when he has to ask: 'What's it all about, Alfie?' For me, it was last night. Suddenly everything turned into ashes. The houses in Holmby, Malibu and the Springs. The wife, the broads, the Lear jet. The lot that turns out more shows than all my competitors *combined*. I have everything. Yet I was unhappy. Why?"

"You'd seen the shows."

"You make a joke but you read my heart. You're absolutely right. My idol was always Thalberg. What was his trademark? Class . . . quality stamped on every picture. Saul, I said, you got to do a series you can take pride in. A series Thalberg would enjoy.

"Don't tell me there's not a Deity up above when the next day you walk in demanding what I want to give.

"Neely, on Buck's show—Everything's first class. Top quality. Forget the budget. I don't care what it costs."

"Got it, Saul."

"So we take a bath on this one. What do I care? So long as we got a Tiffany–Thalberg Production." He held out his hand. "Deal?"

"No."

"How can you say no?"

"Your cameramen are dogs, your sets are shlock, your lab puts a blue haze on the film, your editors are butchers, your scoring must be done in a Tijuana cathouse. When I see the film you grind out, I get sick at my stomach."

Neely gasped.

Saul laughed, slapping me on the shoulder.

"Now I gotta have you. You're cocky. You got balls. There aren't four fucking actors in town who'd dare talk to me like that. But you got that Cagney-Bogart don't-give-a-Goddam attitude. It's gonna make your show a smash. I can smell it. Now, I'd love to talk longer but can't." He hurried me to the door, shoving a contract in my hand. "Ask your lawyer. See if you haven't got me over a barrel. I guarantee to give you everything you want." The white wall slid aside. There stood the old black man in the elevator. "Give my best to Honey. Ask her if I don't give her whatever she wants. Cheap. That's another edge ya got. I'm in love with your wife. Ha ha." The door wiped across his face.

The stooped grey-haired writer in the Harris tweed jacket with the worn leather elbow patches stopped in the doorway and stared at me in surprise.

"Asa," Ted said, smiling, "Buck likes to sit in on all the story conferences."

"Fine," Asa said, sitting awkwardly in the straight chair set in front of Ted's desk. "Just like the Golden Age."

"That's when *Philco* and *Studio One* and *Omnibus* came live out of New York," Ted explained. "They treated writers like playwrights. You'd be there for readings, and rehearsals—"

"I know."

"Buck, did you ever see Asa's *Studio One*, 'The Severance of Ted Lynch'?"

"I don't know. What was it about?"

"*Death of a Salesman* of an account executive. Won everything that year."

"Leslie Nielsen and Virginia Gilmore?"

"That's right."

"Beautiful script," I said.

"Thank you," Asa said quietly. "It all happened to my brother. He was axed from Y & R and couldn't get a job for nine months. Said it was like having leprosy. . . . *But!*" he said briskly. "We aren't going to make any money reminiscing."

"Right." Ted picked up a yellow pad. "What have you got for us today?"

He turned on a salesman's smile. "A fresh locale. A fantastic scuba school. With a fantastic murderess. A Raquel Welch. Never out of her bikini. She pushes her paraplegic husband into a pool full of piranhas."

"That's too James Bond for us."

"I've got a better one with more realism," he said quickly. "The star quarterback of the Rams drops dead in plain view of eighty thousand witnesses. The police are baffled. Buck cracks the case. The Syndicate piped nerve gas under the Astroturf. An MIT Ph.D. worked out all the technical details. . . ."

"No? Well, I've been saving the best for last. . . ."

At midnight, wearing a grey tweed suit I'd bought at Gentlemen's Resale West for a hundred dollars, I spotted a wild-eyed black chick in orange hip-huggers coming out of the drugstore at Hollywood and Vine and followed her west on Hollywood. After a block she got jittery and wheeled around. Taking care not to catch her eyes, I walked quickly past and stayed a hundred feet ahead, using the reflections in the store windows to keep track of her.

Partridge was waiting in front of the Roosevelt.

"Not bad." As we walked across the lobby he asked quickly, "Which one's the house detective?"

"Big guy leaning over the counter talking to the Hertz girl." He grunted approvingly.

Over drinks in the bar he abruptly broke off telling me about old cases. "You getting anything out of this?"

"Hard to say."

He squinted at me, tugging on his earlobe. "How do actors work?"

"Different."

"You?"

"I just keep digging around till I come up with something."

"Hell, you sound like a detective."

I felt that little click and the back of my neck tingled.

"Now—you got something," he said shrewdly.

"Yeah." I tossed ten bucks on the bar. "But if you talk about it, you lose it."

In front of the spotlit columns of Tara II, two limousines faced each other. Glistening grilles not ten feet apart. The bored chauffeurs, smoking, listening to the Dodger game, managed somehow to avoid seeing each other. It was a nice shot. A Mike Nichols shot.

In the big shadowed living room Honey was flanked by Coulter, Nate, Stan, and five or six others awkwardly balancing teacups; Scotty, off by himself, nursed a drink.

"Darling," Honey said reproachfully. "The Guys have been waiting for you such a long time."

I said, "It looks like a bad wake." There was a gloomy silence. "Bad as that?"

"Not when you consider the total package," Coulter said.

"So there *are* a few bad details." Stan smiled. "What deal is perfect?"

"None!"

"Right!"

"You never get everything."

"Never!"

I lit a cigarette. "What are the bad details?"

"The salary and the lot—it's Magnitude."

"I told you I won't shoot there."

They exchanged sidewise glances. Coulter got to his feet.

"Mr. McLeod, there comes a time in every negotiation when you reach final positions. UBC has made it clear these terms are non-negotiable. If they are not accepted tonight—they'll scrap the show."

"Then they have to pay me three hundred thousand dollars."

"No, Mr. McLeod. Then you can sue them for three hundred thousand dollars, which is not at all the same thing. I imagine their legal position will be—"

I cut him off. "What's the salary?"

In the silence I could hear Scotty pouring another drink. Nate spread his hands out apologetically.

"Fifteen hundred."

"I made thirty-five hundred on a half hour three seasons ago."

"Don't think I didn't tell him. I screamed. I yelled. I told him every third and fourth banana in town is getting more. It's insane! But ... that's what it is. It's take-it-or-leave-it time. We've all been there. And we know."

There was a slow nodding of heads.

"And Buck, I beg you, on hands and knees, don't blow it. It's a beautiful deal. With a profit picture that can run to thirty, forty G's a week!"

Coulter said, "We're all in agreement that you should accept."

"Scotty," I said, "I haven't heard a word out of you."

He polished his pince-nez with a handkerchief. "Take it," he said quietly.

"You were the one who told me to take a big salary and forget profits."

"Well, Buck," he said mildly, "things change."

"What about the interlocking corporations and the holding company that were set up to screw me?"

Coulter cut in, "Mr. MacNab is far too modest about his role in the negotiations. UCB *had* slipped some things past me, which *he* caught. With his help they've been rewritten, renegotiated. As a team we've hammered out a contract that we *all* feel you should sign." He slid out of his briefcase a sixty-page contract and set it down on the coffee table.

They sat up straighter, watching me.

Stan cleared his throat. "Frankly, Buck, we're all eagerly awaiting your reaction."

"You're all fired." They smiled uncertainly. "I mean it. I hand you a signed contract. A week later you hand me this piece of shit, and say: Sign it. I say: Get the fuck out."

As they disappeared in the shadows, Honey said softly, "That's just what Josiah wants you to do."

"What?"

"Lose your temper and break the contract."

She jumped up and grabbed my hand.

"Darling, don't you understand? You've won. You beat him every step of the way. You have complete ownership. Final cut. I was number one for three seasons before Irving could get that! The hardest thing to justify to the IRS is low salary and high profits. And you've got that, too. The only loophole UBC could find was salary—"

"And the lot."

She turned away impatiently. "Oh! You can shoot at Magnitude. All that's keeping you apart is the money. And who cares about money?"

"Christ knows, not Nate or Stan or Coulter. Or *you*, Honey! But me? Yes! Vulgar. Crude. Cheap. Grasping. Me! You bet your ass I care about money. Especially when I'm being screwed out of it. That's all this town is about: sex and money."

"You're wrong," she whispered, eyes glowing. "It's *power*. And you have it all right in your hands. Don't throw it away—" She broke off suddenly. "That's not the reason."

"No."

"Then what?"

"Greengauge has gotten to them."

"How could he?"

"I don't know. But the fix is in. I can smell it."

"But what about Scotty? He's your friend. You trust him. Don't you?"

"Yes."

"And, darling, trust me. Lord knows, I'm no lawyer or agent but I have been through an awful lot of negotiations. And this is a marvelous deal. You'll have your own series! On the air! Once it's a hit—and I know it will be—then you can walk off the set and UBC will have to give you whatever you want. Oh, please say yes. Pretty please—for your little Honey?"

As I signed the contracts, Nora passed around glasses of champagne.

Coulter raised his high. "To the show! May it be a huge success."

When the cheers died down, I said, "And when it is, we'll ram this contract up Greengauge's ass—and write a new one."

There was a sudden strained silence. They all looked over my shoulder at Honey.

I turned to her. "What's the matter?"

"Oh, darling," she murmured, blushing. "The guys just aren't used to hearing those *words* in front of me."

Cassidy held a saddle on the back of a colt tied by a long rope to a pole as he walked him around the corral. Kate was sitting on the top rung.

"You're just in time for breakfast," she said.

"Morning, Michael." Cassidy swung the saddle off and gentled the colt down.

"It's Magnitude," I said.

"Good," Kate said crisply. "Then Timothy's out of it and I couldn't be happier."

"I fought as hard as I could."

"Well." Tim swung the saddle back on the colt. "You don't win 'em all."

I asked, "Why won't you shoot at Magnitude?"

"There's no use going into it," Kate said.

"I just wondered," I said. "After all, I've got complete artistic control written in my contract and Saul promised he'd give me anything I want."

"He lies," Cassidy said grimly, swinging the saddle off. "He promised me in *Stampede* that he'd—"

"The subject's closed," Kate said flatly. "I won't let you go through those dreadful battles again."

I took a deep breath and played my last card. "I'm sorry, Kate. I didn't understand. I'd never ask Tim to get into a fight on my account. Not at his age."

"What the hell did you think you were asking for anyway?" Cassidy said angrily. "Don't you know that's all directing is? One Goddam fight after another. Fights with writers, producers, actors, cameramen—"

"Hell," I said, "then you might as well shoot at Magnitude."

He threw his head back and laughed.

"You're going to do it!" Kate said in a fury.

He looked at her in surprise. "How did you know?"

"Agh." She jumped down and ran toward the house. "The hell with the two of you."

Cassidy handed me the rope and went after her. I untied the colt, let him out of the corral, put the saddle in the tack room and walked over to my car.

Kate threw open the front door.

"Well, what are you waiting for? An engraved invitation to breakfast?"

13

Our offices at Magnitude were a madhouse. Shouting workmen carried furniture in and out. There was the stink of fresh paint. Men in white coveralls ripped rugs out from under the feet of a girl dashing frantically around answering the dozen ringing phones.

In the big office, Harriet, Ted's old crow of a secretary, stood on a chair hanging up his Emmy nominations. Three men on their knees in the corner smoothed down his new carpet. Ted said, "Oh, *hi* . . . I must apologize, Tim, since this *is* the producer's office. I took it but it should be yours, so I'll move—"

"Stay where you are," Cassidy said. "You're doing the writing."

"We'll use my office," I said.

"I told them to paint that," Ted said. "It was such a depressing beige."

"What's that?" Cassidy was moving toward a door.

"Nothing. Just a cubbyhole for an assistant."

There was barely enough room for the two battered desks and three straight-back chairs.

"This'll do fine." Cassidy slung his bulging, worn briefcase up on the desk by the window and sat behind it. "Now, what kind of shape is the script in?"

"Pretty rough, I'm afraid. I've been dictating and Harriet hasn't had time to type it out, so—"

"Then tell it to me."

Cassidy pulled a stick out of the briefcase, opened a jackknife, put his boots on the windowsill and whittled.

When Ted finished, Cassidy thanked him politely.

As soon as the door closed, Cassidy snapped shut his jackknife. "You know he can't write it."

"No, I don't," I said. "He's damn good at rewrite and polish."

"Maybe. But he can't write this. He doesn't have the balls."

I told him about Mordecai.

He closed his eyes and sat in the sunlight in his faded denims, thinking. Then he opened his eyes with a snap.

"Yes. Mordecai can do it."

A red-faced man suddenly strode in. He was six-four, weighed close to three hundred. And judging from the bulges in the sleeves of his flashy plaid jacket it was mostly muscle.

"Hi, Tim." He stuck out his ham of a hand. "I'm Cohan. Your new first."

"The name is Mr. Cassidy. Go out in the hall, get rid of that cigar, and wait."

"Yes, Mr. Cassidy."

The door shut. I said, "Wait for *what?* I won't have him on my show. He's nothing but a pig-Irish bully."

"Who would you like?" Cassidy asked calmly.

"A good assistant director."

"I want a name."

"I don't know one on this lot."

"Because there aren't any. Just spies for Neely."

"So we'll take his number one fink?"

"Right."

"Why?"

He looked at me coldly. "Pay attention because I'm only going to tell you once. The only Goddam way you ever get a good show shot is by not wasting any energy on fights you can't win."

There was a knock on the door and Neely stuck his concerned face in.

I said, "What the hell's the idea of assigning anyone without getting my OK or Cassidy's?"

"Jesus, Buck, I was trying to do you a favor. Giving you my best man."

Cassidy said, "If he's your best man we'll take him."

"You won't regret it. Come on in, Killer. That's his nickname. Used to be a pro wrestler."

Cohan came in, cap in hands like a schoolboy.

Cassidy said, "I'll take a chance on you."

"You won't regret it, Mr. Cassidy. I'm a hard worker. And just want to make you and Buck happy."

"It's Mr. McLeod," I said.

"Oh." He sized me up. "It's like that, is it?"

"Yes. And I'll tell you how else it is: Mister and Miss to every member of the cast, said politely and quietly. Yell once at an actor and I'll boot your ass right off the set."

He stared at me with glittering eyes.

Neely slapped him on the back. "Then that's the way it will be. Right, Killer?"

"Right . . . Mr. McLeod."

Cassidy had the protesting Cohan ask all the shooting directors for permission before we visited the stages.

On the set Cassidy would introduce himself to the awed director. Then as he stood in the shadows, poker-faced, his eyes would look first at the camera position, flick to the actors, then check the crosses, fill and backlight. When the scene was shot he'd courteously thank the director and we'd slip out, while he scribbled notes on the crew sheets.

As I walked down the street, blinking in the hot sunlight, smiling people surrounded me. Shook my hand. Slapped my back. Pretty girls brushed breasts against my arm. Agents whispered in my ear of directors who'd been dying to work with me.

I'd been out in the cold so long, I'd forgotten how it felt to have something they want.

The red light stopped blinking, the padded doors swung open, and we stood in the vaulted darkness of another stage.

You could smell the fear. Cameramen screamed at gaffers to hurry it up. Assistants screamed at makeup men powdering actors to stop being Rembrandts. Directors screamed, "It's good enough. Print it." All kept throwing nervous looks over their shoulders at the pale-faced men in dark business suits who, nearly invisible in the shadows, clicked stopwatches and jotted notes on clipboards.

Outside, Cassidy asked, "Every director here shoot with a zoom?"

"They damn well better," Cohan said with a chuckle. "It's a lot rule."

When the sloppy work and sleazy sets and bad dialogue and frightened looks began to blur together, Cassidy said, "Let's start on the dailies."

In dark rooms that had never seen sunlight and smelled of years of stale cigar smoke, we sat and saw all the mistakes frozen forever in the flickering frames of badly focused film.

Back in the office, Cassidy silently poured out drinks, sat down on his desk and looked out the window.

The sun was setting, casting a pink glow on the white sides of the stages, throwing long purple shadows on the crowded company streets where men moved slowly toward the parking lots.

"When the Springsteen brothers owned Magnitude it was a damn good lot," he said thoughtfully. "That's a hard thing to build—a good lot. Harder than making a good picture . . . and God knows that's hard enough."

He took a long swig on his drink.

A tour bus drove by. A taped voice announced: "Coming up on the left is the dressing room of America's Sweetheart . . . Honey Holly!" A dozen nuns peeped out from under the peppermint-striped awning.

"I was here shooting *Stampede* . . . suddenly there were all those Goddam agents swarming all over in their black silk suits"—he shook his head—"like termites."

"The day Saul bought the lot?"

"Yeah. He told me he was going to keep everybody scared. Get more work out of 'em that way. He's ended up turning the lot into the Dachau of the industry."

"Dachau?"

"Yes. Every morning thousands of people come in through those gates and every night when they go home they look a little more like a cake of soap."

The pre-production meeting was held in the big bare room behind Neely's office. The department heads, a dozen weather-beaten men, still uncomfortable in suits and ties, sat drinking coffee around the long wooden table shaped like a cross.

Neely, sitting at the head, waved Cassidy and Ted to seats on his left and right, but scowled at me.

"I didn't expect you, Buck."

Cohan said sharply, "Actors aren't allowed at production meetings."

"I'm the exception." I dragged a folding chair from the wall and sat behind Cassidy.

Neely introduced the department heads. Ted made a little speech about how we were really under the gun and everybody really had to pull together. Cassidy dealt a typed list of names around the table. The men looked at them, at Neely out of the corners of their eyes, then back down at the papers.

The property department finally opened. "This . . . ah . . . says you want Ross on props."

"That's right," Cassidy said pleasantly.

"Well . . . I'll do what I can."

"I don't understand what that means."

The man wriggled uncomfortably. "Ross is assigned to *Doc Shaw and Son.*"

Cassidy smiled. "Then take him off it."

The man shot a questioning glance at Neely. Neely, scowling, sucked on his moustache, scratched the back of his neck, finally gave a little nod.

"I'll do that, Mr. Cassidy."

The head of the camera department laughed, then said disbelievingly, "Maury *Kramer?*"

Neely said, "Oh, I can give you lots better cameramen than Maury Kramer."

"Maury will do fine."

"He's a pain in the ass," Cohan said bitterly.

Camera smiled indulgently. "He *is* a perfectionist. And I'll admit he's slow."

"Always painting," Cohan said.

"He's out," Neely said. "He's old and fussy."

"So am I," said Cassidy. "Have him start tomorrow."

"*Tomorrow?*"

"I'll need him and the art director to scout locations."

Neely leaned back and smiled. "Tim, you're not making a feature." Cassidy didn't say anything. "In television, your cameraman doesn't start work until you start shooting."

"That's dumb," said Cassidy.

The men sat perfectly still.

"That's the lot rule."

"Dumb rule."

"I made it," Neely said flatly.

"Then change it."

"It's policy."

"Does that mean you don't have the power?" Cassidy asked quickly.

Rattled, Neely said, "That's not the point."

Cassidy stood. "Oh, but it is. If you have the power, change it. If you haven't, I'm wasting time talking to you—I'll have to see Saul."

Cassidy was across the room and had opened the door before Neely said unpleasantly, "OK. You've got him."

"That's right," Cassidy said pleasantly. "Good day, gentlemen."

As I pulled up in front of the house, Maria slipped out on the porch, catching the screen door so it didn't bang.

"How's he doing?"

Worried, she shook her head. "The treatments scare him."

"Pretty hard to scare Eddie."

"You don't know what it's like," she said. "They strap him to the table. Then he's left all alone in the big empty room, with that huge cyclotron hanging from the ceiling shooting stuff into him. . . ." She turned away, shivering. "He gets sick afterward. He tries to hide it from me. But I can hear him throwing up."

I hugged her hard.

"Now he's going to be OK," I said, too loudly. "Tell me, is he able to exercise at all?"

"Oh, you can't keep him from that." She'd gotten her voice under control. "He jogs his three miles . . . and does his push-ups and sit-ups."

"Sounds good."

"It's not!" Her voice broke again. "He sits brooding for hours. He pulls himself together when the girls are here. But when they leave he turns mean."

"Mean?"

She nodded. "You better go in before he gets suspicious."

Mean? Suspicious? *Eddie?*

Out in the backyard in the last patch of sun, he sat in a gray bathrobe, a can of Coors in his hand, staring at the girls' sandbox.

"Hi, Eddie. You need a shave."

"I'm not going anywhere," he said with no expression, turning back to the sandbox.

"Don't be so sure of that. You start work tomorrow."

He stared at me. There was a hard, flat, dead look in his eyes I couldn't stand.

"You don't start shooting for eight days."

"That's right."

"You don't need me to lay out stunts tomorrow."

"I need you for other things."

"Like what?"

"Scouting locations."

"Make-work!" he spat out.

"What?"

"That's what they called it in the Depression," he said bitterly. "My father told me. He used to rake leaves back and forth across a street all day for the WPA. That's what I call this charity job you fixed up for your sick friend. Make-work. What do you call it?"

Scared, I took a deep breath and stuck it to him.

"Insurance," I said. "I have to find out if you're well enough to gaff the stunts."

"For Christ's sake, I'm well enough for that. I'm do-ing sit-ups—"

"You say you're well enough but I have to know. If you're not—I'll need time to get someone good."

"I'm telling you I'm all right."

"Prove it."

"How?"

"Come in tomorrow and work at whatever I give you. And, Eddie, if you can't cut it—you're out."

"Wait just one Goddam minute—"

"Can't, Eddie. I haven't the time." I walked toward the house. The look in his eyes wasn't dead any longer. It was so lively, in fact, I wondered if he was going to bounce the beer can off the back of my head.

Next morning as I walked in the office, Cassidy's door opened and Eddie strolled out.

I stared at him. He was all dressed up in his blue blazer.

"Good morning, Michael," he said coolly, and left.

I ran into the office. "For Christ's sake, I wanted to be here when you talked."

"He didn't want you," Cassidy said.

"Why the hell not?"

"He was right. Despite his deal with you he wasn't about to do the show unless I wanted him."

"You've got to give him a chance, Tim. He's the best Goddam stunt man in town."

"I set him."

"You did?"

"Don't you think I can spot a good man when I see one? Do you think I need a Goddam recommendation from you?"

He broke off as Harriet—pale as a ghost—ran in and slammed the door. She pointed behind her and whispered, "There's a junkie out there—with a bomb! He says if we don't give him forty-five hundred dollars he'll blow up the place."

Cassidy said, "Tell him I'll do it for nothing."

Harriet screamed as the door swung open. Mordecai stood there. He wore a filthy, wrinkled trench coat, had a week's growth of beard, and clutched a cardboard box to his chest. He staggered over to the desk.

"Oh, my God," whispered Harriet.

Mordecai shoved the box into Cassidy's hands. "Guard this with your life," he muttered. "It's the Maltese falcon."

"You look more like the last reel of *Sahara*, kid," Cassidy said. "You better sit down."

Mordecai nodded, sat down on the nearest chair, lit up a joint, inhaled deeply and blew out a cloud of smoke.

"When I first came to this town—a shy slip of a lad—you know how producers and directors used to torture me? They made me sit in front of them while they read my script. It was agony. Every time they frowned, I winced. When they'd start scribbling on the pages, I'd die." He laughed wildly. "Now the tables are turned. You've got to shoot that script. So every time you frown, I'll feel good inside. Every time you groan, *I'll* laugh. This is *Mordecai's Revenge*. Lights! Camera! Action! *Read!*"

Poker-faced, Cassidy took the pages out of the box, handed me the carbons and started reading. When he finished the last page, he said, "Mordecai, you've written a damn good script. . . . Hell, he's asleep."

As we walked into Hal's office, he said, "This better be important. I've canceled an extremely urgent meeting; Ted should be home, writing—he's exhausted and—"

"We've got the script."

"What script?"

"The first show."

"Who wrote it?" Ted asked sharply.

"Mordecai Gaunt."

He stared at me suspiciously. "On spec?"

"No. I commissioned it."

"Oh . . . I see." He held out his hand. "May I?" He sounded like an actor from a Thirties drawing-room comedy. Taking the script, standing very straight, he walked stiffly out of the office.

"Buck," Hal said nervously," you can't go around commissioning scripts like this. Our deal with Ted gives him royalties on the running characters because we're treating the first script as the pilot. Now, if Gaunt writes the first script, he'd be entitled to have it considered as the pilot. Ted can sue us. You've put me in a terrible position."

"Adversity develops character," Cassidy said philosophically.

"I suppose so," Hal said doubtfully.

But he cheered up as over drinks we told him the story.

"The only thing I'm not sure of is your co-star being the police chief."

"He's black," I said.

"Oh, *good!* The NAACP and the Urban League will be ecstatic. Whatever happened to that ghastly Walter Brennan clean-up man?"

"He's been turned into Mrs. McNulty, the widow of a cop killed on duty."

"She's got a tongue that can raise blisters," Cassidy said. "She's right out of O'Casey. Y'know who could play her?"

"Who?"

"Maggie Moynihan."

"She'd be mar—"

He broke off as Ted came in.

"It's a good script," he said quietly, setting it down. I suddenly realized he dyed his hair. "There won't be any trouble about our deal, Hal. I'll tell Saul to renegotiate it to cut Mordecai in."

"That's generous of you, Ted."

Ted held up his glass. "To Mordecai Gaunt."

As we put down our drinks he poured himself another. "You know," he said wonderingly, "when I was a kid ... back in New York ... doing *Philcos* and *Studio Ones*—I used to write like that."

Honey was huddled in the far corner of the soda fountain with Carl and Thelma. "Buck! A strange man's been calling you and calling you. He won't leave his name. And I *know* I've heard his voice before."

"I'll bet he's a burglar," Thelma said. "In Beverly Hills burglars always call first to see if anyone's home."

"Stop it, Thelma," Carl said. "You're frightening her."

"It's always better to face facts. A detective told me—"

The phone rang. They all stared at it. Honey carefully lifted it from the cradle. "Hello. . . . Yes, he's here." She put her hand over the mouthpiece. "It's *him*."

"Yes?" I said.

"Don't call me by name. It's Max ... the boom man."

"I know."

"I tried to get to you on the lot but Cohan was always around."

"Yes?"

"Neeley's cooking something up for you."

"What?"

"I can't find out. But it's not nice."

"Can't you pin it down?"

"Not so far. I'll keep trying. But watch yourself— somewhere along the line Neely's going to put the knife in you. . . . That's it."

"Thanks for going to all that trouble, Harry. Let's screen it at nine-thirty."

I hung up. "No wonder you recognized the voice. It was Harry Gridley in editing. He tracked down a car crash he thinks we can use in the titles."

14

Hal introduced Herkimer, UBC's vice-president in charge of Talent. He was thin, tense, very bald, but he had thick, flowing black moustachios he kept pressing against his lip as if he were afraid they'd fall off.

"Mr. Cassidy," he said, pumping his hand, "you have just acquired a good, strong right arm."

"Ah," said Cassidy.

"And you shall find me a very generous right arm. For I'm going to give you many, big, *big* NAMES!"

"That *is* generous of you, Mr. Herkimer, when I have so many small parts."

Herkimer smiled contemptuously. "They will not be small parts when I get through with them."

"Oh?" said Cassidy.

"For example, for the teenybopper junkie, I shall give you . . . Tuesday Weld!"

"It's too small," Ted said.

"She'll never do it," I said.

"*Ordinarily* . . . you'd be absolutely correct!" Smiling, he stroked his moustaches. "But for *me*, she'll do it."

"Girl in the script is fifteen. When Tuesday did *Stampede* for me, she was sixteen and that's thirteen years ago."

"*Technically*, you're absolutely right," Herkimer said silkily. "But, Mr. Cassidy . . . trust me."

"I have a suspicious nature," Cassidy said.

"You'll be surprised how young she looks on camera."

"Sonny," Cassidy said. "Last time I was surprised the way anyone looks on camera was March eighteenth, nineteen twenty-eight."

Hal said quickly, "Herk, let's hold the girl and target in on the top priority part: the Chief."

Cassidy gave me his wink.

A rabbity little man perched nervously on the edge of his chair.

"Mike!" Cassidy said. "Shake hands with Maury Kramer. Our new cameraman."

"Oh, no, I'm not!" His lined old face contrasted strangely with his jet-black hair. "Not that I'm not honored that you asked for me . . . but . . ." He lowered his voice. "Tim, I can't give you what you want—here."

Cassidy beamed at him. "Maury did *Slave Ship* for me."

"A long time ago," Maury said quickly.

"It's still good film. I'll never figure out how you did the uprising in the hold. The only light—glints from the eyeballs and chains—coming together as they climb the ladder." He slapped him on the shoulder. "Damn, it's going to be good working with you again, Maury."

"No, Tim." He jumped up. "I'm not doing the show."

"Maury," Cassidy said easily, "you're afraid that if you give me what I want, they'll fire you."

"You don't understand, Tim," he said desperately. "This is a tough lot. A hurry-up lot."

"What you don't understand," Cassidy said crisply, "is you don't have any choice. Neely just got through telling me you're old, fussy, slow, and love to paint. So, Maury, how many weeks do you figure you've got before they axe you?"

The old man bit his lip.

"And when you're out on the street, who's going to hire you when they screen the shit you've been shooting here? Goddammit, Maury. Don't you understand?

We're going to shoot some *good* film. Something that'll win you an award. Mike has a signed deal for twenty-six shows, and he guarantees you'll do them all." He shot me a look.

"Oh . . . yes . . . right."

"So be here tomorrow at eight. We're scouting locations."

Dazed, Maury walked to the door, stopped and looked back at Cassidy. "I'd forgotten."

"How much fun we had working together?"

"No. What a son of a bitch you are till you get what you want."

Roaring with laughter, Cassidy threw an arm across his shoulder, showed him out, then whirled—bitterly—on me.

"Can't you see the poor bastard has been brainwashed? Wiped out? He's scared of his shadow."

"What am I supposed to do about it?"

"Make him feel needed. Wanted. Loved. Make him believe he's the greatest cameraman who ever lived. For Christ's sake, don't stand there with your mouth open. You're the Star. Remember?"

The studio limousine moved out Ventura slowly in the early-morning traffic. Cassidy was showing Eddie and Maury a book of Hopper's paintings. "See how lonely they look at that lunch counter?"

"It's the light," Maury said.

"That's the look I want for this picture. This is a lonely town. We're dealing with unconnected people."

As we pulled up in the used-car lot, Cohan opened the door. "Morning, Chief."

"It's Mr. Cassidy. And where's the art director?"

Cohan looked around in surprise. "Slinnet? He was here just a minute ago, Mr. Cassidy. He must have been called back on some emergency."

Cassidy took one look at the flying pennants, sparkling cars and flashy salesmen.

"I told you to find a broken-down, shoddy lot with nothing but junk on it."

"That's just what I told Slinnet. Those exact words. He picked it."

Eddie spoke up. "I know one that might do, Mr. Cassidy."

Cohan gave him a hard look. "Better stay out of picking locations. It's work best done by the production department. Because of the many complicated factors involved such as travel time—"

"It's five minutes from here." Eddie gave him the look back with a little extra on it.

The new lot was perfect.

"You've got a good eye, Eddie," Cassidy said. "Maury, what would be the best time to shoot it?"

"Whenever I tell him!" Cohan laughed.

"Go sign this one up," Cassidy said. "Then go back to the lot."

Maury looked around in all directions like a hound that's lost the scent.

"The secret of good color," Cassidy said to Eddie, "is to always have a big patch of black in it."

Maury smiled for the first time. "That's the secret, all right."

"Don't try to shove a lot of colors in the frame. Repeat the ones you have."

"Like taking the blue off that pennant and repeating it in Mike's tie?"

"That's it exactly, Eddie, and there aren't thirty men in town who know it." He turned to me. "What've you worked out?"

"I'd park at the curb. Attract less attention. Then I figure he'll be standing over by that Volkswagen—"

Cassidy grunted. "If I was a fella who didn't want to be seen, I wouldn't stand where anyone driving down Ventura could spot me."

"Good point. Then I guess he'd be in that little shack."

I walked over and opened the door. It was empty, so I went in.

"Cut," Cassidy said. "I think you might get more out of it if you stayed outside."

I went out and peered through the screen door.

Maury, on all fours in the office, shouted, "Tim! If you keep him there, and we can shoot it late in the afternoon, I can give you a helluva brown filter effect through the rusty screen, with a wild red halo around a purple silhouette."

"Great shot, Maury." Cassidy's foot lashed out and caught me on the ankle.

"Right!" I yelled. "Beautiful!"

Honey and the Klipsruders were deep into the cracked crab when I arrived at Chasen's.

"We finally gave you up and started."

"But we saved you some." Judy said.

"Sorry I'm late." I slid in the red leather booth and kissed Honey. "Work."

Ken twisted a forkful of crab in the mayonnaise. "I didn't think actors worked this late unless they were shooting."

"Some do. Some don't."

"Wrong!" Honey said. "No one works as hard as this nut I'm married to. He has to pick out every location, read every bit part. He even ... even ..." She broke into laughter.

"What?" Judy asked eagerly.

Unable to go on, she shook her head helplessly.

"Come on," Ken said, smiling. "Let us in on the joke."

"He ... he ... *wrote* a hundred-page biography of this part he's going to play."

I felt sick to my stomach.

"Let's drop it," I said.

"Silly things like his father being killed when he was ten—he was a cop—and his mother having to become a maid—"

"*Drop it.*"

"For Heaven's sakes, what are you so upset about?"

"You shouldn't have read that. It's worse than opening my mail."

"Well, pardon *me*. How did I know? I thought it was a publicity bio—until I remembered your father wasn't a cop, and you weren't in the Marines, and—"

I kept my voice down. "I don't want to discuss any of it with anyone. Clear?"

"Not even your precious Mr. Cassidy?"

"Anyone."

Ken, interested, asked, "Why would you pretend to be a Marine?"

"Why don't you think you're anyone?"

His fork stopped four inches from his mouth. In the silence I could hear the mayonnaise dripping on the tablecloth.

"Y'know!" Judy said brightly. "That reminds me of a new Polish joke I heard today."

"Oh, good!" Honey said. "I love Polish jokes!"

We started reading actors. Dunwoodie Jones, the Magnitude casting director, a descendant of Jazzbo Jones (who'd once co-starred with Buster Keaton), would slip in the door and mournfully introduce each actor.

It was strange being on the other side of the desk; knowing what the poor bastards were going through; wincing at their too hearty hellos, the terrible lies about why they were late, the lengthy apologies about how they hated cold readings. But once I gave the cue, I saw them through Cassidy's eyes.

Afterward, he thanked them courteously, and darting that desperate, despairing smile, they'd get out as fast as they could.

Cassidy would scribble a note on his pad, and Dunwoodie would glide gloomily in with the next one.

At the end of a long day of bad readings, I took a

deep drink and said, "Why don't we set Haggerty for the Narc."

Cassidy studied me over the rim of his glass.

"Want to give the job to Fred because he's a nice guy, flat on his ass with a sick wife?"

"What's wrong with that?"

"Because the only reason we're here is to hire the best actor for the part. If the world's worst son of a bitch with a million dollars in his pocket is one tenth of one percent better than Fred, he gets the job. Christ, I thought you knew that."

"We're running out of time."

"If you aren't willing to stay here all night and read a hundred more actors to get the best, I don't know what the hell you're doing in the business. Or I'm doing here!"

He stormed out.

"Oh, Mr. Cassidy," Harriet said. "We have a slight problem." There was the murmur of women's voices from the outer office.

Cassidy ushered in a thin, long-necked fourteen-year-old girl with enormous brown eyes. She wore a burlap muumuu and clutched a string pocketbook, a script and a container of coffee.

"Hilary Kruger, I'd like to introduce Michael McLeod—the star of our series."

"No kidding. That's amazing—you being so old and everything." She shook hands, somehow spilling her coffee all over me. "Oh, Jesus, I'm sorry. It's been one Goddam thing after another."

"We all have days like that," Cassidy said.

"Like having that girl tell me after I've been sitting—studying the script for two hours—that there are no more readings? When I've got my appointment all written down on this slip? Five-thirty on the eighth?"

"Today's the sixth."

"Shit. No wonder my horoscope's so fucked up. Excuse me." She looked as if she was going to cry.

"As long as you're here, Hilary," Cassidy said, "and

have had a chance to look over the script, why don't you read us your favorite scene?"

She asked eagerly, "Could I do the one in the car when he's taking me in?"

"Of course."

She slumped into a chair, scowled down at the script, chewed on her lower lip, then slowly raised those enormous eyes and gave a reading that made the hair stand up on the back of my neck.

Finished, she gently set the script down on the desk.

"Hilary," Cassidy said, "you are a fine young actress and that is your part."

"Oh, God," she said in terror. "I love that girl. If I fuck her up I'll kill myself. I hope you know what you're doing."

"I do," said Cassidy.

She looked at him and grinned. "Yeah."

She ran out, bumping into the doorframe.

"God," I said. "It makes the whole day worthwhile."

Going out, Cassidy threw over his shoulder: "*Fred Haggerty*, for Christ's sake."

"James Earl Jones is too deep in primal therapy; Jim Brown is shooting a feature in Spain; Ossie Davis is directing one in New York; Yaphet Kotto is doing a play, and . . ." Dunwoodie helplessly flipped through the pages of the *Players' Guide*. "We've seen everybody else who could possibly do it."

Cassidy, feet up on the sill, whittled for a while.

"Five, six months ago . . . I saw on television this Negro—"

"No more Negroes," I corrected. "Black actor."

"This fella was big. Bigger than you. Moved like a cat. Had a deep bass voice. But didn't lean on it . . ." He frowned. "He was wearing a tiger-skin vest, and the baddies thought that tied him into a murder so they were going to string him up."

"Oh, no!" gasped Dunwoodie. "You don't want *him*."

"Why, Dunwoodie, what brought that on?"

"*Him!* He was starred in a series shot here! Saul canceled it after eight episodes! Because he's a savage. Got in fights. Knifed somebody."

"Let's get him in here."

"Oh, I couldn't, Mr. Cassidy. He's banned from the lot."

"Well, un-ban him. What's his name?"

"I don't know."

"Goddammit, Dunwoodie, don't pretend you don't know his name."

"But I don't, Mr. Cassidy." He was nearly in tears. "It *was* Hardiman but he became a Muslim and now it's . . . something like: Ali—ur—Loyola."

"Thanks, Dunwoodie," I said. "You can go."

As the door closed, Cassidy said: "You made him?"

"Kryellah. He's something! I saw him go on for Brock Peters in *Great White Hope*. Tore the house apart."

"Get him in here."

It wasn't that easy. SAG gave me three agents. All three no longer represented him. Would never represent him. Were suing him. And hoped he was dead or in jail where he belonged. The telephone company had an old disconnect on him. I finally dug up a spade hooker who for twenty bucks got a message to him. She called back to say he'd be there at three.

At exactly three o'clock the door swung open and Kryellah stepped in. He was wearing a dazzling white burnoose; from a gold chain around his waist hung a ruby-handled dagger.

"I'm glad you dressed for the part," I said. "But you were misinformed. We're not doing *Lawrence of Arabia.*"

There wasn't a flicker of a smile on his jet-black hawk-nosed face.

"Mr. Cassidy," I said. "This is—"

"I'll introduce myself. Because I've found people

able to pronounce Antonioni, Van Karajan and Solzhenitzyn somehow never can say Kryellah."

Cassidy bowed slightly. "Mr. Kryellah, I have a part I'd like to discuss with you."

"It's bound to be a Goddam one-way discussion—since you have read the script and I ain't."

"True." Cassidy handed him a script. "Would you like to go outside and read it?"

Kryellah sat down. "Right here's fine with me. Unless you want to talk about me behind my back?"

"That won't be necessary."

Cassidy put his feet up on the sill and started whittling. We must have sat there without saying a word for fifteen minutes.

Kryellah jumped up and slammed the script on the desk.

"That is one motherfucker of a part. And there is no actor in the world who can come close to cutting me in it. And there ain't no fucking way I'm ever going to play it. So up yours, gentlemen."

He started for the door.

"You talk good," Cassidy said. "Can you act?"

Kryellah whirled on him. "What scene?"

"Page nineteen."

Kryellah glanced at the page. "I need the desk."

Cassidy went over and leaned against the door.

Kryellah sat down, carefully looked at the things on top of the desk, then turned his back on us and stared out the window.

Cassidy jabbed his thumb at me.

I read my first line: "I didn't mean to kill him."

He swung around and it felt like having a door slammed in my face. Facing me was a man with a tremendous temper who had taught himself absolute control of it. Who'd clawed his way up every rung of the police force by never losing that control. But now was so mad at me he was afraid he might.

Finished, he turned his back on us.

Cassidy, said, "Yeah, you can act."

Still staring out the window, Kryellah said wearily, "That mean anything?"

"Means you've got the part."

He turned quickly. "You think you can cast me in a show on this lot?" Shaking his head, he walked out. "You are dreamers," he said sadly. "Babes in the wood."

"Darling, you're going to get in a lot of trouble over this colored boy."

"Why?"

"Saul has barred him from the lot. And he won't let anyone else in town hire him either."

"You mean he's blacklisted?"

"Sure. He hasn't worked in months. And he shouldn't. He's a savage. With your temper you're bound to get in a fight and he'll cut your throat with a razor. . . . Wait! I can tell from that look you made a joke. . . . Oh. Sure. I get it. *Black*listed. Buck, listen to me. You're going to find out it's not so funny!"

At the final production meeting, the men Cassidy had named to work the show sat next to their department heads. As Cassidy greeted the leathery old men by name, they smiled and nodded, obviously glad to see him.

"I don't believe we've met," Cassidy said.

"I'm Slinnet," said a red-faced man in a white blazer with maroon trim. "Your Art Director."

"Not mine. If I had an Art Director he'd have been out scouting locations with me."

"I'm sorry, but you see—"

"Out."

As Slinnet left, Cassidy turned quickly to Neely. "Third day I shoot the nightclub set on Stage Thirty-one. I've ordered the RO crane. If you can't get it from MGM, I can't shoot the set."

Neely looked at Cohan. "What's the problem?"

Cohan grinned, shaking his head. "Ya got me. I told him there was *no* problem."

"I brought it up," Cassidy said. "Because I heard you have a rule: no cranes on this lot."

"Oh," Neely said. "That's for kid directors. For you—no problem. However we *do* have a problem. A major problem." He turned slowly to me. "I hear you're considering casting a person whom I have banned from the lot. Now—"

"Stay below the line, Neely."

"*What?* What did you say to me?"

"Keep your fucking nose out of my show."

"Who do you think you're talking to? I'm in charge of all production on this lot."

Cassidy yelled: "Then hold a production meeting."

It had been a long time since I'd heard that voice. It snapped Neely's head around as if he'd been hit in the face with a shovel. The other men dropped their eyes and moved uneasily like infantry replacements coming under their first artillery fire.

"Now," Cassidy said, and they all sat up straight as schoolboys. "We're going through this scene by scene. If you have any questions, ask them. If you don't understand my answer, ask again. I never get mad at a fella for asking too many questions at a production meeting. *But* if anything goes wrong when we're shooting because he didn't ask—I'll have his hide. Clear?"

The men nodded.

"Eddie." Eddie set the board out on the table; Cassidy read from his breakdown: "Scene One. Props: one desk, three by six, wood, battered; one armchair, swivel, imitation red leather, springs sticking through the seat . . ."

Saul said coldly, "Buck, there is a chain of command on this lot. When Neely tells you something—it comes direct from me. So don't insult him."

"I didn't know you could."

Hal laughed; Cassidy and Eddie smiled; Cohan, towering above Neely's chair, glared at me, arms folded across his chest like a cheap roadhouse bouncer.

"Neely was relaying my message. Since it didn't get through your thick Irish head, I'll tell you direct. That black bastard never works on this lot."

"I'll give you the same answer: stay below the fucking line. This is casting."

"You can cast any *schwartze* in the world but this one."

"This is the one I want."

"He's a drunk," he screamed. "A junkie! An *animal!* I pull that bum out of a ghetto gutter. I hand him more money a week than he's seen in his whole life. How does he repay me? By trying to take over the show. He won't say this. Or do that. Because he's setting an example to the black community. Shit! The only example he is setting is to all the *schwartzes* on series who are watching to see what he can get away with. He wins, we're all out of business. So I laid down the law to him. Christ, he tries to tear the lot apart. He knifes a gaffer. Strikes a director in the face! So I made an example of him. I crucified that nigger. *Don't look at me like that!* I'm no racist. That shelf is full of awards from the NAACP and the Urban League. *He's* the racist. Called me—to my face—a Jew cocksucker."

"Which word did you object to?" I said.

"No jokes, schmuck. I'm talking life and death. Let that black baboon rip you off today—tomorrow they're burning down Beverly Hills. I stand for law and order. I own the lot, and I'm telling you, he doesn't work here. Ever."

Cassidy said to me, "Your move."

"Let's shoot somewhere else."

Saul looked quickly at Neely.

"He's bluffing," Neely said. "All his sets are built. It's too late."

"Everything's location," Eddie said. "Except the nightclub set. And I can find a better one in fifteen minutes."

"Easy," Cassidy said, standing up.

Hal picked up a phone. "Ted Ashley promised me Warner's will do anything to get a show."

Saul stubbed his hand down on the cradle and shrugged. "OK. I try to help out some old friends. They refuse to listen to my advice. What can I do? Turn them out in the cold?"

Neely stared at him in amazement. "You mean you'll let him work on the lot?"

Saul nodded slowly. "As long as no one holds me responsible for his safety."

It was very quiet in the black-and-white office.

"What's that supposed to mean?" Cassidy asked.

"He's crazy, hostile, paranoid. Some stagehand sandbags him, don't blame me."

"Oh, but I will, Saul," Cassidy said.

"Right," I said. "Nobody farts on this lot unless you OK it in triplicate."

Hal said, "None of your strong-arm stuff, Saul. I'm warning you—"

"OK. OK. *OK*. Would you mind if I don't walk you to the door? I've wasted enough time on this shit." He picked up the phone. "Get me De Laurentiis in Rome."

In the Chinese restaurant across the street we clicked glasses.

Cassidy said, "Here's to Hal Hundsley."

"Me! Why me?"

Cassidy said, "You looked good in there."

He blushed like a schoolgirl while we drank to him.

"Now," Eddie said, "to—what the hell's the name of this epic anyway?"

"*Hunter*."

We clicked glasses.

"To *Hunter*."

Kryellah stalked into the office and stood ticking like a time bomb. "You want to see me?"

"Good morning, Kryellah," Cassidy said. "Like some coffee?"

"Just the bullshit."

"What bullshit?"

"The bullshit where you tell me I'm the most brilliant, powerful, sensitive actor you've ever seen—but I'm not right for this part because I'm an inch too short."

Cassidy calmly picked up some papers and headed for the door. "Oh, that bullshit. No, I was going to tell you you've got the part."

Kryellah grunted as if he'd been kicked in the balls.

Cassidy murmured, "Now, who's the dreamer?" And closed the door.

Stunned, Kryellah sank into a chair and sat there shaking his head.

Finally I said, "Who's your agent?"

"I'm my agent."

I handed him Scotty's card. "Then go over and start negotiating with my business manager. He's expecting you."

He stood up. "I must have script approval."

"No way. I'm the only one with that."

He scowled. "Then there must be a clause stating I will not do anything I consider demeaning to the dignity of a black Afro-American."

"Why Afro?"

"Why the fuck white *Caucasian*? Your granpappy ever been within a thousand miles of the Caucasus?"

"No. I was just curious. I'll call Scotty and tell him to put it in."

"Then that's it?"

"If you agree on money and billing."

He grinned and held out his hand. "Then I'm a working actor?"

"Except for one thing."

Furious, he slammed his fist in the wall. "Shee-*it!* When you gonna learn they always got one thing up their sleeve?"

"I don't give a Goddam what you've *done*. But on my show you show up on time—sober—knowing your lines; do off-camera; and run lines with the other actors."

"Of course," he said contemptuously. "I'm a professional. What else?"

"I thought this show up. Put it together. Sold it. And I've got control of casting. Script. Camera. Editing. *Everything*. It's mine. And if anyone tries to take it away from me, he's dead. Dig?"

He put his hands down on the desk and leaned slowly across it. His scowling face stopped two inches from mine.

"Daddy, even with all that protection, I'm still going to act your white ass right off that fucking screen."

Exploding in laughter, he ran out the door.

Friday when I came in, Cassidy and Eddie were huddled grimly over the board.

"Mike," Cassidy said, "we have to start shooting Monday."

"The hell we do. That's a rehearsal day."

"Was," Eddie said.

"Look." Cassidy shoved a marked-up calendar at me. "Here's the air date. Here's when UBC has to have the prints. There's the final. The five-star. The dub. The rough cut. The wrap."

"Goddammit, without that rehearsal I won't be ready."

"You never are in life," Cassidy said. "That's half the fun."

"But, Tim—"

"You've walked all the sets. You've read through all the scenes with the actors—"

"Not with Kryellah. And we haven't even set the actor for the grill scene. The guy Eddie doubles for." They smiled. "What's the joke?"

"None, I hope," Cassidy said. "I want to shoot that fight scene close, so I read Eddie. And set him."

"Jesus," I said. "Hollywood's oldest discovery."

"Oh, no," he said. "I couldn't take that honor from you."

Kryellah was more upset than I was about rehearsal.

"Shee-*it!* I was counting on that time to explore our relationship! To dig into the behavior . . . to *investigate*. Now . . . shee-*it*."

"If you'd stop bitching," Cassidy said, "we could get to work on it."

He cocked his head shrewdly. "You mean—rehearse?"

"Sure."

"Love to. As long as it is clearly understood that when we get through there will be a check waiting for me for one day's rehearsal pay."

"Oh, come on," I said.

"Right to SAG, baby, where I'll show you how it's all spelled out in the rules and regulations. I know 'em by heart because on this lot anytime you sit down without crossing your knees you get fucked."

Cassidy called Harriet in, told her to get the check for Mr. Kryellah, and make sure we weren't disturbed for any reason.

"Now," he said easily, "why don't we just read the first scene out loud. Not acting. Not doing much of anything. Just feeling the other fella out."

"That'll do it," Cassidy said, standing.

My God, we'd been at it four hours. Four good hours.

"Kryellah, Sunday my wife and I are having dinner for the cast. Bring wife, girl friend, whatever. One o'clock sharp. I hope you can make it."

"Wouldn't miss it," said Kryellah. "Thank you."

The lights were out in the outer office except at Harriet's desk, where she sat with her coat on.

"I'm terribly sorry, Mr. Cassidy, but I couldn't get the check. Dunwoodie couldn't approve it until I got a written OK from Mr. Neely. And by the time I got it Mr. Dunwoodie had left."

Kryellah laughed bitterly. "Didn't I tell you?"

"How much do you figure it would've come to?" Cassidy said.

"Four hundred and eighty-three dollars."

Cassidy wrote out a check and handed it to Kryellah.

Kryellah read it carefully, then smiled. "You think I'm going to tear it up and say: 'Shee-*it*, Mr. Cassidy, since you're so nice and we had such a good time rehearsing, and you invited me to your house, I can't take your money.' Well, I got news for you. This nigger is e-man-ci-pated! When I work I get paid. So I'm going to cash this—and it's gwine be a big night at de ole plantation. Gwine feast on chitlins, grits, black-eyed peas. And *watermelons? Whoooo-eeee!* Gwine tear up dat ole pea patch. On behalf of all the pickaninnies, I thanks yah."

He made a sweeping bow and, grinning, shuffled out like Stepin Fetchit.

15

Saturday I had to get away from everybody. So I jogged ten or twelve miles, easily, loosely, down the beach, sweating in the hot sun. Not pushing on the show, just letting scenes float up. Hilary's eyes when I took her in. Kryellah's anger when I fingered the Narc.

Suddenly, I stopped. I was in front of my house.

The key was under the loose step. The living room was so clean it looked as if no one lived there. The

Mexican maid Kate had recommended had scrubbed all the pots and pans and hung them up over the stove, where they shone like copper mirrors reflecting spots of the room.

"Shanty Irish," Tabitha said.

I wheeled around, half expecting to see her. Then it all came back: the feel of her hair sweeping across my chest; the soft lips against my throat; that light, deep inside her grey eyes; the husky voice whispering "McLeod"; that dear, funny mind . . .

The pain of her loss slid inside me like the tip of an iceberg. Crying, I turned and ran out of the house, down the beach, into the breakers, and blindly swam out as far as I could, running the show through my head until the pictures got bigger and bigger and squeezed everything else out.

All dressed up in my blue blazer and polka-dot tie, I walked down the curved staircase and was surprised to find the living room full of unhappy writers.

I caught Honey's eye and pointed to my watch; annoyed, she shook her head, then threw her hands out to them.

"You're *wonderful* people—and wonderful *writers.* And what you've written is probably wonderful, too. I'm just too dumb to understand it."

"Honey," Lanny protested. "Everybody understands Women's Lib."

"All you Eastern intellectuals, you mean."

"Right. All us Eastern intellectuals. Like Lucy, Bob Hope, Dean Martin, Carol Burnett—"

"Poor Lanny, I know how you must feel. It's a brilliant sketch and if you were back writing for Carol, she'd do it *brilliantly*—but I can't. It's not me. *Where are you going?*"

I turned back at the arch.

"I'm due at the Cassidys'. Come over when you can."

"Wait!" she called, pouting. "I want to walk in at your side."

"Sweet!" Thelma said.

They all smiled brightly at Honey's sweetness.

"Can't," I said. "See you there."

As I was backing the car out of the garage, there was a staccato explosion of heel beats.

"How dare you humiliate me like that! In front of my employees! I told you to wait!"

"I can't, I told you all about it yesterday."

"*Yesterday!*" she screamed. "Today my show's a disaster. The script is *hopeless*. For the very first time I ask you for help. And what do I get?... This." She threw her hand out. A ring clicked against the rearview mirror.

"Relax, Honey. Stay here. Fix the script. Come over when you can. I have to be there on time."

I gunned the car out on the road.

She ran after me, screaming, "No, you don't. They have to wait for *you*. Now, *you're* the Star."

At Cassidys' the pretty maids were arranging fresh-cut flowers in the vases and lighting fires in the hearths.

Kate kissed me. "Michael, thank you for being on time. What's this?... Oh, what a lovely silver cross. Isn't it Mexican?"

"Yes, with many thanks for the loan of your husband."

She smiled across the room where he was showing Manuel, the head wrangler, how to set up the bar. "He's had a good week."

"I can't tell you how much he's taught me—"

"Good. That's why he's doing it. Now, *I* have to teach you that when you're a married man and arrive without your wife, you're supposed to say something."

"I'm sorry, Kate. Honey has script problems and can't be here for dinner, but hopes to make it later."

While Kate told one of the girls in Spanish to strike her place, the doorbell rang, and Kryellah arrived in his *Lawrence of Arabia* costume with a high-cheekboned black model in a Halston pantsuit.

The others all arrived in the next few minutes. There was the sound of laughter and introductions. Hilary arrived last, alone. She was pale, wore an elegant dark-red velvet dress with a high lace collar, but the bottom of her long skirt looked as if it had gotten caught in a lawn mower.

After one drink we were all in the dining room, looking for our place cards around the long redwood table. As we sat down, the maids set a silver platter with an enormous cut of roast beef in front of Cassidy, who remained standing.

"Artists are always welcome in this house," he said, smiling. "And that's what actors are. The good ones. And you won't find a bad one here. Though Mr. Riordan has yet to earn his spurs. As an actor, I add hastily, facing Mrs. Riordan's indignant glance.

"We have other artists here. That young man in overalls is not a sharecropper but the writer Mordecai Gaunt." There was some applause. Mordecai, pleased, bobbed his head. "Without him, we wouldn't be here.

"Another artist whose name the younger of you may not recognize is Maury Kramer, our cameraman. He is so good that none of you is going to wear makeup."

"Help!" yelled Maggie Moynihan.

Cassidy smiled. "Why, it was your peaches-and-cream complexion that popped the idea in our heads."

He became serious. "Unfortunately, the day before shooting, actors often start gnawing on their knuckles and pounding their heads against the wall. I think it's better if we do it together. This way you'll have a chance to get to know the fella you're going to play a scene with—not meet him on the set as a stranger.

"I hope something else comes out of today. That we'll go on that lot tomorrow as a company. Because it's a bad lot and we're going to have a bad crew. So we'll need each other.

"Now, if you'll join hands."

Some looking around in surprise, we did.

"Lord, we humbly thank Thee for Thy many gifts and blessings, especially that of talent. Though at times it seems heavy to bear, help us to bear it well in Thy cause. In the name of the Father and Son and the Holy Ghost. Amen."

As we got up from the table Hilary grabbed me.

"I'm going to have a nervous breakdown. I worked on our scene last night—and threw up three times."

"Just nerves."

"For Christ's sake! That's all I've got to work with—nerves." Her wineglass slipped through her fingers and shattered on the tile floor. "That's a terrible omen. For a Pisces."

Cassidy patted her shoulder. "I'd be worried if you weren't taut. That's how all thoroughbreds get before a race."

"Yeah," she said gloomily. "But only one wins."

As Mordecai passed she clutched his sleeve. "I love that girl you wrote but you might as well know now that I'm really going to fuck her up."

Mordecai blinked at her, then turned to Cassidy.

Cassidy said, "Why don't we run through it?"

We followed him past the high carved hardwood doors into the library. Row after row of books stretched above our heads; firelight shone on the brass bar that ran around the room to support the sliding ladders. He pulled a bench out parallel to the blazing fire. "Here's the front seat of the car. Action."

Without a beat she turned her tortured eyes to me.

"You're not going to take me in, Mike. I'm just a kid."

When we had finished, Mordecai jumped up excitedly. "You're marvelous, Hilary. You caught every nuance of every line. You—"

"Thank you," she said politely. "It doesn't play, does it, Mr. Cassidy."

"No, Hilary."

"What am I doing wrong?"

Cassidy, head lowered, thought, scratching his chin.

"Do you believe you can change his mind?"

She jumped up despairingly. "No, Goddammit, I know it's wrong, Mr. Cassidy, but I can't. All I see are those fucking jail doors getting closer and closer."

"God, but you're bright."

"I am?" She gulped.

"Of course you can't play that scene in his car. Once you're there he's made his decision."

Excited, he shoved benches and chairs around. "Now, we're back in your apartment. Play the same scene. You may have to change a few lines to make it fit." He tapped the bench. "Here's your bed. Try sitting on it. . . . Action."

Hilary sprawled back. "You're not going to take me in, Mike." She gave me a hard street-smart smile. "I'm just a kid."

All kinds of things began to happen.

"Come on, kid. Let's get going," I ad-libbed.

She came toward me, pleading: "Mike, you know what the slammer's like. What they'll do to me. You know how I'll come out."

"Not my problem."

"Please, Mike, there's so much I haven't had time to do." Suddenly she kissed me, her tongue flicking hungrily in and out of my mouth.

Startled. I began to get a hard-on. She smiled and rubbed against it. "Come on, Mike," she whispered. "Give me a little break." She threw her arms around my neck and bit my lip.

Honey exploded into the room. "Take your hands off him. He's *mine.*"

She drove her nails at Hilary's eyes. I caught her wrists. Face contorted, she struggled with all her strength.

"Mrs. McLeod." She went limp and stared as Cassidy came toward us out of the shadows. "You must forgive me. I was rehearsing a troublesome scene."

"Oh," she whispered. Slowly she turned to Hilary. "My only excuse is that I love him too much," she murmured. "Can you ever forgive me, child?"

"Shit, yes, Miss Holly. It was groovy to see you shoot out of the woodwork, eyes popping like Bette Davis. I've been a fucking fan of yours since I was one or two years old. Could I have your autograph? And wouldja make it out to Hilary?"

"Of course," Honey said weakly.

Coughing, Cassidy turned away.

16

I pushed the car hard all the way in on empty Malibu Canyon, the shoulders of the twisting road dropping off into emptiness, the black broken only by the occasional flash of an oncoming headlight. On KMPC Wittinghill played Goodman's *Sing, Sing, Sing*, and remembering the spotlit Krupa rising out of the Paramount pit, I sang along with the triple-tongued descending trumpets.

It felt great to be up on a cold morning when everyone else is asleep—when you have a job to go to.

In the parking lot in front of Production, five companies were being sent off on location. The confusion reminded me of a division pulling out.

Assistant directors, flashlights fixed on clipboards, called roll. Yawning crew members answered "Yo," stumbled on buses.

"Kremick! *Kremick?*" Much frantic dashing around. "Anyone seen *Kremick?*" An apologetic Kremick appeared. "For Chrissakes, ya been holding up the whole company."

Loaded, the bus roared off into the lifting darkness.

Three sleepy-eyed actresses, Kleenexes tucked under their necks to keep the greasy brown makeup from staining their evening dresses, were handed into a stretchout.

A heavily armored insert car rumbled by like a tank.

Shouts as a mistake is discovered. Swearing dancehall girls and Indian warriors are forced off one bus and onto another.

"Buck!" A screaming Cohan ran toward me. "You were supposed to be in makeup forty-five minutes ago. I was going to put you in the limousine with Cassidy but he's got to leave now."

"I'll go with him."

I opened the door of the old black Chrysler Imperial with the HUNTER #1 sign on the windshield.

"You gonna make up on the set?"

"I'm not wearing makeup."

He gaped at me. "Holy Shit!" He sprinted for the production building.

Cassidy was stretched out in the far corner. Feet up on the jump seat. Hat tilted over his face. He nodded at me, then went to sleep.

Sidney, Cohan's rat-faced assistant, shouted, "Take her away." And the driver took off.

I lit a cigarette and felt the butterflies begin in the pit of my stomach. I flicked on the light and looked through a scene. I caught my reflection staring at me in the window. The lines under my eyes were much deeper than I expected, and there was a lot more gray in my hair.

No wonder Cohan thought I was crazy. I needed all the help I could get.

Cassidy's hat fell to the seat. His head swung back and forth. His mouth was open. His skin was gray and speckled with those brown spots old people have. Jesus, but he looked old! And frail. I felt if I reached over and picked him up he'd weigh no more than a ten-year-old.

Remembering how worried Kate had been about his doing the show, I suddenly thought: *You're going to get him killed. You've never brought anyone you loved anything but pain and death since the day you were born. You're cursed.* Christ, the Black Irish depression had me by the throat.

To snap myself out of it, I thought through the day's work.

The location was an ugly, doughnut-shaped concrete farmhouse perched on the rim of Mulholland with the whole Valley spread out below. The car slid by the honey wagon, prop truck and generator parked on the dirt shoulder. Most of the men stood around the catering truck drinking coffee, smoking, telling jokes; others in the distance scaled Frisbees; a few handed reflectors down from the back of a truck. One flashed blindingly when it caught the morning sun.

As the car stopped, I turned to wake Cassidy, but he was standing outside.

The men all seemed to see him at the same moment and quieted down.

He started walking toward the farmhouse in his purposeful, straight-backed, pigeon-toed way. Then the strange thing happened that always fascinated me. Everyone fell in behind him. It was impossible not to follow that walk.

He stopped. Dug his right heel in the dirt. "Camera. Thirty-five."

Maury pointed. A kid sprang forward, put a wooden T at his foot. Men began wrestling the McAlister dolly toward us.

"Don't move," Cassidy said. "Watch. We're going to walk through the first setup."

When we finished, the operator, a surly kid, all in black leather except for yellow golf gloves, said, "That's a tough set-up."

"Too tough?"

He scowled, shrugged and walked off. Cassidy looked questioningly at Maury.

"Tim," Maury said miserably. "I didn't get any of the men I asked for."

"Neither did I." Cassidy grinned. "Except for you. And that's enough."

He walked off to his chair. It was big and hulking, made out of redwood and buffalo hide with his name branded on the back, and topped by a faded old beach umbrella.

He climbed up and, scowling, studied his script.

Eddie and I had to go through it again for the stand-ins who hadn't bothered to watch the rehearsal.

Then we turned to see how the crew was doing.

Maury couldn't get the gaffer to understand where to put the reflectors. The operator was showing dirty pictures to the camera crew, who giggled and goosed each other. Cohan, Sidney and the driver captain were arguing about where the vehicles should be parked, and the boom man and mixer were yelling as to whether the shot was MOS or not.

"Jesus," Eddie said.

"They're the worst I've ever seen."

"Let's see the fight." Cassidy stood right behind us.

"Tim," I said, "this Goddam crew is—"

"You're not paid to worry about the crew," he said crisply. "Show me the fight."

Eddie and I walked through what we'd laid out. As we worked our way toward the water trough, Cassidy said, "Remember *Shane?*"

"*Shane?*" Eddie, baffled, nodded.

"What was the best thing about it?"

"The shoot-out in the mud."

Cassidy smiled. We turned and stared at the water trough.

"I can take it over," Eddie said.

"Good," Cassidy said. "But why don't you work the haystack in? Makes a nice texture—mud and straw."

We ended up re-staging the whole thing before he

grunted approval. Then we went through it by the numbers: counting out the beats for each punch, each fall, as carefully as ballet dancers. We had plenty of time. It was forty-eight minutes before they had the first set-up lit.

"OK, Mr. Cassidy," Cohan yelled, looking pointedly at his wristwatch. "Let's shoot it."

"So that we all understand each other," Cassidy said, "I never shoot a scene without a full rehearsal. And when I say full, that means everything works. Then when we shoot it, I want the first take. Not the second. Or third. Clear?" Everyone nodded.

"Quiet for the rehearsal!" Cohan screamed. "And that means nobody moves. Nobody breathes. When I say *quiet* I want QUIET!"

"The only sound is you bellowing," Cassidy said. "Action."

I drove the car in. Stopped. Got out. Walked toward the house. Stopped. Felt the shadow. Turned. Eddie kicked.

"Pan's wrong," Cassidy said.

We rehearsed it five times before the operator got the pan right.

"Let's shoot it," Cassidy said.

As I opened the car door, Eddie ran up and pounded me on the chest with both fists. "Break a leg."

"Working with you, I probably will."

I slid behind the wheel and watched the assistant operator hold the slate up.

Cohan yelled: "Roll it."

"Rolling," echoed the mixer.

I could read on the slate:

HUNTER: 23894

DIRECTOR: Cassidy

CAMERAMAN: Kramer

* * *

Get with it!

I put my mind where it belonged, in the pit of Hunter's stomach.

"Speed," called the mixer.

Cassidy slapped his hat over the lens.

"Jesus!" The startled operator cut it.

I was surprised no one had told him. Cassidy was famous for his hat trick. Camera cutting so the editors never had a frame of film to play with.

"Speed," called the mixer.

"Action."

I crossed myself and, remembering where I'd been and where I was going, drove in.

Everything worked—except the pan. Six times.

On the seventh take when he blew it, the operator yelled, "He's off his mark."

"He's right on the money. You're the one who can't cut it."

Cohan ran up. "Jesus, Mr. Cassidy, Neely's screaming. You're hours behind schedule! He told me to tell you: Change the whip pan to a cut."

"Tell Neely I don't change set-ups because he gives me bad operators."

Cohan blinked at him, then ran for the phone.

Six takes later we still didn't have it.

Cohan dashed up, Sidney at his heels.

"Mr. Cassidy, Neely said to tell you: You've got to print the next shot."

"Tell him I'll print the shot when it's right. Until then, I don't want to hear another word out of you."

When Cassidy said, "Cut. Print," it was the twenty-third take.

"Don't fall apart. *Watch*." He walked toward the trough. Dug his heel in. Made a circle with his thumb and forefinger shoulder high. "Fifty. And, Maury, lock off the camera. It doesn't move."

Eddie and I went through the fight for Maury. He threw out the reflectors, tarped off the sunlight and used the arcs to get deep black shadows and sharp sparkling highlights.

"Nice, Maury," Cassidy said. "Let's shoot it."

On "Action" I dove in past the lens. As I turned to get up, Eddie kicked me in the face and we were into it.

Eddie and I can do fights nobody else in the business can touch. We're damn near the best alone, but put us together and we're dynamite. It's not just the timing and precision. It's the absolute trust. With anyone else I have to take a few inches on a punch for protection. But with Eddie I know just what he's thinking. When he stabbed the pitchfork at my throat, someone gasped, "Jesus." But it was just where I could block it. His kick gave me perfect leverage to take the trough over. Sloshing and sliding in the mud, I was a little late getting out of the way as he swung the shovel down, so he slowed it imperceptibly, before I cut his legs out and we rolled over into the haystack. Finally, I hoisted him over my shoulders, gave him the old airplane spin, then smashed him down into the ground. The split second the overturned trough blocked him from camera, he twisted, taking the fall on his shoulder.

"Cut. Print. Don't move." Cassidy came over and looked down at Eddie. "You all right?"

"Fine. How was the fight?"

"Not bad." He squatted down on his heels.

Cohan rushed up. "What's the coverage?"

"That's it."

"Oh, you gotta shoot more coverage. Neely insists on lots of coverage on fights." Cassidy looked up. Cohan swallowed and ran for the phone.

"Mike, sink down and pull him up to you. Maury, I was wondering if you were six inches to my left on a thirty-five . . . very low . . . maybe on a high hat. What would you have?"

Maury's face lit up. "Why, I'd have their two profiles—almost in silhouette—from the mud, and behind them, way below, the Valley floor, with that street running off into infinity and tiny little cars buzzing between their faces like bugs."

"I bet you would at that. Mike, you see where I'm cutting. It's tight. Now bang his head against the trough. Yeah, that'll work. Second team."

He stood up. As Sidney began screaming for the stand-ins, I asked, "What are we doing?"

"The scene inside the farmhouse where you beat the information out of him."

"But that's my *acting* scene!" Eddie yelled.

"We'll soon see." Cassidy walked away.

Eddie ran after him. "That doesn't shoot until Friday."

"Didn't."

"Jesus, Mr. Cassidy, I don't know my lines!"

"Better learn them."

"But, Tim," I said, "I hit him with a chair. Bounce him off the wall. What do I do in the mud?"

"Think of something."

"It's a tight shot."

"Not too tight for thinking."

"Mr. Cassidy." Cohan ran up, breathing hard. "This is no time to shoot something scheduled for Friday. We're hours behind on today's schedule—" He broke off as Cassidy climbed up in his chair and, stone-faced, stared at his script.

I couldn't blame him. Up there Cassidy was absolutely unapproachable.

Eddie and I worked on the scene. I kept trying to figure out when to slam his head against the trough and choke him; Eddie, completely gone, kept murmuring his lines like the Rosary.

When the shot was lit, Cassidy looked at it through the lens. "Pretty, Maury. Let's do it."

"Mr. Cassidy," Eddie said desperately. "I haven't learned my lines."

Cassidy got up from the camera. "What's the difference?"

Eddie stared at him as if he'd gone crazy. "What's the difference?"

"Right. It's a grill scene. He keeps asking where a man is. If you can't remember the line, just say 'I don't know.' Till the very end. Then you damn well better remember. Let's go."

"Wait a minute," I said. "Aren't we going to rehearse it?"

"Rehearse *what*? You can't think. He can't talk. Jesus, what a scene this is going to be. Roll 'em."

"But, Mr. Cassidy," Eddie pleaded. "You just said you never shoot anything without a rehearsal."

"I lied. Roll 'em."

On "Speed" he slapped his hat over the lens.

"Hit the dirt." Eddie dove to the ground.

He whipped his hat away from the camera. "Action."

I knelt into the shot and pulled Eddie up by the lapels.

"Where's Hastings?"

"Hastings? Why—" Sheer terror suddenly shone out of Eddie's eyes. He was up. "Uh . . . I don't know."

"You better remember." I banged his head on the trough and pulled him back. "Where is he?"

Paralyzed, Eddie gulped, "I . . . uh . . . don't know."

But at the end he said: "Nine-eight-three-seven Sunset." And collapsed in the mud.

Cassidy's hat hit the lens. "Cut. Print."

"What's the coverage, Mr. Cassidy?" Cohan asked.

"That's it."

"My God, Mr. Cassidy," Eddie said. "I took a lot of awful long pauses in that. You better shoot some close-ups—to tighten it up."

"Jesus, Riordan," Cassidy said. "Two minutes ago you'd never acted. Now you're trying to direct. *Wrong set.*"

*　*　*

We pulled up at the sleazy, sagging, two-story motel on Ventura. Our cops had the side of the street roped off, and a curious crowd stared at us.

Kryellah, arms folded angrily across his double-breasted blue suit, waited stormily at the far side of the chipped, faded pool.

"Good morning, Kryellah," Cassidy said pleasantly. "Hope you haven't been waiting too long."

"Long enough," he said ominously, "to have played this scene back and forth in my head and come up with a *problem*."

"I don't need problems." Cassidy looked around. "How about some solutions?"

"This *problem* happens to be Goddam serious—"

"Excuse me. Hans, how good to see you!" He darted off to shake hands with Hans Lenroy. In the Thirties Lenroy had played the elegant desk clerk in all the RKO comedies, arrogantly ordering Grant and MacMurray and Melvyn Douglas out of the posh bridal suites; now he was old and shabby and embarrassingly grateful for the three lines as the motel manager.

"Shee-*it*." Kryellah smashed his fist against a palm tree. The poor bastard was uptight. He didn't have that first scene under his belt. And the crew straggling in were probably old enemies.

"What's your problem?"

"For disobeying my orders, I'd bust you right in the mouth when you come out that door. I missed it when we rehearsed in the office—but here, having you right on top of me, makes me so fucking mad—"

"Now, Kryellah, what's the problem?" Cassidy asked.

"It's that I don't know how to play this Goddam scene. I—"

Cohan and Sidney trotted up. "Sorry I'm late, Mr. Cassidy, but pulling out the generator smashed into the honey wagon. Luckily nobody was hurt."

"Too bad," Cassidy said. "On the sidewalk there's a

sixty-year-old bleached blonde putting nail polish on a toy poodle she's carrying. Sign her up. I want her spotted—*there.*"

"Yes, sir." They ran off.

"If I could bother you for one Goddam second about this Goddam *problem*—"

"First, Mr. Lenroy, let me introduce Mr. Kryellah."

Ready to explode, Kryellah shook hands, went through his three lines with Lenroy.

"Very nice, Hans. Now as you go back to the office throw a nasty glance over your shoulder. Good."

Kryellah erupted. "Now, I shout: '*Hunter,*' he comes out, and we are finally facing the motherfucking problem I've been trying to tell you about for the past fifteen minutes—"

"One second, please," Cassidy said. "Michael, instead of coming out of the door directly behind him as we rehearsed it, try the one above it on the second story."

"Right." I ran up the stairs.

"Now, Kryellah, what's your problem?"

Kryellah looked up at me standing on the balcony, then turned and stared at Cassidy for a long, deadpan beat.

"Ah," said Cassidy. "You solved it. Good. Maury, we'll play this whole scene on a low shot, across Kryellah's profile to Mike, trucking with them as they walk toward that stairway. Let's rehearse."

Later Kryellah grumbled, "This isn't comfortable."

"Neither is childbirth," Cassidy said. "But it's creative."

Maury shook his head. "It's a beautiful set-up, Tim, but we'll never get it with this operator—"

"Heads up," Eddie called.

A long black Mercedes limousine pulled up with screeching brakes.

Neely, two flunkies and Ted behind him, stalked toward us, yelling, "You're going to have to reshoot everything you've done this morning. It's a lot rule everyone has to wear makeup. I—"

Cassidy cut him off, his voice so low I had to strain to hear it. "Where are the men assigned to work this show?"

"And where did you find these assholes?" I said.

"I don't understand." Ted looked at Neely. "Aren't these the men who were at the production meeting?"

"Not one," I said.

"How could that happen?"

Neely yelled, "For Christ's sake, you changed your shooting schedule at the last minute so obviously I had to make some personnel changes."

"Without telling me," Cassidy said.

"That does sound strange," Ted said.

"What's strange," Cassidy said softly, "is that with some of the finest craftsmen in the industry sitting home drawing unemployment you gave us these scum."

"Now wait a minute."

"The worst fucking crew I've ever seen," I said.

"Complete incompetents," Cassidy snapped. "I can't get a decent shot with them."

"Does that mean you're walking off the set?"

"I don't walk off sets—I throw snotty production men off them."

Ted, scared, said, "Now, gentlemen—"

Neely said, "I'd like to see you try."

And Cassidy went for him. Neely turned and ran. Not far. Just a step. It was just a second before he stopped himself. But everyone saw it. And he knew they had. He turned around, brick red, eyes on the ground.

"Well," Ted said, "I guess there isn't much we can accomplish here . . . and I have a lot of work to do."

Cassidy said, "You can take that Micky-dazzler of an operator back with you."

Neely said slowly, "Where am I going to get another operator in the middle of the day?"

Eddie said, "Big Joe Greenberg is shooting a promo on Stage Eleven."

"Lunch!" Cassidy called. "Forty-four minutes! And when it's over I'll expect to see Joe's face behind the camera."

Neely, defeated, climbed in the Mercedes with the operator, and it shot out the drive.

Kryellah was furious. "What the fuck he call lunch for? I don't want to eat! I want to ACT!"

I explained. He shook his head gloomily. "The new operator'll be just as bad. They're nothing but pigs on this lot . . . Shee-*it*." He folded his arms across his chest, leaned against the palm tree and stared moodily off in the distance.

"You want to play Emperor Jones by yourself or the scene with me?"

He grunted bitterly but started walking through it.

As the lunch break ended, a studio car pulled up and Big Joe Greenberg sauntered toward us. His big frame was going to fat; his grey hair was getting thin—but his hands and forearms were still muscled like a weight lifter's and he had the delicate touch of a heart surgeon. He was one of the dozen top operators in town and knew it.

"Joe, welcome aboard."

He took a quick look at the crew as we shook hands.

"Must be a sinking ship."

"Why, we're the hit of the season."

"Then I've been misinformed. I was told you were playing the lead."

Kryellah chuckled. I introduced them.

When we went through the scene Joe stood beside Cassidy, ignoring the camera—just watching.

"Mr. Cassidy, I'll need a few minutes to talk to the camera crew."

I couldn't hear what he said but they stopped smiling and wriggling around; and by the time he finished they stood straight as soldiers. Cassidy winked at me.

"Ready for rehearsal, Mr. Cassidy."

Joe, shifting on his seat like a jockey, pointed a finger at his assistant, gentled the pusher with the back of his hand and talking quietly, pulled them together.

Finally he said: "We're ready to shoot it, Mr. Cassidy."

Kryellah kicked a metal film can viciously. "I'm glad *he* is. I was ready two hours ago."

I took a chance. "That's what I hear about you niggers—never have it when you need it."

He whirled on me in a fury.

Cassidy said: "Places, please."

I ran up the stairs and into my room.

I watched through the curtains as Kryellah stormed up the path, argued with Lenroy, then turned and shouted: "Hunter!"

I opened the door and stepped out. As our eyes connected I felt a jolt. Steaming out of him was black hate for all the years of chicken shit he'd had to take from whites. We were into it so deeply that when Cassidy called "Cut," we stood motionless on the stairs—not breaking the eye contact—still feeling it.

"That all right for you, Joe?"

"When it isn't, Mr. Cassidy, I'll tell you."

"Then that's a print."

Kryellah stepped to the rail. "I want to do it again."

Joe pulled his neck into his shoulders as if he expected a hurricane to hit.

Cassidy looked up coldly. "Why?"

"I can do it better."

Cassidy studied him. "I don't think so, but I'll let you try. *Kill the print. Make it a hold.*"

We did it three more times, Kryellah getting bigger each time, before he yelled, "Yes! Goddammit! That's the one. Print it!"

"No," said Cassidy. "Print One. *That's a wrap.*"

Kryellah jammed his hands in his pocket and glared

after Cassidy; the one motionless figure in the noisy confusion of men tearing down the lights and shoving out the camera.

"He was right," I said. "The first was the best."

"Shee-*it*. I know better than to expect you to disagree with him. He's your fucking tin god. Well, I don't like the bullshit he's giving me."

"No. You're mad because he's not giving you the bullshit. All the 'you were *tremendous,* and *marvelous,* and *thrilling.*' When he says print that means you were good. And if he says you were good, that means you were unbelievable."

"He's sure got you conned. He fooled me some too, that day in the office. But," he said bitterly, "I got no use for a man who prints the wrong take."

Worried about the two big scenes we had tomorrow before he'd get to see the dailies, I said, "Do me a favor. When you get in I'll have them screen *Gallant Patrol* for you. Then first thing tomorrow tell me what you think of Cassidy as a director."

"Deal." He scowled and jabbed his finger against my chest. "You call me nigger again—and you're dead."

There is a small piece of time I always love early morning on location. It's just after the equipment trucks have backed into place but before the crew has arrived. Over your first cup of coffee and cigarette you bullshit. It's a point of rest between the warm bed you crawled out of in the cold dark and the long day's work lying ahead.

Big Joe, Eddie and I were arguing about last night's exhibition game and whether Prothro could turn the Rams around.

Twenty feet away silhouetted against the low hot red sun, Cassidy, Stetson jammed low on his forehead, pointed to a pack of fleecy clouds and, sniffing out the wind, talked over the weather with Maury.

The bus pulled up in a cloud of dust. The men started climbing out.

The black Chrysler Imperial pulled up and Kryellah got out. I hurried over, reaching him just as he got his cup of coffee.

"Morning, Kryellah."

He nodded. Cut off, cold.

"How'd you like *Gallant Patrol?*"

"Why, I adored it," he said bitingly. "All those clean-cut young kids killing all those dirty old Indians. And the jokes they played on their old colored messboy. Like the night they told him they're camped on an Indian burial ground. The way his teeth chattered! And he stuttered and rolled his eyes around. Man, that was one scared nigger! You must have bust a gut laughing."

"OK."

"OK *what?* You the one sent me to see that fucking movie."

"I forgot that bit."

"Beautiful." Hurt, barriers went up.

"What about the rest of it?"

"Same old racist rip-off. Baby, when you see the kid on guard duty falling asleep while the Indian's creeping up, you're rooting for the kid. I'm for the redskin. What right those honky soldiers have to break treaties, invade their land, and practice genocide?"

He slammed his coffee cup to the ground.

"I can't figure where the fuck your head's at to show me such a piece of shit. You ever see *The Battle of Algiers?* That's a fucking war. And that's a fucking movie. And Pontecorvo—that's a director. But *Gallant Patrol?* And Cassidy? Shee-*it.*"

He walked away, turned back abruptly.

"Just so you don't think I'm writing him off because I'm a bigot. There's one thing your Mr. Cassidy directs brilliantly."

"What's that?"

"The horses."

As he walked through the cluster of laughing,

coffee-drinking men, not one said hello or nodded. And suddenly I realized we were all white.

Starting the day's work, Kryellah was aloof and detached, but since that was his attack in the scene I didn't know how much Cassidy was picking up.

By eleven-thirty we were shooting my scene with the pimp at the outdoor table at Cyrano's. We had tied up Sunset completely. It was a sunny day and the crowd of hippies, tourists, and Jesus freaks gave it a colorful, carnival atmosphere.

Cohan called out, "Phone call for you, Mr. McLeod. From Hornblower."

"OK to take it?"

Cassidy nodded. As I squeezed behind him, he said quietly, "It's the dailies. Remember: never ask how they were."

"Right."

Cohan led me inside to a wall phone opposite the big silver espresso machine.

"Yes, Ted?"

"I've seen the dailies . . ."

"Unh-hunh."

The son of a bitch waited *and* waited.

Christ, I was dying to ask, *how was Kryellah? How was the fight? How was Eddie in the grill scene? But most of all: How did I look? How did I act? How was I?*

"Ted, I'm holding up shooting."

"Oh . . . well, the consensus is: Cassidy's not shooting enough coverage."

"That it?"

"Nothing else that can't wait. Will you tell Cassidy about the coverage?"

"We'll talk about it after I've seen the dailies tonight."

"I haven't set up a screening for you tonight."

"Then set it up."

"Overtime for the projectionist is not in the budget."

"Then put it in the fucking budget. And be there when I get in."

I went back and told Cassidy what had been said, ending with "So the jury's still out."

"No," he said. "We won the first round."

"What did I miss?"

"They didn't tell you we had to reshoot it."

"That's right. So it must've looked damn good without makeup."

He growled, "Agh, what the hell do *they* know? Let's go to work."

It was nine-ten when we pulled up in front of Production and climbed wearily out of the limo.

"Coming to see the dailies?" I asked Cassidy.

"If I didn't know what they looked like when I shot them, you're in a hell of a lot of trouble."

Ted was waiting under an arc light shining down on the concrete wall of the editing building.

"How'd it go? At least you're back on schedule." He handed me a slip of paper. "That's the viewing room. I've got to run."

"I want you to watch the dailies with me."

"But, I can't. I don't have the time. I haven't had any dinner. I'm exhausted. My ulcer's acting up. I'm late for a story conference on Mandeville."

"On what script."

"*Desperate Hours* in the motor home."

"That doesn't work. I don't do anything for three acts except watch while they drive to San Diego. In the second act I've got to get the jump on them."

Ted sagged against the wall. "You're talking about a whole new script. I don't know if I can get the writers to buy it."

"If you can't—bring them out to location for lunch tomorrow."

"We going to see some rushes?" Kryellah said impatiently.

Ted, shaking his head, hurried off. I wondered what had upset him.

We walked up two flights of iron stairs and pushed open the swinging doors with *18* on them.

On the screen one cowboy knocked another through a candy-glass window. There were screams:

"Close the door."

"We're looking for the *Hunter* dailies."

"Not here!"

"Out."

In the hall we studied the paper.

"That eight might be a nine," Eddie said.

We walked down the hall. Nineteen was locked.

"Shee-*it.*"

"Then," Eddie said, "the one must be a seven. It's seventy-eight."

"That's in the other building."

As we got outside, Kryellah said, "I'm splittin'."

"You've got to see the dailies."

"There ain't gonna be no dailies."

"Why not?"

"Because Saul don't like actors to see dailies—makes 'em uppity."

"But it's all been set up."

"You'll see. This is one of Saul's little"—he brought his fingers together like scissors—"snip-snaps. That's how he cuts your balls off. So watch out. Remember, there ain't no stars at Magnitude—only steers. Snip-snap."

Chuckling, he walked off in the soft night.

We climbed the stairs to 78. Inside, a plump girl in a low-cut evening dress picked up a jar of poison.

"There."

The editor pushed a button. The picture froze.

"Isn't that her nipple? Or am I crazy?"

"No, Harry. That's her nipple."

"How the hell can that happen with a crew and cameraman and operator standing around? *Are they all blind?*"

Down the hall I kicked in the door of an editing room and called Production. They said it was an editorial problem. I called Editing. They said *Hunter* was too new a show to be on their schedule and I should call Emergency Screenings. There was no answer at Emergency Screenings. When I got Editing back I couldn't find the man I'd been talking to and everybody else said I'd have to wait until tomorrow.

"Darling," Honey said, "some clerk goofed."

"No. Neely set it up that way."

"Buck"—she took my hand—"you'll break your heart until you learn that the people we have to work with are stupid and lazy and sloppy—and make mistakes. We don't but that's why we're Stars. Because we can do everything better than anyone." Smiling, she un-zipped my fly. "Here—I'll show you."

Next morning, Neely—sucking coffee out of his moustache—apologized profusely. "When you wrap, I'll have your editor show you both days. So we had a few growing pains. From here on"—he gave me a bad smile—"we're just one big happy family."

It was cold in the parking lot as we worked out the double car chase. Eddie was driving one car and Shorty Ottleigh, the best driver in the business (thank God), the other.

I slapped my arms against my sheep-lined coat and took a belt of Jack Daniel's.

"Let's get a slate on all three cameras," Cassidy called. The brutes and arcs cut slashes of light through the darkness.

On "Action" I strolled through the dark, nearly empty parking lot toward my car, when Eddie in a souped-up Camaro shot out of the dark straight for me. I ran for the nearest parked car. Jumped behind it just as Eddie sideswiped it with a shattering crash and zoomed off in the dark.

I hauled ass in the opposite direction when Shorty

came blasting in with his yellow Porsche. I barely got behind the Chevy when Shorty hit it, tearing the front fender off.

Then they chased me back and forth. Sweat got in my eyes. The arcs were blinding me. I was gasping for breath. Headlights barreled at me. I'd run. Tires screaming, they'd cut for me. Smash into the parked cars.

Sweet Christ, please keep that knee from caving in.

I whipped through the two parked cars. Got maybe five feet past them, when Shorty smashed into them. There was the screech of shearing metal. Something shot by my ear. Shorty was really up my ass when Eddie hit his horn and I turned and dove right at the headlights zooming at me, landing between the oncoming front wheels on my padded forearms, feeling the bumper shoot over my head. Then it was gone, and I looked up and saw the Porsche shoot by the camera, missing the matte box by inches.

"Sit up—if you can," Cassidy said.

I could, so I did.

"Cut. Print."

"You Irish bastards are crazy!" Kryellah said.

"But talented," Eddie said.

"We got rhythm," I said. "You'll see it in the dailies."

"Unh-*unh*," said Kryellah. "I saw them last night. Remember?"

"That's the wrap."

"Kill the arcs," Maury called. The lights began banging out.

"Where's the editor?"

A lanky, long-nosed man with a blond toupee parted in the middle stepped up. "I'm Simpson. The film's all ready for you, Mr. McLeod."

Eddie took Kryellah by the arm. "You've got to see the Edward Riordan Film Festival. I act him right off the fucking screen."

"You, too?"

We called out good-nights to Cassidy, who waved, not looking up from the call sheet he was going over with Cohan and Sidney.

We sat down in the viewing room in the dozen plush armchairs surrounding the console. Beyond them stretched the threadbare cheap seats.

Leader flashed by: 6 5 4 3 2. A band began playing *The Yellow Rose of Texas* and the title GALLANT PATROL came up.

"Kill it."

The music wailed like a run-down record as the picture flickered and disappeared.

"Where are the *Hunter* dailies?"

Lit only by the dim blue bulb on the console, Simpson looked from Eddie to Kryellah. "They're being broken down."

"Who told you to show me this?"

He dropped his eyes. "I don't remember."

I stood and pulled him to his feet by the front of his shirt. "We're going to see Neely. By the time we get there, if I were you I'd remember."

In silence we walked down the iron staircase, out across the perfectly cut dark lawns, past the white bungalows where in the lit windows black women dusted desks and vacuumed rugs, and into the production building.

We pushed through the swinging doors and stopped dead. In the big room fifty men stood staring at a white-faced Cassidy, who, hands clenched at his sides, faced Neely, insolently sprawling back on the edge of a desk.

Neely said, "So there's no RO crane on your call sheet. So what?"

"I ordered it eight days ago."

Neely looked at Cohan.

"If he'd ordered it, Chief, it would be on the call sheet."

Cassidy said, "I brought it up at the production meeting—and you said no problem."

"I would never say that," Neely said. "I have a rule against cranes on this lot."

"I heard you say it, Neely," I said, stepping forward.

"So did I," Eddie said.

"Stay out of this, Actor. This *is* below the line."

"That's right," said Cassidy. "And it's between you and me."

Neely took his time lighting a cigar. "Tim, I'll be frank, I didn't want you on the lot. I knew something like this would come up."

Shirt-sleeved clerks elbowed each other aside to get a better view. Cohan pointed to a dozen stunt men from *Cattle Country,* still in costume, who stopped signing vouchers, and turned around and looked us over.

"You see, Tim, you're not as young as you used to be. You old-time directors say—behind my back—that I run an assembly line. Well, if getting the job done cheap and fast and playing no favorites is running an assembly line—then I do and I'm damn proud of it.

"But that means when *you* think you've said something but haven't. And cause a mess. I can't take you by the hand and solve your problems. *You haven't got a crane.* Shit, I've got twenty directors shooting tomorrow without a crane. Now, you've taken up enough of my time."

Cassidy said in a flat voice, "I told you at the production meeting if I didn't have the RO I couldn't shoot the set."

"Oh? Boys, pay careful attention. Because there may be legal issues enjoined here. I'm telling you: your services are of a rare and unique and irreplaceable function on this production. Now, knowing this—because a piece of technical equipment (which you forgot to order) is not forthcoming—you refuse to perform your contractual duties? Is that what you're telling me?"

"Not quite," said Cassidy. "I'm telling you: you're a liar, a cheat, and a yellow son of a bitch."

He plucked the cigar out of Neely's mouth with his left hand, slapped him hard across the face with his right, then knocked him sprawling across the desk with a short left.

Cohan jumped forward and pinned Cassidy's arms to his side. Neely grabbed a gooseneck lamp and slashed Cassidy across the face with it.

By then everybody was moving.

I hit Cohan in the side of the throat. He staggered back with a strange choking sound. I drove a beautiful right hand straight into his solar plexus. His mouth flopped open. As he fell to the floor I saw over his shoulders Cassidy dancing around Neely like Gentleman Jim Corbett—hands held high, knuckles up, peppering him with left hands.

White shirts swarmed over me. But they weren't much. A few cracked heads, a few back-kicks in the balls, and they scattered for protection behind their desks. Eddie yelled. As I turned, the stunt men were on me. I had a flash of Kryellah, standing where I'd left him, arms folded across his chest.

I split the two on my left, getting clubbed in the ear. Turning, I got one with the heel of my hand in the balls, drove an elbow in the face of another. Eddie dropped one with a chair.

A forearm slammed across my Adam's apple from behind and twisted up, spreading the muscle, cutting off the blood flow through the carotid artery to the brain. It's a judo choking hold.

I knew I had six seconds and that it was Cohan. I clawed for his eyes and tried to throw an elbow into him, but he knew where to stand. I drove my right heel down on his feet, feeling bones break, but he only tightened the grip. The fluorescent lights were spinning, darkening. Then there was a sound like a two-by-four hitting a sandbag. The grip was gone. I fell on the floor. Cohan landed face down beside me like a side of beef.

Kryellah stood over me, one fist clenched. The other hand pulled me up.

"Get the nigger!" Neely shouted, pointing.

Kryellah ran lightly toward the door, a wedge of cowboys after him. He jumped on a desk. Turned. Kicked twice. Two men fell. He war-whooped and dove on the rest, taking them to the floor. I down-punched one. Eddie got two with his chair. But a red-headed man in a purple neckerchief kicked Kryellah in the side with the heel of his boot. Kryellah grabbed him by his neckerchief, smashed his head into the side of a desk, splintering it. Then lifted him to his shoulder and heaved. The man flew over the desk and crashed through the window.

I was rabbit-punched so hard I thought my spine was broken. I stumbled around. Eyes out of focus and coming toward me, blood pouring out of the corner of his mouth, was Cohan. His huge hands were circling. He drove one for my eyes and tried to pick up my knee at the same time. An old wrestler's trick. I jumped back. But he moved in. My back touched the wall. I was trapped. He smiled, and as his hands went for my throat I grabbed the lapels of his coat and, pulling him toward me with all my strength, drove the top of my head into his face.

When I stepped back there was nothing where his face had been but a red pulp. As he fell to the floor, two men turned away and threw up. And it was all over.

I grabbed Cassidy, who was puffing like a walrus but still cutting up Neely, and pulled him over to where Eddie and Kryellah stood together. Then we backed for the door.

"Last chance to get the nigger," Kryellah said politely. But nobody moved. As the door closed, we turned and ran down the corridor.

Sirens were going off all over the lot. We sprinted across the lawn. Piled in Cassidy's Bentley. I took off like a big-assed bird as cop cars came screaming in from everywhere. I cut around the corner on two wheels. As we screeched toward the gate, they were trying to set two cars up as roadblocks. I shot between them, and studio cops dove in all directions as we smashed through the orange-and-white barrier and headed for the freeway.

As I pulled up in front of Cassidys' we were on the last eight bars of *A Thousand Miles*.

> *"Look awayyyyy ...*
> *Look A-waaaaaay*
> *Over yon*
> *Hedge ROOOOOOOOOOOOOW."*

"We're getting there," Cassidy said as we piled out of the car. "But there's still room for improvement. Once more from the top."

> *"Oh, who will glove your hand?*
> *And who will—"*

Kate, in a bathrobe, stepped out the front door.

"Tim, where in God's name have you been?"

"Katharine." He kissed her. "We have had some lively doings."

"Fighting. At your age."

"And he looked pretty good in there," I said.

"For a white man."

"Kate, darling, Kryellah here is not only a drinking Mohammedan—"

"Not Muslim. Afro-American."

"—but an Irish tenor."

"Bass."

"Jesus," said Cassidy. "His voice has changed. We're in a terrible state of chassis with no tenor."

"I'm the tenor," Eddie said.

"Well, you better all come inside, whoever you are," Kate said, smiling.

We sat around the kitchen drinking and singing while she bandaged us up and cooked some steaks.

"Listen, men," Cassidy finally said. "You're all right in a fight but you don't know when to go home."

Tiptoeing up the stairs in the dark, I missed one and sat down hard. Lights blazed on and Honey came running toward me, tying her white bathrobe together.

"Buck! Where have you been? Saul's been calling all night. He's furious. He's going to swear a warrant out for your arrest! He's going to cancel the show! What are you going to do?"

"Fuck you."

"You're *drunk*."

"Yes. But I'm still going to fuck you."

She slapped me hard across the face. "Get out of my house. You disgust me." I grabbed the rail and pulled myself to my feet. "You make me sick. You stink of alcohol."

I unzipped my fly and pulled out my cock. It was hard as a rock.

She stared at it, then turned and ran, but I grabbed her robe at the neck, ripped it off her, caught her around her naked waist and pulled her down to the stairs. She rolled quickly over on her stomach, grabbing the banisters on either side.

"Nora! Help!"

I tried to turn her over without hurting her, my cock bumping against the cheeks of her ass.

"Nora! Call the guards!"

"Oh, shut up and turn over."

"Never!" she hissed. "Never! *Never! Never!*"

"Suit yourself." I spit on my hand, wet down the head and slid my cock up her ass.

She gasped, then with all her strength tried to buck me off, but I had her by the shoulders. She was tight and fighting me, but I strained, forcing the head past the cord, then rammed it home.

"*Stop it!* ... You're hurting me ... oh! ... That's sodomy! ... Oh. I've never felt so degraded in my life. How dare you? ... *I'll have you killed for this* ... I swear it. NORA! *NORA!* HELP! ... oh ... oh ... *oh, God!* Don't stop. ... Don't come, darling. ... Oh, I love it ... oh ... yes. Yes! *YES!* ..."

We met in the parking lot of the Chinese restaurant. Hung over, beat up, blinking in the sunlight, we climbed silently into Cassidy's car.

As he pulled up at the front gate, the cop pushed the button that raised the barrier and grabbed a phone.

"They know we're here," Cassidy said.

He parked in the no-parking zone right in front of Stage 38. I pushed open the padded door and we walked onto the empty stage. The work light threw our flickering, magnified shadows up on the white nightclub set looming over us.

Cassidy slung his briefcase up on a plywood table, pulled out a big Thermos and a bottle of Johnnie Walker Black. We helped ourselves to the coffee, everyone adding a slug of Scotch, and sat there drinking and smoking without saying anything.

Finally Kryellah said, "Goddam gloomy in here. Shouldn't we meet 'em outside?"

"No," Cassidy said. "Always be on a set if you want to control it."

"Guess you been in a fight or two, huh, Mr. Cassidy?"

He grinned. He looked awful in that bad yellow light with the big purple mouse under his eye and the long iodined cut across his face. "Generally not as rough as this, Eddie. But hell, we were always fighting. Trying to get the good actors and not the contract players. Trying to get rid of the Goddam happy endings. Trying—"

There was a sudden creak and we started.

"They're coming in."

"No," Cassidy said. "That's the sound a set makes settling. Don't get jumpy."

Eddie said, "So things weren't all good in the good old days?"

"You hear a lot of talk that movies would be better today if the old studio heads were back. Don't you believe it. Cohn was the worst son of a bitch I've ever known; the Warner brothers weren't any better and L. B. Mayer brought in the gangsters. Christ, the only way we made any good film was by fighting those bastards every inch of the way." He took a swig from the bottle. "Even so, we didn't accomplish much."

I said, "You made some great movies."

"Great?" He shook his head. "No . . . Some that weren't so bad. Some that were pretty good. But, *Jesus,* when you think who we had!

"Just take the writers I worked with: Bill Faulkner, Scott Fitzgerald, John O'Hara, Bob Sherwood, Sidney Howard, Phil Barry, Ben Hecht and Charley MacArthur. Think of the movies we should have made!"

"You did all right," I said. *"Scarface, Stagecoach, The Maltese Falcon, Bringing Up Baby, The Philadelphia Story, Mr. Smith Goes to Washington, Citizen Kane, Wuthering Heights, My Darling Clementine—"*

"For Christ's sake," he said savagely. "Can you put any of them up against Renoir's *Grand Illusion* or Kurosawa's *Ikiru* or *Seven Samurai?*"

I knew what he meant, so I didn't say anything.

He looked off in the shadows, scratching his chin. "I guess we didn't fight hard enough. . . . *Heads up!*"

Sunlight streamed in as the double doors were shoved open. Saul strode in surrounded by a dozen studio cops, Neely (his face taped) at his side. Still moving, he jabbed a finger at me.

"*You* wouldn't listen to me. What's the result? Bloodshed. Anarchy. A man in the hospital at death's door."

"It's Neely's fault. He lied about—"

"What am I—a rabbi? Who cares who's right? Who's wrong? I own a lot that cranks out television. You're costing me money because you've halted production and—"

He broke off as a truck pulled up outside with screeching brakes. Through the slats, sunlight sparkled on the gunmetal-grey shape of the RO.

"There's your fucking crane. So start shooting. But understand you're on parole. Anything happens—it's jail for all of you. And probably not for the first time."

He walked away.

"Saul," I said, "I'm not working until I've seen my dailies."

Neely whirled around, screaming, "I'll sue you! Your contract has a clause which specifies—"

Saul slapped him in the face.

"Who the fuck are you? My lawyer! Shut up! Show him his dailies." He smiled at me and said softly, "Want to know how they look, Buck? I'll tell you. They look just like all the other shows . . . like shit."

After they left, the crew stuck their heads around the door. Maury and Big Joe came up, grinning, and shook hands.

A rangy bald man stepped up. "Mr. Cassidy. I'm Amundsen—your new first."

"Amundsen, we'll walk through the set-up with the first team. While we're lighting they'll go see the dailies."

Up on the grid lights began banging on.

"Yes, sir. Hold it quiet for rehearsal."

Big Joe slid on the seat of the RO, the men twisted the counterweight lock, and—released—the arm slowly swung him up high above our heads.

"Now that I've got it," Cassidy said, "I better think of something to do with the damn thing."

Outside the screening room, I let Eddie and Kryellah walk off toward the stage ahead of me. I leaned back against the wall, warm from the hot sun, closed my eyes and relaxed for the first time in a month.

Son of a bitch, I thought, *it's a hit.*

Simpson's voice said testily, "He's camera cutting, you know."

"I know."

"He slaps his hat over the lens so I can't use cuts *I* might like."

Christ, I thought, *that's the one thing you can count on. You're only given maybe a dozen marvelous moments in your life and some son of a bitch will louse them up.*

"Simpson, you—"

"Harry," Honey said. "Can I borrow my husband a sec?"

I opened my eyes. She stood a dozen feet away on the lawn, wearing a yellow angora sweater, a yellow pleated skirt, a yellow ribbon in her hair, and black-and-white saddle shoes.

"Oh, sure, Honey." Smiling, he slipped off through the sliding doors.

"Never argue with an editor," she said seriously. "Fire him."

I laughed. She took my hand and slid it around her waist.

"You're so bad!" she whispered, rubbing the back of my hand against her ass. "You were just *terrible* last night. What are you so happy about today?"

"I've got a hit."

"You mean you've got two days of good shooting."

"No," I said. "I've got a hit."

"*If* you do, you owe it all to me. Oh, don't look like that, Mr. High and Mighty. While you were waiting on Stage Thirty-eight, I was in Saul's office on the phone with Josiah.

"You were canceled until I told him I'd walk right off his network. Signed contract or no. That's how you got your old crane. Well, aren't you going to say something?"

"Thanks."

"Oh, you're *terrible!*" She stuck her tongue out, whispered, "Get home early."

And ran off across the green lawn, her ass jiggling as sweetly in her yellow pleated skirt as a high school cheerleader's.

I wondered if there was a word of truth in what she'd told me.

The rest of it went as well as a show could go.

We wound up in a ratty second-floor apartment on Moorpark near Laurel. The last setup was my taking Hilary off to jail. It was a bitch to light. The camera was out on the landing, backed up against the rail; there was a forest of eye lights clamped everywhere. Maury kept sighing, shaking his head and readjusting them. Hilary kept wandering around, mumbling her lines, bumping into furniture.

"Oh, Mr. Cassidy," she begged, "can't we do this before I burst?"

Cassidy patted her cheek. "Soon."

He took me aside. "She may throw in some new bits. Keep it going. I have a hunch she's only got one take in her."

"Right. What's this for?"

He held out a clean, pressed handkerchief. "Might come in handy.

"Roll 'em."

"Rolling."

"Speed."

"Action."

She turned and everything was in her eyes. I just played to them. The men and the lights and the camera faded off at the edges. She was one marvelous moment after another. Fearful. Conning. Angry. In my arms all frantic sex. Then she stepped back and, seeing death in my eyes, stood frozen. I slipped the coat over her shoulders. The contact made her cry; tears streamed from her hopeless eyes. I held out Cassidy's handkerchief. She blew her nose as loud and long as an eight-year-old.

Then did a beautiful, unexpected thing. She threw her head back proudly and swept out like a queen.

Cassidy's hat hit the lens. "Cut. Print. End of show."

Kryellah started clapping, then Eddie and Maury and Joe. Then the whole crew.

Hilary looked up at me, puzzled. "Is that because it's the last shot?"

"No. It's for you."

"Me?" Her little elf face lit up. She threw herself in Cassidy's arms.

"Oh, I can't stand it being over. I want it to go on forever."

I couldn't think of anything to say as I walked Cassidy out to his car.

He tossed his battered briefcase in the back seat, slammed the door and turned to me.

"We got most of what we went after. Not all. You never do. But it's tough, and funny, and moves, and it's as honest as we could make it. Good job, Mike."

I was afraid I was going to cry. "Jesus, Tim, I can't thank you—"

"None of that," he said crisply. "You've got forty-six minutes and forty-five seconds of good film. Protect it. I'm not going to do the cut. I'm tired. Besides, it'll be good for you. If they say you're short and want you to shoot an added scene, they're lying. They've yanked something. Eddie has the footage count. I left you some frames to play with at the top of the farmhouse drive-in. You can start that as late as your look camera left."

"Right."

He thought for a moment in the warm summer night, oncoming headlights sweeping across his face.

"From here on it's up to you. From all I could find out, on these TV series it's the star who's in charge. Not the director."

"It's a good thing. You should see the next one."

"Use Eddie. He has a good eye for acting. I've been checking him out. He's especially good on you. I'd think about turning him into a director."

Surprised, I said, "That's a damn good idea."

Worried, he scratched his chin. "Pace yourself on the fights. Remember even Bronko Nagurski had some fella running interference for him."

"I've got a business manager and agent."

"By definition they go with the money. And Magnitude has more than you. It's a bad lot. They backed off. But they'll be back. They're going to go all out to break you."

"I know."

He punched me on the shoulder and got behind the wheel.

"See you soon, Tim."

"God willing."

"Yes."

"And when I do," he said, "don't be looking like a cake of soap."

17

When I was a kid, slouched in my seat in the Great Neck Playhouse Saturday matinees, I always loved the montages by Slavko Vorkapich. I was fascinated by the jumble of pictures on top of each other: the belching factory chimneys, the whirring machinery, the happy workers leaving the gate, the graph going up, up, *up* 1927 ... 1928 ... 1929. Then 1930 zoomed out and all at the same time the chimneys stopped smoking, machinery stopped turning, the graph plunged down, the workers sadly walked out the gate.

For the next three weeks Slavko could have been directing my life.

Alarm clocks exploding in my face. Hands set at four-thirty, four-fifteen, four o'clock.

Lights shining in my eyes. Keys. Fills. Kickers. Crosses. Barndoored. Kooked. Inkies.

Lenses pushing in on me. 35's, 50's, 135's.

Script pages handed to me on the set. All colors. Pink. Yellow. Green. All bad.

Directors' eyes. Burned out and careless. Or sly and ambitious. All calculating how to be well enough liked to pick up another show.

Night after night—in various viewing rooms—plates of Chinese food. Hamburgers. Tacos. Pizzas. All cold.

Women. All sizes. All shapes. All beautiful. Coming toward me. Smiling. Frowning. Kissing me. Cursing me. Shooting me.

Fights. The ones Eddie laid out. Stunt men coming at me with fists, feet, canes, clubs, chairs, bottles, knives.

Then the other fights. The real ones.

"Buck, baby, as you enter I *zoom* in from behind the chandelier to a big close-up of you."

"No zooms on this show, Zab."

"You *must* be kidding! That's how I get my dynamics. I end each scene on a close-up and *zoom out*, then POW! Cut to the wide shot and zoom in. That's my style."

"It's not the style of the show."

"Buck, you can't do this to me. I've laid out the whole show with a zoom. I wouldn't know how to shoot it without one."

"Put the camera there on a fifty. Pick me up at the door. Pan me right to the bartender. As he walks away truck with him to the cash register. Stop. When he turns I'll step in and you'll have an over-the-shoulder."

Late at night. Three editors smoked angrily in a screening room.

The one with waxed points on his gray moustache, wearing the safari jacket, said, "You've got to face facts, Mr. McLeod. Your first show is three and a half minutes short—"

"Wrong," I said.

He threw his hands up. "The script girl already told you it was three twenty-six short."

"She's wrong."

"Well, if everyone's wrong but you, Mr. McLeod, this is no place for me." He started up the aisle.

"If you go through those doors—it won't be on your feet."

He stopped quickly, his thick lips open in a surprised little O.

"You've been hiding film on me. Now, you can admit it, put it back in and save us a lot of time. Or we'll run it on stop and go. Well?"

He didn't say anything but sat down.

We were four minutes into the film before I spotted it. "There." The frame froze. Ran backward. It was the two-shot of me and the pimp sitting outside Cyrano's.

"When you cut to my close-up, you chopped out a nice beat where he tried to stare me down."

"I dropped it because it dragged."

"Don't direct."

"That's editing."

"Editors work on newspapers. Cutters on film. Now cut in the footage you cut out."

By four-thirty I had the cut the way Cassidy had shot it, then we only had to take out six frames at the top of the farmhouse drive-in to have exactly 46:45.

"Cut. Oh! That's a *print!* Buck, you were marvelous!

You had all of Marlon's animal vitality, but somehow made it completely your own."

Behind his maroon-veloured shoulder, Eddie shook his head.

"Let's do one more, Stu."

The handsome young face turned petulant.

"Won't you trust me? Once? It was . . . *magic*."

Amundsen sidled up. "If you shoot it over we'll have to break for dinner. I'd sure like to send the boys home early. They're beat."

He was right. They were buckling.

"Coming back to it, you'll be cold," Stu said. "You'll never recapture the spontaneity."

I took Eddie off in a corner. "It felt pretty good to me, Eddie. I think we can get away with it."

"No fucking way. You were empty and pushed. There wasn't an honest beat in it. Just one cheap trick after another. It was absolute shit."

"You've got to watch that, Eddie."

"What?"

"Now that I'm a big star, telling me anything—just to make me feel good. *Dinner!*"

The montage ground to a halt at two o'clock one cold morning in Griffith Park, when we finished shooting our fourth show.

Exhausted men coiled cable in the background while Maury, Eddie, Big Joe had a slug from the bottle, shook hands, then stumbled off in the darkness to do nothing for the month every television series shuts down until the first show is aired.

While I was suddenly catapulted across the country on an endless round of one-night stands to publicize *Hunter*.

The country was struck down by a heat wave. In the plastic airports and motels and interchangeable TV stations the air was clammy from air conditioning and smelled like the green soap in the bottom of urinals. Outside, the dusty air could sear your lungs.

The local UBC flack would meet me at the airport and rush me around the circuit: lunch with the station manager; drinks with the newspaper people; the talk shows—two or three per town—where I'd sit in a circle fighting to get my pitch in ahead of the four or five other guests.

Our paths kept crossing. I must've run into the soggy seersuckered author of a sex manual in five or six airports—sitting alone, eating Hershey bars. I'd wave but he'd always ignore me.

I was banging anything I could get my hands on. Carhops, receptionists, Hertz girls. At first I didn't care who or what. But as I flew over this Godforsaken country that scorching summer, Harrisburg to Birmingham, Birmingham to Memphis, I learned the locals take too much out of you. So I shifted to stewardesses. There was something comforting about another drifter and they were as rootless as I was.

In endless hotel rooms, head on my chest, they'd talk on into the night about the men in their lives, cigarette smoke curling up to the ceiling as Johnny faded into the waving Stars and Stripes, which dissolved into the unchanging test pattern.

Next morning, sharp and crisp as Marines in uniform, they'd flash a brief, professional smile and, heels tip-tapping briskly, disappear into the airport crowd.

I'd had the sticks by the time I hit New York. The Algonquin lobby looked great. Shabby and run-down, with shabby run-down New York faces drinking and arguing.

There was a message that a Shirley Povnar had called. I called her from my room.

"I didn't think you'd remember me. You must meet a lot of stews."

"Not like you, Shirley," I said, trying to place her. "Come right over."

Shirley turned out to be a slim twenty-two or -three with a heart-shaped face splashed with freckles. I couldn't remember if I'd balled her or not.

"Oh, no," she said over a drink. "I couldn't do it right away with you—for the first time—just like that. Not without having dinner or something first."

But she did, screaming so loudly when she came that I was sure the phone was the manager.

"Hi, it's Ginger. The National flight to Chattanooga? I'm downstairs. Can I come up?"

"Sure."

When I opened the door Shirley sat up in bed, holding the sheet to her chest. "What is this? Some kind of Hollywood orgy? What kind of a girl do you think I am?"

"A very pretty girl." Ginger was slipping out of her dress. "Hi, I'm Ginger."

"This is Shirley."

"Never mind introducing us. I'm leaving."

"Oh, I *am* sorry to hear that. You know who you remind me of? Shirley MacLaine. A much *younger, prettier* Shirley MacLaine."

She tossed her dress on a chair and pivoted around. She had a lean dancer's body, with high heavy breasts and erect dark-brown nipples. Shirley stared at them as she moved toward us.

I said, "Do you go both ways?"

"You mean with a *girl?* NEVER! I never have and I never will."

"You're sweet, Shirley." Ginger patted her cheek. "Don't worry, nobody's going to ask you to do anything you don't want to do. We just want you to have a good time." She slid into bed.

After an hour I got bored trying to pry them apart, so I showered and left.

At Clarke's there was a long line waiting to get in the back room. But Danny was sitting at the big table and waved me over. He was with a couple of sportswriters, a tight end from Buffalo, and an outside linebacker from the Jets. We talked about Namath's knees and Gabriel's elbow and if Prothro could turn the Rams around.

Suddenly I knew Tabitha was in the room. I turned quickly. She was at a red-checked table at the back against the brick wall, staring at me.

As I walked across the room she looked down.

"Tabitha . . ." I said. "My God—Tabitha."

"Mr. McLeod. Mr. Hollister."

He was a big, nice-looking kid in a J. Press blue pin-stripe with a vest. He nodded at me warily.

"Mr. McLeod is just passing through. He's a denizen of Hollywood."

I just stared at her, stunned by that Irish setter hair, and the way that skin was drawn across those cheekbones, and those grey eyes looking up at me.

"God, how I've wanted to see you."

"Then your prayers have been answered. Again. Mr. McLeod was once a poor man, Chet. But he had Great Expectations and prayed a great deal. And today he has a rich and beautiful wife."

"I think you'd better go back to your table," he said.

"Tabitha, I've got to talk to you."

"No," she said.

He stood. "Now."

"Careful, Chet," she said. "He doesn't fight fair. He hits below the belt."

"No problem, Tab."

"For Christ's sake, Tabitha. Give me two minutes to talk to you."

"Damn you," she said quietly. "Go away. This is my city. It has the theater and snow and *The New York Times* and people you can trust. Get the hell out of it."

"Tabitha . . ." I put my hand out. She jumped up, striking it away. Her chair fell over.

She started to cry and ran across the room, pushing through the people waiting to get a table.

I thought Hollister was going to hit me, but he picked up her coat and purse and went after her.

I paid their check and mine, said good night to Danny and his friends, picked up my bags at the Algonquin without waking the girls, took a cab to Kennedy and sat all night in the empty TWA lounge—thinking—until five-thirty, when I took the first plane back to the Coast.

18

Three hundred people were invited to Tara II to see the first shows. They all accepted but Tim and Kate and Ted and Laura.

There was a chorus of oohs and ahs as Honey floated down the staircase in a white ball gown with long white gloves and a tiara.

I had to hand it to her—she knew how to work a room. A smile here. A handshake there. A cheek kiss. A few serious words. She timed it perfectly, too. Sliding her arm in mine just as System went on the ten big color sets UBC engineers had set up in the drawing room.

I said, "You know more names than Jim Farley."

"Sweet!" She kissed me as flashbulbs popped.

We sat down as her show went on.

It was a disaster.

Endless film clips of her preparations for the wedding, a sketch where she was an angel arguing with St. Peter to let in a rock-and-roll singer.

Everyone laughed so loudly I had trouble hearing the straight lines. When she started singing her closing theme, they swarmed around us.

"Oh, Honey!" "You're so marvelous!" "So funny!" "So darling!" "So cute." "So dear."

My opening credits were up and I couldn't hear a word, so I quickly led my group to the library.

When the closing credits came up, I asked, "Well?"

Kryellah said, "It works."

Maria said, "I like it."

Hilary said, "I'm terrible."

Eddie said, "No, you're not. It's good except for the music."

I called Cassidy. "How did you like it?"

"I liked it when I shot it. Before you put the improvements in. Who the hell did the music?"

Kate got on. "Stop it, Tim. It was marvelous. I was proud of both of you. Michael . . ." There was a catch in her voice. "I hope you're ready. You're going to be a star."

I felt the hangover next morning as I walked into the breakfast room. There was too much sun streaming in, and Honey's heels were making a hell of a racket as she paced up and down the black and white squares. I poured myself a cup of coffee and picked up the trades.

Variety:

Hunter Looks Like Hit

New UBC private eye entry takes off like gangbusters. Mordecai Gaunt's script is hard-hitting, tightly plotted yarn about junkie using tetanus as murder weapon. Co-star Kryellah is stand-out as black Police Chief constantly bumping heads with McLeod. Academy Award winner Margaret Moynihan, series' only other regular, shows she's lost none of her comic cunning. Supporting thesps (mostly unknown) are all top drawer but Hilary Kruger's teenage junkie has the stuff Emmy awards are made of.

Tim Cassidy's TV debut shows strictly class megging in every frame.

Maury Kramer's lensing is superb, as are sets by Allan Slinnet and incisive editing by Clyde Krautz. Other technical credits all OK except for gimmicked-up, shlock score.

But when all's said and done, series' success will depend on public's reaction to star. McLeod's been around and looks it. But his tough, rugged, dangerous quality could pay off big. If so, his backup of wife's variety skein would wrap up the Sabbath for UBC.

Reporter:

HUNTER SEASON'S SLEEPER

Move over, Lee Marvin and Steve McQueen. McLeod looks like another who can go from Tube to Big Screen Stardom. He's rough, tough and mucho sexy. His kidding around with old-timer Margaret Moynihan will make you laugh; his dramatic work with sensational newcomer Hilary Kruger will make you cry; and his blow-up scene with co-star Kryellah will blast you out of the room.

Honey's heel clicks were becoming impossible to ignore. I looked at the next column.

HONEY BOMBS

Honey Holly gamely battled her bottom-of-the-trunk material—but lost. Who'd a thunk the old pro wouldn't know enough to give the Heaven sketch the heave-ho?

I turned back to *Variety*.

Old Pro off Pace in Opener

"I'm sorry about your reviews."

"Old pro!" she cried. *"Old pro!"*

"They meant it as a compliment."

"Oh, they did, did they?" she said wildly. "Well, Mr. Sexy New Star, just wait until they call *you* an old pro and see how you like it."

"Variety said I'd been around and looked it."

"Oh! You're a *man*. Who cares what a man looks like?"

She ran out. I could hear her sobbing all the way up the stairs. Then the bedroom door slammed.

I knew I should go up and try to make her feel better. But instead I poured another cup of coffee and read my reviews again.

The cops on the gate loved the show. So did the sexy messenger girls on their motor scooters. So did Harriet.

There must have been twenty people waiting in Ted's office. All talking at the same time, trying to shake my hand.

Ted shouted, "Buck, you won't believe *The New York Times*. Shut up, everybody, and let him read it." He shoved the paper in my hands.

Hunter, UBC's new Sunday-night series, must have been confected by a kleptomaniac. The dialogue has been lifted from Dashiell Hammett; the hard-eyed look at the seamy underside of Los Angeles from Raymond Chandler; even McLeod's excellent portrayal of the existential private eye is deeply in debt to the immortal Bogart.

But this horrendous season one finds it hard to complain of stealing from such exemplary sources. Especially since the show ends up creating its own style. A gritty, honest attention to nickel-and-dime details that must be respected.

"Boys," I said, "I'm due on the set in five minutes and want a few words with Ted."

"My God, Buck, *The New York Times!*" Ted said. "How marvelous that they appreciated all the things we fought and bled for."

As the door closed behind the last man, I said, "Ted, the only fucking thing in the whole show I let you handle was the music. What happened?"

I hadn't been shooting half an hour before I felt I'd never left. Some of the good men were gone—replaced by bad. The director, Benedetto, was a kid fresh from NYU who talked about Jean-Luc Godard but printed anything so that he could get a reputation for being fast.

"Heads up," Eddie said.

Saul was running across the set, flunkies stretched out behind him.

"Buck!" he called out in his thin, high-pitched voice. "We made it, Baby. We're a smash."

He handed me the overnight Nielsen.

It read:

		Rating	Share
(1) *All in the Family*	(CBS)	26.8	34.6
(2) *Hunter*	(UBC)	24.3	34.2
(3) *Honey Holly*	(UBC)	24.1	32.0

* * *

"Now, it's only down one little point," Honey said sweetly, sitting on her stool, the writers in a semicircle around her. "But it hurt me."

Thelma said, "What size is the Nielsen sample? A hundred families. So someone went to the can. Big deal."

Honey frowned. "Thelma, you swore by the ratings when they were good. It's not right to knock them when they're bad."

"Honey," said Lanny. "You're number three. You can't call that bad."

"Oh, yes, I can," she said softly. "And so should anyone on the team who plays to win."

The writers exchanged quick sidewise glances.

Honey clapped her hands and grinned at them.

"You know my very favorite show-business story in the whole world?"

"What?" three people said.

"Once when Jack Benny was the biggest star in radio—and he was number one for years—his ratings began to go down. Week after week they slipped. Finally he called all his writers in.

"And dear Jack said: 'Boys, something's gone wrong. Maybe it's me. Maybe it's you. I don't know. But I do know that we've been together so long I feel as if we're a family. And like a family we're going to lick this—together.' And they all worked like dogs and in a few weeks he was back on top and didn't have to fire anyone. Isn't that a beautiful story?"

"Inspirational," Thelma said.

"Well, that's how I feel about all you. You're *my* family."

"We all love you, too, Honey," Thelma said fervently.

"Then like a family, let's roll up our sleeves and pitch in—Oh! Hi, darling! 'Scuse me, Gang."

She skipped down the aisle and kissed me.

"Thanks for coming right over."

"What's the problem?"

"I just got a teeny bit worried that your head might get turned by your reviews."

"I'm happier about the ratings."

"You're going to think me a terrible wet blanket. But Josiah called—his research boys sampled your audience. They looked in out of curiosity. Everyone wanted a peek at my new husband. They predict it's going to take a big drop next week. Promise you won't be disappointed."

Next week *Hunter* went up from 24.3 to 24.9, staying in second place behind *All in the Family*. *Honey* went from 24.1 to 22.8 and slid into fifth place behind *Flip Wilson* and *The Wednesday Night Movie*.

As I walked into the soda fountain, Honey, Thelma and Carl Ushley abruptly broke off an angry discussion.

"Private?"

"No, darling, Thelma was just leaving."

Thelma stalked out grimly.

I went behind the bar and built myself a drink.

"Honey," Carl said, "this season Thelma's an absolute *disaster*."

"Oh, you've noticed, too," she said sadly.

"She hasn't had *one* halfway decent idea. And she's been *hell* to work with."

"I thought it was just me."

"She just doesn't have it anymore. Honey, she's got to go."

"Carl, how can you say that? Thelma's my friend."

"Honey, you're loyal and sweet and dear, and God knows I love you for it. But Thelma is *destroying* you. Slotnick and Stram aren't joining us."

"Thelma told me it's just money."

"They told *me* they wouldn't work with Thelma—at any price. And you know how desperately we need them."

"Yes." She sighed and shook her head wearily. "But where can I find a producer overnight?"

"Promote me. You won't lose any time breaking a new man in. I'll get twice as much work out of the writers. *And* we'll have Slotnick and Stram."

She reached over and squeezed his hand. "My good, strong right arm as producer . . . well, it's certainly something to think about."

He set his martini glass down on the marble counter with a click.

"I'm afraid you're going to have to do more than think about it."

She withdrew her hand and, twisting a pearl in her necklace, waited.

"Andy Williams has asked me to do his eight specials as *producer*-director. I'm meeting him in half an hour to give him my answer."

"Buck, dear, would you ask Nora to hold dinner for half an hour?"

Nora sighed and shook her head. "Oh, dear, I'm afraid it's not going to be the way you like it, Mr. McLeod."

She bent down, slid the roast out of the oven, put the pan up on the tile counter and started covering it with aluminum foil.

Something about the slump of her shoulders and the wisp of gray hair across her thin neck reminded me of my mother in the big kitchen in Great Neck when word came down that dinner was delayed. Suddenly I pulled all the bills out of my pocket—there must have been close to two hundred dollars—made a wad of them and slipped it in the pocket of her apron.

She pulled it out and stared at it. "What's this for, sir?"

"The late meals and early breakfasts. All the trouble I've caused you."

"Oh, it's been a pleasure, Mr. McLeod. Here, I couldn't take it."

"Buy yourself a new dress to set off your pretty blue eyes."

"Now, Mr. McLeod, I don't waste money on fancy clothes. Not at my age."

"There must be something."

"Well . . . if you promise you won't tell *anyone?*"

"Promise." I crossed myself.

She whispered, "I've got a bit put by, enough so in a few months I'll be giving my notice and going home to live with my widowed sister in Roscommon."

"To Roscommon then." I toasted her, then handed her the glass. She downed a good stiff one.

"Oh, Mr. McLeod," she said, smacking her lips, "you're a real gentleman."

"Nora," I said, "you're the first woman in the whole world who ever said that to me." I bent down, kissed her and left her blushing like a schoolgirl.

As I turned into the dark hall something in Honey's voice stopped me.

"Carl, don't think that after taking all those bows when the show was number one you're going to walk out as soon as it starts to slip. I won't allow that."

"Luv," he said, "despite my begging you—every season—you'd never give me a contract. I was your faithful dog Tray you'd toss the bone of a show to every week. So now, when I say toodle-oo, luv, and walk out the door, there's nothing you can do except say good-bye."

The stool creaked as he stood.

"Carl," Honey said in a new, thoughtful tone. "That Canadian boy you adopted is still a minor, isn't he?"

"Anthony. Yes." There was fear in his voice. "Why?"

"On his seventeenth birthday party," she went on lazily, "after the guests had left, the two of you went skinny-dipping and then—"

"No one saw us!"

"Someone shot some film of it on a long, long lens."

"Oh, God . . ." he said so quietly I could barely hear him.

"If the immigration people should see it, or the district attorney . . ."

"Oh, Jesus, don't hurt Anthony." He was crying quite hard. "He's just a child. Honey, I beg you—"

"Carl! What a way to talk! No one's going to hurt anyone. Why, you're going to get a contract with a raise. And the way Thelma's been behaving you may turn out to be producer any day, too. But it will have to be when I think it's best. Understand?"

"Yes."

"Well, gosh, stop looking so gloomy! Give Andy my love. And, say! Why don't you see if you can get him for guest star next week?"

The next Nielsen read:

(1) *Hunter* (UBC)   29.3
(2) *All in the Family* (CBS)   28.7

Honey was tied for fifteenth place with *Gunsmoke*.

Nate, Stan, Coulter and Scotty, drinks in hand, cheered as I stepped in Ted's office.

"Numero Uno!" Stan yelled.

"Yay!"

"You're fantastic!"

They stopped shouting and pounding me on the back when I slammed the X-rays and letters down on the bar.

"What the hell's this?" Nate said.

"My back has been broken in three places. The red circles show where. That letter was written yesterday by Dr. Kennicut at UCLA, with two concurring opinions. It states that I'm suffering from excruciating pain from old lower-back injuries, a cracked disk, and severe muscle spasms. They have prescribed absolute rest. Any attempt to work would aggravate my condition and be extremely dangerous to my physical and mental health."

They all stared at me. In the silence Coulter quickly slipped glasses on his nose and studied the letters.

Scotty said quietly, "Buck, if you break your contract, you'll put your profits in jeopardy."

"If these profits that everyone keeps talking about are so fucking good, how come I haven't seen any?"

Scotty blinked at me. "You must be joking. There isn't a series in town that breaks even the first season."

"Because they've sunk six or seven hundred thousand in a pilot thay have to pay off. What are we paying off?"

Coulter put down the letters. "I've gone over all the financial arrangements in detail and found them sound."

I tapped my fingers on the X-rays. "What about these?"

"Mr. McLeod, you have a doctor—"

"Three doctors."

He shrugged. "Three doctors who say you can't work. UBC will produce twenty who'll testify you're in perfect health. Doctors will say anything in court."

"Like lawyers."

"No," he said dryly, "a lawyer is in a somewhat different position if his client acts like a Goddam fool— he has to go into court to protect him."

"Buck." Nate threw his tiny hands toward me. "For Christ's sake forget all this talk of lawyers and courtrooms. When a star walks! It never gets that far. I've been through it a hundred times. And things don't get decided by a judge in his black robes but by a *blood-bath*. It's kick-'em-in-the-balls-and-gouge-their-eyes-out time. And I've won a helluva lot of them."

"Has he ever," Stan murmured.

"But I'm against this. One hundred percent! You know why?"

"Yes," I said. "Because it doesn't make a fucking bit of difference—*to you*—how much money I make.

Since this is a TUL package you skim ten percent right
off the top. You get twenty-three G's a week for doing
nothing."

"Are you impugning my integrity?"

"I'm informing you—as my agent—that I am in
such severe pain that on the advice of my physician I
cannot report for work tomorrow."

I opened the door.

"What'll make you all better?" Nate asked nastily.

"What you get, Nate."

"Twenty-three G's," he said in a strange, choked
voice. "For Christ's sakes, Buck, I haven't got a chance
of getting that out of them."

"Then pay part of it out of your commission."

"Buck!" he screamed, running toward me. I
slammed the door in his face.

I swam forty laps in the pool, then stayed sweating
in the sauna until I got drowsy, and, wrapping myself in
towels, stretched out on the red leather rubbing table
in the pool house.

When I came to, Honey was running her hands over
my nude body. The only light came from the fireplace,
and I could see she wore a white silk bathrobe that
showed a lot of cleavage.

"You don't look as if you hurt so bad you can't go
to work tomorrow," she murmured, smiling down at
me.

"I do though."

She frowned and sat down, still running her hands
over me. "Oh, Buck, you're making a terrible
mistake."

"For Christ's sake, you were the one who told
me when I signed the contract, as soon as I had a hit,
walk."

"But not this quickly. Darling, remember when
Vince Edwards had *Ben Casey* and what a hit that
was. Even so Abby waited a whole season before he
had him walk."

"I don't give a Goddam. I'm doing it now. Why the hell does it upset you so much?"

She opened her eyes wide and looked at me very seriously. "Because we're married, and marriage means helping out each other. And you don't know what's going to happen."

"What?"

"As soon as you walk out, you've broken your contract—and that means you don't have artistic control any more. So UBC and Magnitude will start re-cutting all your shows and shooting added scenes—"

"Christ." I sat up.

She rested her breasts against me and pouted. "And then you'll get all mad, and you won't play games with your little Honey."

Her hands kept on stroking me.

"Oh, look, he's standing up straight as a soldier. Oh, he's so cute. He has a little smile on his face."

She pulled up my hand and not taking her eyes off mine sucked my thumb—hard.

"Bucky, tell your little Honey that you're going to work tomorrow. So Honey can stop worrying, and kiss him, and slide her tongue in his little mouth."

"Sure," I said. "Suck it, baby."

And she did.

"I want off this lot."

Saul, behind the clean sweep of desk, said, "No. Buck, it's like a marriage. For better or for worse. I haven't got a ring but I've got a contract. Now if, as in all marriages, some friction has arisen—"

"It certainly has," Nate said. Stan, Coulter and Scotty nodded solemnly.

"Then"—Saul spread his hands out—"let us alleviate it. Buck, what would make you happy?"

"I want to hire my own people: art director, set director, costume designer, editors, everyone. I pay them. They work only for me."

"He can't have his own unit!" Neely said. "That's a vertical concept, and we have a horizontal system."

"Then change your fucking system."

"Now, Buck," Nate said nervously. "We're not going to get anywhere attacking the system."

"True," Stan said.

"Your fucking *system* turns out nothing but bad film. *Hunter*'s the only good show on this lot—and I've got the reviews to prove it. And the only reason is because we fight your system every inch of the way."

"It seems to me," Coulter said, "that Mr. McLeod has presented a very strong case. I'd like to hear the rebuttal."

"Mr. Coulter," Saul said, "the Magnitude system is the most efficient and economical in the industry. Present show excepted."

"Don't blame that on the system!" Neely said angrily. "Like he said, he's fighting us. Tearing the lot apart. Shooting night for night. Editing on golden time. Re-scoring. His costs are unbelievable."

Saul said, "Buck, no one has more respect than I for artistic temperament. But when that God-given drive for perfection runs head into reality and it costs too much money, I have to lower the boom."

"What do you care what it costs, Saul—since you don't own a piece of the show?"

Neely shot a stunned glance at Saul, who was on his feet, moving quickly toward me.

"Many reasons. Our reputation for economy. Our commitment with UBC. But most importantly—my word. What did I promise you? That I'd put money in your pocket. Well, that's what I'm fighting for, my friend—*your* profits."

Outside we stood in the dark parking lot, Mercedes drawn up in a circle around us like a wagon train.

Coulter said, "Seems to me, Mr. McLeod, that you have a top-flight team fighting for your profits." There was a murmur of agreement.

The cars drove off. Eddie and I stood there in the warm starry night.

"What do you think, Eddie?"

"Two questions. One: Why was Neely so shocked when you said Magnitude didn't own a piece of the show?"

"You saw that, too?"

He nodded. "And two: How come no one else on your top-flight team did?"

"Buck, old buddy, don't just stand there gapin'. Come in. Come in."

"Jesus, Jud, this is your dressing room?"

"Not like the one we shared on *Wagon Train,* eh?"

He held out his hand proudly at the big stone fireplaces, the cowhide armchairs, the pool tables, the paneled walls with stuffed animal heads, the twenty-foot-long mahogany bar with a Japanese bartender behind it.

"Never forget the day Saul handed me the key to it. Eight years ago, when *Cattle Country* hit the Top Ten. Bourbon for my friend, Kato. You know when we did that *Wagon Train* you told me to stop dyeing my hair. Best advice anyone ever gave me." He patted the famous silver thatch. We clicked glasses. "Welcome to the R & F Club."

"The what?"

"Buddy, you're on your way. You're going to be Rich and Famous! And let me tell you, it's the only way to be. Money! That thirty-five G's a week with hundred percent residuals I get is chicken feed. I do a hundred rodeos. They pay me twenty-five G's just to ride out on my horse and sing a few songs. Buck, you knew me when I didn't have a pot to piss in. Well, now I own ranches and oil wells, condominiums, car washes, fried chicken franchises. Christ, I own every fucking tax shelter in the country. And I love it. And you will, too. But it isn't just the money.

"I mean, who the hell has it better than me?

"Laurence Olivier? He has to act his ass off on a stage eight times a week. McQueen? Newman? They got to read scripts. Pick directors. Worry. The only thing I worry about is that they write me out of everything. 'Cause I only shoot two days an episode. The rest of the time I hunt and fish and fuck.

"I mean I have it *all!* And Buck, you can too."

He grabbed a silver rod and clanged it noisily inside a silver triangle hanging over the bar.

"Chow time! Come and get it while it's hot!"

Four pretty long-legged California girls with straight blond hair scampered in.

"Girls, say hello to my old buddy, Buck."

"Hello, Buck," they said.

"Diane's for you. She sucks like Dracula."

"Some other time, Jud." I headed for the door. "I've got to get four minutes out of a second cut."

"Let the hired hands do it. And have yourself some fun!"

I stopped and studied him curiously. "Jud, how do you feel when you see a bad *Cattle Country?*"

He stared at me in surprise. "Why, shit, Buck, I haven't seen a show in years."

19

As I walked in my office, Coulter said: "I'm on a tight schedule."

"Me, too," Nate said. "This better be top priority."

"It is," I said. "You've met Juan Lares."

"I introduced them," Eddie said.

They all smiled at Juan in that pleasant way important people do at the hangers-on around stars. In his worn blue jeans, with his wiry build and deep tan, he looked like a wrangler.

"He'll do the talking," I said. "He's my new lawyer."

It was very quiet as I sat down.

"Christ," Coulter drawled in his Groton accent. "I should have warned you. Every time an actor has a meteoric rise some two-bit ambulance chaser tries to cut himself in."

Juan smiled at him. "I've always wanted to take on one of you Sullivan and Cromwell bastards."

"Unfortunately for your ambitions I'm not with Sullivan and Cromwell."

"I know. I was." He laughed at Coulter's surprise. "Went there straight from Harvard Law. I was their token spic. Made junior partner before I went to Salinas to work for Chavez."

Coulter, bored, murmured, "I'm not particularly interested in your credentials."

"You should be. I put in a year with the district attorney before I set up private practice. And he'd love this case. The poor but honest TV star stolen blind by his lawyer, agent and business manager. He'll go for criminal fraud."

Nate jumped up. "I don't have to listen to that kind of slander from no fucking wetback—"

"Sit down, Nate," Coulter said lazily. "And keep quiet. He's dealing."

Nate sat slowly down.

Juan shrugged and drank from his can of Coors. "Who knows—yet? I've just had a few hours to poke around. I know about Abel and Baker. But tell me about Oran."

"Why, of course," Scotty said. "Buck owns one hundred percent of the stock—"

Juan slammed his fist on the table. "Fuck it then. We'll subpoena everything and see you in court."

Coulter said coolly, "Mr. MacNab was referring to the common stock."

"Then there's also preferred?"

"Yes."

"Preferred pays the profits?"

"Yes."

"How does the preferred break down?"

Scotty looked questioningly at Coulter, who nodded. "Two percent is Buck's; eighteen percent is Magnitude's—"

"You told me Magnitude didn't have a point."

Scotty looked away from me and poured himself another drink.

"They told you lots of things," Juan said. "Who owns the other eighty?"

"Jasmine."

"Never heard of them," I said. "Eighty percent! Jesus. It's a good thing we didn't make any profits."

"Not so fast," Juan said. "I think they've been disbursing profits from the first show. Right?"

Coulter nodded.

"How much?"

Scotty, still looking at the floor, said in a shaken voice, "The show netted twenty-two, twenty-three thousand an episode."

"More," Nate said grimly. "We had to kick back two-thirds of our commission to Jasmine."

Juan jotted down figures. "Eighteen plus twenty-two. That's forty thousand a week. Times eight shows . . . I figure Magnitude has fifty-seven thousand six, and Jasmine's ripped Buck off for two hundred and fifty-six thousand dollars."

I walked over to Scotty.

"Scotty," I said quietly, "I knew what they were from the beginning. But you and I were friends. . . . How the hell could you sell me out to UBC?"

"*UBC!*" He looked up at me in amazement.

Coulter said, "Jasmine is a wholly owned subsidiary of Lollypop Productions."

"But that's Honey," I said.

Coulter and Nate nodded.

Nate added bitterly, "He's her business manager—now; controls the cash flow of all her packages."

Scotty caught my sleeve. "It wasn't that, Buck." He started sobbing. "It was *her* ... I knew what I was doing was wrong ... but I just couldn't say no to her."

Juan pulled papers out of his briefcase.

"Now, shall we start dealing you bastards out?"

But I didn't hear the answer. I was out the door.

Far away—up on the stage—Honey sat on her stool, talking to eight men I hadn't seen before.

"So, once again, from the bottom of my heart ... welcome! I know I'm going to love working with you—because you're all such *wonderful* writers. Does anyone have a question?"

"I do, Miss Holly—"

"*Honey!* We're just one big happy family here!"

"Out," I said.

Surprised heads swiveled around. Stared at me.

"*Out.*"

She nodded. Carl quickly herded them off through the wings.

"What is it, darling?"

"I know."

"Know what?"

"Everything. Jasmine. Your getting to Scotty. The whole fucking rip-off."

"I see," she said calmly.

"You really shoved it up my ass and broke it off, didn't you? '*Sign the contract, darling, don't worry about the salary.*' And just the other night ... '*That's what marriage is, isn't it, darling, helping the one you love!*' And all the time you were helping yourself to forty G's of mine a week. You cunt! You two-bit, lying, cheating, double-crossing cunt!"

"Don't act so surprised." She spoke evenly without moving. "You know how it works. As soon as we were

engaged, you went behind my back to Greengauge promising you'd get me to do another season if
he put your package on. You were still negotiating two
minutes before the wedding. Everything you said about
me goes double for you."

I thought it over.

"You're right. I'm not one damn bit better than you
are. We're both the same."

"No." She slid off the stool and walked very slowly
down the ramp. "There's on big, *big* difference. I
loved you. You never loved me. I love you still.
Despite all the terrible things you've done to me. The
lies. The other women. I can't stop. And God knows
I've tried." She stopped inches away and whispered.
"But as long as I live, Buck, I'll never stop . . . loving
you."

"You're good," I said. "The hands. The voice. The
pauses. The blinking to keep the tears back. As good
as I've seen. The words are crap—dialogue's never
been your strong point—but I wouldn't want a syllable
changed. I want to remember you always . . . just like
that."

I turned and started up the aisle.

"No. Don't go. I need you. I love you. You said
we're both the same. We belong together."

She grabbed my shirt.

"It's over." I kept going. The shirt ripped. She fell,
tackling me around the knees.

"I won't let you go. You're mine. You belong to me."

I pulled her hands off and walked on.

"You're going to *her.* That young whore! No one
walks out on me. *I'll have you killed! NO! I'LL HAVE
HER KILLED."*

Then the door swung shut, putting her behind me,
as I walked quickly down the crowded, noisy, sunny
street.

20

The door of the small Spanish house on La Peer south of Wilshire opened and a frail old man with a white beard, glasses stuck up on his forehead, peered out.

"Mr. McLeod?"

"Thank you for seeing me so late, Mr. Bernstein."

"Any friend of Tim Cassidy's is always welcome."

Most of the living room was in shadow. We sat down. There was a long-necked reading lamp behind his worn armchair.

"Before you say anything, it must be a picture. And it must be in trouble. And I've been retired for two years."

"Do you like it?"

He shrugged slightly. "I miss the excitement. The people. Making good film. That's bad."

"What's good?"

He smiled and patted the thick leather book on the coffee table. "I've made the acquaintance of Spinoza. It would have been a terrible thing, dying, not having known Spinoza."

"I don't know what to say to that, Mr. Bernstein. So I'll get right to the point. I star in and own *Hunter*. A new television series. A hit. We've been shooting at Magnitude. My lawyer caught them and some other people with their hand in the till. Monday morning I have to start shooting on a new lot."

"That's impossible. This is Friday night."

"Everything's location. Except my office set. So we can schedule that the last day."

"Mr. McLeod, I'm not interested in coming out of retirement to work on a *television series* that's in trouble."

"Mr. Bernstein, I know you made only features. The best features. I know you were head of production for Selznick when he was the best. That you handpicked your crews and they were the best."

"Mr. McLeod, why flatter me after I've said no?"

"Because you care about making good film. Forget this is television. Cassidy's directing. The script is good. And I want you to put together the best crew you ever had."

"You can't afford them. Not for television."

"You're wrong, Mr. Bernstein. We can—*if* we pay them a bit over scale, and give them a piece of the action."

"Profit-sharing?"

"Why not? Now, the only way they can make extra money is by being slow and getting overtime. Figure out an incentive pay plan to make them work faster."

"I've always wanted to do that, Mr. McLeod. But I've never found a producer who was willing. . . . Hmmm . . . with so little shooting, personnel shouldn't be such a problem."

"They may be, Mr. Bernstein. This is delicate. But I don't know how to meet it except head on."

"Please."

"My co-star is black. I wouldn't feel right working with a lily-white crew. I want blacks, Mexicans and Orientals on it."

Bernstein stroked his beard thoughtfully.

"Some of the very best men won't like working with inexperienced minority boys—when old friends with years of seniority can't get a job."

"Then I don't want them."

"That's going to make putting together a fine crew extremely difficult."

"When it comes down to it, Mr. Bernstein, though

I don't mean to be rude, if *you* don't think it's worth the trouble, I don't want you, either."

The little old man slowly smiled.

"Mr. McLeod, Spinoza and I think it's well worth the trouble. Do I have a free hand in picking the men?"

"Yes. But I have final authority on everything. I'm bringing three men with me: Maury Kramer, Big Joe Greenberg—"

"They're both first-rate."

"And Eddie Riordan, who gaffs all the stunts and has been picking locations and checking the bills. He'll be associate producer. Unless you want the credit?"

"Production manager has always been good enough for me. Who's the producer?"

"Mordecai Gaunt. A writer. He knows nothing about production and I don't want him to learn. His job is scripts."

"What about money?"

"UBC pays me two hundred and thirty thousand an episode. There's no agent's commission off the top."

"I was referring to my salary."

"Pay yourself whatever you think is fair, then add fifteen percent of the profits."

He stared at me in amazement. "Do you know what you're saying, Mr. McLeod?"

"Sure. I'll get you cheaper that way. Don't smile. You also have to be my business manager. And everything's in a mess. You'll want to go over all the details with my lawyer."

He picked up a yellow lined pad. "What's his number?"

"He's outside in the car. I'll bring him in."

He chuckled and shook his head.

After he and Juan started going over the figures, I said, "Good-bye, Mr. Bernstein."

"Where are you off to in such a hurry?"

"New York."

"New York! You can't go to New York at a time like this!"

"I have to."

"No, you don't, Mr. McLeod——"

The phone rang. It was Eddie.

"She's here."

"You're sure?"

"Been here two days. She's testing for *Nicholas and Alexandra*."

"You're right, Mr. Bernstein. I don't have to go to New York."

I shot up Laurel on two screaming wheels. She'd rented a little wood-shingle house out on the point of Lookout with all the city lights blazing before it.

I pounded on the door.

"Yes?" she asked calmly. "Who is it?"

"McLeod."

There was a long, long pause, then the door swung open and she stood there. She was in a pink-and-white Victorian bathrobe and the long red hair was tied back with a pink and white bow, and that nose and mouth and cheekbones were all there——right in front of me.

"Yes?" she asked crisply.

I didn't know what the hell to say. Where to begin.

"It's about a part," I said stupidly. "In my series. You'd be perfect for it. It shoots Monday. It's the lead. The heroine."

She started to laugh. "Oh, Michael," she gasped. "That's so . . . *tacky*."

Then we were in each other's arms and I was kissing that marvelous warm mouth.

I broke away. "Tabitha, I owe you an explanation."

"No," she said. "Just tell me how it stands with her."

"It's over," I said. "From now on I'm with you."

She studied me. "Yes," she said very seriously. "It may not be for long. And I don't see any castles in Ireland——but we'll have everything else."

Then shyly she leaned her head against my chest, and I gently picked her up and carried her into the bedroom.

God, I was nervous as we sat reading the scene in Cassidy's high-ceilinged library, the late-afternoon sun glistening on the brass bars stretching across the walls.

Tabitha had the first speech—a long one. Mordecai had done another lovely script. A tough call girl—the only witness to a syndicate hit—and I do the dumbest thing in the world, fall in love.

I sat up with a start. They were both staring at me.

"What's the matter?"

"It's your cue," Cassidy said gruffly.

"Oh." I read my line.

She went on. It was her big emotional scene, but she was reading it quietly, thoughtfully; frowning at some of the lines; taking long pauses.

Jesus! I thought. *What if he doesn't like her?*

I studied him. He sat there poker-faced, head tilted slightly.

For Christ's sake! Tabitha! Show some flash! Some fire! She was coming up to the end. *Go! Go! Go!*

But she trailed off quietly, and thoughtfully closed the script.

"Thank you," Cassidy said gravely, then picked up a stick and began whittling.

"Well!" I said. "One of the things that's so useful in a reading like this is that I can see where Mordecai is going to have to make some line changes."

"The lines are fine," Cassidy grunted.

"Yes," Tabitha said. She stood. "Excuse me," she said politely to Cassidy, and walked across the room.

He didn't take his eyes off me. After the door closed, there was a long wait. Finally I said, "How did you like the reading?"

"Not much," he said.

"Tim," I said desperately. "It's the way the kids work these days. They learned it all from that Goddam

Strasberg at the Actors Studio. They're always *exploring*. They don't want to get *results* too quickly. And they . . . mumble!"

Those hooded eyes were watching me like a hawk.

"Tim," I begged, "let me go talk to her. Run over the scene a few times. It won't take long. Then we'll do it again. She's really one helluva actress."

"Oh, *she's* fine." He stood up with the flicker of a smile. "I didn't like you."

Dinner was a crown roast of lamb, crusted and dark on the outside, rare pink on the inside; new potatoes no bigger than the first joint of your thumb; platters of delicate, fresh asparagus in melted butter darkly speckled with fresh-ground pepper.

Tabitha spoke easily and openly and was funny. Maria and Eddie and Kryellah laughed a lot. Kate from her end of the table watched her with a strange expression. Luciana and Antonella, who sat poker straight in their Sunday dresses, shot adoring sidewise glances at her.

"What's the wine?" I asked.

"La Tache," Cassidy said.

"It's something," Kryellah said.

"We save it for special occasions."

Dessert was a piping-hot soufflé that tasted of orange and vanilla, and the pretty Mexican maids, shyly glancing at Tabitha, brought in ice buckets of champagne.

My God, I thought, *I'm going to have Tabitha sitting at the other end of my table with our children between us saying grace*—

Luciana pinched me sharply on the elbow.

Cassidy was standing at the head of the table.

"To Tabitha . . . we've waited for you for a long time."

"Oh, *yes!*" said Kate.

And we all stood and drank to her.

* * *

Early Sunday morning, Bernstein stood outside the Goldwyn gate, black umbrella protecting him from the grey drizzle, reading Spinoza.

I opened the car door. "I'm glad you got this lot, Mr. Bernstein."

"It's appropriate," he said, climbing in. "It's a quality lot." He looked at me over his glasses. "I ran your shows yesterday. They're quality, too, Mr. McLeod. And so is your performance."

I thanked him and to change the subject nodded at the empty road ahead, with the rain slanting against the big white stages. "Nothing more deserted than a lot on a Sunday morning."

"Appearances can be deceiving, Mr. McLeod. Park here, please."

He showed me into the office suite.

The phones were ringing. He picked one up.

"No. No one will be in today. I have nothing to say." He hung up.

"Have you got a press agent, Mr. McLeod?"

"No."

"I think you better get one. You're big news, Mr. McLeod. We're getting hundreds of requests for interviews."

"I won't talk to them."

"All the more reason to have a press agent. If you have no objection I'll get one."

"Fine."

Fifteen minutes later we started the crew interviews. Eddie, Cassidy and I sat behind the desk while Bernstein brought in, one by one, three candidates for each job: best boy, boom man, dolly pusher, etc. There were the leathery old-timers we all knew well and had worked with many times.

Then there were the new faces—

A small wiry brown-black man in an elegantly cut double-breasted white suit bowed to us, very sure of himself.

"I am Alfred de Burry." He had a soft West Indian accent. "I am the *best* first assistant director in the world."

Cassidy grinned and tugged at his ear. "Why?" he asked.

"Because as an ex-dancer I am offended by wasted movements. I must have maximum energy with minimum effort. My deck must not make the click-clank of obsolescent machinery but *purrrrr* like a happy tomcat, who, incidentally, also never makes a wasted motion. You must meet my assistant, for I do not work without him."

He opened the door.

A huge coal-black man came in, grinning warmly.

"This is best *second* assistant director in the world. I call him Al, too. Not because it is his name but, thus, we are known as Big Al and Little Al. It is a touch theatrical, perhaps, but, after all, that is our métier. *N'est-ce pas?*"

They bowed and left.

We looked at each other and nodded.

Then there were the kids with no money from Watts and the Barrio who—somewhere—had worked in film and fallen in love with it. And—somehow—had managed to claw a card out of the union. And now stood before us with desperate eyes, wanting the job so badly that nerves knotted up—they'd stammer, make mistakes, contradict themselves.

The thin, whispering Chinese boy with a degree from Cal Tech, who'd photographed an award-winning 16-millimeter film on azaleas.

The stolid, powerful Navajo who'd helped out the prop man when a feature shot on his reservation, followed him back to Hollywood, worked for years on non-union commercials.

The good-looking, slim young black, tall as Jabbar, with a Fu Manchu that couldn't cover a livid scar that ran from one ear across his mouth.

"LeRoy, all these companies you say you gaffed these porno flicks for," Eddie asked. "They still in business?"

"Shit, man, you gotta be kidding. They outa business day they finish shooting. They just one step ahead of the Vice."

"If we can't check the companies, how do we know if you're good?"

"Hire me and I'll show you."

"Thank you. We'll let you know."

He shrugged and hopelessly walked out.

Eddie tossed a wad of paper against the wall. "How the hell can you tell if he's any good from those credits?"

"By the man," Cassidy said. "LeRoy will do fine."

When we came to the last category—gaffer—Bernstein came back inside alone and closed the door sharply. He was upset.

"There is a man outside I didn't send for."

"That would be Houlihan," Cassidy said. "He called me late last night and I told him to come over. I don't know how you feel about him, Ira, but I think he's the best gaffer I ever worked with."

"Sober. Drunk he's as dangerous and destructive a man as I've ever seen."

"Agreed," Cassidy said. "But he swore to me he's off the sauce."

"I'm not running a rehabilitation camp."

"Well, since he's here, Mr. Bernstein," I said, "let's talk to him."

Houlihan came in pulling off his cap, revealing his huge white shaved skull. I'd forgotten the sheer bulk of the man. He was only a few inches taller than I was, but twice as thick from the chest through the spine. His biceps bulged through his cheap coat, wet from the rain, as he sat down.

He stared at us desperately, twisting his cap in his

hands. Suddenly he reminded me of Victor McLaglen before the IRA court in *The Informer*.

"I haven't worked in over a year. No one will give me a job. Oh, I've been *house painting*," he said scathingly. "But, my God, I've been in pictures all my life." He held his enormous hand out straight before him. "I still have my touch. And drunk or sober I'm the best. No!" He slammed his fist into his hand. "I didn't mean that. Drunk I'm no good to anyone.

"What I meant, gentlemen, was if you give me a chance, I'll break my back to repay you. And if you decide not to, bless you for seeing me, and the best of luck to you on your show."

There was a long silence after he closed the door, then Eddie said, "Jesus, give him a break."

"I would," said Cassidy.

Bernstein sat cold and motionless at the end of the table.

"What do you think, Mr. Bernstein?"

"I think you Irish are sentimental about drunks. Alcoholism shows a flaw in a man's character. A major flaw."

"Mr. Bernstein," I asked, "doesn't Spinoza believe in Redemption?"

He sighed and softly drummed his fingers on the desk. "The problem is—does Bernstein?"

It was a strange, marvelous feeling to open my door and see her stretched out in front of the fireplace, frowning over the script. She smiled and threw her arms out wide. "Hel—*lo*, McLeod," she said in her lovely, husky voice.

We made slow, gentle, floating love, there on the bearskin. Then ran laughing, naked through the rainy night down to the surf, and hand in hand dove through the dark booming waves until, chilled to the bone, we raced back to the house. After we toweled each other off, I threw myself down on the bearskin, gasping for breath.

"Poor old geezer. You're suffering from exposure. I'll have to give you mouth-to-mouth resuscitation."

"Ummm ... ummm ... you give such splendid resuscitation, Miss Weston, I hate to point out that's not my mouth—*ouch!*"

21

The early morning red sun glinted on the posh Singles Only complex towering over the ramshackle rooming houses on the beach in Venice.

I pulled up in the parking area, noticing all vehicles were parked under neatly numbered signs.

"Good morning, Mr. McLeod. Miss Weston." Little Al opened the door for Tabitha. Big Al, smiling, handed us steaming coffee mugs with our names stenciled on them.

The Old Timers, in their neatly pressed sun-tans, and close-cut neatly combed grey hair, stood smoking, drinking coffee, smiling, chatting; reminding me of a group of master sergeants in an Army stockade surrounded by young, long-haired, blue-jeaned prisoners.

The studio car pulled up. I nudged Tabitha. Cassidy got out. Squinted at the rooming house, then walked quickly through the men in that pigeon-toed, straight-backed, loose-kneed walk. They stared at his back, then fell in behind him.

"He's marvelous," Tabitha whispered.

He stopped. Dug his heel in the sand.

"Mark it," Maury called. The wooden T was dropped.

"Gentlemen," Little Al said crisply. "Mr. Cassidy

will walk through this with the first team. Do not work. Simply watch. When he has finished, if you have any questions, ask them."

He bowed to Cassidy, who nodded at the crew. "Morning, gentlemen. Maury, might be nice if you put a riser on the McAlister. Get on a fifty about three feet above Mike's head. Don't want to know where he is. Walk, Mike. . . ."

"Dolly track."

"Just shoot his face and the sand at his feet . . . Stop."

"Mark him."

"Now, Mike, knock on the door."

I did. Tabitha opened it, scowling. "Who are you?" She played the whole scene wrong. Sullen. Down.

"Cut."

"Let's go to work."

Little Al snapped his fingers. Two stand-ins stepped instantly on our marks.

As the crew slowly, stiffly, uncomfortably started to work, Bernstein, looking at his wristwatch, crossed his fingers and toasted me with his coffee cup. I toasted him back. Then hurried over to where Tabitha stood frowning over the script at the foot of Cassidy's chair.

"Tabitha, it'll play better if you don't—"

"Fuck off, Movie Star." Her eyes were blazing.

"Now wait one damn minute, I—"

"You heard the lady," Cassidy snapped.

Steaming, I walked over to where Eddie was watching them lay the dolly track.

"What's bugging you?"

"Goddam Actors Studio bullshit. All of a sudden she decides to play the scene mean. All wrong. I told her how to play it last night."

"Maybe she didn't like what you told her."

"Then she should at least have had the simple professional courtesy to discuss it with me. After all, I am the star of the show."

"That's what it says in *TV Guide.*"

"I'll just have to teach her a lesson."

"What are you going to do?" he asked nervously.

"Underplay her into the ground. I'll start so low she'll never be able to——"

"Now, Mike, she's——"

"Stay out of it, Eddie. It's for her own good."

Al called places. In rehearsal, to fool her, I hit the lines hard. She squinted at me thoughtfully, and said hers so low the mixer had to ask her for more projection.

"OK. Let's shoot it," Cassidy growled.

Slate.

"Speed."

"Action."

I walked through the sand, knocked on the door.

"Hi," Tabitha said, with a big smile, flirting. "Who are you?"

Thrown, I gulped, "Unh . . . Mike Hunter."

I never caught up the whole scene.

"Cut. Print."

Cassidy walked off, smiling. Eddie was doubled up.

Tabitha kissed me.

"You're going to have to do better than that, Movie Star," she whispered. "Or I'll act you right off the fucking screen."

Cassidy staged us from one side of the slum alley to the other. Out of dark shadow into dazzling sunlight. Kryellah sensed I was witholding information about the girl and was pushing me—hard. I'd get mad and walk away into a single, he'd stop me, I'd turn it into an over-the-shoulder, then he'd step up into an even two. I'd walk away again.

Eight pages, all in one, long, stop-and-go, pulling dolly shot. It was beautiful and a ball breaker.

As the stand-ins stepped on the first of a labyrinth of chalk marks, Kryellah and I walked off and joined the others, standing together, watching the crew.

Houlihan, floppy Panama hat bobbing, darted

around, huge fingers delicately pointing exactly where he wanted lights spotted. LeRoy bounded in, set down a lamp, clicked it on and flooded it all in one motion.

Houlihan gave him a grin and an AOK sign.

Big Joe Greenberg was showing the dolly pusher— the Navajo boy—how to cut the wheels when it was stopped.

The Chinese boy racked focus. Big Joe checked what he was doing, changed something, patted him on the shoulder.

"They're going to make it," I said.

"It's too soon to say, Mr. McLeod," Bernstein said cautiously.

"No," Cassidy said. "They're falling together."

Tabitha came over and slid her hand in mine.

"Damn, but it's a pretty thing to watch," Cassidy said.

"What?" Tabitha asked.

"The new crew coming together," Eddie said.

"I don't see anything," she said after a moment. "What should I look for?"

I smiled. "Do you know what a gaffer does? Or a boom man? Or a dolly pusher?"

"Of course not, darling."

"Then even if I pointed it out to you, you couldn't see it."

"That's ridiculous. I can tell if a man's good at what he does. A fisherman or a hod carrier or a ditch-digger."

"No, Tabitha," Cassidy said. "Women just think they can. Like Kate. I used to take her to the Friday-night fights. She'd take a fancy to some kid dancing around throwing a lot of leather. Was sure he was doing a helluva job. Never could understand how he'd end up flat on his back."

We laughed.

"I see," Tabitha said dangerously. Smouldering, she studied the sweating men, some stripped to their waists, working up and down the length of the alley.

"I've discovered one thing wrong with your crew."

"Why, what's that, Miss Weston?" Bernstein asked.

"There are no women on it."

"Women?" Bernstein said, amazed.

"You can't have women on a crew!" I said.

"Of course not," Eddie said.

"It would never work," Kryellah said.

"How would you know?" She was furious. "You stand around taking bows for being such enlightened, liberal, equal-opportunity employers, when you're practicing the worst kind of discrimination. That crew should be half women!"

"That's impossible!" I said.

"No! You're impossible! You smug, reactionary, bigoted Neanderthal *men!*" She stormed off.

Stunned, we stared after her.

"Remember, it's only her first day," Cassidy murmured. "By tomorrow the shyness should have worn off."

The last location we shot that day was the old merry-go-round on the Santa Monica Pier. The scene where we fell in love. It was full of strange, interesting beats. We were tough and street-smart, watching each other warily as knife fighters, but somehow, somewhere we had to fall in love. Cassidy ignored our pleas to pin it down.

Struggling, we kept walking through it in the echoing old all-wooden building. The late-afternoon sun slanting in turned us fire-engine red as we rode the beautifully carved wooden horses, sliding up and down in tempo to the calliope playing as we whirled around; and always we were right on the edge of something marvelous that we couldn't get.

"Ooooh!" She threw her hands out in frustration. "I could explore this all week!"

"You do that," Cassidy said. "I'm shooting it. Now."

"Roll it!" Little Al yelled.

She grabbed my hand. "No, I've got to have more time."

"That's life," I said. "You never get all the time you need."

She looked at me strangely.

"Action."

Immediately she was the strange, half-tough, half-vulnerable hooker. Everything seemed a little off. There were marvelous moments when we connected completely, and others when we slid by each other. We were coming up to the end and still hadn't fallen in love, and I was getting panicky. I didn't know what the hell was going to happen. I held out the box of popcorn. She took a handful. Suddenly her jaw stopped as if she'd bit a stone. She stared at me and stared at me. Then leaned quickly forward, kissed me, and stepped back, blushing like an awkward fifteen-year-old. I reached out, took her hand, and we stood there—in love—in the shadowy, echoing hall.

"Cut. Print," Cassidy said. The men stood still, staring at her. Then began applauding.

"Was I all right?" she shyly whispered to me, bobbing her head to them.

"Great," I said.

"Oh, thank God, Michael, I've been so afraid I'd embarrass you."

I walked quickly off in the corner behind the base of the boom because I didn't want anyone to see me crying.

We pulled on the lot at six-thirty, said good-bye to the crew, had a fast drink with Eddie, Cassidy, Kryellah and Bernstein. After they left, she said, "I'm bushed, darling. Do we have to go out to the beach? My house is closer."

"Why not stay here?"

"Here?"

"Sure. That sofa turns into a bed. This, Miss Weston, is a *star's* dressing room."

She clapped her hands in delight. "How lascivious!"

We showered together, and tired as I was the suds and hot spray and the feel of her soaped body against mine excited me, and we made love, standing in the tub.

Later we cued each other over sent-in Chinese food. She fell asleep in the middle of a line. I took the script out of her hand. Tucked her in. And, looking down on her marvelous, sleeping face, thought: *this has been the best day of my life.*

"Cut. Print."

Kryellah stared at her. "Je-*sus*. That's some actress."

"Yeah." I tried not to sound too proud. But he grinned. He knew. They all knew. You could tell the way they watched our scenes.

Cassidy didn't say much to us. We didn't say much to each other. You never have to when things are good. A grunt here. A "How's this look?" A "Little more" or "Little less" is all you need.

After "Cut. Print," Cassidy often would say, "That's good." And the crew, stripped to the waist, watching intently, would nod agreement, then smile proudly as they'd start work on the next setup.

That night when we drove on the lot the crew trooped in with us to the viewing room. Part of the Bernstein-McLeod system was that they were paid to watch dailies. There was cold beer, Cokes, pretzels and cheese and crackers.

The lights went out.

Tabitha's first close-up flashed on. There was a gasp from the crew.

Sweet Christ, but she was something to see! Maury had caught the sparkle in her eyes; the fill didn't flatten out the hollows under the cheekbones, and that dark mane of red hair was broken only by the kick of a few highlights.

She grabbed my hand and scrunched back against the seat, frowning at herself.

As Cassidy's hat slapped across the lens, I shouted out into the dark, packed room, "Maury, that's the best damn close-up I've ever seen."

There was a deep grunt of agreement.

The scene with Kryellah in the alley was a stunner. When the merry-go-round master came up, everyone gasped. Maury had gotten a fabulous soft, foggy pastel into it. I couldn't watch it from outside but was right back there walking around with her. She bit into the popcorn, kissed me, blushed, and as we fell in love through the windows in the back a sailboat slid slowly across the screen above our heads.

The lights banged on. They started clapping. I shoved Tabitha up on her feet. They cheered. She blew them a kiss and hauled me up. I pulled up Cassidy, Kryellah, then Eddie and Maury and Joe. We applauded them and more people were pulled up until we were all standing, applauding each other.

Afterward out in the dark summer night, Bernstein said, "By feature standards—any standards—that is very fine film."

Tabitha kissed him. "Congratulations, dear Mr. Bernstein."

"For what?"

"Putting together in one day such a great crew."

"They are not yet a great crew," he said.

Startled, she said, "Why not?"

"First," he said severely, "like a man—they must be tested by adversity."

Cy Cerutti, the editor, stepped up. "I haven't seen anything like that since *To Have and Have Not.*" He walked away, shaking his head.

"What's he mean by that?" Tabitha said.

Cassidy said, "It was Bacall's first picture; Bogart fell in love with her and Hawks got it all on film."

"Oh, I'd love to see it."

"You really should," I said. "The similarities are

amazing. A great male star, using all his technique to make a talented newcomer look good."

"You bastard." She threw her beer can at me. I ducked and took off down the street.

She chased me, shouting, "You insensitive, illiterate, Mick bastard!"

The boys, getting into their cars, cheered. "Go get him, Tabitha."

I whipped into the apartment, tore off my clothes and stretched out on the bed.

She threw open the door.

"OK. You've caught me. What are you going to do about it? ... Oh ... *oh* ... OH! ... That's really a low blow."

We had dinner across the street in the Formosa. After we ladled out the beef with snow peas, lobster Cantonese, and Peking duck, she frowned thoughtfully at me. "I want to talk about your acting."

"I never thought you'd get around to—"

"Shut up, McLeod. This is serious. ... I can always see what an actor's doing. He decided to play boredom instead of anger. And I say: good choice or bad choice. Except when it's *really* good.

"Example. In *On the Waterfront,* after they've killed Brando's pigeons, Eva Marie says: 'We've got to get out of here. Let's go upstate.'

" 'What'll I do?' he asks.

" 'We'll get a farm.'

" '*Farm* . . .' he says."

"I remember." She held out her hand to silence me.

"What he did with one word was hand me a Greek tragedy. A man's whole life in one *syllable*. And I couldn't see how he did it. I saw it over and over again. And still don't know what he did. Well, that's real acting.

"And you're that good. Oh, not all the time. But neither was Brando. I can't tell when I'm working with you. But in your scene with Kryellah, you had three moments when I couldn't see the gears shift. Seamless moments I couldn't take apart."

She reached over and took my hand.

"I'm proud of you, Michael. You're a real artist."

I didn't know what to say.

"Oh, darling, I've embarrassed you. Poor baby, hasn't anyone ever told you how good you are?"

"Sure. But they didn't know anything."

She laughed, threw her arms around my neck and kissed me. Past her hair, I saw the bartender watching us closely, and remembered as we came in that he'd left a busy bar to go to the pay phone.

"Let's go." I signed the check.

As we walked up the street, a car pulled up and a man carrying a camera ran into the Formosa.

"Let's live on our lovely lot forever," Tabitha said dreamily. "We'll make good film all day with our marvelous crew that has yet to meet with adversity, and poontang all night."

"*Poontang?* Where did you learn—"

"Excuse me, Mr. McLeod," said the cop on the gate. "There's a Mr. Hundsley from UBC come to see you. I let him wait in your dressing room. Hope that's OK."

"Fine."

Hal had on white buckskin shoes with black rubber soles, white flannel trousers, a striped red-white-and-blue blazer, and he held an old-fashioned straw hat.

"A boater!" Tabitha said happily. I introduced them, Hal complimented her on the dailies, she thanked him, excused herself. Hal thoughtfully tapped a cigarette on his gold case.

"I'm not here as your friend."

"I understand."

"Honey forgives you and wants you to come home."

"No way."

"She has important things she must say to you."

"I have nothing to say to her."

"Now, Buck, there's always something to be said between man and wife."

"Her lawyer to my lawyer."

He lit the cigarette with a snap of his Dunhill.

"Now that I've discharged my duties to UBC could I have a vodka and tonic?"

"Sure." I expected him to relax but he sat there frowning, stirring his drink. It's quiet on a lot at night. The only sound came from music editing, where a few bars of a chase theme were played again and again.

He said abruptly, looking straight at me: "Y'know, Buck, Honey's been top dog in a tough town for years. She makes Lucy and Loretta and Marlo and Cara look like Girl Scouts."

"What are you trying to say, Hal?"

He sighed and rubbed his palms on his thighs. "If this split came about because of the pressures of work and the show—and there was no other woman involved—she *might* accept it . . . eventually. But when her show's slipping—to have it hit the papers that you left her for Tabitha, a more beautiful woman, a much *younger* woman . . ."

He shook his head.

"She won't let it happen."

"It already has."

"Buck." He was very upset. "She's a dangerous woman."

"Meaning?"

"Hire some bodyguards."

I laughed. "For Christ's sake, Hal, I can take care of myself."

"You probably can." He set down his drink and stood. "But it wouldn't be you she'd go after. Good night."

I opened the door to the bedroom. Tabitha slept soundly, head thrown back, mouth slightly open. I leaned against the doorframe and, smoking, thought for a long time.

*   *   *

The next night as we drove up to the gates, extra cops were trying to hold back the mob of photographers.

"Duck," I said, as I drove through and the flashbulbs began popping.

"No," she said. "I'm not ashamed of anything."

As we got out of the car, Eddie asked, "You eating off the lot?"

"I was planning to."

"I better let you out the back gate."

We sat in the corner booth at Dom's, running lines, eating the marvelous smoking-hot barbecued chicken and drinking his tart Italian rosé.

There were only two couples finishing dinner at the red-checked tables. But the bar was crowded, and there was the usual sound of arguments, jokes and laughter. Suddenly it stopped.

I looked up. Honey was coming through the kitchen door, Benjy behind her. She wore a blue suit and a blue beret with a white pompon that bounced with every step.

Tabitha looked up as she stopped—smiling—before us.

"Hello, Buck, long time no see."

Benjy pulled a chair out from the next table, and she sat down.

"Aren't you going to introduce us?" she asked.

"No," I said.

"Benjy, it's terribly quiet in here."

He went over to the jukebox, slid some money in, and the intro to her *Little White Lies* floated out into the silent room.

"Honey, either you get the hell out or we will."

"No," Tabitha said. "I want to hear what she has to say."

"Good for you, Tabitha. I hope you don't mind if I call you Tabitha. You're just as I'd imagined you'd be. Young and lovely with a level head on your shoulders.

That's what I'd hoped for. Because Buck *is* impulsive. He drinks and gets into fights and is always having a little something with an extra or bit player. Not that I'm complaining; I knew that when I bought him."

"Bought him?" Tabitha said carefully.

"Oh, didn't he tell you? Yes, indeed. Buck cost me forty-nine thousand in old debts and another seven thousand—before the wedding—for haircuts, shoe-shines, razor blades—"

"You got it all back plus two hundred thousand interest."

Tabitha put her hand on mine, signaling me to be quiet.

Honey saw it and her mouth tightened.

"But all that was part of our deal. You, Tabitha, are not."

She paused. When Tabitha didn't say anything, she went on.

"I think a girl has to know what kind of a deal she's going to get from a man. Especially if the man's Buck. I have a hunch, Tabitha, that he looks pretty good to you. The big star of his own hit series. Lots of money for clothes and jewelry and trips. . . . *But it won't be that way.* If he walks out on me, he'll have nothing. No divorce. No show. No house. No money. He'll end up with nothing but bills and lawsuits, and I'm sure a level-headed girl like you won't be happy shacked up with an over-the-hill actor on unemployment insurance."

"It sounds marvelous. I hope you're through because you're beginning to bore me."

Honey's eyes narrowed. "I certainly wouldn't want to do that, Tabitha. But I do have a few more things to tell you—"

"There's a word I've always despised," Tabitha said. "But it suits you perfectly. It's cunt." Honey gasped. "Get out of here, cunt."

Honey stood up abruptly. Benjy slid her chair back under the other table. She looked as if she had more she wanted to say, but started instead toward the kitchen.

From the jukebox her voice purred:

> *"The moon was all aglow*
> *And heaven was in your eyes . . ."*

"Look out," I yelled.

Honey wheeled and drove her nails for Tabitha's eyes. Tabitha blocked her hand away and, on her feet, hit her hard in the stomach with her right.

Honey took two quick steps backward, then sat down heavily on the floor, her skirt up to her crotch, her pretty long legs stretched out in a V.

The bar became a freeze-frame. Everyone stopped dead in the middle of a gesture, gaping at her. She scrambled to her feet and ran off through the kitchen while her voice sang out lushly:

> *"The night that you told me*
> *Those little white lies."*

22

Late afternoon of the last day. Blazing hot. Everything brown. Brown ground. Brown rocks. Brown leaves on brown trees. And we were in trouble.

The pickup truck far below, snaking its way up Malibu Canyon, was bringing the new camera. An hour ago our Mitchell had buckled.

The Santana blew harder. We turned our backs against the flying brown dust. Cassidy and Maury stood at the end of the ridge, studying the puffy black clouds building up over Hollywood, our next location.

The truck pulled up in a cloud of dust. The waiting men sprang into action: grabbing the camera; running it over to the dolly; bolting it to the plate; loading the magazines; threading the film.

"Three minutes," Little Al said.

We stepped on our marks so they could check our light.

Tabitha kicked at a rock. "Dammit. I'm dried up. Empty."

"Find something new to play."

"What?"

"Are you a city girl or a country girl?"

"Why?"

"City girl—up here—might be afraid she'd turn her ankle in the dirt. Jump at the sound of a cricket."

"That's *good*. Don't say another word."

We shot it without rehearsal.

"Cut. Print."

"Oh, I know I can do it better," Tabitha said. "Please, let's do it again."

"No," Cassidy said. "That's a print."

Bernstein said, "After you load, we're going to eat here. The catering trucks are on the way. Thirty-eight-minute lunch. Then we'll make the move."

Houlihan slammed his hat on the ground. "Christ, let's get out of the Goddam dust. Make the move and then eat."

"What the hell is this—a debating society?" Cassidy asked icily.

Ashamed, Houlihan picked up his hat and they went to work.

We shot down the canyon toward the blue sweep of the Pacific, and the tiny red tile roofs on the border of the highway and the white stretch of sand.

"I was awful," Tabitha said angrily. "The crew didn't listen. They were bored."

"They're tired. They've been shooting night for night all week."

"So have I."

"It's not the same. Ever try to sleep in the daytime with kids playing and your wife vacuuming?"

"No, I never have," she said snottily.

"Don't get a hair up your ass. We've got a rough night ahead of us."

"Damn Cassidy! Why wouldn't he let me do it again?"

"Because his job is getting the whole show shot. Not manicuring one scene. He's got one hell of a rough night ahead. He's figuring out now how good we're going to be at three o'clock this morning."

"All that Hemingway bullshit about grace under pressure. Well, don't worry about me. I'll be fine."

"I hope so," I said carefully. "But you're going to have to do a lot better than this."

She didn't say a word for a while, then touched my hand on the wheel. "I had that coming. I've been a brat. I'm sorry, darling."

"A swim will do us both good."

But the water was hot and oily with heavy ground swells.

As I got in the car she was staring at the house so strangely I asked, "What's the matter?"

"I was remembering the end of summer vacation when I was sixteen. I sat in the beach wagon, weeping, while Father locked up the cottage at Falmouth. I kept saying, 'I'm never, ever going to see it again!' 'Why, of course you are,' Father said. 'Next June.' But he sold it that winter and bought the house at Quogue. I was right. I never did see it again."

I took Sunset in. She sat in the corner wrapped in her thoughts. Once I turned on KMPC for some music, but without saying a word she flicked it off.

* * *

It was about eight as I came up to Vine. The setting sun shining through the thick black clouds turned everything a poisonous green. Gusts of wind spiraled newspapers up off sidewalks, struck down wire trash baskets.

I turned north on Vine, glancing at the men unloading the arcs in front of the old ABC theater.

Tabitha screamed. I hit the brakes. Reporters swarmed over the car. Mikes were stuck in our faces. Cameras ground away. Lights blinded us.

"How do you feel about your wife's suicide?"

"Suicide?"

"This must be the girl?"

"Look this way, dear!"

"Did you have any idea this would happen when you broke up the marriage?"

Eddie, shoving heads aside, jumped on the running board. "Hard right, slow."

I swung the wheel and drove straight toward the shouting faces. Big Al shoved them out of the way. Then our cops held them back while I drove in the parking lot, and slammed the Cyclone gate shut behind me.

"What happened?"

Eddie said, "She's alive. Drive to your trailer. A hundred cameras are shooting you."

Inside the trailer Hal waited with a TV news crew.

"Get 'em out," I said.

"It's all right. They're ours," he said calmly.

"How's Honey?"

"Fit as a fiddle. She took an overdose of sleeping pills. But by one of those incredible coincidences Benjy found her five seconds later, and rushed her to Cedars, stopping en route only to release her suicide note."

"What's it say?"

"She begs *you,*" he said to Tabitha, "to give him up."

"Christ," I said.

"I've roughed out a statement for you to give. You know Harry Gordon?"

The white-haired, lantern-jawed anchor man grinned and waved. "Sure. Hi yah, Buck?" Then, remembering the circumstances, shifted to a somber expression.

I sat Tabitha down in the corner.

"Can I get you a drink?" She shook her head. "You all right?"

"Fine," she said. "I'm mad."

Harry said, "Want to rehearse it?"

I glanced at the cue cards and shook my head. They lit up the clip-ons.

Harry said, "I'm here in Buck McLeod's dressing room, right in the heart of Hollywood, where he is shooting his tremendously successful UBC television series, *Hunter*. I think I hear him coming."

I walked into the shot.

"Buck, what's your reaction to this tragedy?"

"It's a shock, Harry. A terrible shock. But I understand she's going to be all right."

"That's our information."

"Thank God for that."

"Amen. Tell me, Buck, is it true that your marriage was on the rocks?"

"Harry, as in any marriage, there were strains—tensions. Plus the pressures of both shows. I wouldn't be honest if I didn't admit there were problems."

"Buck, do you think you can work them out?"

"All I can say at this time is that must be between Honey and me."

"I understand. Buck, do you have a word for Honey's fans?"

"I know how much your cards and letters mean to her. So please write."

"That's Honey Holly, care of UBC-TV, Hollywood, California. And thank you . . . Buck McLeod."

"Cut," Hal said.

"Jesus," I said.

"I know, but we've got to get something from you

on the air." He flicked his eyes outside. I followed him out. "Honey's been on CBS begging you to come to her bedside. Josiah wants you to go."

"No."

He started to say something, then shrugged and left.

The reporters and television crews jammed against the gate had gotten the Jesus freaks, junkies, hookers and midnight cowboys all stirred up. They were jabbering away to each other, jumping up, trying to spot us. Behind them on Vine the cars crawled by; drivers' heads craned out the windows. On the roped-off far sidewalk, our men unloaded the trucks, the wind pushing their clothes flat against their bodies.

Tabitha joined me.

"There she is!"

An ugly blond girl with mad eyes pointed a cross at Tabitha. *"Repent!"*

"Repent!" chimed in a bunch of Jesus freaks.

The girl screamed, *"Repent! Or you'll roast in hell-fire and brimstone through all eternity."*

I took Tabitha back in the trailer, then called a council of war.

"What do you think of the crowd?"

"They're trouble," Cassidy said.

"Then let's forget the scene. Make the move now, and come back and pick it up Monday."

"We can't," Eddie said.

"We've got to shoot it now, Mr. McLeod," Bernstein said.

"Why?"

"There's a clause Juan couldn't knock out of your new contract that states if we go forty percent over budget on any one episode, Jasmine resumes control."

"Are we forty percent over?"

"The move to Goldwyn was expensive. Your contract settlements were generous. Mr. Hornblower's, for example—"

"I don't want an apology, Mr. Bernstein, just an answer."

"No, Mr. McLeod. We're not forty percent over. And we won't be—as long as you finish the entire show tonight. I don't care how late we go. But it must be tonight."

Cassidy, Maury, Big Joe and Houlihan went across the street to light it with the stand-ins, while Tabitha and I rehearsed it as best we could in the trailer.

There was a knock. "All ready, sah."

Outside, the men were lined up in a rough diamond.

"Now, Tabitha," Cassidy said easily, taking her by the hand, "you stand right in the center here between Kryellah and Big Al. We're going to walk across the street in this formation. Then shoot the scene. During the take don't stop if someone yells or a horn goes off. We can wild line later. On the 'Print' re-form just the way we are. And we walk back. Keep it closed up. Whatever they yell. Don't say anything. If I say 'Go'—charge. Got it?"

They nodded grimly.

He took his place at the point of the diamond. Waved to the sergeant. The city cops went out and stopped the traffic. Then our cops swung the gate open and cleared a path through the crowd on the sidewalk.

"Heads up," Cassidy said, and led us out.

As we marched by, they murmured, "That's her." "Where?" "Between the two niggers."

Then we were out on the street passing the stopped headlights, then up on the other sidewalk in front of our own lights.

"Roll 'em."

We did the scene.

"Cut. Print."

We re-formed the diamond and started back across the street.

On the far sidewalk hundreds of faces, jammed together, stared angrily at us.

But they weren't Strip people. Bitter red-faced men with crew cuts; stringy women with pursed lips. Bible Belt faces.

Christ, I realized, *they're Honey's people.*

A lanky woman shook an umbrella at Tabitha.

"You hurt Honey!"

"Slut."

"Whore!"

An overalled man shook his fist. "Don't think you're going to get away with it."

"No!"

"We'll teach you to hurt Honey!"

A rock whizzed past my head.

Cassidy said, "Go." And we charged.

There was the shock as we hit the wall of struggling, screaming, shoving bodies. Twisted faces flashed by, screaming, spitting at us.

Women's hands clawed for her. Men's fists pounded at us. Cassidy fell. As I pulled him up, a woman stabbed her umbrella over my shoulder for Tabitha. I hit her. Blood pouring from her nose, she fell over backward. Then we were past them through the gate, and our cops, billies swinging, fought them back and closed it behind us.

I grabbed Tabitha. She was pale and breathing hard.

"You all right?"

"Yes, darling."

Cassidy asked, "Anybody hurt?"

Eddie said, "Just cuts and bruises."

"Mr. Bernstein," I said, "this looks like a good place to get the hell out of."

We climbed the steep new dirt road that led to our last location. Far below on the wide parking area off Mulholland the caterers were setting up tables.

We reached the top. An acre of freshly bulldozed raw land stretched ahead. Perched on it, the wooden skeleton of a half-built house was outlined by the lacy, blinking city lights.

Tabitha gasped. "Oh, Michael, it's perfect."

Kryellah and I ran our scene inside the doorframe.

He wanted the girl. I said I wasn't going to turn her

over. He said she's my only witness to Murder One. I
said I didn't care—I was in love with her; we were going to Mexico together. "Then I'm taking you in," he
said. As he pulled out the cuffs, I hit him.

Then Eddie showed us the fight—piece by piece—
he'd be doing with Smoky Reed, Kryellah's stunt man.

They worked their way upstairs for a nice chase
over the beams of the unfloored rooms. Some good bits
with props. Eddie'd show us where to cut in for the
close-ups of Kryellah and me. Cassidy would nod.

They ended up in the master bedroom—outlined
only by a ridgepole, two-by-fours and window frames.
Running across the middle of what would be the floor
was a narrow strip of planks less than two feet wide.
Eddie walked backward on it, trading punches with
Smoky.

Finally, Smoky knocked him down and took out the
cuffs.

"Not bad," Cassidy said. "Is that the finish?"

"We don't really have one," Eddie said, "unless you
like this."

He knocked Smoky back suddenly, ran across the
room, leaped up on the window frame and jumped out.
Smoky dove off from the floor, tackled him in midair,
and they fell into a sandpile thirty feet below.

Tabitha, screaming, ran over to them. "Are you all
right?"

Eddie rolled over. "Sure." He looked up at Cassidy.
"What do you think?

"You're right," he said. "You don't have a finish."

Kryellah and I laughed.

Tabitha looked from Eddie and Smoky at her feet
up to us. "Men," she said.

For dinner we had great steaks plus beer and wine
and hard stuff. The bottles were going up and down
the long tables at a good clip. There was a lot of kidding and laughing.

Bernstein studied the men gloomily. "I hope they don't think the work's over."

"Cheer up, dear Mr. Bernstein," Tabitha said. "They have been tested by adversity."

"Besides," I said, "we're due for a break."

"Mr. McLeod, it's been my experience that's just when you don't get one." He called out, "Three minutes."

The first truck up the hill broke its axle.

Tabitha studied our faces. "What's it mean?"

Bernstein nodded at the sheer, steep slope above us.

"All the equipment—lights, booms, the crane, cables, everything—has to be carried up by hand."

"I'll simplify the fight," Eddie said.

"No," I said. "We've only got one chance. Kryellah and I will do the fight. Shoot it all tight, in one piece, on the crane. We'll drop eight cut-ins. And pick up the time we've lost."

"It's too dangerous," Bernstein said. "What if you should get hurt? How will you play the next scene?"

"Hurt," I said.

So on that strange, heavy hot night Kryellah and I swung at each other as slowly as astronauts on the moon's surface, while lightning flickered in the black sky above the ridgepole; and, stretched out below us, a stumbling, sweating, gasping, cursing chain of men heaved gear up the crumbling hill.

Big Joe sat off in the dark on top of a stepladder, drawing lines with a stick in the dirt to show where the tongue of the crane had to be positioned.

We came to the end of it. Kryellah threw the punch across my jaw. I fell. He took out the cuffs.

"That's the cut," Cassidy said.

"Hell, no!" I hit Kryellah back, ran toward the window, jumped up on the sill—

"Freeze," Cassidy said.

"Come on, Tim," I said. "Kryellah and I can do the fall."

"Christ, yes," Kryellah said. "That's the fun part."

"That's the cut," Cassidy said with an edge to his voice.

There's nothing to be said when he has that look. Some of the lights had arrived. Maury began positioning them as Eddie and Smoky started at the beginning.

I found Tabitha sitting on a sack of cement above a comma-shaped black hole that someday would be a swimming pool.

I gave her a bear hug while she snuggled up, kissing the spot on my neck she liked.

I checked her out. She was pale and the circles under her eyes had turned dark blue.

"You better take a nap."

She shook her head. "Once I fell asleep I'd never wake up. Stop worrying. I'm fine." She looked around. "All this is fascinating. It must be like a war. The way men are when there are no women."

"While they're lighting the fight, would you like to walk through our scene on the set?"

She nodded gratefully. "I'd love to."

Our scene began after Kryellah, leaving me in the sandpile, called out to her: "I'll give you five minutes," then went and waited in his car.

She came out of the pool house, helped me into the house and wiped the blood off my face. She looked around at the beams and said: "You know, I haven't lived in a house since I was eleven—since my father died. I always promised myself I'd have one. But I never did—lots of fancy apartments but no house. And now I never will."

"Sure you will," I said.

But she saw through my lie and smiled. "You're right," she said. "This is my house . . . our house. What's that?"

The rest of the scene was just her pointing to things and asking what they were. I'd tell her: joists and stud sills and cross-hatching. And she'd repeat the words after me simply, lovingly. Then she showed me where she'd put the furniture. It may not sound like much, but she was tearing me to pieces.

"That's right," Cassidy whispered out of the dark. "Do it just that way. Honest. Flat. Don't try to pump any emotion into it."

Little Al snapped, "Don't move that light!"

Houlihan said, *"They've changed the set-up."*

LeRoy said, "You're wrong, man!"

"Don't *man* me, you black bastard."

"Nobody move. Nobody talk." Cassidy walked over to the knot of men. "What's the problem?"

"Houlihan started tearing down the lighting."

Houlihan said, "Because you changed the set-up."

"Wrong," Cassidy said.

Houlihan stared at him in disbelief and pointed to us. "But when I saw you rehearsing them *there* I thought—"

"Don't think," Cassidy said. "That goes for all of you. You're too tired. Your brains won't work right. I'll do all the thinking for everybody. Understand?" They nodded. "Now it's not going to get better. It's going to get worse. So be very polite to each other."

When they had it lit, Kryellah and I, all padded, walked through it, indicating, so Joe could get an idea of the timing for the crane.

While they were fiddling with the adjustments, I walked over to the window and looked down at the sandpile. There was a lot of spill on it. Kryellah came up beside me.

"You game?"

"Shee-*it*."

I walked over to where Big Joe behind the camera floated out in the darkness, giving orders to his men down on the ground.

"Joe," I said quietly, "there enough light on the sandpile?"

His eyes probed mine.

"You going to do that stunt?"

"If you can get it."

"Oh, I wouldn't miss that," he said bitterly. "Be worth a lot. The last shot of you alive."

Down below they moved the base and his worried face slid away from me and disappeared in the dark.

Eddie checked out pads as we twisted and stretched to limber up.

"Ready?" Cassidy asked. We nodded.

"Roll 'em."

Kryellah held out his pink palms. I slapped them— hard.

"Action."

The scene played. When he pulled out the cuffs, my fist grazed his chin. He staggered back. I ran up the stairs, feeling Joe boom up alongside me. Kicked down the keg of nails. He jumped over it. We played hide-and-seek through the rafters. Then I went after him with the rubber hatchet and he caught me across the face with the balsa two-by-four. As I went down he tackled me, and we rolled around, nearly falling once, but we made it into the master bedroom. He was pushing me hard and it was tricky fighting backward on that narrow planking. I wasn't quite balanced when he threw the punch, and fell faster than we'd rehearsed it. As he pulled out the cuffs, Cassidy called, "Cut. Print."

I knocked Kryellah back. Ran for the window. And hauled myself up on the sill.

Jesus, it looked a mile down.

I dove out and the air was rushing by and the ground was rushing up and Kryellah tackled me and WHAM! I hit on the point of my shoulder and Kryellah landed on me. Something snapped and I screamed.

When I came to, I was turned over on my back and Eddie had my coat off and was carefully slicing through my shirt with a razor blade.

In the air twenty feet above me Big Joe was peering down over the edge of his camera.

"How was it?" I asked.

"We'll get it next time," he said.

"What?" screamed Kryellah. *"You tellin' me that was no fuckin' good?"*

"You weren't," Big Joe said, deadpan. "But I was. So we got it."

Tabitha, crying, knelt beside me. "You damn fool, are you all right?"

"Fine," I said.

"Shoulder's dislocated," Eddie said.

"What?" she gasped.

"Pop it back in," I said.

Kryellah held out his hands. I grabbed them. Eddie squeezed.

When I came to, Eddie was slapping my face while Tabitha yelled. *"Smelling salts! Hasn't anyone any smelling salts?"*

"Here." Cassidy held out his bottle of Johnnie Walker Black. I gulped it down. It burned my throat but cleared my head. "Grandstander," he growled.

"How'd it look?"

"Not too bad," he admitted grudgingly. "OK. Let's go to work."

"Work!" Tabitha said in horror. "He has to go to a hospital. He has a dislocated shoulder!"

"Use it," Cassidy said to me. "Might add something to the scene."

"Don't joke," she said fiercely. "He's hurt. He's in pain."

"I'm fine," I said, getting up.

She stared at me.

"He's all right," Eddie said.

"Sure," Kryellah said. "He's fine."

"You're all crazy! You're like little boys in a Spartan conspiracy. You think if you pretend it doesn't hurt, it won't. *But it will—*"

Lightning ripped across the sky. There was an immediate deafening rumble of thunder. And a raindrop splattered against her forehead.

Cassidy shouted, "Joe. Get the ridgepole."

Joe swung the camera around, yelling at his boys to shove him in.

LeRoy shot by the openmouthed Houlihan, spun an arc around, raced to another, turned it so the bar of pink wood was crosslit.

"Roll it," Cassidy called. "Double X. No slate."

"Rolling."

"Nobody move," Cassidy said. "I want the track."

"Speed."

A drop streaked like silver thread through the lights. Then another. The splats they made as they hit the wood picked up tempo like a tap dancer until a solid sheet of silvery rain blotted out the beam.

"Cut. Print," Cassidy called.

Men had already draped the camera in black rubber ponchos. Bernstein loomed up before me, his dripping wet suit plastered to his body, his beard glued to his chin, holding up a useless black umbrella.

"Mr. McLeod," he said in despair. "We've lost."

"The hell we have, Mr. Bernstein. We're going to shoot it in the rain. Look under the stairs. It's dry. We'll play the scene there."

"Right," said Cassidy. "I'll use that piece of the ridgepole to bridge Kryellah's exit. Put the camera there, Joe."

He put his arm around Maury's shoulder. "Light it like Von Sternberg. Forget about sources. Make it theatrical. Symbolic. Throw big black prison bars across their faces."

Maury smiled. "LeRoy, set the key over there. On the ground. I'm going to want some patterns made out of wood."

The men in their glistening black ponchos slipped and slid in the mud as they shoved booms and lights around while Tabitha and I went through the scene.

"My God, Michael," she said, amazed. "It's better this way."

Her face vanished. The hot blue-white beam of the arc swung across the faces of blinded men who, curs-

ing, threw arms up over their eyes. Then it stopped on
an empty patch of mud.

Houlihan stepped into the circle of light. He was
stark-naked and held a bottle of whisky. He sang in a
surprisingly high tenor:

> *"Me and my shadow,*
> *All alone and feeling blue . . ."*

He danced gracefully around the circle, pointing to
his shadow. "Everybody join in. When Houlihan sings,
everybody sings." He pointed to his cock. "Just follow
the bouncing balls. All together now."

> *"Just me . . . and my shadow,*
> *I've no one else*
> *To tell my troubles to . . ."*

As he cakewalked back and forth the rain pelted
against his heavily muscled body. Dead white except
for the red circles around his neck and wrists, and the
red bush above his bouncing cock.

The light swung back to the set. There was a curse.
A blow. The light swung back. And LeRoy was
stretched out on the ground.

"No nigger touches Houlihan's lights."

The men went for him.

He smashed the bottom of the bottle on a wheelbar-
row. Then whirled back, holding out the jagged edge
like a knife. The men stopped.

"Come on, niggers. Make your move and I'll have
dark meat for dinner."

Cassidy walked out toward him.

"You're drunk, Houlihan."

"Well." Houlihan grinned slyly. "Maybe I took a
drop or two. Because of the rain. Only to keep from
catching my death of cold."

Cassidy stopped in front of him. "Give me the
bottle."

Houlihan's eyes flicked suspiciously around. "I can't do that."

"Give it to me," he said.

"No!" Houlihan shouted angrily.

Cassidy slapped him hard across the face.

"Holy Mary, Mother of God," breathed Eddie.

Houlihan, one hand rubbing his cheek, glared at Cassidy.

Cassidy held out his hand. "Now," he said quietly.

Dropping his glance, Houlihan turned the bottle around and held out the neck to Cassidy, who pulled it out of his hands.

"Now get off my deck, Houlihan. You're fired."

He turned on his heel and walked quickly toward us, tossing the bottle away. "What are you all standing around for?" he said crisply. "We've got a lot of work to do." He knelt beside the stirring LeRoy.

Suddenly in two great bounds Houlihan was on him. His hands slammed against his throat; he swung him over his head and, screaming with rage, shook him at the sky like a rag doll.

Then Eddie was kicking him in the balls and Kryellah and Big Al were pulling at his hands and somehow I had a two-by-four and brought it down again and again on that glistening white skull until he fell.

Even then we had to pry his fingers off Cassidy's throat. Christ, Tim looked so slight, all crumpled up. I gently lifted his white face out of the mud, blood trickling out of his mouth. I felt his pulse.

"He's alive."

I picked him up like a baby, left hand cradling the back of his neck.

I walked slowly and carefully down the hill.

Kryellah went in front of me walking backward, arms held out to catch him if I tripped.

Tabitha was stanching the flow of blood with handkerchiefs the silent men handed her from the dark.

Behind me, Bernstein held up his black umbrella to protect Tim from the rain.

"Alfred de Burry!" I called.

"Yes, sah?"

"Have our cop call ahead on the radio. Find out where the nearest hospital is with a fully equipped emergency ward. Alert them. And tell them to send for a throat specialist."

"Yes, sah." He dashed ahead.

"And a priest," Eddie yelled.

"Then call his wife."

"I'll handle that." Eddie ran ahead.

The cold rain cut into my face, the mud sucked my shoes as I walked down the hill surrounded by the silent men in their glistening black hoods.

On the level ground Eddie had a weapons carrier backed up, motor running, tailgate down. Inside was a stretcher. Kryellah jumped inside and we gently put him down on it. As I folded the blankets across his chest one eyelid flickered slowly open, then the other. His eyes drifted aimlessly around, then stopped on me. Puzzled.

"You're all right, Tim. Don't try to say anything. You've had an accident."

A terrible choking sound came out of his mouth.

"It's the death rattle," someone moaned.

There was the sound of a kick. Little Al hissed, "Shut your mouth!"

Tim's eyes caught mine and he made that ghastly, rasping noise again.

His voice box must be crushed, I thought. Then I understood what he was trying to say.

"Whisky," I shouted. "He wants whisky."

Someone handed me his bottle of Johnnie Walker. I lifted his head and wet his lips.

He gasped. "How's LeRoy?"

"I'm fine, Mr. Cassidy," LeRoy said through swollen, bloody lips.

"Good." Tim managed to say in that terrible voice. "Now take me back."

"Tim, we're taking you to the hospital."

"It's my deck," he gasped fiercely. "And I haven't finished shooting."

Eddie ran back from the driver's seat. "What's the fucking holdup?"

"He wants to finish shooting."

"Well, he can't," Eddie said angrily. "It could kill him."

Eyes glittering furiously, Tim shook his head. *"Take me back."*

"I can't, Tim," I said. "This is too serious."

His hand reached out for mine.

"If I'm going to die, Michael," he whispered, "I'm the one to say where and when. Not you."

Bernstein said, "He's right."

"The hell he is," Eddie said angrily. "You don't understand. There's no priest here. That means he wouldn't have received last rites. If he—"

"He knows that," Bernstein said gently. "Old men know quite a lot about death."

"For Christ's sake, Michael," Tabitha said. "You can't kill him for your lousy television show."

"Right," said Eddie.

Not knowing what in Christ's name to do, I studied Tim's face. His eyes were fixed on mine with tremendous intensity—measuring me, weighing me, testing me.

Then a slight smile creased his lips and he gave me his wink.

I picked him up off the stretcher and turned toward the hill.

"Let's go to work!" I shouted.

"Oh, no, Mike," begged Big Joe. "For God's sake—"

"What the hell is this, a debating society? Haul ass."

I walked past their stunned faces, holding Cassidy against my chest, and started the climb up the steep wet hill.

We strapped him in the stretcher and like a papoose propped him up against the base of the boom. Eddie stood close and relayed his commands, while Bernstein held the glistening black umbrella over their heads.

The men, fighting the numbing fatigue, stripped off their ponchos and shirts to feel the cold rain lashing against them. They'd stop and stare at Cassidy now and then, as if to draw strength from the fierce spirit in that hurt old body.

It was three-forty-two when we were ready to shoot. Tabitha looked like a ghost.

"Yell," I told her. I screamed like Tarzan pounding my chest. She joined in.

"It helps," she said. "Thanks."

"Roll 'em," Eddie called.

"Rolling."

"Speed."

"Action," Eddie shouted.

Tabitha helped me out of the wet sandpile and through the rain into the house. Then she really turned it on. As she talked about the house she'd never had, she was heartbreaking. She made me cry. That made her cry. We sat there—the two losers of the world—trying to choke the sobs back.

Then Kryellah shouted, "Time's up." And holding onto each other, we walked out past the lens.

The cheering crew mobbed us. They screamed and hugged us. I broke through them and ran to Cassidy.

Glaring, he shook his head.

"What?"

The men fell silent and stared at him. He held out his hand thumb down.

"Was something wrong technically?"

"No," Joe said. "It was perfect."

"It wasn't the acting, Tim. The acting—"

"Stank," he rasped furiously. "Christ, stop admiring each other. She's a whore. You're a bum. Cut out all the fancy acting. Just say the lines. Now do it—"

He moaned, and his head flopped over, blood pouring out of his mouth.

"Get him to the hospital."

Eddie and Kryellah grabbed the stretcher and took off.

The men started to follow.

"No one else moves. Put a hold on the last take. And roll 'em."

"I won't do it again," Tabitha said. "I can't."

She ran after the stretcher. I caught her and spun her around.

"I don't care anymore," she screamed. *"He's dying!"*

I slapped her hard across the face.

"He may be, Tabitha. And if he does, we're going to have honored his last request. We're doing it again."

She nodded slowly.

"Have we got speed?" I shouted savagely.

Little Al snapped out of it. "Sorry, sah. *Roll them.*"

I went over and fell in the sandpile.

"Speed."

I yelled, "Action."

Tabitha helped me up and we went and did the scene. God knows it was flat and empty. Then Little Al shouted Kryellah's line, and we walked out past the lens.

"Cut. Print," I yelled over my shoulder as we ran for my car.

In the emergency room at Cedars, a jostling, shouting, green-gowned crowd of interns and nurses were all over him, sticking needles in him, taking blood, giving plasma, listening to his heart. Kate, smiling down at him, held one of his hands between hers. A skinny young redheaded priest was giving him last rites.

Someone shouted, "Operating Room Three." And they all shoved him down the corridor and ran around the corner.

The big white-faced clock in the waiting room said five-forty-seven when Kate came out of the door. We all got to our feet.

"They have just finished an emergency tracheotomy," she said clearly. "His condition is critical but his vital signs are stable. We won't know anything more until tomorrow. But before you go home I want you to know my husband told me: 'They're the best damn crew I ever worked with.'"

They went past her in single file, wiping off their hands on their pants before they shook hers. She stood there, smiling, thanking them by name. When only Kryellah, Eddie, Tabitha and I were left, she opened the door.

"He wants to see you—but it can only be for a second."

"Kate," I said. "Christ, but I'm sorry—"

"Stop blaming yourself, Michael, and get that hangdog look off your face. That's not what he needs."

He was propped up in the big bed with a forest of tubes in his nose and mouth and throat and arms.

He made a gurgling sound.

"No talking," Kate said sternly. "If you have something to say, write it down here."

She held out a pad and pencil and he scribbled something. She read in her lovely voice, "'How was the last take?'"

"Why, hell, Tim," I said. "Once we got rid of you, everything was great."

His shoulder shook as he made strangled, scratching noises.

"No laughing, either," Kate said. "Now, you all go home and get some sleep."

23

I eased around the pink coral shoulder and swam out into the soft warm green-yellow water. Suddenly I was shadowed. I saw the grey shark hurtling down. Sick with fear I swam for my life. He struck. But with only one tooth. One sharp tooth poked into me. Jabbing and poking and . . .

I was looking up at a dark ceiling. A black shadow of a man pushed the hard toe of his shoe into my side.

"Coming to," he said.

I was on the mattress on the floor of the house on Lookout.

Tabitha?

Lying beside me. Her face covered with a white cloth. I tore it off. It had a strange sickly-sour smell.

"Perfectly harmless." Greengauge's voice came from across the dark room. "Merely to ensure her sleeping a few more minutes—while we talk."

I went for the man above me but he sapped me down, then kicked me in the gut a few times. He had metal tips on his shoes.

"Please, Buck, promise me you won't do anything heroic. I deplore violence."

His gold lighter flared up. He was freshly shaved and powdered.

The man looking down at me had a beefy mean face, a sap in his right hand, brass knuckles on his left and a .38 stuck in his belt.

"Allow me to introduce Detective Withers of the Narcotics Squad."

"Where's your warrant?"

He kicked me in the ribs. The lighter went out.

"Buck, if you take that attitude we'll never solve our problem."

"What problem?"

"Dealing," Withers said. "Three bags of uncut smack. Forty G's worth. I got three witnesses."

"Junkies!" I said.

"Be reasonable, Buck," Greengauge said. "You could hardly expect them to be ordained priests of the Episcopal Church. Though these days, perhaps you should." He chuckled.

Suddenly fighting mad, I yelled, "Book me, you son of a bitch. Try to nail me in court with this two-bit frame."

"Not you," Withers said. "Her."

All the fight went out of me, and I was scared.

"It seems to be an open-and-shut case. But in the past Detective Withers has helped save the careers of some of our rock stars, and since you were involved, he called me—at once—for which I shall be everlastingly grateful."

He puffed on his cigar. The glow shone on his powdered cheeks. I was trying desperately to put it together but nothing fit.

"Through some technicality I don't pretend to grasp, Detective Withers *could* put his report in some sort of locked file instead of through the regular channels. Then, say, at the end of a year, if he was convinced she had reformed, he would destroy the evidence."

"Reformed how?"

"Stop fucking her," Withers said.

"Detective Withers feels you have been a bad influence on the child, and once you've separated she will be on the road to rehabilitation." He blew out a smoke ring. "He also has a fervent belief in the sanctity of marriage. You must return to your wife."

"Right," Withers said.

Everything fell into place. It was Honey.

"Josiah, can I talk to you alone?"

"Why, of course."

The floorboards creaked. Withers stopped a dozen feet away. I leaned toward Greengauge and whispered, "Honey's had it. She's through. Washed up. I'm hot. Just beginning to take off. I'm going to be your biggest star. Bet on me."

"I agree. Your star is on the rise; Honey's is on the wane. And, Buck, you know how fond I am of you personally, while Honey *is* difficult and deceitful."

"Then go with me on this."

"Alas, Buck, morality doesn't decide these matters. Money does. And the economics of the situation are that Honey owns outright twenty seasons. Buck, her reruns are the backbone of our daytime programming. We handle the syndication of her shows overseas. She's number one in Italy, Spain, France, Germany, Japan, Korea, the Philippines . . . it's astounding.

"So my affection for you must be weighed against thirty or forty million dollars."

Withers spoke impatiently out of the dark. "Deal or no deal?"

Tabitha stirred beside me.

"Deal," I said.

A 707 took off. We were drinking a bottle of Cordon Rouge at a table by the window at LAX. It wasn't cold enough so we drank it out of water glasses over ice cubes.

"Don't look so glum, McLeod. My old buddy Edwina Alsop has a house in the hills near Antibes where she's painting and she'd love to have someone split the rent. So I'll be fine."

She didn't have any makeup on. Her hair was tied back in a bow, and she wore a red-and-white-checked shirt and an old, worn, beautifully cut suit of blue jeans.

"Good," I said, smiling, and poured more champagne.

She studied me. "It's bad, isn't it?"

"It's just because of the morals clause in my contract Juan thinks it's smarter for me to move back in with her for a few months—as a face-saver for her—so she'll drop the charges against me."

"For a good actor, you're a lousy liar."

"OK," I said. "It's bad. But it's not for long. And we can take being apart for a few months. Then we'll be together in Paris in April. Now there's a song title for you: *Paris in April*."

She didn't smile, but reached out and took my hand.

Bernstein came up to the table and bowed. "I got here as quickly as I could, Mr. McLeod."

"Thank you, Mr. Bernstein. They're holding a seat for her on the SAS polar flight that's boarding. But it isn't paid for."

"I'll take care of it immediately."

"We better get going."

Frowning, she nodded and slung her bag over her shoulder.

As she went through the inspection area, I spotted a ten-year-old kid pulling a ring out of a Cracker Jack box. I bought it for five bucks.

I caught up with her at the loading gate. She was hugging Bernstein.

"Oh, dear, *dear* Mr. Bernstein. Take care of him."

"I shall do my best, Miss Weston," he said solemnly. "God-speed." He bowed and walked away.

I took her left hand and slid the ring on the third finger.

She studied the huge glass diamond.

"Why," she said thoughtfully, "that is the most beautiful ring I have ever seen."

"It's an engagement ring."

"That must be the reason."

"It means I'm going to marry you this spring in Paris or Dublin."

"You should, McLeod," she said. "Since I'm carrying your son."

"You're *what?*"

She nodded shyly. "Ever since that first night."

"Why the hell didn't you tell me?"

"Because I knew you'd act ... *dumb.* And you are. . . . Oh, Michael." She began crying hard and threw her arms around me. "Oh, God, how I love you. I couldn't bear to have anything happen to you."

I nodded to the correct, blond, concerned SAS people, who quickly separated us and pulled her on the plane.

I lay on the bearskin rug listening to old Billie Holiday records, drinking Jack Daniel's with Heineken chasers, studying the patterns the fire threw on the ceiling.

And I marveled at how that lovely, slim body I loved so could have my child growing inside it.

When the phone rang and they told me the plane had landed safely in Copenhagen, I left.

The columns of Tara II were floodlit but there were no other lights on in the house.

As I stepped in the dark entry hall, I was surprised to see Nora sitting in the small straight-backed gilt chair. She was sound asleep. She wore an old blue hat, a black coat. A battered straw suitcase was at her feet. I touched her shoulder.

She woke with a frightened start.

"Oh, thank God it's you, Mr. McLeod," she whispered, jumping to her feet. "I've given my notice. I'm leaving. I've been waiting for you—for hours. I had to warn you."

"Warn me?"

"You can't go back to her. If you do she'll never let you go. Not her. She'll kill you first. Just like Irving."

I stared at her pale, frightened face. There was the smell of whisky on her breath but she didn't seem drunk.

"Irving died of a heart attack."

"For God's sake, listen to me! I was standing right

over there when he came bursting in like a madman. He took those stairs three at a time and him just over a coronary. Then he ran in the bedroom and screamed: 'You whore! I should have known. You were a whore when I married you. And you still are. But a spade cornerback!' (That's nigger football player.)"

"I know."

"Oh, she's a great one for the niggers. There's one from then calls her still."

"Nora." I took her gently by the shoulders. "Forget all that. Go back to when Irving was yelling at her."

"He called her every name you can think of. Said he was leaving and she said no, she wouldn't let him. A terrible ruckus broke out with her screaming and him cursing. A lamp crashed, and a chair fell. Then there was a groan and a body hit the floor. There's a deathly silence. Then he gasps—so weak I can barely hear him but desperate—'Honey, the pills ... in God's name don't stand there ... hand me the pills.' He had those nitroglycerine things for his heart, the doctor—"

"Then what happened?"

"I let out a scream and raced up the stairs but by the time I got there the door was locked. I beat on it with my fists yelling at her to let me in, but one of her damn records blares on so loud I couldn't hear my own voice.

"By the time she unlocks the door and lets me in, everything's picked up neat as a pin, and he's stretched out dead as a mackerel."

"Buck?" Honey's voice floated down the dark staircase. "Is that you, dear?"

"Yes," I called out. "Be right up."

"Don't," she whispered. "For God's sake—"

"I have to, Nora. Thank you for telling me." I kissed her old cheek. "God bless."

I stopped at the head of the staircase. Far below the carved wooden railing the pink smudge of Nora's face stood out faintly from the black and white squares. She turned slowly and went out the door. Down the corridor a sliver of light slashed between the slightly ajar white satin doors.

Honey had arranged herself as carefully as for an old pinup shot. Her black negligee blended into the black satin sheets. Pinpoint spots flattered her stretched-out legs, emphasized her cleavage, threw hollows under her cheekbones and picked up her eyes.

"Welcome home, *husband*," she said throatily.

"I want a divorce."

"That's not the deal," she said quietly. "And if you don't go through with your part, someone's going to get hurt."

So it was her. I had to be sure.

"I was kidding," I said, laughing. "Hell, you know I never welshed on a deal in my life."

She never took her eyes off me while I undressed. As I started to get into bed, she was suddenly all over me. Hungrily biting, licking, chewing on me as if I were a piece of raw meat. She went down on me, sucking so hard I thought she'd tear the skin off.

The strange thing was that feeling about her as I did, I couldn't keep from getting a hard-on. She straddled me and rode it up and down, moaning in delight.

Suddenly, she grabbed me by the hair and pulled my head back hard. She lowered her face to mine.

"You belong to me," she whispered. "I'm never going to let you go. Ever. Understand?"

"Yes," I said.

And I knew I was going to have to kill her.

24

The pretty blonde girl with the pale blue eyes and the tiny, almost invisible gold hairs at the corners of her mouth sat in the rowboat telling me all about the disappearance of her husband.

While I wondered: *how long I would have to hold her head underwater before she drowned. Could they tell anything from the autopsy? By the look on her face? The way her lungs had filled with water?*

"Cut," Eddie said. He was squatting alongside the Mitchell on the pier.

"What's wrong?" I asked.

He looked at me thoughtfully. I'd told him Honey had framed Tabitha on a grass charge, which she'd drop if I moved back in for a few months.

I couldn't tell how much he bought. It's hard to sneak anything past Eddie, but he was directing his first show and had his head full of other problems.

"You weren't listening. This time listen as if you think she's lying."

From then on I concentrated during the takes. But at each new location I studied the terrain, searching for opportunities.

Driving back to Goldwyn, I looked down at the sharp drop off Mulholland.

I'd get Honey to drive me up here. Have her stop. Knock her out. Open my door so it would look as if I'd jumped clear. Then get out in the road, drive it over, and watch it bounce from ridge to ridge until it burst into flames.

The cops would ask why she'd suddenly driven off the road. . . . I'd get her drunk. I'd pour whisky down her throat and all over her—

Christ, I'm going crazy. I'm stealing scenes from old movies. That's how Garfield did in Cecil Kellaway in The Postman Always Rings Twice.

I walked into the office, locked the door, knocked down a double Jack Daniel's and looked at the tuna-fish salad set out on the table. I put the spoon in the mayonnaise.

Arsenic! I'd poison her.

I suddenly flashed back to Partridge in the Roosevelt Bar talking about his days on Homicide.

"If the husband's murdered, the wife may not have done it. It may have been her boyfriend. But if it's a wife, it's always the husband."

"Why?"

"He's got the motive. It's always sex or money. *Cui bono?* a DA friend of mine always used to ask. My Latin's not too good but I translated it, 'Who stands to gain?' So I'd just read the will and insurance policy, haul in the one who got the loot and sweat 'em until they'd confess."

I threw the salad across the room. The plate smashed against the wall.

There's no fucking way I can get away with this. Honey's death will be all over the papers and television. The cops and the coroner and the DA will go over her with a fine-tooth comb. Cui bono? Me. Who has the motive? ME! Forty fucking million dollars' worth.

Cy buzzed to tell me he was waiting with the scenes I wanted.

I sat down in the dark screening room.

Up came the first take on the scene in the half-built house in the rain.

Thank God for Cassidy. We were terrible. Sentimental, self-indulgent, hokey. I couldn't wait for it to end.

But the second take was flat and sparse and absolutely clean. You couldn't see any acting in it—anywhere.

"Cy, can you run these for Cassidy at Cedars?"

"On a Moviola."

"Do it as soon as you can. I think he'll get a kick out of it."

As I walked toward the stage, I thought: *She's your one true love and where is she? Sleeping in some lonely bed in the South of France with your child growing inside her.*

I went back to figuring how to kill Honey.

Silhouetted against the lit set, Hal in a Cardin suit was arguing bitterly with Eddie and Bernstein.

"*Buck!* Thank God you're here. You've got to help me! UBC has just started a minority training program. You know. They start out on props and end up in my job. It's Josiah's pet project. *Well,* I brought over the trainee assigned to your show for the next few weeks—"

"And I told him to forget it," Eddie said.

"Buck, as a *personal* favor, say it's all right. We're due *now* at Scandia, Josiah's giving a lunch for the Urban League and it's going to be covered by *Time, Newsweek* and *Ebony*—"

"Save your breath, Mr. Hundsley." A tall, well-built black man stepped out of the shadows. He wore a dark suit and tie and wraparound sunglasses.

"I didn't know it was *his* show. There's no way McLeod's going to give me a job. We've tangled ass before."

He peeled off his shades and damned if it wasn't little Stevie Cavalry. One of his ladies must have lent him four or five G's for the plastic surgeon because he was even prettier than before.

"Oh, if Buck didn't work with people he's had fights with, we'd never get the show cast each week. Ha ha. It's all right, Buck, isn't it?"

Suddenly it hit me!

"Sure, fine." I walked quickly off the set. Out through the padded doors. And leaned against the wall of the stage and laughed.

I was home free! I had no fucking motive.

Before the wedding Coulter had made me sign that waiver so in case of her death I didn't get a cent from her estate. No. To be exact, I got one thousand dollars. But what big, successful TV star will do anything for a G—especially murder his wife?

25

The red plastic pillow arced in the air and plunked down in the green swell of the sea.

"Man overboard," the six men in the cockpit said half-heartedly.

"Sing it out. Goddammit!" snapped Ayers, the peppery white-haired Yankee skipper. "Keep pointing at it. Don't take your eyes off it. Ready to come about! DUCK! Hard alee."

He shoved the tiller over. The boom shot across over our heads, slammed taut, the sail bellied, and the boat heeled on its new course.

"That's damn dangerous," Big Joe said.

"Where's the man overboard?" asked Ayers.

They stared stupidly at the empty, heaving, silvered waves.

"He's dead," Ayers said. "Because you didn't keep your eyes on him. Learned your lesson?" They nodded. "Now, who's going to be handling her?"

I slid over and took the tiller. After I brought her about, he relaxed.

"Where'd you learn to sail?"

"Long Island Sound."

"That's for schoolgirls. Storm comes up, you're five minutes from a yacht club. Here the coast is eight miles behind, Catalina fourteen miles ahead, and if you miss Catalina there's nothing till you hit Hawaii. Ever feel anything like that Pacific Swell?"

"Never."

" 'Course not. It started off the China coast."

Eddie looked anxiously at the sloop a hundred yards ahead, and the ferry on our starboard he'd hired for the camera ship.

"Can we start chasing the other boat? We've got a lot of work to do."

"Yip." Ayers squinted at the horizon. "And you've got three hours to do it in."

"Why only three hours?"

"By then the fog will have moved in."

Eddie looked at the sun, sparkling in the cloudless sky, and winked at me.

Three hours later we were tied up at the Marina. Socked in.

The fog was so heavy that sitting in the cockpit I couldn't see Eddie and Bernstein standing three feet away on the dock, deciding where to eat. Their voices moved off, and Ayers stepped lightly into the cockpit.

"Understand you want to see me."

"I want to buy your boat."

"She's for sale at the right price."

"What isn't?"

"A lot of things," he said, frowning.

I let it pass. "Mr. Bernstein will do all the negotiating. But I have to have her this Friday."

"No problem."

"Good. Would you like a drink, Mr. Ayers?"

"Not till sundown."

I took a slug of Jack Daniel's and said casually, "You can keep the ship-to-shore."

"That's not going to lower the price."

"Doesn't make any difference. I want it gone by Friday."

He looked at me curiously. "You know your way around boats. Why?"

Knowing I had to convince him, knowing what I said would be repeated to the cops, I said carefully, "Mr. Ayers, my wife is Honey Holly." I could see that meant nothing to him. "She's a big television star." No reaction in his blue eyes, deeply creased in the corners. "Well, the reason I'm buying your boat is so the two of us can get off by ourselves. Have a second honeymoon. Now, if there's any way her agent and business manager and director and writer can get to her, she'll be on the phone all weekend." I smiled at him. "So I want it out."

"It's dangerous to sail without it."

"I'll just have to chance it."

"Suit yourself." He jumped up on the dock and immediately vanished in the fog.

His footsteps faded quickly away. There was only the sound of water slapping against the hull, the creak of the mooring, the far-off hoot of the foghorns.

Hungry, I stepped on the dock and moved through the grey fog that eddied and swirled around me.

I stopped dead.

Stretched out on the bow was a man wrapped in a black rubber poncho. Without making a sound I walked to the edge of the dock, squatted on my heels, reached out and gently raised the poncho.

Under it was Cavalry.

What the fuck was he doing here? Spying on me?

I played back the conversation in my head. All he could have heard was that I bought a boat for a second honeymoon and wanted the radio taken out.

I studied Cavalry. His too-good-looking face was completely relaxed and his breathing was deep and regular.

With two fingers I jabbed him hard under the rib cage.

He gasped and sat up, staring at me stupidly. "Lunch over?"

"No."

"Then why'd you wake me?"

"I was afraid you'd fall overboard."

"In a pig's ass," he said angrily and, rolling up in the poncho, stretched out again.

Smiling, I went off down the dock. He hadn't heard a word.

Honey waited impatiently in Chasen's best booth. She wore a suit of big black and white squares with one white glove, one black.

"What's all this about? Why did I have to meet you here in such a hurry?"

"Because we're celebrating!" I kissed her, using a lot of tongue. She slid away.

"Celebrating *what?*"

"Our second honeymoon."

"We never had a first," she said tartly.

"Good. That makes it even better. Today I bought this beautiful yawl."

"A *what?*"

"A sailboat. And Mr. and Mrs. McLeod are going to celebrate their *first* honeymoon by sailing her to Catalina this weekend. Now what do you say to that?"

"You must be crazy! Buying a boat! Deciding to sail to Catalina without even asking me! I can't go this weekend! My schedule is—"

"Honey," I said very quietly, beginning the speech I'd rehearsed. "Do you want this marriage to work?"

"Why, you know I do."

"I know—no, I should say I *hope*—that if we can get the hell away from Josiah and the phone calls and the script conferences, just you and me—alone—on the sea with the sky and the fresh wind, that all the past will blow away and we can make a fresh start.

"I think it's worth a try. Honey, say yes, so we can forget the damn past and start having a real future."

The violet eyes studied mine suspiciously through her long, false lashes.

"It really means a lot to you?"

I answered honestly, "More than anything in the world."

She smiled. "Then I'll do it."

Mr. Bernstein huddled miserably in a yellow slicker at the far end of the cockpit. He didn't know it, but he was Honey's understudy.

Behind me the shoreline had dwindled down to a blue-brown shadow with scattered twinkling lights.

It was time for the dress rehearsal.

I opened the locker at my feet and pulled out a Polaroid.

"Mr. Bernstein, I'd like a picture of you."

The flash froze him in an astounded Jewish shrug. I took two more of him. I would take four of Honey, hoping I could get her to clown around. So the cops would see that she was happy just before it happened.

"Mr. Bernstein, just one more of you standing up there."

"Up on that little piece of deck?"

Honey would probably have the same reaction. I might have to do it for her.

"Just hold onto those wires that run down from the mast and you'll be perfectly safe."

He seized them and stepped up on the deck. As soon as the flash went off he stepped quickly back in the cockpit.

"Why don't you go below, Mr. Bernstein?"

"Below *what*, Mr. McLeod?"

"In the cabin. You'll be more comfortable. It's warmer."

As soon as the door closed behind him, I pictured Honey standing on the gunnel, one hand holding the stays. I looked around the horizon to make sure there was no boat in view, shoved the tiller hard. The boom shot over my head and smashed into her knees, knocking her overboard. I threw a red pillow to mark the spot. It shot past me in the white furrow of the boiling wake. About now I would bring her about and start the search. How long could she last? A woman who didn't know how to swim.

I turned around. Bernstein was staring at me through the cabin doors. "What was that vicious sound?"

"Good news, Mr. Bernstein. Everything checks out. We're heading home."

I pulled up in front of Tara II. It was completely dark. Honey must be taping late. Good.

As I turned the key in the lock, the black hall exploded into light.

"Surprise! Surprise!" shouted the Klipsruders, the Kidders, the Truscotts and a dozen more—all in paper party hats.

Honey called out, "I hope you're not mad, darling. I just had to tell the Gang."

"Of course."

"We're so glad you two came to your senses," Judy said.

The Gang sang: *"Happy Honeymoon to You."*

Ken slapped me on the shoulder. "Buck, I'm going to call you up tomorrow at noon for a weather report." He nudged me in the ribs. *"Whether she did or whether she didn't."*

The men guffawed.

Christ, should I tell him now I took the phone out? How will it sound at the inquest? "I told him I was going to call him. And he never mentioned there was no phone."

Judy said, "I'm going to have to wash your mouth out with soap. That's dirty."

"No, Mother. It's funny."

"Buck doesn't look as if *he* thinks it's funny."

"I'm still surprised."

"Good. There's no fun tossing a surprise party if you're not surprised."

Honey said, laughing, "I've got another one."

"What?"

"I have to be on your boat—all alone—for an hour before we sail."

What the fuck was she up to?

"OOOOH!" Judy clapped her hands in delight. "You *really* surprised him."

"It's just that I wanted to get an early start. Six-thirty."

"Then I'll be there at five-thirty."

"That means that I'll have to get up and take you down there—"

"No. Your Mr. Bernstein is meeting me at the Washington Street turnoff at whatever time I tell him. I just spoke to him."

"I hate to make him get up that early on his day off—"

I broke off because Judy and Ken were looking at me strangely. I grinned at her. "Won't you give me a hint?"

"No fair!"

"No clues!"

Honey considered. "Let's just say—if you eat one bite of breakfast I'll push you overboard."

"That's *cute*," Judy said.

"Hey!" Ken shouted. "If you lovebirds are through surprising each other, us landlubbers would like to propose a toast." They raised their glasses. "Anchors aweigh!"

The alarm went off at four-thirty. Honey got right up and went into her dressing room. I pretended to be asleep when she walked out wearing a trench coat and carrying a bulky cloth suitcase. She paused at the door and blew me a kiss.

Silence. Then a clatter of pots and pans from the kitchen. A long silence. Her car started. The garage doors slid up. She drove off slowly down the gravel drive.

I went to the window and looked out. *Christ, there was heavy fog everywhere.*

I dialed 554-1212. A woman's voice said: ". . . low-lying coastal clouds and heavy, early-morning fog should burn off the beaches by ten-thirty."

Perfect.

I showered, shaved, cut my fingernails very short. Put on brand-new jockey shorts, white wool socks, blue jeans, black sneakers and a heavy, ribbed black turtleneck sweater.

I had matching clothes aboard so if blood got on these, I could sink them.

Downstairs, I opened the door to the crypt, and stood watching Irving's gold profile sparkle above the flame.

The guardhouse gate clanged shut behind me, and I took Carolwood to Sunset. As I drove slowly west on Sunset, the fog made strange swirling patterns like the dry-ice effect in a vampire movie.

Suddenly it lifted and I saw the wet playing fields of UCLA. Then it socked in hard. I slowed down. Ahead on my right there was a strange white blob I couldn't place.

It materialized into the Marymount statue of Mary.

Suddenly, I desperately wanted to jam on the brakes, bolt out the door, throw myself at her feet and pray for forgiveness.

But instead, I punched up KMPC and stepped on the gas while Blood, Sweat and Tears sang:

> *"What goes up*
> *Must come down. . . ."*

Honey's white Rolls loomed up in the empty parking lot like a beached whale.

As I walked down the sloping gangplank, a woman on a radio sang softly:

"*I'd like to get ya on a slow boat to China.*"

I walked past the gently bobbing sterns. As I stopped in front of the one freshly lettered *Honey II*, I realized the singing came from one of Honey's records.

I tried the cabin door but it was locked.

"Hi, darling," she called. "Happy honeymoon."

"Happy honeymoon. Open up."

I could smell spicy food cooking.

"Not on your life. I'm saving my surprise until we're way out at sea."

Perfect.

I started the motor, turned on the running lights, cast off the moorings and eased her out into the channel. The bow slid through the black water. Our movement caused the fog to lift, briefly revealing empty, rocking boats that slipped behind us. I eased her out past the crushed-stone breakwater with the loudly clanging bell buoy.

When I felt the Pacific Swell hit, I set the course by compass and we beat steadily out into the gray darkness.

Far ahead the deep foghorn of a freighter sounded. It was quickly answered by the nervous bleat of a fishing boat.

In two hours the fog had burned off and the coast had disappeared behind us. I headed her into the wind, killed the motor and hoisted the sails. She took off like a gull, and I played with her—seeing how high into the wind she could point, enjoying the swift and sensitive feel of her in my hand.

A clatter of pans in the galley brought me back to business. The only ship in sight was the topmasts of a schooner far off to the southwest.

Honey's record sang:

> *"If she gets weary,*
> *Women do get weary*
> *Wearing the same shabby dress . . ."*

I brought her up on the tack I needed, opened the locker and took out the Polaroid.

"Ahoy below. The captain requests the pleasure of your company on deck."

"Aye, aye, sir."

The varnished mahogany doors opened and she stepped out, carrying a tray. She set it down carefully and closed the doors behind her. She was wearing a captain's hat with lots of gold braid, a blue blazer, white silk bell-bottoms, and shiny slippery black patent-leather shoes.

Perfect.

She tossed me a salute. I snapped her picture.

She set the tray down beside me and poured a drink out of the frosted silver cocktail shaker.

She lifted silver covers off dishes of steaming hors d'oeuvres. "Eat. Oh, I sound like Molly Goldberg."

"My God, they're good. This one's some kind of lobster curry, and this is creamed crabmeat and something—"

"And you thought I couldn't cook."

I kissed her. "I've got the perfect wife." I picked up the camera. "And I want pictures of her."

Laughing, she danced a sailor's hornpipe while I took two more.

"Let's try one up there."

I pointed to the spot.

She looked at it and frowned. "That looks scary."

"It's perfectly safe—just hold onto those wires."

She shook her head.

"Here, sit down and I'll show you how it's done."

She took the tiller gingerly. "I can't turn us over, can I?"

"Not as long as you hold it like that. Now watch."

I leaped up on the deck. "Da dum!" Holding onto the stays, I made a low sweeping bow.

"Oh, I want a picture of you. Just like that."

I bowed again while she snapped it.

"Now you."

"OK. But first, darling, scan the horizon like a ferocious pirate."

I glanced quickly to the southwest. The schooner was gone.

"No. Look over that way. I want to see more of that gorgeous profile."

Holding onto the stays, I put my palm over my eyes and scowled off ferociously.

"A teeny bit more . . ."

The deck heeled under me. I twisted around. Something sharp thudded against my chest and cut sickeningly into me. I grabbed it. It was a bayonet. Lashed to a boothook. Held by Stevie Cavalry, who stood in front of the swinging cabin doors. Then the boom smashed against my knees. The sky spun above me, and the cold dark waters closed over my head.

I went down, down, down, in slow motion while fast cuts of film flashed across my brain.

Cavalry slumped over the hood of the car. Kryella saying: "He's kept by white women."

Nora's pale face in the dark hall. "A spade cornerback. Oh, she likes the niggers. One still calls."

Lifting up the black poncho and seeing his face. "He's spying on me."

Honey in the hall, the gang behind her. "I have to be on your boat—all alone—for an hour before we sail."

I burst back up into the sunlight and gulped air into my lungs. I was surprised at how far away the yawl was. Cavalry was washing my blood off the deck.

The stereo sang:

"You are too wonderful
To be what you seem. . . ."

* * *

Honey—at the tiller—blew me a kiss, then waved good-bye.

I had to hand it to her, she'd set me up beautifully.

Treading water, I quickly turned my back on her because I didn't want her to see me laugh.

With all her tricks and planning, she'd blown it. She didn't know there's no fucking way you can kill me in the ocean. Christ, with two bayonets in me I could swim the eight miles back to shore in two hours. Three at the most.

I'd won. I'd get Juan and we'd nail her on attempted murder.

I checked the wound. The bayonet had sliced the nipple in two and bounced off the ribs, cutting into the lats under the left arm. I stripped, bandaged it as best I could with my jockey shorts. Took a sighting from the sun and struck out in a crawl. I'd swim for fifty minutes, then take a five-minute break.

After five minutes the left arm wasn't worth much. So I shifted to a sidestroke. After twenty minutes I had to turn over on my back and float.

Christ, I felt cold. And my stomach was beginning to cramp. I wondered if she had put something in those drinks. I was bleeding too much.

You're starting to get sleepy. So no more breaks. Just hang in there until you hit land.

As I rolled over I saw about two hundred yards away the grey triangular fin cutting straight toward me.

I screamed and sprinted away, flailing both arms.

Oh, my God, I am heartily sorry for having offended Thee—

mother was ahead—shadowed but young again with her hair dark and down

And I detest all my sins because of Your just punishments. But most of all because they offend Thee—

father's great bulk appeared beside her

My God, who are all good and deserving of all my love—

there was Tabitha—bathed in a lovely golden light

I firmly resolve with the help of Thy Grace to sin no more. And to avoid the near occasion of sin—

Great nuclear explosions went off inside and outside me. And I saw the whole chain of creation. The first fish crawling up on the land; salamanders turning into dinosaurs; dinosaurs into fossils; apes leaping down out of trees and becoming men.

And dead center, under the terrible sky of Golgotha, the Christ Crucified. Nearer to me, the dark, loving presence of Mary.

Suddenly I realized the spark of life in me was eternal. And thanking Her for Her Intercession and Him for His Gift of Grace.

I laughed, turned around and, hoping to get a piece of the son of a bitch, swam straight for my old enemy . . . me.